THE
UNICORN CHRONICLES
BOOK IV

THE

LAST HUNT

BY
BRUCE COVILLE

SCHOLASTIC PRESS
NEW YORK

LIBRARY OF CONGRESS CATALOGING-IN-PUBLICATION DATA

Coville, Bruce.

The Last Hunt / by Bruce Coville. — 1st ed.

p.   cm. — (The Unicorn Chronicles ; bk. 4)

Summary: Beloved and her Hunters have commenced the final hunt for the unicorns
by ripping through the Axis Mundi into Luster. As the magical world begins to
collapse from the wound, Cara seeks the help of Graumag the dragon and other
friends across Luster to fight the Hunters in a concluding battle, while the unicorns
come to discover an old and dark strength within them — Provided by publisher.

ISBN 978-0-545-12807-0 (hardcover)

[1. Unicorns — Fiction.   2. Dragons — Fiction.   3. Fantasy.]   I. Title.

PZ7.C8344Las 2010

[Fic] — dc22   2009043125

10 9 8 7 6 5 4 3 2 1   10 11 12 13 14

Printed in the U.S.A.   23
First edition, June 2010

Map by Katherine Coville copyright © 2010 by Scholastic Inc.
The text was set in Adobe Garamond Pro.
The display type was set in Mantinia.
Book design by Phil Falco

For Adam and Charlotte

ACKNOWLEDGMENTS

To say this book has been a long time in the making would be an understatement. When Jean Feiwel invited me back in 1991 to create a unicorn series, neither of us could have imagined it would take me nearly two decades to reach the end of the story.

In those years I have been helped enormously by the good eyes and even better ears of many friends, including Daniel Bostick, Cara Coville, Katherine Coville, Kelly Lombardo, Naomi Miller, Tamora Pierce, Michael Stearns, and the late and much-missed Paula Danziger.

I also owe thanks to Pat Brigandi, my editor for the first book, and Zehava Cohn, who guided me through the second. Both helped me shape the world and the story that continues to evolve. For this book, as for *Dark Whispers*, the editorial reins were taken up by Dianne Hess and Lisa Meltzer, ably assisted by the wonderful Grace Kendall.

Additionally, my beloved writer's group — Tedd Arnold, MJ Auch, Patience Brewster, Cynthia De Felice, Robin Pulver, Vivian Vande Velde, and Ellen Stoll Walsh — listened patiently in and out of nearly a decade, trying to keep track of the strands of the story even when I would return to it after leaving them hanging for six months or more. Their patience was monumental, and their contributions invaluable. In the last year I added a second writer's group — Ellen Yeomans, MJ Auch, Suzanne Bloom, and Laurie Halse Anderson — and their input has been likewise invaluable.

I want to express not only gratitude but apologies to all the booksellers who have spent years dealing with the queries — eager, anxious, sometimes cranky — about when the next book would be released.

I also need to give a special call out to a young fan named Tori Hutchinson, who provided the name for Seeker. Though he only appears in one brief scene, his name felt very right to me.

Appreciation of a very deep kind goes to Petar Meseldzija, whose cover art made me almost giddy with delight. Petar thoroughly captures the spirit of wonder and adventure and mystery that I am trying to create in these pages.

And a major tip of the hat to Phil Falco for his beautiful and elegant design work on volumes 3 and 4 — and for re-creating the look of the full series. Nicely done, Phil!

But most of all I must thank the fans who urged me (with varying degrees of patience!) to finish the darn thing. Many who started reading the Chronicles as children have grown up while I have been trying to write this concluding volume, and I am both chastened and heartened by their continuing emails letting me know they are still eager to read it. If I hadn't been painfully aware that so many people were waiting for this story, I might have given up at any number of points along the way. So thanks, dear fans. It's been a long journey, and I literally could not have done it without you!

Which is not to say there could not be more books about Luster. After all, there are hundreds of scrolls and books in Grimwold's cavern, and they are filled with the tales of the adventures the unicorns and their friends have had across many centuries. So there are certainly stories left to tell, though none quite so epic as this one.

Last, but not least, I should acknowledge my cat, Luna, who is my personal Squijum.

— Bruce Coville

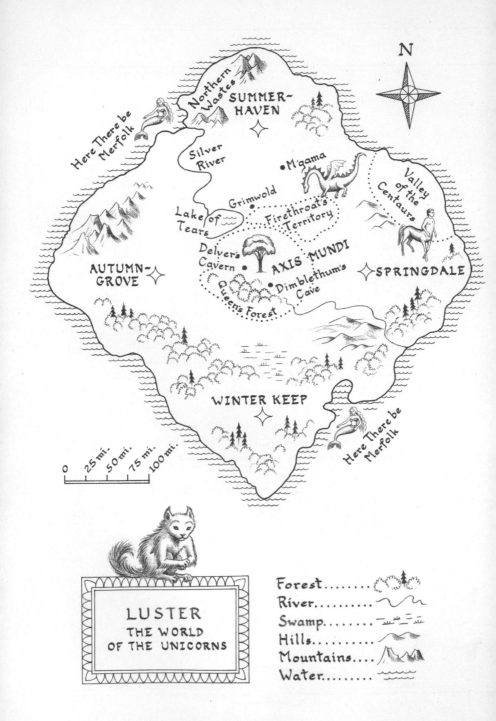

N

Northern Wastes

SUMMER-HAVEN

Here There be Merfolk

Silver River

M'gama

Grimwold

Valley of the Centaurs

Lake of Tears

Firethroat's Territory

Delver's Cavern

AXIS MUNDI

Dimblethum's Cave

AUTUMN-GROVE

SPRINGDALE

Queen's Forest

WINTER KEEP

Here There be Merfolk

0   25 mi.   50 mi.   75 mi.   100 mi.

LUSTER
THE WORLD
OF THE UNICORNS

Forest........
River..........
Swamp........
Hills..........
Mountains....
Water........

THE LEGEND
OF THE
HUNT

For the last time I, Grimwold, Fourth Keeper of the Unicorn Chronicles, take pen in hand to record the story of how the Hunt began, a task that has been repeated once every ten years since the unicorns first came to Luster. From this story flows all that has happened to the unicorns in the centuries since, and this retelling has been our way of keeping the story fresh in memory.

*   *   *

Where the unicorns came from, no one knew. But there was no question that their appearance on old Earth made it a sweeter, richer place to be. In that time, humans and unicorns lived largely apart from one another. However they were not enemies.

Now, while unicorns live very long lives, they are not immortal. And the day finally came when the first of the unicorns passed away. Alas, his horn — which was all that was left of him, for his body dissolved, as is the way of unicorns — was found by a man who soon discovered that it still held powerful healing magic. This should have been enough for him. But seeking to make himself seem brave and bold, he boasted that the unicorn, who had died before the man even saw the horn, had been a fearsome foe, and that he had battled it to the death.

Lies being what they are, the story of the fierce unicorn spread — as did the truth of the way its horn could heal.

This was the state of things when a man, who was a true hunter, found himself with a daughter sick and in danger of dying. Deciding to go in quest of a unicorn's horn to cure her, he prepared himself to face a terrible beast. As his wife was already dead, he took to carrying his child — whom he called Beloved, for his entire heart was filled with her — into the forest on his back.

One fateful day the hunter left Beloved to rest in a clearing while he continued his quest. That afternoon an ill-timed breeze caught the scent of the child and her illness and carried it to a unicorn named Whiteling. Wanting to help, Whiteling came to the clearing. Approaching with care and tenderness, the unicorn knelt and pressed the tip of his horn to Beloved's chest, piercing her flesh in order to heal her.

The hunter returned at that moment and cried out when he saw — or thought he saw — a unicorn trying to kill his daughter. Swiftly he loosed an arrow, which pierced the unicorn's heart in the very same moment that the unicorn's horn pierced the heart of the ailing girl.

Whiteling snapped his head up in shock and pain, a

movement so sharp that it broke off the tip of his horn, which lodged in Beloved's heart.

The hunter charged, and before Beloved's horrified eyes, man and unicorn fought unto the death. As the girl watched both of them die, her father's words about the evil of unicorns seared their way into her heart, which had become the most unusual heart in the world. For in every moment, it was both wounded by the shard of horn that was lodged there and at the same time healed by the horn's powerful magic.

Fueled by pain and anger, kept alive by this strange magic, Beloved became the fierce and eternal enemy of the unicorns. She sought ever to destroy them in vengeance for her father, and also as repayment for the pain that constantly wracked her ever-wounded, ever-healing heart.

So began the Long Hunt, which stretched across centuries as Beloved continued to seek the destruction of the creatures she blamed for her misery.

Now, at last, it is over. Here in what remains of my cavern, I must turn my pen to recording the joy and the sorrow, the triumph and the tragedy, that filled the last days of the Hunt . . .

Grimwold

Fourth Keeper of the Unicorn Chronicles
The Queen's Forest, Luster

PROLOGUE

IN THE BEGINNING

He looked at the seed. Glowing gently, it lay cupped in the palm of his enormous hand.

Having to steal the seed to carry out his plan had troubled him, but only a little. Seeds were meant to grow, not to be hoarded and hidden away. So stealing this one had seemed, to him, a moral act.

Still, he knew that if his plan were to be discovered the punishment would be great.

In his other hand he held the remnants of a fallen star. This, too, was forbidden, for the star's power was enormous, despite its fall, and not allowed to those of his level.

Again, this troubled him but little.

In truth, it was neither the seed nor the star that weighed heavy in his thoughts. It was the blood. To shed blood — even his own, which was what he intended — was the highest crime of all. Yet what he had in mind could not be done without it. Absent that life-giving fluid, the seed and the star were worthless.

Pressing the seed into the still warm star, he took a blade from his belt and drew it across his palm.

His blood oozed out, silvery-crimson and warm.

It fell onto the seed, which quickened at its touch.

He smiled.

It had begun.

BLOOD
MOON NIGHT

The onrush of a conquering force is like the bursting of
pent-up waters into a chasm a thousand fathoms deep.

Sun Tzu, *The Art of War*

CHAPTER
I

THE RISING OF THE MOON

Cara Diana Hunter edged closer to her grandmother, Amalia Flickerfoot, Queen of the unicorns. Neither girl nor Queen were able to keep their eyes from the sky, where the scarlet circle of the Blood Moon rose higher and higher.

Not far to Cara's right stood her friend Medafil, who had flown her back to Autumngrove after their journey to the Valley of the Centaurs. Medafil was a gryphon, with a head and wings like those of an eagle, though vastly larger, and a lower body like that of a great, tawny lion. Right now his sharp, curved beak was opening and closing — a sign, Cara knew, that he was muttering to himself, something he did when he was nervous. Additionally, his tufted ears — the only part of his head not like that of an eagle — were twitching. So was his long, lean tail, which — save for the burst of fur at its tip — looked almost like a serpent in the moonlight.

Around the gryphon, the girl, and the Queen, stretching beyond sight into the woods, was a glory of unicorns. It was likely the greatest glory ever assembled, for word of the danger had gone out, and nearly every unicorn in Luster had now traveled to Autumngrove. All had heard the dreadful news that Beloved had gained one of the Queen's Five, the powerful amulets that allowed passage back and forth between Earth and Luster. Normally the amulets would carry only one or two people — or unicorns — between the two worlds. Alas, there was little doubt that Beloved intended to use the amulet to create a gate through which she could bring an entire army of Hunters. And there was little doubt that she was planning to exterminate the unicorns.

And now another rumor was circulating, one that said the delvers had stolen a powerful item from M'Gama, the Geomancer — an item that would allow Beloved to choose *where* in Luster to make her attack.

Where that spot would be no one knew, for it was unclear what, if anything, Beloved had learned of Luster. The Queen had asked M'Gama to use her magic to determine the most likely spot for the invasion. The Geomancer had agreed, but then had fallen mysteriously silent — a silence that only added to the Queen's worries, since M'Gama was one of their closest and most powerful allies.

Before she fell out of contact, M'Gama had given the Queen one useful piece of information, telling her *when* the attack would most likely occur: tonight, the night of the Blood Moon, the anniversary of the death battle between Whiteling and Beloved's father.

Gazing at the crimson orb as it rose slowly above them, Cara felt a fresh shiver of terror. Her fear was not simply for the unicorns, but for Luster itself. She had come to love this world intensely, and the thought of it being invaded made her sick.

To make the situation even worse, Cara knew that Beloved was seeking her, personally, though for what reason she had no idea. The girl moved closer to her grandmother, and was about to lean against her, when the Queen cried out in pain.

"What is it?" asked Moonheart, who was standing nearby. "What has happened, sister?"

The Queen shook her head, causing her mane to ripple like silk and silver over her neck. "I don't know, brother. It was as if something had struck me a blow. I felt —"

Before she could say more, the ground rippled beneath them.

The assembled unicorns trumpeted in panic, rearing on their hind legs and pawing at the air. That no such thing as an earthquake had ever troubled Luster's surface made the trembling of the stones beneath their hooves all the more terrifying.

"Do not fear!" bugled the Queen. *"Do not fear!"*

Her voice was lost in the chaos. But the tremor only lasted a moment, and as the world settled the worst of the glory's panic ebbed away.

"Do not fear!" called Amalia again. "Remember, this

happened from time to time on the old world. It is called an earthquake."

"But it has never happened in Luster!" said Moonheart. "What does it mean?"

Amalia Flickerfoot gazed at her brother, clearly uneasy, before finally answering, "I believe it means that Beloved has opened her gate into Luster." She paused, then said, almost to herself, "But a new gate should not cause *that* much disruption. What has she done?"

Though she tried to mask it, the fear in her voice was so palpable it made Cara shudder.

CHAPTER
II

THE BREACHED TREE

Even as Cara and her grandmother were watching the rising of the moon, far away Prince Lightfoot stood trembling in astonishment at what he had just seen in that same bloodred light.

Not twenty feet ahead of him loomed the Axis Mundi, the very center of Luster, a tree so vast it filled the unicorn prince's field of vision. Between Lightfoot and the tree was a cairn, its stones rising as high as the Prince's shoulder. On that cairn had rested a ball of wire. He had watched his friend the Dimblethum place it there but moments before. Lightfoot knew all too well what it was: the "anchor" that would let Beloved choose the spot where she would enter Luster.

The explosion that followed the Dimblethum's placing of the wire sphere had knocked the Prince to the ground, momentarily blinding him. When his eyes had cleared and he finally managed to stagger back to his feet he had seen two things that frightened him: The Dimblethum had disappeared, and the wires were glowing a fiery orange.

Immediately Lightfoot had flung himself toward the cairn, hoping to knock it down and trample that glowing ball. But despite three attempts, some magical barrier had prevented him from reaching it.

Then, as he had watched in horror, the wire sphere — untouched — had lifted from the cairn. When it was hovering about a foot above the stones, it began to spin, spitting off flecks of red and yellow light. They fell, still glowing, onto the silvery-blue leaves that covered the forest floor. For a moment Lightfoot had feared they would spark a fire. When he saw that was not going to happen, he had returned his attention to the spinning sphere.

Slowly, silently, it had drifted toward the great tree. His heart pounding, Lightfoot strained with all his might against the magical barrier that held him back.

It had not budged by so much as an inch.

When the glowing sphere struck the trunk of the tree, the Prince had averted his eyes. A blast of power and energy had rolled past him, its force knocking him back to the ground, which was now shaking beneath him.

Twisting toward the tree, Lightfoot had cried out in dismay. A ragged hole had appeared in the trunk. Starting at ground level, it stretched to half again the Prince's height and was wide enough for five men to walk abreast.

From the darkness overhead, Lightfoot heard a keening, as if the branches themselves were calling out the tree's pain.

*   *   *

Within the opening that had pierced the tree shimmered a curtain of mist. Past that thin veil Lightfoot could see, dimly, another world, a world bounded by stone walls.

It took the Prince a moment to realize he was glimpsing the kind of castle he had heard sung of in the old stories the unicorns had brought with them when they departed Earth for Luster.

But it was not the castle that transfixed Lightfoot with fear. It was what he now saw approaching from beyond that veil of mist: row after row after row of grim-faced, angry-eyed men.

The Prince shuddered. These were not just "men."

They were, quite clearly, *Hunters*.

Even worse, in front of the Hunters strode another human, one Lightfoot knew all too well from his last encounter with her: Beloved, the ancient and eternal enemy of the unicorns.

A quiver trembled along the Prince's flanks as Beloved drew close to that shimmer of mist. Her dark eyes blazed and her silver hair moved freely about her, as if somehow lifted and attended by its own private breezes.

Lightfoot scrambled to his feet. His first instinct was to flee across the meadow that surrounded the tree. But that would surely attract the attention of the invaders. And it would do the unicorns no good. The more useful, if far more frightening, tactic, would be to try to spy on them.

With that in mind, and thankful for the darkness, the Prince moved quickly around the tree, which was so huge it could easily hide him.

Unable to see, but listening with keen ears, he heard the astonished shouts of the arriving men. It was obvious that whatever they had been expecting, whatever they had been told, they were still amazed to find themselves in another world.

To his own shock, Lightfoot felt a sudden urge to move back around the tree *toward* the men, a compulsion so strong and powerful it was almost impossible to resist. He was baffled, until, peering around the curve of the trunk, he spotted the reason for it: Arriving with the men was a group of young women.

Lightfoot shuddered again. From the time of the slaying of Whiteling, unicorns had been driven by a powerful compulsion to come to the aid of maidens in the wood. With new horror, the Prince realized why Beloved was bringing these young women to Luster: They were *bait* — lures intended to draw unsuspecting unicorns to their deaths.

Sudden anger overwhelmed Lightfoot's fear. He wanted to charge trumpeting among the Hunters, slashing with his hooves, stabbing with his horn, wounding and killing as many as he could before their swords and spears brought him down. He shook his head as he realized that would not be wise. The Queen must know of this, and he was the only one who could tell her. He must not fall, must not be captured. With that thought, any remaining fear for himself the

Prince might have felt vanished, replaced by a greater fear for the fate of his kind. For centuries Beloved had wanted to wipe out the unicorns. Was it possible that now, at last, she was going to succeed?

Lightfoot edged back around the tree, hoping he could determine how many Hunters were now entering Luster. But even peering around the curve of the great trunk did him no good. Unicorns do not have much use for numbers, and he had never learned to think in terms of the many, many men he saw streaming forth. Were there more of them than there were unicorns in Luster? For that matter, how many unicorns *did* live in Luster? *Why had he never paid attention to such things?*

The men kept coming, so many that they nearly filled the area in front of the tree, spilling well past the spot where the magical barrier had prevented Lightfoot from knocking down the cairn. He wondered if that meant the barrier was down now or if it only blocked passage in one direction.

Stop! he told himself fiercely. *Think about that later. My main task right now is not to be seen, not to be captured. And that means . . . that means . . .* Lightfoot found himself losing his focus as he was suddenly overcome by a powerful attraction to the maidens walking with the Hunters.

How strange. Even though I know why they are here, my heart is still drawn to them. I wonder if they understand the treachery expected of them — understand what will die if they are successful.

17

Forcing himself, with considerable effort, to ignore the maidens, the Prince returned his attention to the procession of Hunters.

Suddenly the men stopped. Lightfoot realized it was because Beloved herself had stopped. The men and the maidens gathered around her.

Beloved turned to face them. Raising her arms, she cried, "My children!"

Her voice was clear, strong, and compelling — even for Lightfoot, who both hated and feared her.

She began to rant. The Prince could make out some of what she said. His father, Dancing Heart, had always claimed that Lightfoot's greatest gift was for language, which was why he could talk to such strange things as the delvers and the Dimblethum. And his connection with Cara had let him pick up numerous human words and phrases. So even though much of what Beloved now said was lost to him, he could tell, quite clearly, that she was urging the men to go out and kill as many unicorns as they could, as quickly as they could. He caught the words "blood" and "evil" fairly frequently and began to feel frustrated that he could not understand all she said. Yet even without knowing each of her words, Lightfoot found that the hate in Beloved's voice made him feel unclean. He wanted to find some clear stream where he could wash himself free of the filth of her anger.

Then the enemy said something that he *did* understand and that filled him with new fear. "Above all, I want the girl — Cara Diana Hunter. Bring her to me!"

With that, Beloved seemed to be finished. Dropping her arms, she murmured, "It's autumn here. A good time for death." With a shiver, she rubbed her arms and said something about a cloak.

One of the Hunters stepped forward. He seemed to be offering to do something for her. Without waiting for an answer, he started for the tunnel in the tree.

Beloved uttered a sharp command that stopped him in his tracks.

Lightfoot strained to understand, trying to untangle the meaning of Beloved's words. As near as he could make out, it would be dangerous for the man to go back through the tree so soon — something about opposing magics that would fight each other. According to Beloved, he must wait a certain number of hours before he could return to Earth.

Lightfoot knew from Cara that hours were a measure of time. But he had no clear sense of how long an hour actually was. And he didn't understand the number that Beloved had used.

The Hunter, looking embarrassed, nodded and backed away from the tree. At the same time, Beloved clutched her chest. "Go!" she shrieked. *"Go!"*

This was followed by more words the Prince couldn't quite understand, followed by final words that were all too clear: "Go and kill unicorns! Kill them! *Kill them all!*"

The Hunters erupted in a mighty cheer. Then, without uttering another sound, most of them broke into groups of three and four. The maidens, who had been standing in a cluster, split up, each going to join one of the groups. Lightfoot noted that there were not enough maidens to go around, so that most groups were maidenless.

"Go!" cried Beloved again.

Lightfoot stiffened and held himself as still as possible, hoping none of the Hunters would come near him. One group did pass close to his right side — too close for comfort, but, to his relief, not close enough to spot him. Within moments, Hunters and maidens had faded into the forest, leaving Beloved alone.

At least, Lightfoot thought she was alone. So he was surprised when she turned to her right and said, as if answering a question, "Yes, it is indeed as you promised."

Is she talking to someone else? wondered Lightfoot. He moved closer, then pointed his ears forward, straining to hear.

The hint of a whisper came to him, too faint to make out the words.

Smiling, Beloved said, "I will not forget what I owe you."

So intent was Lightfoot on trying to hear the voice that responded to Beloved that he neglected to pay attention to closer sounds, such as the lightest of footfalls approaching from his right. It was only when a spear grazed his side that the Prince realized what danger he had been ignoring. He spun and bugled a challenge. Two men were sprinting toward him, their swords drawn, their faces twisted with bloodlust. The second man, who still held his spear, raised it and threw. It hurtled through the air to lodge itself in Lightfoot's shoulder. The Prince bugled again, this time in pain.

The men were almost on him. In that instant, Lightfoot knew what he must do. Turning from the Hunters, ignoring the searing pain in his shoulder, hoping the barrier truly was down now, he galloped toward Beloved. If he could move fast enough, fiercely enough, perhaps he could trample her beneath his hooves.

Beloved saw him coming and exulted. "First blood!" she cried, her voice filled with an unholy joy.

The spear embedded in Lightfoot's shoulder drooped, then snagged on a root. The impact ripped it free, tearing open a wound that sent scarlet-silver blood flowing down his chest and a lightning bolt of pain shooting into his leg.

As the Prince staggered, Beloved drew a dagger from beneath her robe. Its blade flashed red in the Blood Moon's light.

Lightfoot reared, intending to send a rain of silver hoof-blows onto her head. But he had underestimated his enemy. She flung the blade. It penetrated his chest between his fore-legs, causing him to stagger again.

Reaching into her robe, Beloved pulled out another dagger.

Raw terror seized Lightfoot, and he knew, with every fiber of his being, that he did not want to die on a blade wielded by this madwoman. In that same moment, he saw the answer, shimmering beyond her: the gate to Earth!

Gathering what was left of his strength, Lightfoot hurtled forward, racing past Beloved.

"Stop him!" she shrieked. *"Stop him!"*

The Prince was almost at the opening now. Ignoring the fiery pains in his chest and side, Lightfoot jumped into the wounded tree and galloped along the wooden tunnel. With a leap that took most of his remaining strength, he soared through the shimmer of light. A strange tingle ran the length of his body as he did, causing him to gasp.

He continued forward, carried by his own momentum, and seconds later found himself in the very last place he — or any unicorn — would have ever thought to seek for shelter: the courtyard of Beloved's castle.

A shout of rage from behind made Lightfoot realize he was not safe yet. One of the men had leaped through the tree in pursuit.

"Die, unicorn!" roared the Hunter, his words far too easy for the Prince to understand. "Die in the name of Beloved!"

The man raced forward, his blade pointed straight at Lightfoot's heart.

Though the Prince was eager to do battle, his wounds were too much, and he found that the last of his strength was gone. Lacking the energy to fight, or even to run, he braced himself for the end.

The Hunter raised his sword to strike. But as the blade began its downward arc, the man's face twisted in pain and terror. He cried out, an uncomprehending shout that echoed eerily from the castle walls. His sword clattered to the cobblestones when he dropped it so he could beat helplessly at his skin.

Watching in horror, Lightfoot saw the man's flesh start to bubble. The Hunter fell to the ground, screaming as he writhed in agony.

A moment later, he was dead.

Staring at the twisted, blackened corpse, Lightfoot remembered Beloved's warning to the other Hunter about opposing magics. Then his own wounds overcame him. His knees buckled, and he collapsed onto the cobblestones.

At least they're only wounds, he thought, *not two kinds of magic warring within my flesh.*

He was still trying to remember exactly why that was important when everything went black.

The unicorn prince lay unconscious in the courtyard of his greatest enemy.

CHAPTER III

THE RUBY FAILS

In the red shaft of the Rainbow Prison, Ian Hunter knelt in front of an ancient tree, holding a dying street urchin in his arms.

That boy, Rajiv by name, had just reached out his hand to touch the cheek of Ian's wife, whose ghostly form, insubstantial and seemingly insensible, was sitting inside the tree's hollow trunk.

Though Ian had tried desperately, he had been unable to rouse his wife from her magical sleep. But at Rajiv's touch Martha Hunter had opened her eyes and whispered, "There you are!"

Ian had shouted with joy. Martha drew back, as if she found the sudden outburst painful.

Behind him, Ian heard his friend Fallon breathe a sigh of relief. That sigh was easy enough for Ian to translate: *Maybe, just maybe, we will escape this strange prison after all.*

Most of the inmates of the Rainbow Prison — including

24

the aggravating woman Felicity, who stood watching from a few feet away — could remain indefinitely without experiencing harm. That was because, like Martha, they were present in spirit only, their bodies safe back on Earth. But Ian, Fallon, and Rajiv had rashly entered this scarlet hell *with* their bodies. And because the Rainbow Prison was made only of light, they had been without food or water since they arrived. Which was why Rajiv now had but hours to live; dehydration had taken hold of him. Ian figured he himself might have only another day before he suffered the same fate. Fallon, who seemed to have an unnatural vigor, would probably last longer, but even *he* must succumb sooner or later. Finding Martha had been the key to their chance for escape — and survival.

Turning toward his mysterious friend, Ian lifted Rajiv. Fallon bent, causing his long, golden hair to fall past his shoulders, and scooped the boy into his muscular arms. Looking up, Rajiv murmured, "Good news, Sahib Fallon! Now that we have the memsahib we can go home." He sighed, then added, "If not, at least I got to see her. I am glad of that, since we worked so hard to find her."

He sighed and his head lolled to the right as he drifted back into unconsciousness.

Ian's gut tightened. He had to get them out of here before it was too late for the boy. Aching to hold his wife, but knowing that her form was less substantial than mist, he whispered her name, packing a world of love and longing into that one small word: *Martha*.

25

"Ian," she whispered back, and he winced at the fear he heard blossoming in her voice. *"Ian, where am I? Why is everything so red?"*

"You are in the Rainbow Prison, my love. At least, your spirit is. I came to fetch you, but we're going to have to work together to escape. Can you step out of the tree? I'd help, but, well . . ."

He put his hand on her arm to demonstrate.

Martha screamed when his hand passed through her arm as if she were nothing but a ghost.

"Shhhh! Shhhh, love. It's all right. Like most people here, you are present in spirit only."

"Ian, I don't understand! It seems as if I've been wandering in dreams for . . . for I don't know how long. I had strange dreams, about you and a boy and a very tall man, dreams that you were searching for me. Before that I sensed Cara, once. At least, I think I did. Except she was so much older than she should be . . . almost a teenager!"

Ian flinched, but said nothing.

"It seemed like a dream," continued Martha, "and at the same time it felt more real than life." She paused, looked around, then asked again, "Where are we? And why is everything so red?"

"We're in a place called the Rainbow Prison. Beloved sent you here."

Martha's face darkened. *"I hate that woman!"*

"You have good reason. We both do. Even so, without her I would not have found Cara."

"You've found Cara? Where? *Where is she?*"

"In Luster."

Martha looked blank, and Ian realized that Beloved must have kept more things from his wife than he had realized. "Luster," he said gently, "is the world of the unicorns."

Martha closed her eyes and said sadly, "I've lost my mind."

Ian cursed himself for revealing too much too quickly. "Sweetheart," he urged again. "Can you leave the tree?"

"Don't be silly. Of course I can!" But when she tried to stand, it proved impossible. Her face twisted in panic. "Ian, I can't move!"

The fear in his wife's voice pierced Ian Hunter's heart, which was already sinking under the burden of his own fear. All through his search for Martha he had expected that she would be as the other prisoners in this place, free to wander about. But now it seemed that Beloved must have double-ensorcelled her, not only sending her to the Rainbow Prison but at the same time somehow binding her to this spot.

He called to mind the directions given to him by the Blind Man back in India — directions for which he had traded the occasional use of his eyesight.

"Here is what you will have to do, Mr. Hunter," the man had said. "There must, by the laws of magic, be some object of power that was used to place your wife in the Rainbow Prison. Very likely, it was a ruby similar to the one you carry. If that is the case, then once you find your wife you should be able to use your own ruby to send her back to her body."

"And if that is not the case?" Ian had asked.

The Blind Man had smiled ruefully, shrugged, and said, "That is a risk you must take. Now, assuming you *do* manage to send your wife back to her body, she must then find the focus object that matches yours. With that in hand, the two of you should be able to sing a connection into being."

Ian would have queried the Blind Man on this, except that he knew that such singing was how Cara had pulled her grandmother out of the green shaft of the Rainbow Prison several weeks earlier.

"It is not easy to do this," the Blind Man had continued. "It requires a deep connection of the heart. Obviously, the song must be one that is of special meaning to both of you. And, of course, absent the focus object here on Earth, it will not work at all."

That was the big gamble, the one on which he had staked everything: that Martha would be able to find the matching ruby. Praying that his own ruby would indeed send her back, he reached into his pocket and said, "Martha, listen carefully. I am going to try to return you to your body."

Her eyes widened. "How?"

"With a ruby that Cara gave me . . . the same ruby that let you see her. If this works, then as soon as you are back in your body you must try to find a similar ruby that I hope will be hidden somewhere nearby. Once you have it, you and I should be able to use the jewels to pull the rest of us back to the physical world."

"How do we do that?"

He smiled. "Your mother was trapped in a place like this —"

Bitterness twisted Martha's face. "Do not speak to me of that woman! She is no mother of mine!"

Ian was startled by the venom in her voice, then understood. "Martha, there is a great deal you don't know yet. Once we're out of here, I'll tell you everything. At least, everything I know myself."

She looked as if she were about to cry, but it seemed tears were impossible in her current condition. With a heavy sigh she said, "I don't understand any of this, Ian. I just want to go back to where we were before my mother stole Cara. *I want us to be a family again!*"

Without thinking, Ian reached for her, then remembered he could not yet hold her. His voice thick with sorrow, he murmured, "We can't go back, Martha. And we can't retrieve those years. That doesn't mean we can't find something good in the future, all three of us — you, me, and Cara. But first we have to move through this."

Martha nodded, then said softly, "I'm sorry, Ian. We'll save that for later. What do I do once I find this jewel?"

"Sing to me."

She gave her husband a skeptical look.

Lifting the great ruby, he said, "Hold the matching gem and start to sing. Cara has done this once, managed to connect to . . . to someone in the Rainbow Prison and sing her out. We'll have to be open to each other, sweetling. Sing with open heart. Once I hear you, I'll sing back."

Martha shook her head, baffled, but said, "All right, I'll try. But what do I sing?"

"How about, 'The Heart That Stays True'?"

She smiled slightly, her face pained. It was "their song," the one they had claimed as a mark of their love before their marriage, back when they were both teachers and the world had still made sense.

"Fallon and Rajiv will be coming with me," continued Ian, hoping as he said it that this would indeed be the case.

She nodded, then said softly and with an odd mixture of anger and tenderness, "You have a lot of explaining to do, buster."

"I know," said Ian, though, in truth, he was not looking forward to those explanations. "All right, let's try. Are you ready?"

Martha nodded again.

Ian extended the ruby.

Nothing happened.

"Touch it," he urged.

"I can't," she whispered, her eyes desperate. "Ian, I can't lift my hands!"

He moved the ruby closer, put it against Martha's face, ran it along her arm.

Still nothing.

Desperate, but knowing he could not hurt flesh that was not there, he thrust the ruby directly into her chest.

Still nothing.

His own chest constricted. Everything, all their plans for

escaping from the Rainbow Prison, had depended on finding Martha and using the ruby to send her back to Earth. And now the ruby had failed. He wanted to weep, to scream. Had they come so far, survived so much, for this?

Kneeling in front of the tree trunk, placing his hand close to the cheek he could not touch, Ian whispered, "I'm sorry, Martha. I'm so sorry."

Before she could answer, a moan from Rajiv caught his attention. When he turned to ask if the boy's condition had worsened, the look on Fallon's face frightened him. Ian scrambled to his feet and hurried to the big man's side. "Is he . . ."

Fallon shook his head. "He still lives. But I fear it will not be for long. I think —"

"*Ian!*"

Spinning toward the tree, Ian Hunter was astonished to see his wife fading from sight. He flung himself toward her and reached into the tree trunk.

She vanished even as he tried to close his hands around her.

Ian staggered back, stunned, then wheeled on Felicity. "What have you done now?" he roared.

The woman shook her head, and he could tell by the expression on her face that she had no more idea what had happened to his wife than he had.

"Perhaps the ruby had a delayed effect," said Fallon.

"Possible, but not likely," said Felicity. She crossed to the tree and peered into the now-empty hollow trunk. "Gentlemen, I am as baffled as you are." She smiled. "Isn't it fascinating how mysterious this all is? If it weren't a matter of life and death for you, I'm sure you'd be enjoying this as much as I am."

Rajiv moaned again, so softly it was like the slightest whisper of wind through leaves.

Ian sank to the ground and leaned against the trunk, staring at the space where his wife, who he had crossed two worlds to find, had, quite literally, just faded away.

With her had gone their last hope for escape.

CHAPTER IV

IN THE HALL OF THE DELVERKING

When the Geomancer was captured at the base of the Axis Mundi by a cove of delvers, she had expected torment, perhaps even death. So she had been surprised when the creatures treated her with what seemed like a degree of awe . . . though whatever awe they might be feeling did not stop them from binding and gagging her before they carried her underground.

They grumbled and complained as they did all this, and M'Gama was startled to realize that she could make out their words, or at least most of them; their language seemed to be nothing more than a badly mangled form of the speech used by dwarves. The thought brought a pang of memory, as it made her think of her own dear Flensa, so recently killed in the delver attack on the home they shared.

M'Gama's captors carried her into their underground world through a cave not far from the Axis Mundi, five of them in a row holding her bound form over their heads as if she were a log. She did manage to shoot one glance backward before they went underground, looking to the great world tree as if it could somehow save her. In truth, her greatest hope at the moment was that she had managed to save *it*, by means of the rootwood spell she had been casting when the delvers overcame her.

Once underground, they traveled down a steep slope for several minutes. The Geomancer was intrigued to see that the passage was lit, dimly, by glowing orange lines that ran along the walls. At the bottom of the slope, her captors stopped and put her down in order to add one more element to her imprisonment: a blindfold.

A moment later M'Gama heard one of the delvers chant something. They picked her up and began to move again. Almost at once a strange tingling ran across her entire body. She bit her lip to keep from crying out, but the sensation passed in an instant.

This odd prickly feeling was repeated twice during the next several minutes, and she wondered what caused it. Shortly after the second repeat, she heard a grinding sound, followed by a gravelly voice screeching, "Halt! Who seeks to enter the Great Hall of Gnurflax, King of Delvharken?"

"I am Braxton, leader of the Twelfth Cove. My cousins and I return from the great tree with a gift for the King."

"What is this gift?" demanded the first voice.

Braxton could scarcely contain his glee. "We bring him . . . the Geomancer!"

"Oh, I envy you," said the first voice. "This is a great prize indeed. Enter, and be welcome."

Beyond him, M'Gama heard another delver voice, deeper and richer than most delvers, bellowing, "I want Namza! Where is Namza? He can't simply have disappeared!"

"This is a good time to bring such a gift," whispered the guard who had challenged their arrival. "The King is unhappy."

"With Namza?" asked Braxton, and M'Gama could hear the surprise in his voice. "I thought he trusted the wizard with his life."

"He does," replied the guard. "Or did. The problem is, Namza is nowhere to be found. The King has been furious. We will all be glad of something that might change his mood."

A bit more carrying followed, then the delvers set her down. Rough hands stripped off her blindfold, revealing an enormous cavern dimly lit by pots of glowing fungus. Arrayed at the cavern's far side were nearly two dozen delver guards, each gripping a spear and standing at rigid attention. Pressed against the walls — or, in some cases, against thick stalagmites — the guards seemed so much a part of the cavern that it would have been easy for eyes less sharp, or less accustomed to the dark than M'Gama's, to miss them.

Even so, they were a minor concern for the Geomancer at the moment. Her focus was on the large delver directly ahead of her, who wore a crown of reddish brown stone. He sat on a throne, which was situated on a raised platform. With a start, M'Gama realized that both throne and platform had been carved from what had once been a massive stalagmite rising from the cavern floor. It was beautiful work, but also, to her mind, something close to a sacrilege.

Though her hands were still bound, she managed to bring herself to a standing position. At well above six feet the Geomancer towered over the delvers, most of whom were barely half her height. Her ebony skin, high cheekbones, full mouth, and broad nose were also a stark contrast with the pale delvers, whose lips were thin and whose noses were little more than two gaping holes in the center of their faces. Only their eyes, made for seeing in the dark, were larger than hers.

M'Gama was dressed in traveling clothes — sturdy trousers, a linen shirt, a simple but beautifully made brown cloak. Her proud stance gave even these humble garments a look of elegance — as did the many rings she wore, the stones of which seemed to glow with their own light even in this dim cavern.

As for King Gnurflax, he was dressed in a gray tunic and a short brown robe, both coarsely made, but still of better weave than was typical of delver clothing. His eyes burned with feverish intensity, and it was clear that he was delighted to discover who had fallen into his clutches. Digging his fingers into a bowl of freshly gathered grubs, he popped a handful of the squirming things into his mouth and chewed contentedly.

"So," he said at last, pausing to push half of a grub off his lower lip and back into his mouth, "the famous earth magician has finally come to visit the Children of the Earth."

M'Gama blinked at the reference to "the Children of the Earth." That was also how dwarves thought of themselves. Despite her surprise, she did not bother to answer Gnurflax. Instead, she simply returned his stare with a fierce dignity.

Her gaze infuriated Gnurflax, who snarled, "Don't play your silent games with me, woman. You and I have loathed each other at a distance for years now. Why not say what you think?"

M'Gama replied by spitting on the floor.

The King leaped to his feet. But before he could say or do more, a look of shock crossed his face.

The other delvers were silent, clearly not feeling whatever it was that had made the King pause.

M'Gama, however, did feel it, and felt, as well, a wave of loss and terror. Even as the King began to shout, "He did it! He did what he promised!" the Geomancer threw back her head and unleashed a wail that drowned the King's voice. Her cry was still echoing from the walls long after the guards had knocked her to the floor and gagged her once again.

M'Gama did not struggle as the five delvers carried her out of the Great Hall, again holding her over their heads as if she were no more than a log they were taking from one place to another. The reason was simple: She was overwhelmed with dread at what had just happened. She knew from her connection to the stone and soil of Luster, which were home to the roots of the Axis Mundi, that Beloved had not merely created a gate into Luster. Somehow she had managed to damage the world tree itself. What that would mean, not only for the unicorns, but for Luster, the Geomancer did not know. Of only one thing was she certain: The results were bound to be dangerous — horribly dangerous.

The delvers carried M'Gama into a room-sized cave, lit, barely, by orange stripes like those that ran along the passageways. Without a word, they chained her to one of the walls. In an odd way, the imprisonment was almost kind, for they secured only one ankle and one wrist. Both chains were of sufficient length for her to sit on the stone outcropping to her right, even to lie down if she wished. Additionally, she noticed a small pool, fed by a trickle of water, in a declivity to her left. So, she would not want for something to drink. She suspected they might even provide food, though she also suspected it would take two or three days of hunger to make whatever they gave her seem edible.

Still not speaking, the delvers left the chamber. A few minutes later the orange stripes faded, and the darkness around her was complete.

M'Gama didn't mind; she spent much of her time underground and was used to darkness. In truth, she was relieved to be alone at last. She needed to think.

The big question, she decided, was how much damage had been done to the Axis Mundi. She had tried her best to save the tree from destruction by weaving a spell of protection as she placed four pieces of enchanted rootwood into its trunk. Unfortunately, the delvers had captured her before she had completed the spell. So she was not sure how much effect it would have.

As she continued to think, she changed her mind. The truly big question was whether there was any way to *heal* the Axis Mundi. She leaned back against the wall, then pressed herself to it, trying to draw strength from the stone around her. It worked — she did feel strength flowing into her. But at the same time she felt something that filled her with new terror.

The world was quivering.

It was the tiniest of vibrations, nothing that anyone not as attuned to stone as she was would even notice. But she had no doubt about it.

And then the Geomancer felt something else, something that caused her to stretch her senses in the way of someone trying to discern a faint smell caught on the softest of breezes.

Yes, there it was again! This time she could tell what it was, and she nearly cried out in shock. Not too far from her someone of great power, power much like hers, power rooted in stone and tied to Luster, was held in some strange enchantment.

Who was it? Where was he — or she — imprisoned?

The Geomancer opened her senses, reached out all around her. But the touch of magic was gone, as if whoever it had come from was exhausted.

CHAPTER
V

DRAGON TASK

In the first moments after Beloved breached the border between Earth and Luster the panic among the unicorns had been horrible. But the terror had subsided, at last, into an uneasy quiet.

Now the Queen's Council had gathered to discuss the situation.

Cara had been invited to attend. She felt honored to be asked, but soon found herself frustrated, for it seemed there was much of fear in the discussion and little of practical ideas.

To make things worse, she was still exhausted from her journey to the Valley of the Centaurs. Struggling to stay awake, she leaned against the silvery-blue bark of an eldrim tree, staring at the golden hoofprint in the center of her right palm. It had appeared there after she had killed the Chiron, the King of the centaurs. She had done this, which was his last and greatest wish, in return for the story she had been sent to seek. He had vowed he would only tell it to her if she agreed to crush the magical egg holding his life force, which had kept him unnaturally alive for many centuries, until he had become little more than a withered husk.

Now, much as she tried to focus on the talk of the council, she found her mind drifting back to that story, which had cost her such torment of heart to learn. It was a tale both startling and disturbing, for it revealed that the unicorns had an enemy even more dangerous than Beloved. Even worse than that, this secret enemy — known only as "the Whisperer" — had been created from the unicorns' own darkest feelings.

The council had been arguing about this story and what it might mean when Beloved's invasion had begun. Now all attention had turned to the immediate crisis. As Cara listened — *tried* to listen — she began to wonder if that long ago ceremony, in which the unicorns had tried to rid themselves of all that was less than perfect within themselves, might not also have robbed them of the fire they would need to fight Beloved's invasion.

Moonheart's deep voice caught her attention, bringing her back to the moment.

"*Where* has the enemy entered?" he was saying. "That's the most important question right now, Amalia. How far away are the Hunters?"

"M'Gama was trying to discern where Beloved would make her attempt," replied the Queen. "But she has not been in contact — which is one more thing I am concerned about.

It is not like her to remain silent at a time like this. I fear something has happened to her."

"Without word from M'Gama, we have no way of knowing how quickly the Hunters will be upon us," said Fire-Eye. "They might be anywhere!"

Cara wished Lightfoot were beside her, so they could talk mind-to-mind, as they often did during such meetings. Then she wished she hadn't wished it, because wondering where he was, what had happened to him, only added to her fear and despair.

The conversation went on. And on. When the Squijum came bounding out of the darkness to curl in her lap, she yawned and shook her head. His silly, furry presence was comforting. Despite the terrifying events, the night was cool, the air sweet. And she was, with good reason, exhausted. . . .

In her dream Cara was searching for the Dimblethum. She was troubled, because she could not find the shaggy creature — who always made her think of a bear who had gone halfway to becoming a man — and she was beginning to fear for him. The gruff beast had saved her from a delver when she first fell into Luster. Now, for some reason, *she* needed to help *him*.

But where was he?

Suddenly she heard him calling, as if from a great distance, "Cara! Cara, the Dimblethum has done a bad thing. The Dimblethum is sorry."

She ran, trying to reach him, to comfort him, but found herself tangled in darkness. Her legs would not work, refused to run as she commanded them. The frustration was reaching panic level when the sound of her name being called woke her.

Cara blinked and sat up. The unicorns — and Alma Leonetti, the only other human present — were all looking in her direction.

"I am sorry to wake you, granddaughter," said the Queen. "But we need you to join this discussion."

Cara scrambled to her feet, embarrassed to have fallen asleep when so much was at stake. "I'm sorry," she said quickly. "Sorry!"

"No need to apologize," said gentle Cloudmane. "Your sleep is well-earned. It is we who are sorry to wake you. However, the conversation now concerns you."

"Do you have something for me to do? Just tell me. I'll do anything you ask!"

"Generally better to know what you are agreeing to before you make a statement like that," said Alma Leonetti.

Cara remembered vividly the story that Grimwold had told during their journey to the Valley of the Centaurs, the tale of how Madame Leonetti had come to Luster as a young woman in order to plead for the unicorns to return to Earth. They had not done so, of course. But the old Queen had agreed to send one unicorn back, as a reminder of the beauty and the magic that had been lost when the unicorns fled. That unicorn, known as "the Guardian of Memory," volunteered to spend twenty-five years on the home world, at which time it would be relieved by another. Their job was simple: For those humans sensitive enough to feel it, the Guardian's very presence kept alive the memory of what it meant to have unicorns in the world.

In more than one case, the Guardian had fallen prey to Beloved and her Hunters.

Cara wondered what it must be like for Madame Leonetti to know that her request had cost the lives of several unicorns. Yet, it was clear she had an honored position here at the court. In fact, she had been allowed to drink from the Queen's Pool, which was why she was still alive now, hundreds of years after she had first come to Luster.

It was all so hard to understand. . . .

"We have been talking about who might help us in our hour of need," continued the old woman, "and Fire-Eye has put forth the idea of asking for assistance from one of the dragons."

Cara felt a tightening in her heart. She had an idea where this was heading. "Which dragon?" she asked. "And why?"

Alma Leonetti smiled. "The why is easy. We need allies in the struggle to come, and there are none more powerful than the dragons. Even one of them would be an enormous aid to our cause. The question at hand is: Would you be willing to go and make the request?"

"Why me?" asked Cara, her voice smaller than she had intended. Immediately she felt embarrassed. Why question it? She had offered to do whatever was necessary. But . . . well, she had already faced two dragons, and while she knew she could, potentially, survive such an encounter, she also knew how terrifying it might be.

It was the Queen who answered. "We make the request of you for two reasons, granddaughter. The first is speed. None of the dragons are close at hand, and it would take days for any of us to reach them. However, Medafil has offered — with much fussing — to fly you to the dragon's lair. Which means the journey will only take a couple of days."

"And the second reason?"

"That should be obvious," said Moonheart, never one to phrase things gently. "You have the gift of tongues and can speak to dragons in their own language. They respect this and will be more likely to respond as a result."

"So which dragon would you like me to visit?" asked Cara. "Firethroat?"

She hoped that would be the case. She knew Firethroat and felt she would not be in great danger in her presence. The dragon would at the least be polite and might even be pleased to see her.

Alma Leonetti shook her head. "While the Lady Firethroat is fond of you personally, she is not especially a friend of the unicorns."

"Certainly you don't want me to ask Ebillan!"

Ebillan had been her second dragon, and he was another matter altogether. Cara had barely survived her encounter with that angry beast and had pretty much promised never to bother him again.

Alma Leonetti shuddered. "No, that one is best left at peace."

"Then who?"

She knew Luster held five more dragons, but of these she knew nothing but their names: Red Rage, Fah Leing, Graumag, Bronzeclaw, and Master Bloodtongue.

"That question was debated at great length while you were sleeping," said the old woman. "Though Fah Leing is likely to be on our side, he might choose to take no side at all. Red Rage is far too unpredictable, and not one we would send you to speak to. That leaves Bronzeclaw, Master Bloodtongue, and Graumag. Of these three, we think the one most likely to come to our aid is Graumag."

"Can you tell me about him?"

"Her, actually. She is young, as dragons go, though she was one of the first to arrive in Luster."

"Why was that?"

Her grandmother shook her head. "I do not know. There has always been a bit of mystery about the Lady Graumag, even more than the others, all of whom keep to themselves."

"Then why do you think she would be the most likely to come to our aid?"

Alma Leonetti rubbed her chin. "Though Graumag is basically a solitary beast, she is friendlier than most and will gladly talk with anyone who comes through her territory." She bit her lip, then added, "Unfortunately, that territory is on Dark Mountain, which rises on the southwest shore of the Lake of Tears, and is more exciting than it is pleasant."

"Why is it called 'Dark Mountain'?" asked Cara nervously.

"Eternal clouds loom over its peak, so that the mountain lies in deep shade at all times. Very little grows on its slopes, since so little light falls there. As Moonheart told you, Medafil has agreed to fly you. That is assuming you accept the task, of course. You are free to say no. But we asked you because the fastest way to reach her is by flying, and your gryphon friend cannot carry a unicorn — or even, until his wing is more fully healed, a large human."

"You do not have to accept this task, Cara," said her grandmother gently. "You have already done more than your share by making the journey to the Valley of the Centaurs."

"I'll go," said Cara. "Of course I'll go!"

She was pleased that she was able to hide her fear so well that her voice barely trembled.

CHAPTER
VI

THE CALLING OF THE COVE

After leaving the Valley of the Centaurs, the delver who Cara had nicknamed Rocky had spent the better part of two nights wandering in a vaguely homeward direction.

In a very undelver-like way, he traveled aboveground. This was partly because the tunnels of Delvharken would be dangerous for him. He was, after all, still supposed to be locked in the King's dungeon, and he was fairly certain his fellow delvers all knew it.

His other reason for staying aboveground was that he was deeply confused by what he had learned about the origins of his people. He could not decide what, if anything, he should do with the information, and simply did not want to see any other delvers until he had been able to think it through.

Normally he would have taken the story to King Gnurflax. However, since it was Gnurflax who had stripped Rocky of his true name and then sent him to the dungeon, it was unlikely he would find a willing ear there. He thought several times about trying to contact his teacher but feared that even the attempt would endanger the old delver, whom he loved and honored above all others. Not that danger wasn't all around now, anyway. But his teacher would be in no position to help when things got worse — as they were sure to — if the King had already disposed of him.

Finally Rocky decided to act as any proper delver would and seek out a cave where he could think in peace.

It did not take long to find a place that suited his needs. It was a great relief to hide himself in the cave's darkness, which was even blacker than that of the night outside. After unbuckling the short sword the centaurs had given him, Rocky settled into a corner. It was nicely cold and hard. He crossed his hands over his chest and closed his eyes.

By the time the sun's rays began to spill in at the front of the cave, Rocky was unhappy to discover that he did indeed know what he must do next. It was not a pretty thought.

Sighing, he got to his feet and began to search the cave for the things he needed. The task took longer than he expected, for the tools had to be exactly right. But in time he had eleven stones arranged in front of the place where he had been sitting.

Picking up the first stone, he named it — being careful to get the pronunciation precise and exact. Then he spat on the stone and put it back on the cave floor. He lifted the second stone and performed the same ritual, though with a different name. He repeated this until he had named all his cousins. He then returned to his place and sat facing the semicircle of stones. Closing his eyes, Rocky crossed his arms, placed his palms flat against his chest, and began to chant.

Rocky's cousin Razka was the first to feel the call, which started like an itch at the back of his brain. He didn't know what it was at first and shook his head, trying to dislodge the strange feeling. It did no good; the itchy-tingly tickle persisted. It reminded him of the sensation you get when you run into a cobweb in the dark, except that instead of being on his skin it was *inside* his head. Razka felt a rising panic, wondering if some strange night creature had crawled into his ear while he was sleeping and was now burrowing through his brain.

"Razka!" growled Pedrak, the leader of his new cove. "What's wrong with you?"

"Nothing," said Razka quickly.

"Then stop that blasted twitching!"

Razka hated Pedrak, and didn't want to give the *skwarmint* any excuse to apply discipline. He sighed. In truth, Pedrak wasn't all that bad. It was just that Razka didn't belong with this cove, and neither Razka nor Pedrak could forget that fact. But the King had assigned Razka here after sundering Razka's proper cove, and who were they to argue?

The maddening sensation continued. Finally, Razka recognized it for what it actually was: the nearly irresistible cousin-call. All delvers knew of this, but it was rarely used, since cousins almost always traveled together, anyway.

Who was calling?

Razka stopped, let the feeling wash over him, and sighed again. It was the nameless one, of course. Hadn't that dratted delver — Razka couldn't even think of what to call him — caused enough trouble? Stones and bones! He was the main reason the cousins had been scattered to different coves, flung like a handful of pebbles to places where they did not belong and were not truly welcome.

Razka tried to shut out his cousin's call, but it did no good. The itchy feeling grew stronger.

In the cave, Rocky could feel the connections begin. First Razka, then the twins Erkza and Rendzi, then Gratz, who was the youngest of the cousins — came within his web.

But he needed more.

His arms began to ache, but he did not lower his palms from his chest. His throat grew parched and dry, but he did not cease his chanting. His head throbbed from the effort, but he did not break his focus.

He had more connections to make.

Zagrat was scrabbling over a slope of broken shale when he felt the call. Like Razka, he experienced it first as an itching at the back of his skull. Unlike Razka, he knew immediately

what it meant and did not resist. He looked ahead. The rest
of his new cove was moving on, ignoring him as usual.
Without another thought, Zagrat turned and began trotting
in the other direction. Curses and rockfalls to the King and
his orders! The cousin-call was sacred, and the King was
crazy, anyway.

Rocky was relieved when he felt the connection to Zagrat.
He was the oldest and wisest of the cousins, and the one
who most agreed that the King had indeed gone mad.
Adding him to the four who were already responding left
only two more to pull in. He would have greatly preferred
to bring together all eleven of his cousins, but that was
unlikely. Some would be too far away, some too stubborn,
or angry, or frightened to answer the call. Even getting seven
(enough, with himself, to make a *kurtzen*, a working cove)
was going to be difficult.

He was tempted to furrow his brow and concentrate
harder, but knew that would do no good. You couldn't force
this kind of magic. In fact trying too hard could actually
block it. He needed to try not to try, which was hard in
itself. The secret was to sink further into his own mind, to
send the call from a deeper, stronger, more real part of his
own being. It was dangerous, but it had to be done. Setting
aside his fear, breathing ever more slowly, Rocky abandoned
himself to himself.

As he did, the Stone began to reclaim him.

DAY ONE OF THE INVASION

In every separation lie the seeds of reunion, in
every reunion the seeds of separation.

Sebastian the Scrivener
First Chronicle Keeper of Luster, Second Scroll

CHAPTER
VII

EARTH

Lightfoot raised his head. Everything was dark, and he was in pain. The world felt strange beneath him, and he realized he was lying not on forest floor or grassy meadow, but smooth stones.

Slowly, memories came drifting back — first the horrid sight of that gaping hole being ripped through the great world tree as Beloved blasted her way into Luster; then the invasion of the Hunters, with Beloved herself at their head; and finally the memory of being attacked by two of those Hunters and of leaping, in order to escape, through the very opening that Beloved had created.

He shook his head in disbelief. *He was on Earth!* He had to get back to Luster, get back to warn the others. But something Beloved had said to one of her men floated up from memory, something about not passing back through the gate too quickly.

With a shudder, he remembered the grisly death that had taken the Hunter who followed him through the tunnel.

That was what Beloved had been talking about! Clearly he had to let some time pass before he could return to Luster. The question was, How *much* time? Beloved had spoken of hours. But how could a unicorn measure an hour? And how many of them had gone by while he was unconscious? It was still dark, as it had been when he came through the gate. Did that mean he had slept only a little while, or that he had slept straight through another day while his body tried to heal his wounds?

Of course, that was assuming day and night in this spot were perfectly matched to where he had come from in Luster, which seemed unlikely.

He stretched, then shuddered as a throb of pain shot through his chest. Well, at least that was a clear sign that not too much time had gone by. If he had slept through another day, his natural healing magic would have done more work by now. Then he realized that even the passage of time would not have been enough to heal him, since there was still a dagger protruding from his chest.

Lightfoot bent his head to grab the hilt of the blade with his teeth, but failed on his first and second tries. Twisting his neck painfully, stretching, straining until he thought his veins would burst, the Prince finally managed to get a grip on it. With an agonizing wrench he extracted it. An arc of silver-crimson blood spurted from the wound, but quickly ceased to flow. Lightfoot waited, breathing slowly and carefully, as the wound sealed itself. It was not completely healed and still pained him, but the worst was over.'

He closed his eyes and tried to think. The question remained: How long had he been here? He was aching to return to Luster, but could not go back too soon. He shivered again at the memory of the Hunter who had pursued him through the tree and the grotesque way the man's skin had bubbled as the warring magics of his too-swift round-trip between Earth and Luster had quickly, and painfully, brought on his death.

The gate to Luster, waiting only a few yards away, seemed to beckon him. Lightfoot gazed longingly at the opening, which was embedded directly into the main gate of the castle itself. Unlike the opening in Luster, the edges of this gate were smooth and even. The sight of it was agonizing to him. The war had begun, he was needed, and Luster was only steps away. Yet he would do the unicorns no good if he leaped back into their world only to die moments after arriving!

With a sigh, the Prince heaved himself to his feet. His eyes were growing accustomed to the darkness, which was alleviated by the shreds of moonlight that made their way through the heavily clouded sky, as well as the faint glow of the opening to Luster. In the dim light, he could see the remains of the Hunter who had followed him — little more than bones now, the skeleton twisted by the man's final agonies.

The Prince turned away.

Looking around, he was able to discern that he was in the courtyard of a great fortress. Cara had told him about human buildings, and he had seen a few in Luster, M'Gama's house being the most elaborate. But he had never imagined anything such as this, so grand and vast, with towers that seemed to scratch the sky itself.

What kind of power and skills did these humans have to create such wonders? And how much did they cut themselves off from the world by doing it? You could stay within those towers and never feel the rain, or the sun on your skin, or the bite of cold.

The very idea made Lightfoot sad, and he felt sorry for the humans.

He was trying to decide what to do next when his body suddenly informed him that his first need was for food and water. Glancing around, he thought, *Well, if Beloved and the Hunters were living here, the castle must have some source of water. It shouldn't be too hard to find.*

It didn't him take long to discover that there was indeed a well in the courtyard. But unicorns are not made to turn handles or raise buckets, so whatever water was there would do him no good.

Frustrated — and far thirstier than he had been before discovering the useless well — Lightfoot continued his explorations. Soon he came to the castle doors. They towered above him, a pair of massive wooden slabs carved with strange images and, like the well, clearly not designed for a creature without hands. But Lightfoot was desperate, and after several minutes he managed to use his horn to trip the latch. At once the door on his right creaked open a fraction of an inch, just enough for him to insert the tip of his horn and ease it a bit farther. Into that new space he hooked his right front hoof. He gave a sharp tug — and the door swung smoothly open.

The Prince stepped inside, shuddering to think that he, a unicorn, was entering the very heart of Beloved's domain.

He found himself in a large room, most of its space taken up by several long tables. This must be where the Hunters gathered to eat. Unfortunately, the tables were bare.

At one side of the room he saw a broad stairwell.

He sighed. *I suppose I'd better see what's up there.*

He started up the steps, thankful he had had a chance to practice using the confounded things at M'Gama's home. Though he suspected Beloved had brought all her Hunters to Luster, he moved with a unicorn's silence, anyway. No point in taking any chances.

On the first level above the great hall, he found a long corridor lined with bedrooms on either side. Not one of them looked as if it had been used in many years.

The next floor contained more of the same.

The main stairwell ended here. But at either end of the corridor was another set of stairs, each of them tightly winding. These, guessed Lightfoot, must lead into the towers he had seen from the courtyard.

He resisted the thought of climbing them. The curve of the stairwell was so tight that his body would be twisting all the way up. He feared slipping and, even worse, reaching a point where he could not turn around, so that he might have to go backwards all the way down.

Still, the chance that he might find something, anything, that would be of use in the struggle against Beloved was not to be denied. So up he went, ignoring the pain that his half-healed wounds still gave him.

The tower had five levels, each level holding a single room, each room empty. The stairwell continued on, ending at last at a ceiling. Oddly, the stair went right up to this barrier.

Examining it more closely, the Prince realized it was actually a door, held shut by a latch. Though he did not have words for either of these things, he could see the outline of how it was supposed to open and a metal device that held it shut.

Frustration boiled within him. He closed his eyes and tried to calm himself, then studied the situation again. Soon he figured out how the latch worked and realized it might be possible to move it with his horn.

Possible, but not easy. Forcing himself to take slow, careful breaths, he poked at it with the tip of his horn. He was fearful of breaking off the point, for though the horn was strong and sturdy, it was not invincible. Just thinking of the way Whiteling's horn had broken off in Beloved's chest made him cautious.

His patience was finally rewarded when the latch slid aside. Bowing his head — he did not want to push up with his horn — he braced his neck against the barrier.

It lifted easily.

The sun was rising as Lightfoot came out onto the roof, a broad, flat area surrounded by a chest-high wall. He went to the edge. Far below stretched an exquisite landscape of woods and small lakes, gilded with rose and gold from the morning light. In the distance he saw snow-capped mountains.

The sight twisted something inside Lightfoot and an unexpected ache pierced him. *Home,* he thought. *This is home!*

Confusion swept over him. *Luster* was his home, and he loved it. But this place, this Earth . . . this was where the unicorns had been born, where they had lived until driven out, and *this* was his home, too — home in some deep, ancient way that he could not understand but that ripped at his heart.

The Prince felt a stinging in his eyes and his vision grew blurry. He felt a moment of panic before he realized with astonishment that he was doing something he had thought only humans were capable of.

He was weeping.

CHAPTER VIII

BLESSINGS AND FAREWELLS

"Are you ready to make our good-byes to your grandmother?" asked Medafil.

Cara looked up at the gryphon and nodded.

He twisted his enormous eagle's head to one side to stare at her. "You're sure?"

She nodded again.

"Well, then, dag-flammit, let's do it."

By "it" the gryphon meant their visit to Cara's grandmother, a necessary precursor to their mission. Though they both loved Amalia Flickerfoot, neither of them were entirely comfortable with her, since until a little while ago they had known her only as Ivy Morris. For Medafil, she was still, in many ways, the girl he had befriended long ago. For Cara, she was not only the grandmother who had lovingly raised her, but also the person who had stolen her from her parents. And now, restored to her true form, Amalia Flickerfoot was, for both of them, the Queen of the unicorns.

"Let's do it," agreed Cara.

They set out for the Queen's clearing. As they walked, Cara reflected on the fact that some of her uneasiness came simply because her grandmother was so different than she used to be. It was not just her shape that had changed. Ivy Morris was changing in other ways, too. As a human, she had been quiet and gentle. In her true form of Amalia Flickerfoot, however, she carried herself with a strength and pride Cara did not recognize. Oh, there was still enough of the old Ivy Morris in the Queen that Cara knew without a doubt who she was, who she had been. Even so, it hurt that the last seemingly solid foundation in her life had been shattered.

And that was not the only thing troubling her. Cara was also aware that she still harbored deep anger over the discovery that her grandmother had stolen her as a child, then let her believe that her parents were dead. The two of them had talked that out, and she now understood, at least somewhat, the reasons for her grandmother's actions. But understanding was not the same as forgiving, and not all of the bitterness had faded.

Cara's thoughts were interrupted by a soft sound from Medafil. Blinking, she realized they had reached the Queen's clearing. She did not know the unicorn who stood guard at the entrance, but given the hundreds of unicorns that had poured into Autumngrove over the last few days that was no surprise. The unicorn, on the other hand, knew at once who she was. That was no surprise, either, since she was the only human girl among them.

"The Queen is waiting to see you," said the guard. Then he stepped aside so Cara and Medafil could pass.

Cara's grandmother stood with her back to them, her head drooping. She turned quickly when she heard them enter the clearing. Though clearly glad to see them, she could not hide the weariness and concern that marked her face.

Cara wanted to say something, but "You look so worried" seemed flat-out foolish. How could the Queen not be worried? All of Luster was under attack, and the responsibility for defending it fell on her shoulders. Not knowing what else to do, Cara simply said, "I wish I could do more to help."

Her grandmother shook her head, causing her mane to ripple like silk spun from moonlight. "The regrets are all mine, dear child. You have already done far more than was fair of me to ask. And now you and Medafil have accepted yet another mission. This means a great deal to me, though my own wish is that I could shield you from all this."

"You shielded me all my life!" cried Cara. Then, unable to resist, and a bit more sharply than she had intended, she added, "Longer than you should have, with *some* things."

Amalia Flickerfoot sighed, knowing what she was referring to. "I learned my lessons as a human all too well, granddaughter. Stealth, slyness, deceit — they are not the unicorn way. And yet —"

Cara gasped. "And yet they may be just what we need!"

Her grandmother looked at her in puzzlement.

"Think about it, Gramma. Beloved expects you all to act like . . . well, like unicorns. But remember what Alma

Leonetti said just before the Blood Moon rose? 'Maybe you need to take in some of that darkness you once released.' Out of all the unicorns, *you* are the one who has some of that darkness. You learned it as a human. Don't do what Beloved expects — don't act like a unicorn — and maybe we'll have a better chance at survival!"

The Queen laughed, but not derisively. "Wouldn't it be an odd stroke of luck if the years I spent in human form, not even knowing who I was, turned out to be the key to our salvation? I've been fighting that part of myself, trying to return to being fully unicorn. But what I learned as a human may be the key. It may, indeed, be the key."

Cara smiled.

"Given the quality of that advice," continued the Queen, "you make me reconsider the mission I've given you. I'm tempted to keep you here as one of my councilors. But we really must try to enlist Graumag to our cause, and you are the best one to make this journey."

"I know. And I'm glad to accept the task."

"As I was certain you would be."

Cara's heart lifted at the pride she could hear in her grandmother's voice.

"And you, old friend," said Amalia, turning to Medafil. "Once again you come to my aid."

"As you have more than once done for me."

The Queen sighed. "Those were interesting times, were they not, Medafil?"

"Oh, very interesting. I think of them often. We were frequently in a biff-snippled pile of trouble."

"But never trouble such as this," whispered the Queen, looking past Medafil, past Cara, as if trying to peer into the future.

"May the time of simple troubles come again," replied Medafil softly.

Cara went to her grandmother and put her arms around her neck. As always since the transformation, she felt a pang of sorrow that her grandmother could not return the embrace.

"Travel safe, travel well, little wanderer," murmured the Queen. "May those who have gone before be always with you."

"And with you," replied Cara, tightening her grip on her grandmother's neck and burying her face in the silken mane.

They stood that way for a long moment, both acutely aware that it was possible they might never see each other again, and not only because of the dangerous task Cara was undertaking. Now that Beloved was in Luster, everyone was at risk.

"I love you," whispered Cara at last.

"And I you," replied her grandmother.

Cara released her grip and stepped back. Medafil, too, said his farewell to the Queen. Then the girl and the gryphon left the clearing. Cara glanced back once as they did.

The Queen had turned away. Her head was drooping again.

*   *   *

Alone in her clearing once more, Amalia Flickerfoot reflected on what her granddaughter had said.

Maybe the key did lie in her human side.

She thought, too, about the strange story Cara had brought back from the Valley of the Centaurs. Could it be true? If so, was this "Whisperer" at large in Luster even now? If they managed to survive the Hunt, what were they to do about him?

She sighed. It was too much. But Luster was hers to defend, and she would rise to the occasion — or die trying.

CHAPTER
IX

A DREAM WITHIN STONE

Namza, the king's wizard, slept the sleep of Stone.

This sleep was deep, undisturbed . . . and unintended.

It happened because Namza had decided to spy on King Gnurflax as the monarch conferred with the mysterious voice that seemed to be not only guiding but also warping his decisions. After silently following Gnurflax to the cave where Namza knew he spoke to the voice, the old wizard had pressed himself to the tunnel floor just outside the entrance. Then he had inched forward until he could see around the edge of the cave's opening. Once in place he had lifted a thin slice of mica into which he had poured an enormous amount of magic. Peering through it, he had tried to see who spoke to the King. But his attempt had attracted the bodiless voice, and at once Namza had felt its fierce attention shift toward him, felt the strange power of its eyeless gaze. Unexpectedly terrified, the old stone wizard had willed his heart to still its ferocious beating, his lungs to still their need for air, his body to still its functions, slowing,

slowing all signs of life as he tried to make himself unnoticeable.

In this attempt the wizard had succeeded all too well, passing from living delver to stone. Though he was not dead, it was possible he might never return from this sleep.

As he slept within the Stone, Namza began to dream. The images sometimes shifted, as they will in dreams, merging and sliding into one another. But they were also crystal clear, for they were not inventions, but true memories of his youth . . .

Namza's first dream was of his *nakken-gar*, the year of wandering that was part of his apprenticeship to his own teacher, Metzram, who was the king's wizard at the time. On the eve of the *nakken-gar*, Metzram had charged him with a task, as was traditional. In this case, it was to fetch some stones from the edge of a dragon's cave.

"The stones there will have absorbed great power," Metzram had told his pupil, "a power we can use in our spells." His scratchy voice had been solemn as he added, "Let me wish you success, my student. I would not like to lose you, as I did the last two students who undertook this task."

Then Metzram brought out a map, which showed the locations of the seven dragons that lived aboveground. Together he and Namza decided that it was Bronzeclaw's cave to which Namza would travel.

"I will not see you again for a year," said Metzram. Which was only right, for to return before the year was up would be a great shame. Crossing his arms over his chest, he said softly, "Earth and water, air and fire, may you find your heart's desire."

Namza repeated the gesture and the words. The next morning he began his journey.

He set out with high hopes, traveling at night, as was proper, and finding dark places to rest during the painful daylight hours. It was interesting to see the strange world aboveground on his own, rather than with his cove, as was the usual way. He took his time traveling to Bronzeclaw's cave; no need to hurry, since even if he succeeded in gaining the stones, he could not return before the year was out.

At the half-year mark, Namza reached the dragon's cave, which was set well above the tree line on a high and desolate mountain. He approved; the starkness of the stone held great beauty to his delver eyes.

The next stage of his task was to learn the dragon's patterns. To do that, he needed to find a hiding place far enough from the beast's lair not to be easily spotted, yet close enough to observe its comings and goings. Wherever he found would also have to shield him from the relentless sun. It took hours of searching, but he finally located a small cave that would serve nicely, and after driving out the furry creature that inhabited it, he settled in to watch.

It didn't take long to discover that the dragon hunted by dark. This was a great relief to Namza, as it would spare him having to cross the wide expanse of stone while exposed to the hideous sunlight.

After several nights he felt confident he could predict when it was safe to gather the stones he was seeking, and the next time Bronzeclaw left to hunt, Namza began the trek to the cave.

Alas, he had been overconfident. To reach the dragon's lair took more hours than he had expected. And finding the best stones, the ones that radiated the magic Metzram had taught him to look for, became deeply absorbing; there were many to choose from, and he wanted the best for his teacher. He smiled with pleasure each time he located one that had special strength.

Even though this took more time than he had planned, all might still have been well had not Bronzeclaw returned far earlier than Namza had thought likely. He was just tucking the last of the stones into the pouch at his side when he heard a rustle of wings. The sound struck terror into his heart. Spinning, he saw the great beast — fiery orange, save for its enormous claws, which were indeed bronze — swooping toward him out of the darkness. Namza opened his mouth to cry out in terror. At the same moment, the dragon opened its own huge mouth and unleashed a gout of flame that came within inches of searing off the delver's skin.

Namza turned and fled. Bronzeclaw was approaching far faster than he could run, but he knew it would take a few moments — how many he wasn't sure — before the flying horror could again breathe fire.

Reaching a ledge, Namza scrambled over. In his haste and fear, he misjudged the terrain — something shameful for a delver — and began a long, painful fall down the mountainside.

In his dream, the fall into darkness seemed to go on forever.

CHAPTER
X

A SLUMBER LIKE DEATH

Lightfoot found it harder to descend the stairs than it had been to climb them. After managing one flight, he stepped into the adjoining room so he could turn and back down the rest of the way. That method proved easier after all, even if somewhat nerve-wracking.

He finally reached the long hall from which the two towers rose. His thirst and hunger were worse, his wounds still ached, and the effort of going up and down the spiral stairs, so unnatural for a unicorn, had tired his still-healing body to the bone. Wearily, he stared along the corridor. It seemed unlikely the tower at the other end would hold anything different. Even so, and much as he tried to talk himself out of it, the Prince realized he *had* to explore it.

The war has started, he reminded himself. *Unicorns may be dying already. If I'm not in Luster to help, I have to do whatever I can from here.*

He sighed, then walked the length of the corridor and started up the other tower stair.

The first three rooms were empty. But when he peered into the room on the tower's fourth floor, one level below the topmost chamber, he found it well furnished, with a plush carpet, several chairs and dressers, and a large, canopied bed surrounded by scarlet curtains.

His first thought was that this must be Beloved's room. Then he spotted, through an opening in the curtains, a body on the bed.

Cautiously, Lightfoot crossed the room. Using the tip of his horn he pushed aside the curtain.

On the bed lay a beautiful woman dressed all in white. She was as unmoving as one dead, yet somehow the Prince sensed that she still lived.

Though he had never seen her before, Lightfoot knew at once who she must be. In this place, and with that flowing red hair, who *could* she be if not Cara's mother?

He tilted his head and studied her more intensely, thinking, *If she really is Cara's mother, that means she is the child born to the Queen during the long years she was trapped in human form.*

Which — strange as it seemed — meant that he and she were some degree of cousin.

Lightfoot shook his head in puzzlement. The sight of Martha Hunter — so like a grown version of Cara — filled him with an odd mix of feelings, the strongest of which was a new pang of fear for what might be happening to Cara right now.

He dragged his thoughts back to the present. Deciding

he should try to wake the woman, he snorted and tapped his hooves against the floor, softly at first, then harder, until the room was filled with a sound like the ringing of silvery bells.

The woman did not shift or stir.

Lightfoot shook his head, this time in vexation. Why did she not wake? Had he been mistaken in his belief that she still lived? But if she was dead, why was her body here on this bed?

Then he remembered: Beloved had exiled Martha Hunter's spirit to the Rainbow Prison, just as she had done to the Queen's spirit when she was still Ivy Morris. The reason he could not rouse Martha was simple: She was not here to *be* roused! What he saw before him was only an empty shell. The real Martha Hunter was far, far away, her true self trapped in another world.

Lightfoot cast his mind back to a night in Ivy Morris's house — his first and only trip to Earth before now, though he had scarcely experienced the world then. That night it had been a song that pulled Cara and her grandmother from the prison. The Prince shook his mane angrily. He couldn't sing! Besides, it had taken both the song *and* the ring M'Gama had given Cara to make the connection that allowed their escape.

He studied the woman again. Though she lay as if dead, he realized at last that she did indeed breathe. It was slow and shallow, and you could only notice it if you watched long enough. But there was no doubt of it once he saw it.

Well, there was one more thing he could try. Perhaps a healing would work. He hesitated. He was still weak from his own wounds, and attempting this would further drain his energy. Maybe he should rest first and try the healing later.

He shook his head in irritation. Things were moving too fast, there was too much happening for him to wait.

Taking a deep breath, Lightfoot placed the tip of his horn against Martha Hunter's chest. Pushing forward, he pierced the fabric of her gown, then her flesh.

The Prince expected the jolt — a healing always drained him of power. What he did not expect was the horrifying feeling that a giant hand had grabbed his sides and squeezed them, forcing out not only all the air in his body, but all the energy as well.

With a gasp of surprise he pulled his horn free and staggered back. He managed only a few steps before the world went black and he collapsed onto his side.

CHAPTER
XI

ON THE WINGS OF A GRYPHON

Alma Leonetti came to help Cara pack, though in truth there was not much to take, as she had so few clothes. Happily, the old woman brought some bread, some cheese, and some dried fruit for Cara to take with her.

"Thank you," said the girl as she accepted the food. Looking at it, she asked, "But where does this come from?"

The old woman smiled. "As you know, there is a scattering of humans in Luster. We do for each other what we can."

"But to make cheese, you have to have milk . . ."

"Humans aren't the only ones who occasionally stumble through one of the gates, Cara. Goats, in particular, seem to adapt well to this world."

Cara laughed and shoved the food into her pack. She was about to call for Medafil when she heard a whicker at the edge of the clearing, followed by a deep voice asking, "May I enter?"

"Of course, Moonheart," she replied, though she dreaded what Lightfoot's cranky uncle might have to say. With a start, she remembered that he was not merely Lightfoot's uncle, he was actually her own great-uncle!

Though she anticipated some stern words of advice, Moonheart simply stepped close to her and said, "There will not be a big farewell today, Cara. So I come on behalf of the council to offer formal thanks for what you are about to do."

Pleased, she nodded and said, "You know I am glad to help."

She expected Moonheart to give her the ritual words of parting and then leave. So she was surprised when he said, "I know you think I am hard on Lightfoot, Cara. And I suppose I am. But it is only because I want him to achieve his true potential. Though you may not believe it, I am as worried about him as you are. May the Bright Powers keep him safe."

"May the Bright Powers keep him safe," replied Cara with all her heart.

Moonheart leaned closer. "Travel safe, travel well. May those who have gone before be always with you."

Then, without another word, he turned and left the clearing.

"There's more to that one than you might think," said Alma Leonetti softly. She looked down for a moment, then raised her head and locked eyes with Cara. "These are dangerous times, child, the worst I have seen in my hundreds of years here. It pains me that we are sending you off on such a mission. But it is going to take everything we have to survive this, and what you are attempting now is vital. I hope to see you again in better days."

Then she, too, repeated the ritual words of farewell. Wrapping her mist-gray cloak around her, she left the clearing.

Minutes later, with the Squijum bounding along beside her, Cara joined Medafil. Fallen leaves rustled silver and blue around their feet as they left Autumngrove. Cara found the rich smell — earthy, slightly spicy — oddly comforting.

Once they were clear of the trees, Cara and the Squijum climbed onto the gryphon's back. Medafil spread his wings and began to run. A moment later he took a great leap. Great wings beating against the cool air, he carried them into the sky.

CHAPTER
XII

THE SLEEPER WAKES

When Lightfoot woke his body ached, and he was so weak he could scarcely move. He recognized the symptoms as those which always came with a healing, but he had never experienced them with such fierce power. Lifting his head a few inches from the floor, which was all he could manage at the moment, he saw that Martha was also awake. So the healing — he assumed it had been a healing — had worked.

She was staring at him with a frightened look.

Of course, thought Lightfoot. *If she has spent time with Beloved, she must believe I am a ferocious monster, bent on killing her. I should have thought of that!*

Though what he would have done differently if he *had* thought of it he couldn't have said.

What do I do now? If I could just communicate with her, explain to her . . .

He didn't dare try to touch her, since she would almost certainly think he was attacking. Though the idea that he could attack in his current condition was laughable.

79

She spoke. Lightfoot could only make out a few of the words, but her confusion and her concern were clear.

Come to me! he thought desperately. *Just come to me. Put your hand on my side and we can talk.*

At least, he hoped that would be the case. The energy flow he had felt as he tried to wake her was so unlike anything he had previously experienced he wasn't sure any of the magic had actually gone into creating the kind of connection he had with Cara.

He tried again to get to his feet, then gave up.

The sight of his struggle seemed to stir something in the woman. She rose from the bed. Lightfoot could see that, like him, her legs were weak. Even so, she managed a wobbly step forward, then another, before they buckled. She kept herself — barely — from collapsing. Lowering herself carefully to the floor, she began to crawl. The Prince assumed she planned to flee, to get out of the room before he could get to his own feet and attack. So he was astonished when, instead, she crept to his side and placed a hand upon his shoulder.

"Thank you!" thought Lightfoot.

She gasped and drew back, her eyes wide with the shock of hearing him in her mind.

Lightfoot longed to pull himself toward her and reestablish contact but was afraid of frightening her off. So he remained motionless, scarcely daring to breathe. After a few seconds, she reached forward again. As she did, he tried to settle his mind, so their second connection would not be too chaotic. Focusing himself, he thought as calmly as he could, "It's all right."

Though Martha's eyes widened again, her return thought arrived in Lightfoot's mind almost immediately. It was not, as the Prince had expected, some question about how they were able to communicate. Instead it was an immediate warning: "You should not be here! They will kill you."

Despite the urgency carried on the words, Lightfoot was oddly touched. He knew questions must be exploding in the woman's brain. Yet her first instinct was to warn him of his danger.

"Beloved and the Hunters have left," he replied. "No one remains in the castle except you and me."

As if released by this answer, now the questions did come tumbling out of her. "Where have they gone? Who are you? How did you wake me? Do you know how long I have been asleep? Why are you here in this horrible place?"

In spite of their predicament the Prince could not help but laugh. "I can tell you're Cara's mother! She's the only other person I've met who can ask questions that fast."

"I'm sorry. I'm very confused, and frightened, and —" Martha broke off the thought and stared at him in astonishment. "You've met my daughter? Wait! Yes — yes, you have! I can tell."

It was Lightfoot's turn to be astonished. "What do you mean, you can tell?"

Martha furrowed her brow. "I don't know, exactly. It's just that I can somehow sense her in you." She shook her head impatiently. "The why doesn't matter now. Have you really met her?"

"I have indeed. Met her, and healed her, and bonded with her, and been through many adventures with her."

"Adventures? She's just a little girl."

"Not that little," replied Lightfoot evasively.

"My god! How long have I been sleeping here? How much of my life has Beloved stolen?"

For this, of course, the Prince had no answer.

"Where is Cara now?" thought Martha fiercely. "Where is my daughter?"

Lightfoot tried to clamp down on his last sight of Cara, the image of her being carried into the forest by delvers. But the memory must have escaped his control, for the woman gasped in horror and pulled away, trembling and wide-eyed.

Words tumbled from her lips. Lightfoot could pick out a few of them, but they were mostly a babble of meaningless sound. Finally he lurched forward, placed a hoof against her leg, and thought sharply, "I cannot understand you when you speak out loud! We must be in contact, and you must *think* your message to me."

The woman took a few gasping breaths. "But that *can't* be Cara!"

"It was."

"No, no! She's too old! Cara is only . . ."

Taking a deep breath, Lightfoot thought, "She told me during our last journey that her birthday had passed, and she was now twelve years old."

Martha Hunter's cry of grief pierced the Prince's heart. "*Twelve?* Oh, god, oh, god . . ."

Lightfoot had no idea how to deal with the pain and loss that marked the woman's face. They were far past anything he could heal with his horn.

"My little girl," moaned Martha, curling into a ball. "My little girl!" Then, in a transition so swift it baffled the unicorn, she sat up and cried, "But she's in terrible danger!"

Lightfoot, who had had to keep shifting his own position to remain in contact with her, replied ruefully, "I'm sorry. I didn't intend to show you that."

"And why not? She's my daughter, isn't she?"

"I didn't intend to show you because there is nothing we can do right now. Also, I thought you would have too many other things on your mind, having just been woken this way."

"But she's my daughter! And she's in danger! What were those creatures? How long ago was this? What will they do to her? How can we get to her?"

Because of their connection he received not only Martha's questions, but also a sense of her terror and anguish, and beneath that, of the deep love she had for Cara. Which made his answer all the more difficult. "I do not know how long ago it happened. I've lost track of the time. I will confess that I am dreadfully worried about Cara myself. But I will also tell you this: She is brave and strong — probably braver and stronger than you would guess — and she has already survived things I would not have thought possible. Though I am concerned, I also have great faith in her."

"But what were those . . . creatures?"

"Delvers. They are enemies of the unicorns. Even so, I have hope they will not harm her."

"Why?" Martha asked eagerly.

"I believe their king is working with Beloved and that it was at *her* urging that the delvers were seeking Cara. If so, the delvers will want to deliver her to Beloved safe and sound. There is danger in that possibility, too, of course. But not of the same kind."

"Beloved," murmured Martha. She turned away from Lightfoot. When she finally turned back and placed a hand on his side, her face was red and stained with tears. It was also set with a fierce determination. "How can I get to Cara?" she asked. Before he could answer, she cried, "Wait! Wait!"

"What is it?" asked the Prince, alarmed by the look on her face.

"I just remembered — right before you woke me I was talking to Ian!"

This time it was Lightfoot's turn to flinch away. Martha's thoughts of her husband carried with them such a welter of emotions — anger and desire and fear and longing and loss and love all roiling together — that simply receiving them made his heart ache and his head pound.

She leaned forward, not willing to let him sever the connection. "I saw Ian," she repeated, and now the feeling that flowed most strongly on her words was confusion.

"I don't understand. Where did you see him?"

"He was in that horrible red place Beloved sent me to. But how can that be?"

Lightfoot was relieved to have a question he could answer with some certainty: "Your husband is a Hunter, is he not? The last time I saw him, he was setting out on a hunt to find *you*. So it does not surprise me that he made it into the Rainbow Prison."

"You've met Ian? I'm amazed he didn't kill you!"

"Your husband has left the service of Beloved."

She let out a little sob as she thought to him, "Has he truly?"

"Yes. And now, in return for that good news, may I please ask a question?"

Martha gave a tiny, rueful laugh. "Ian always said that my questions carried me away. All right, I do have more questions, urgent ones, but you certainly have one coming."

"After you woke, why did you touch me instead of running away? Surely, if you know Beloved, you must have been told I would be a fierce, ravening beast."

Her reply burned with anger, though it was not directed at him. "That's simple. Because I know Beloved, I know enough not to believe a single thing she has said. If she told me the sun rose in the east this morning I would have to check for myself to be sure."

"Ah, I understand. And why —"

"Later!" thought Martha fiercely, cutting him off. "Ian is trapped in that horrible place and I have to get him out!"

She put her head in her hands. Lightfoot moved one leg so they would remain in contact.

"It's all foggy," she thought to him, "but I'm starting to remember. Yes! He had someone with him — a boy. The boy was ill. Dying, I think." A new urgency filled her thoughts. "But what was it Ian told me to do?"

She was silent for a time, but Lightfoot could sense the fierceness of her concentration and knew at once when the answer came to her.

"I remember! He told me I had to come back here and look for a scarlet gem! He had a gem, too. It was supposed to send me back, but it didn't and we thought I was still trapped." She shook her head. "If the ruby didn't work, how *did* I get back here?"

"*I* brought you back, when I tried to wake you."

"You tried to wake me?" she asked, puzzled.

"With my horn. I tried first by making noise. When you didn't stir, I decided you must be trapped in some magical sleep. So I pierced your chest with my horn, thinking I might be able to break the spell."

Martha cried out, and her fingers fluttered to her breast.

"Oh, the spot where I pierced you healed instantly," thought Lightfoot, trying to sound reassuring. "But that piercing is what woke you. It's also the reason we can speak to each other. The horn makes a connection."

Martha nodded, looking dazed. "I wonder why Ian's ruby didn't work. I suppose it could have been because of Beloved's extra spell."

It was Lightfoot's turn to be puzzled. "Extra spell?"

"She didn't just put me in the Rainbow Prison," said Martha absently. "She used another spell to lock me in a kind of endless sleep while I was there." She shuddered at the memory, then pushed herself to her feet. Lightfoot could see she was growing stronger, as if full use of her body was returning.

He wished his own energy would come back as quickly!

She glanced around, muttering to herself and causing Lightfoot to wish, yet again, that he had paid more attention to Cara's human speech. But it was so much easier to communicate mind-to-mind, and he had not anticipated the need to talk to yet another human — much less Cara's own mother.

Martha began searching the room, appearing to grow increasingly frantic. Lightfoot tried to rise, as if he might help, but was still too weak from the healing. So he watched from the floor as she wrenched open drawers and pawed through their contents. Finding nothing, she stripped the sheets from the bed, then overturned the mattress. The Prince was astonished by the fury and determination on her face as she threw the pillows to the floor then pounded each with her hands, clearly feeling for a hard lump that would reveal a hidden gem. Finally she growled and bolted from the room.

Lightfoot was not sure how much time had passed when he heard a cry of delight from somewhere above. A moment later Martha rushed back into the room. Standing before him, she opened her hand to reveal a great scarlet jewel. She said something Lightfoot couldn't understand, then held the ruby so that it caught the morning sun pouring through the window. It blazed with crimson fire.

Lightfoot whickered to get Martha's attention.

She moved to his side, knelt, touched him. "What is it?"

"Cara had a stone almost identical to that one. It came from Grimwold."

"Grimwold?"

"The Chronicle Keeper of Luster. He gave Cara a similar jewel to use in bargaining with a dragon —"

"A *dragon*?"

The horror in her thought made Lightfoot flinch. "She handled herself well," he replied reassuringly. "But the jewel itself became a problem for her."

"Why?"

"Because she saw you in it — saw you in the Rainbow Prison, though she didn't know, then, that was the name of the place."

Martha's eyes widened. "I remember that! I sensed her — called out to her. But I thought it was only a dream. Besides, she was too old to be Cara. At least, that was what I thought." She choked back another sob.

"It really happened," thought Lightfoot. "Because the gem was her only connection to you, she didn't feel she could give it up. Happily, it turned out that the dragon wanted something else."

"Where is that jewel now?"

"You saw it in the Rainbow Prison. Cara gave it to her father, to use in his quest to find and free you."

Martha barely seemed to notice his response. Her face set and grim, she stared at the jewel, as if willing it to give her the answer. She stared and stared, then smiled as a scarlet light began to shine into her face.

With a nod of approval, she began to sing:

> *I looked far and wide*
> *For a heart to stay true . . .*

CHAPTER
XIII

THE ENCAMPMENT

Beloved's moon-white hair lifted and flowed about her shoulders as if it were a living thing. Looking across the growing village of tents, carefully arranged in neat lines, she said, "You have done well, Kenneth."

The muscular Hunter standing beside her, a tall man with reddish-golden hair smiled. "Thank you, Grandmother Beloved. You know I live to serve you."

The two stood at the edge of a wide field about half a mile southwest of the Axis Mundi. Beloved had sent out several of her Hunters to locate a good spot for their base of operations. Kenneth, one of her favorites, had been first to return, and she was well pleased with the place to which he had led her. Not only was the field large enough for their needs, it had a clear river, some fifty yards in width, running alongside it — protection and a good water source, all in one.

She decided Kenneth would receive a special reward when all this was over. Before she could say that she gasped, her approving thoughts interrupted by a fierce throb of pain in her chest — the eternal reminder of the ever-wounding, ever-healing piece of unicorn horn embedded there.

Though she controlled her face, Kenneth knew what that gasp meant. Beloved was never without pain, pain that rose and fell in intensity, sometimes cresting to a level that left her, briefly, speechless. He waited for the spasm to pass before saying, "We easily have room for all the tents."

"True. But we won't be using them much. I want most of the men out on the Hunt at all times. We have a lot to learn about this place, and I don't intend to spend years on the task. I want the slaughter of the unicorns to begin as quickly as possible."

"As you say, Grandmother Beloved."

"Please see to having my pavilion set up. I want to use it soon."

She shook a hand to indicate he was dismissed. Kenneth bowed, then quickly departed.

No sooner was he gone than — seemingly from nowhere — a voice whispered sweetly, "Is it not good?"

"It is everything you promised," Beloved replied, feeling a rare moment of content. She made a quick turn, as if hoping to catch a glimpse of her unseen visitor. As always, she saw nothing. "I have been waiting for you," she said plaintively. "Where have you been since we came through?"

"Doing my work," answered the voice, so casually she could almost hear a shrug. "And you? What have *you* accomplished in this time?"

"I have sent four hundred men out on their first Hunt in Luster. Most of them are after unicorns, of course. But I gave five teams, of twenty men each, tracing packets. The packets are seeded with my own blood, which the child shares. With the spells they carry, the packets should lead my men to her quite efficiently."

"Excellent," purred the voice. "And what of the unicorn who fled through the tree?"

"I have another twenty men waiting to go after him the moment it is safe to return to Earth."

"Very good."

"The men now out on the Hunt are charged with making notes of what they find," she continued. "We have a great deal to learn if we are to track down every last one of the beasts. It is going to be wonderful, though, to finally —" She stopped, flinching at another stabbing pain in her heart. When it had passed she continued, "to finally, after all these centuries, bring this to a close. I can almost smell the blood even now."

She paused, as if waiting for an answer. When none came, she said, "It does help to know that this is a fairly small world." Then, almost pleading, she added, "Can you not explain the place to me more thoroughly?"

"Is it not sufficient that I have helped you to come here?" asked the voice, suddenly sharp. "That I am with you even now?"

Beloved flinched, not from pain this time. "I do not wish to seem ungrateful."

"Nor do you," replied the Whisperer smoothly, gently. "Just overly curious."

"I am sorry. I seek only to know the things that will help accomplish our mission."

Again no answer came, but this time she knew the voice was gone. She could tell not from the silence but from a kind of emptiness in the air. With a sigh, Beloved turned her attention to the matters at hand. She was pleased to see her pavilion — a colorful tent larger and better furnished than the others — rising at the center of the field.

She paused to wait for the next surge of pain to pass, then went to where Kenneth and the other men were working.

"We will have your furnishings in place before the hour is out, Grandmother Beloved," said one of them.

"Good. I especially want my clock, so I can see when it is safe to send some men back to the castle."

"I envy them," said another of the men who was working on the tent. "That unicorn who went through will be an easy catch."

"Never underestimate them!" snapped Beloved. "*Never!* They're brutal and vicious."

Chastened, the man returned to his work.

Beloved nodded her approval to Kenneth and walked on, heading for the river. When she reached its banks and was able to gaze on the clear water, she thought, as she had so many times before, *Where did this place come from?*

It was a mystery she had contemplated ever since the unicorns fled from Earth.

A tremor shook the ground beneath her feet, causing the river to surge over its banks. The water sloshed against her feet.

Beloved found herself wishing the Whisperer were still close at hand. She wanted to ask what was happening to Luster now that she had finally managed to enter it.

CHAPTER XIV

"THE HEART THAT STAYS TRUE"

Still clutching the ruby, Ian crouched in front of the hollow tree, staring into it as if he could somehow will Martha's return.

He didn't truly want that; he wanted her free of this scarlet prison. But he didn't know if she had really escaped, or if Beloved had somehow discovered their attempted "jailbreak" and managed to intervene. The possibility terrified him.

The woman Felicity stood nearby, watching him as hungrily as he watched the tree.

The minutes crawled on. He had no way to check the time; in truth, for him time seemed to have stopped. So he had no idea how much of it had passed before Fallon, who was standing somewhere behind him, whispered, "Ian! Listen!"

He strained, not understanding at first. Then he caught it. Coming from the hollow trunk, faint but growing steadily louder, were the words of a long-loved song, sung by a long-loved, long-lost voice:

I looked far and wide
For a heart to stay true,
I found it at last
When at last I found you.

Ian leaped to his feet, crying, "Fallon, put a hand on my shoulder. Quickly! This may be it. We'll have to be touching for you and Rajiv to come with me."

Still clutching the boy in his free arm, the big man instantly did as Ian asked.

Martha's song continued, growing stronger and more clear. Opening his heart, setting aside his fear, Ian joined his voice — parched and rough though it was — to that of his wife:

Though I may wander
In paths far from you
I'll always return
To the heart that stays true.

In his trembling hand, the ruby began to glow. He heard Felicity gasp as a tendril of scarlet light snaked out from the jewel. The light moved slowly at first, as if puzzled, almost hesitant. But, when an answering glow appeared in the hollow trunk, the tendril of light thrust toward it.

"Hold tight, Fallon!" cried Ian.

The moment he broke from the song, the light began to falter.

"Keep singing!" replied the big man, tightening his grip on Ian's shoulder. *"Keep singing!"*

Ian picked up the song again. As he did, they were pulled toward the tree.

"Wait!" cried Felicity. "Wait! Take me! *Take me!*"

She lunged for them. But her insubstantial hands could not touch, could not grasp, could not hold. Ian, Fallon, and Rajiv whirled into the red, leaving Felicity's voice fading behind them.

CHAPTER
XV

RAZKA AND GRATZ

Gratz the delver felt a surge of relief when he spotted his cousin Razka. He, Gratz, was the youngest of their cove, and he had feared it might have been a deep foolishness on his part to respond to their nameless cousin's call. So it was good to know he was not the only one who was answering.

He waved his spear in greeting.

Gratz had traveled from a considerable distance to respond to the call. It would have taken him longer but he had slipped underground shortly after he started and used several transit points to speed him on his way. Now he was aboveground again, which he disliked intensely — especially because it was morning and growing uncomfortably bright. Any sensible delver would have sought shelter from the horrid sun by this time.

"We'd best hurry," he called when Razka, who was climbing the rocky slope below him, was close enough to hear.

"I've been hurrying since I felt the call — and hurrying even more since I felt it begin to wither," snapped Razka. "I just hope we're not too late. After all the trouble that nameless idiot has caused, I want him alive so I can throttle him myself."

A moment later the two delvers scrambled into the cave. Their eyes quickly adjusted to the darkness — such a relief after that hideous morning brilliance! Even so, it was not easy to find their cousin.

It was Gratz who finally spotted him, and then only because he noticed the array of stones on the cave floor. Looking beyond them, squinting, he made out the form of the one he was no longer allowed to call by name — who, in truth, had no name. The delver still sat cross-legged, as was proper for cousin-calling. But he was as gray as the rocks around him. His skin was starting to crack.

"Razka!" screeched Gratz. "Come here!"

Razka hurried over and stood next to Gratz, who was trembling. The two delvers stared at their cousin for a long time before Razka said, "He must have wanted us to come very badly."

"Do you think it's too late to call him back?" asked Gratz.

"That depends on how soon the others arrive. We'll need a full *kurtzen* to pull him out of this."

"Do you really think another six of us will show up?" asked Gratz.

"We only need five. That will make seven of us plus . . ." Razka fumbled for a word, and finally said, "plus *him*. That will be enough, since bringing our cousin back will complete the *kurtzen*. That's a powerful magic."

"So," mused Gratz, "the question is, do we have five cousins as foolish as we are?"

"Hard to say."

"Well, even if we don't, the sooner we start, the better our chances of saving him."

"I don't know if we should," said Razka, his voice soft, frightened.

"Why not?"

"Because, you fool, we can't call him back without using his *name*!"

Gratz frowned. The King had stripped their cousin of his name as retribution for his treason. This was the greatest punishment possible for a delver — in fact, it meant the nameless one was not really a delver anymore at all, since he had been set outside civilized society. Using his name to call him back from the Stone would mean they, too, had become traitors. "What do we do?" he asked, wringing his knobby hands in despair.

Razka sighed. "I don't know." He noticed that his legs were trembling and decided to sit. He stared at their nameless cousin. How far into the Stone had he gone? If he was too deep already then even if they attempted this wicked deed it would be for nothing. He could not return, and they would have marked themselves as outcasts for no good reason. He heard Gratz sniffling. "Stop that!" he ordered harshly.

"Sorry. I was just remembering how Ned . . . how our cousin taught me to play 'ponds and pebbles' when we were little. He was always good to me."

Razka smacked him on the back of the leg. "This is no time for sentiment. Do you understand what it will mean if we try to call him back?"

"Yes. It will mean we are no longer delvers. But is that a good enough reason to let him return to the Stone so young?"

Razka shook his head. "It's not just that, Gratz. Think of all the trouble he has caused. He truly is mad. If we do manage to call him back, who knows what terrible thing he might do next?"

"He is our cousin," said Gratz stubbornly. "Our tie to him is stronger than our tie to the King."

Razka turned toward the cousin under discussion and murmured, "If he is stone, he will cause no more trouble."

Gratz, hearing the note of uncertainty in Razka's voice, sank to a cross-legged position on the floor. He picked up the stone that had been designated with his own name. Closing his eyes, hoping desperately that Razka would join him, and even more desperately that the others would arrive in time, the young delver did the most dangerous thing he had ever done in his life.

He thought his cousin's name.

CHAPTER
XVI

RETURN TO EARTH

Lightfoot watched in fascination as Martha Hunter sang. Her eyes were fixed on the scarlet gem. Her voice was surprisingly pure. Though the Prince could not make out all the words, he caught enough to know that what he was hearing was a love song.

Suddenly Martha's voice was joined by another, this one distinctly male. A shiver rippled across the Prince's shoulders, for the cracked, husky voice seemed to come out of nowhere. It was oddly familiar and a moment later Lightfoot recognized it as the voice of Ian Hunter.

Ian and Martha continued to sing, the words seeming to wind around each other like vines, a seeming that became more real when a tendril of scarlet light erupted from the gem Martha was holding. A moment later a pulsing red cloud materialized in front of her. From it came another tendril of light. The twisting rays of crimson light joined, merged, grew thicker.

As Martha's voice grew stronger, more confident, the air in front of her began to shimmer, as it will over a bare patch of ground on a hot summer day.

A moment later Ian Hunter, still singing, stepped through the crimson cloud. He looked weak, worn, and unkempt. Even so, his face shone with triumph.

Behind Ian came an extremely tall man, brown-skinned and with long, golden hair. His right hand was gripping Ian's shoulder. In his left arm, he clutched the limp body of a boy, as if guarding some precious treasure.

A sob from Martha drew Lightfoot's attention in time to see her lunge forward and throw her arms around her husband. Ian, in turn, swept up his wife and held her so tightly that Lightfoot was surprised she didn't cry out in pain. Ian croaked a few words. Lightfoot wished, yet again, that he had learned more of Cara's human speech.

He also felt an odd twinge of jealousy for what was made possible by having arms.

Martha pressed her face to Ian's shoulder; Lightfoot could see that she was weeping.

After a moment the tall man spoke. Though his voice was as dry and cracked as Ian's, Lightfoot understood enough to realize that he was worried about the boy, who seemed near death.

Ian looked up, and Lightfoot easily understood his reply: "You'll find a well in the courtyard."

The tall man shifted the boy so he was holding him

with both arms, then started for the door. He paused for just a moment, looking startled when he spotted Lightfoot, then continued out of the room and down the stairs.

The Prince struggled to his feet, with the vague idea of following. He had been far too long without water himself. However after only two steps he realized he was still too weak to negotiate the stairs and decided his main interest was in Cara's parents, who were wound in each other's arms again, as if oblivious to everything around them.

Fallon moved swiftly and silently down the winding stair of the tower. Rajiv's dry skin and shallow breathing had him deeply concerned. He had seen dehydration before — there wasn't much he hadn't seen in his time on Earth — and he knew the boy was in serious danger.

The lack of food and water in the Rainbow Prison had bothered Fallon, of course, but nowhere near as much as it had affected Ian and Rajiv. He had pretended his discomfort was worse than it really was, a habit so old he had scarcely realized he was following it.

As he wound his way down the stairs, his thoughts went back to the scene in the room above. What in the world was a *unicorn* doing in this place?

A moan from Rajiv returned Fallon's thoughts to the immediate situation and he began to move faster. At the bottom of the tower a wide corridor led to another, larger, stairwell. Soon he found himself in a great hall. Though the room showed signs of recent occupancy, it was now silent and empty.

Where was everyone?

Passing through the space, Fallon realized that neither it nor the bedchambers above showed any signs of having been modernized. It was not just the lack of plumbing in the tower; he saw no electric lights, nor any sockets in the walls. He moved quickly to the great doors at the front of the room. The one on his left stood slightly ajar. He pushed it with his foot. It swung open to reveal a large courtyard. Two things immediately caught — and warred for — his attention.

The first, and by far the more spectacular, was an oval opening, a good ten feet high, that seemed to have been carved out of the rough wood of the castle gate. Gazing into it, Fallon saw a smooth-sided tunnel that, after several yards, came to a thin curtain of mist. Beyond that mist, dimly visible at the far end of the tunnel, was an open meadow bordered by a forest of silver-trunked, blue-leaved trees.

Fallon felt a throb of joy as intuition and something deeper — some heart-connection for which there was no name — informed him that the one he had sought for so long was on the other side of that opening.

He ached to plunge through it.

But the boy . . .

"You've waited centuries," Fallon told himself fiercely. "You can wait another day."

So he turned his attention to the other thing he had seen: a well. After placing Rajiv gently on the paving stones beside it, Fallon drew up a bucket. The water it held was cold and clear, tempting as a spring day. Ignoring his own thirst, he dipped his hands into the bucket, then dribbled a little water on Rajiv's parched lips.

The boy didn't move.

Slowly, tenderly, the big man continued to drip water onto Rajiv's mouth. When his hands were empty he plunged them into the bucket once more. This time he gently laved the boy's face in order to cool the hot, dry skin. Then he dripped more water on the mouth.

Rajiv's lips parted slightly, enough to utter a low moan.

Fallon let the precious water fall even more slowly, being careful not to choke the boy. Not until he saw Rajiv's throat make a swallowing motion did he release the breath he had barely realized he was holding. He lifted the bucket and drank deeply himself.

Then he went to stand in front of the mysterious opening that beckoned to him so strongly.

CHAPTER
XVII

MEDAFIL'S STORY

If gliding and not in a hurry, Medafil could fly for several hours without resting. Given the urgency of the situation, and the fact that he was carrying a passenger, he was working much harder. Consequently, he needed to stop for a break every two hours or so.

Cara was just as glad. Though she loved flying, loved seeing the beauty of Luster as it flowed below them, clinging to the gryphon's back with hundreds of feet of open air beneath her was exhausting, both physically and mentally.

The second time they stopped to rest, the ground trembled under their feet. An hour later, while they were flying above a range of stony hills, she heard a distant rumbling. Looking down, she cried out in horror as she saw a gap wrench open in one of the hillsides. What was happening to Luster?

Dusk was starting to darken the sky when they made their final stop for the day, coming to rest in a small clearing a good distance northeast of Autumngrove. The Squijum nestled close to Cara's side, quiet for once even though he was not asleep, while Cara shared with him some of the nuts and dried fruit Alma Leonetti had given her. Medafil went off on his own, returning about an hour later and looking quite satisfied with himself.

"Good hunting?" Cara asked, guessing what he had been up to.

"Excellent," replied the gryphon, licking his beak. He glanced around, found a likely spot, and began tamping down some grass to make a more comfortable resting place.

Cara yawned and rolled out her blanket. As she did, she said, "Medafil, there's something I've been wondering about."

"Yes?"

"Well, Luster is the world of the unicorns. But I know there are seven dragons here, and delvers, and a whole population of centaurs. And you told me yourself there are merfolk off the coasts."

"Unfortunate, but true. Fribble-brained water people are a bit too given to jokes for my taste. Anyway, what's your question?"

"Well, there are lots of all those other creatures. So, what about gryphons? Are you the only one?"

"Gaaah! I'd rather not talk about that."

"I'm sorry. I didn't mean to offend you."

"I'm not offended, nud-splorkle it. I just don't like to talk about it. But if you must know, there's a fairly large flock of us in the Grand Aerie. It's in the mountains north-west of Autumngrove."

"Ah. But you don't stay with them?"

"Those savages? Can't stand the mub-fuzzled ignora-muses. They can hardly string two words together. Besides, they, um, don't really care that much for me, either."

Cara sat for a moment, trying to sort through this. Finally she said, "So is that where you were raised?"

"Hmmph. You can call it that if you want. Shoving drip-ping gobbets of recently killed rabbit down a fledgling's throat is not *my* idea of proper child rearing."

"So you're not entirely happy with your parents?"

The relationship between parents and their children was always a matter of interest to Cara.

"Well, no unhappier with them than they were with me," he sniffed. "They never did understand me. Nor did anyone else for that matter. Not that they ever said that in so many words. They can barely talk, you know. I don't mean just my parents, I mean the whole lot of them. Oh, they know some words, and they could talk if they wanted to, but with them it's mostly squawks and screams, with an occasional 'Gaaah!' thrown in for variety. So they had no idea what to do with a poet."

"You're a poet?" asked Cara.

"Given what a sensitive spirit I possess, not to mention my inventive way with words, I'm surprised you hadn't real-ized that by now. I would have thought it was obvious."

"Of course," said Cara gently. "I should have known. So what happened?"

"Well, one morning I was sitting on a rocky crag, composing an ode to the sunrise. Which wasn't easy, since I didn't have that many words yet, and the gryphon language isn't really made for poetry. Anyway, I wasn't bothering anyone, you know, just minding my own business." He shook his wings in irritation. "But apparently that's not good enough for some people. Oh, no. Three young toughs — one of them my own brother! — decided I needed some kind of lesson. I'm not sure what lesson they had in mind, since all they said was 'Gaaah!' along with some other inarticulate squawks. Anyway, they drove me off the crag, then kept coming at me. But — hah! — I was faster than they were, for all they liked to think they were the best at everything. Except, um, I didn't stop flying for a long time."

"How long?"

"A really long time. All day, actually. By the time it was starting to get dark, I had no idea where I was or how to get back. Not that I really wanted to go back. A poet can only take so much of that kind of treatment."

"What happened then?"

"Well, as I said, it was starting to get dark. Given how long I had been flying, I definitely needed to rest. But just as I was about to land, I realized I was in the worst possible place."

"Why? What was wrong with it?"

"It wasn't finished! I had heard about spots like that, all kind of blank and misty, but I didn't think they were real."

Cara shivered. "I remember seeing them listed on the map M'Gama showed us."

"Well, they're pretty terrifying, let me tell you. You're not sure what's going to happen if you land on one! So I flew back up and went a little farther. But the next spot I tried was just as bad."

"Why?"

Medafil looked from side to side, then said softly. "I had come to the Caves of the Cockatrices."

"Cockatrices?"

"Deadly things. You wouldn't necessarily know it to look at them — you might even laugh, since they're pretty stupid looking. Actually, they *are* stupid, near as I can make out. You could take out one of their brains and not have enough to spread on a slice of bread. But deadly? Oh, my dear, you have no idea!"

Cara shuddered. "In what way? Do they eat people?"

"Hah! Wouldn't be easy for them to do that, since if one of them looks you in the eye . . ." He went silent and shuddered.

"What? What happens?"

The gryphon dropped his voice. "Stone. Just like that, you turn to stone!"

"Yike!" murmured the Squijum, who had climbed onto Cara's shoulder and was listening from behind her hair.

Medafil ruffled his feathers. "The only good thing is, there aren't very many of them."

"Where did they come from?"

"Oh, who knows? One of nature's little mistakes if you ask me. Anyway, I certainly couldn't stay there! So I flew on through the darkness, which I don't like very much, except for the part about seeing all the stars above me. Then . . ."

He paused. The silence stretched on for so long that Cara finally snapped, "Then *what*?"

"I don't like to say what happened next."

"Why not?"

"It's embarrassing."

"Oh, for heaven's sake, Medafil, just tell me what happened."

"I fell asleep."

"While you were flying?!"

"Gaaah! I told you it was embarrassing! Never mind. I don't want to talk anymore."

And with that he tucked his head under his wing.

"Medafil?"

Silence.

"Medafil?"

Nothing.

"Medafil, please tell me the rest of the story. I was just surprised is all. I didn't laugh, you know I didn't laugh."

"I am ignoring you," said the gryphon, his voice muffled by his wing.

"But I really want to know what happened! I'm worried about you. What if you didn't survive?"

From beneath the wing she heard a chuckle.

"If you don't tell me what happened I'll tickle you!"

"Gaaah! All right, I'll tell you! But you have to promise not to make fun of me."

"I promise."

"All right. I woke up before I hit the ground, which was a blessing. But I had been flying fairly low, looking for a spot to land, so I didn't have time to recover before I, did, um . . . land."

"Did it hurt?"

"Hurt? I invented seven new curses on the spot! Then I passed out."

Medafil was silent for quite a while after that. Cara was about to urge him to continue, when she heard him snore.

"Drat!" she said. She considered waking him and insisting that he continue the tale, but then reminded herself that he had been flying all day, while all she had had to do was hold on for dear life.

Full darkness had descended and the night was growing cold. Taking her blanket, she crawled across the clearing and snuggled against the gryphon's side, fitting in as neatly as a kitten could have curled against its mother.

She heard the low rumble of a purr.

A moment later the Squijum cuddled against her, sighed, and quickly fell asleep.

Cara, however, did not sleep, at least not right away. She lay awake late into the night, jumping at the slightest sound and worrying about Lightfoot. When at last she did drift off, she had slept for only a few moments when a shuddering in the ground hurtled her back to wakefulness.

"Frim-spazzit!" cried Medafil, springing to his feet.

"Hold still!" shrieked the Squijum, leaping up and down and slapping at the ground. "Hold still, you bad dirt!"

Cara couldn't have agreed more.

CHAPTER
XVIII

A MATTER OF TIMING

In the tower room, Ian Hunter pulled his wife even closer and whispered, "I'm sorry, Martha. Sorry for all of it."

"I don't know what to say, Ian, what to do. You've been gone so long —"

"Only so I could continue to search for Cara! We agreed to that, sweetheart. Neither of us had any idea that Beloved was going to . . . to do what she did to you. But now I've found Cara, and I've come for you as well."

"Yes, you've come for me, but Cara is lost again!"

Ian gripped his wife's shoulders. "What do you mean?" He felt as if he had just received a blow to the stomach.

"She's been kidnapped by some creatures called delvers."

Cold fear twisted Ian's heart. "Why do you say that?"

She gestured toward Lightfoot. "He told me. Or showed me."

Ian, whose entire attention had been on his wife from the moment he had appeared in the room, turned and saw the unicorn for the first time. "Lightfoot?" he cried in surprise.

The Prince whickered a response.

"He's the one who broke the spell," said Martha. She crossed to the unicorn, knelt, and put her hand on his shoulder. "That's what pulled me out of the tree."

Ian nodded, then said, "Listen, I have had occasion to deal with the delvers. I know they look horrifying, but I do not think they will harm Cara. More likely they are planning to deliver her to Beloved. That's bad, but at least it should keep her safe for now."

Martha nodded grimly. As she did, Lightfoot thought to her, "Please give my greetings to your husband."

"How do you know him?"

"It's a long story. Please, just greet him and ask him, "'Who was the other man who came through with you?'"

Martha spoke the question aloud.

"His name is Fallon," replied Ian. "We met while I was searching for a way into the Rainbow Prison. He . . . helped me when I had a problem." He felt a pang in his heart as he realized he had nearly forgotten about Rajiv. "Fallon was carrying a boy with him. The boy was ill — I need to check on him."

He hesitated, then extended his hand to Martha.

"I am not yet ready to go down the stairs," Lightfoot thought to her. "My legs are still too weak from waking you, which took a great deal of energy. But I need water, very badly. Could you ask your husband to bring some?"

Martha repeated this information to Ian, adding, "I'll stay with him until he is stronger."

Ian nodded, and headed for the door.

When he entered the courtyard Ian expected to see Rajiv and Fallon together. So he was stunned to spot Rajiv's body lying alone by the well. Terror stricken, he raced to the boy's side. To his relief, Rajiv was still breathing.

Glancing around, Ian spotted Fallon standing in front of a large oval opening in the castle's wooden gate. Stretching beyond the oval was a tunnel that Ian knew, with immediate certainty, led to Luster.

He called to his friend, then dropped to his knees and lifted Rajiv's head into his lap.

Fallon immediately trotted back to join them. "I have already given him a little water," he said, kneeling beside Ian. "We can give him more in a few minutes. We should mix some salt with it, to help his body rebalance, but I did not want to leave him alone while I went to look for it."

"I can find some easily enough," said Ian. He slid Rajiv's head from his lap, then gently lowered it to the cobbles. "I'll get some, as soon as I have a little water myself."

Cupping his hands, he reached into the bucket.

"Not too much," cautioned Fallon.

Ian didn't answer; he was too busy sipping the water, which at this moment tasted better than the finest wine ever made. Sighing deeply — the relief was enormous — he stood and headed into the castle. He returned a few minutes later with the salt, as well as some cups.

"Excellent," said Fallon. He mixed a little salt into a cup of water, then let some drip onto Rajiv's lips, which parted hungrily in response. Fallon let just a bit more water fall into the boy's mouth, then murmured, "Ian, that opening over there — it leads to Luster, I'm sure of it."

"I agree."

"The friend I seek is on the other side."

"As is my daughter."

Fallon smiled. "Then we can continue together for now. I'm glad, for I was not looking forward to parting from you."

Ian was unexpectedly pleased to hear this. "Nor I from you," he replied with genuine affection.

"We'll need to wait until the boy recovers, of course," said Fallon. "He should be well enough to travel tomorrow."

Ian shifted uneasily. "I cannot wait until tomorrow."

Fallon raised a questioning eyebrow.

Ian sighed. "My daughter has been taken prisoner. I need to rescue her, and time is important."

"Where did this information come from?"

"I'm sure you noticed the unicorn in the tower room. He told me. Well, he told Martha. She passed the information to me. He is still exhausted from waking her. I need to take them some water."

Fallon, who was gazing longingly at the opening in the gate, nodded but said nothing for a moment. When he finally did speak, it was to say, "In front of the gate lies a corpse, blackened and badly contorted. I am not sure what it indicates, but I do not like it."

Ian spotted the body, and shuddered. But all he said was, "I have to take some water to my wife."

Ian carried a bucket of water, along with an empty cup for Martha to use, up the tower steps. Halfway to the top he lost his sight, and nearly his footing. He stood in silence, unwilling to call out; he had not yet told his wife of the price he had paid to find his way to her side. Hoping the Blind Man would not need his vision for too long, he settled cautiously on the steps to wait. After what seemed hours, but was in reality only about twenty minutes, his vision returned and he got to his feet to resume his climb.

Martha was still sitting next to Lightfoot. From the way her hand rested on the unicorn's shoulder, Ian was sure they were talking mind-to-mind, just as Cara had done with the Prince. He stifled a gasp as he suddenly realized something that had been lost to him in the desperate hours of their escape from the Rainbow Prison: Martha and Lightfoot were cousins!

He wondered if Lightfoot had informed her of this fact or if that was going to be left to him.

Perhaps the Prince doesn't even know yet himself, thought Ian ruefully. *I have no idea what happened after Ivy and Cara returned to Luster. Has my mother-in-law revealed her true identity to the other unicorns or not?*

If the task of telling Martha was to be left to him, he was not looking forward to it. How in the world do you tell your wife that her mother was born a unicorn?

Silently, he set the bucket on the floor beside Martha.

"Oh, thank you," she said. "I'm parched, too, but didn't know if I could stay awake much longer. Lightfoot says that is to be expected — that I'll need to rest awhile to recover both from the healing and my time under Beloved's spell."

He could hear the frustration in her voice and knew she wanted to start their search for Cara instantly. "Rest will be good," he said gently. "I'll wait for you in the courtyard."

Ian and Fallon took advantage of the time Martha and Lightfoot slept to plunder the castle stores. Knowing better than to gorge themselves after nearly starving in the Rainbow Prison, they snacked lightly on cheese and dried fruit. Then Ian set to work preparing a light meal, using lentils and some salted fish, while Fallon went to keep watch by Rajiv's side.

Ian carried the meal outside when it was ready, and the two men ate in companionable silence. When they were finished Ian said, "We should take advantage of being here to get weapons and fresh clothing. Well, weapons at least. I'm not sure there are any clothes here that will fit you!"

Fallon laughed. "I'll wash up a bit while you're gathering things."

* * *

Beloved's armory was well stocked, and Ian made a number of trips, carrying out weapons — a variety of blades, as well as bows and arrows — that he hoped would suit not only Fallon and himself, but Martha and Rajiv as well.

That done, he shifted his attention to the matter of clothing, returning after a time with his arms loaded with fresh garments not only for himself, but for Martha and Rajiv. When Fallon expressed wonder that the castle contained such an array of clothing, he explained about the Maidens of the Hunt. "Also, new Hunters are sometimes recruited at a very young age, particularly if a young man of the right bloodline becomes orphaned."

Fallon looked troubled, but said only, "This Beloved has quite an operation."

Ian nodded grimly. "She has used her centuries of life to gather money, power, and arcane knowledge. Leaving the Hunt, knowing that she would see it as a betrayal that must be punished, was one of the most frightening things I've ever done."

Dusk was falling as Martha and Lightfoot entered the courtyard. The Prince appeared a bit wobbly, but otherwise seemed fine.

After Ian had introduced Fallon and explained who Rajiv was, Martha pointed to the gate-within-the-gate and said, "What's that?"

"Our entry to Luster," replied Ian.

"You shouldn't have let me sleep. Let's go!"

"Rajiv is not ready to travel yet, Mrs. Hunter," said Fallon. "I am hoping he will be well enough by morning. Children recover from dehydration quickly."

"We can't wait until tomorrow," said Martha sharply. "We have to go after Cara right now! Tell them, Lightfoot."

The unicorn looked at her in puzzlement. She sighed, then placed a hand on his shoulder and thought: "They want to wait until tomorrow to go through that gate. I can't wait, I want to go look for Cara right now. Will you come with me?"

The Prince hesitated, then replied, "I need to show you something."

Puzzled, keeping one hand on Lightfoot's shoulder, Martha let him lead her toward the gateway.

Ian rose to join them.

A few feet from the gate, Lightfoot stopped in front of a blackened form, so grotesquely twisted that only by studying it carefully — which was hard to do, since it was sickening to see — could you tell it had once been a man. Martha cried out in disgust.

"That is what happens to anyone who passes back through the gate too soon after having first come through it," explained Lightfoot. "I heard Beloved say it, and a short time later this poor fool proved it when he chased me here. The problem is, I don't know the human language that well and don't know how long I must wait. For that matter, I have no idea how long I've been here, since I fell unconscious from my wounds when I first arrived and again after I woke you."

Martha stared at the misshapen body, her horror shifting to mounting frustration. She could not ask her new friend to risk such a fate. She was tempted to make the journey on her own, to plunge through the gate right this moment. But without a guide how could she find her daughter in the vastness of a world she had never seen before? Despair, which she had been trying to hold at bay, overcame her. She staggered for a moment, and Ian caught her. "What is it?" he asked.

Fighting off horrid imaginings of what the delvers might have done to Cara — might be doing even now — she whispered, "We can't go yet."

"Why not?"

She pointed to the grisly remains of the Hunter and explained, ending with, "I'd go alone, if I had to. But it doesn't make any sense to go to Luster without Lightfoot." She paused, and her chin began to tremble. "How will we ever know when it is safe?"

"Oh, we'll know," said Ian unhappily. He gestured to the Prince. "I didn't realize Beloved was aware Lightfoot had come through the gate, much less that she had watched him do so. Now that I do know, I can guarantee you this: The moment it is safe, she'll be sending Hunters back to kill him."

CHAPTER
XIX

WHISPERS

When the unicorn named Belle left the Valley of the Centaurs, her intent had been to return to Autumngrove as quickly as possible. She didn't mind traveling alone; she welcomed it, actually, since it gave her time to think. And she had a great deal she needed to think about.

First was the matter of the centaurs, who had turned out to be friendlier than she had anticipated. Even more interesting — from her point of view — they clearly had a strong warrior code, something her fellow unicorns sorely lacked. She would have loved to remain with them and watch the trial-by-combat that would determine their next king, who they referred to as their "Chiron." Princess Arianna and the warrior Arkon had invited her to do so. Belle had been tempted, and even had good reason, since the naming of a new Chiron would be useful information to carry back to Autumngrove. But things were moving too fast for her to dally, and she had felt she must decline.

The second and far greater matter of confusion was the story the old Chiron had told about the birth of the Whisperer. Could the unicorns really have been so foolish as to perform that Purification Ceremony he had described? Had they really tried to become perfect?

Belle shuddered at the thought.

Even more troubling was the Chiron's claim that their own worst instincts, pulled from them in that misbegotten spell-casting, had congealed into a strange being called "the Whisperer," who was now their most terrible enemy, more dangerous even than Beloved.

Equally bizarrely, he had said that the Whisperer had subverted a band of dwarves and turned them into the delvers. According to the Chiron, since the Whisperer was — however unintended — a creation of the unicorns, this explained why the unicorns and the delvers were forever locked in conflict.

Belle had been pondering all this as she made her way back toward Autumngrove. Then, on the night of her third day of travel the Chiron's story was confirmed in the most horrifying way possible.

A voice began to speak to her.

"I know what you want," it whispered, seeming to come from nowhere and everywhere all at the same time.

Belle stopped, startled. "Where are you?" she demanded. "*Who* are you?"

"That doesn't matter," purred the voice. "What

matters is that I know what you want. And I can give it to you."

"What do I want?" she asked, her voice defiant.

"You know."

She snorted. "Just because I know doesn't mean that you do."

"You want to be in charge, because you think the Queen is a fool."

Belle's eyes widened. Then she turned and ran.

CHAPTER
XX

RAJIV

Rajiv had been expecting to die. So when he opened his eyes and saw that he was no longer in the Rainbow Prison he was not sure, at first, if he was back on Earth or had entered the afterlife. Certainly the stars that spangled the dark sky above him were not in any pattern that he recognized. Nor had he ever seen so many, except on his journey into the Himalayas with the two crazy men who he had convinced to let him accompany them.

He groaned slightly. Almost instantly, so fast it was as if he had summoned a djinn, the face of the big sahib, Fallon, appeared above him. Such an odd face! Oh, very handsome, to be sure. But his skin was as brown as if he had been Delhi-born, while his hair was of purest gold. Rajiv never tired of trying to figure out where he might have come from.

Right now the sahib's kind eyes were filled with concern.

Rajiv tried to greet him, but found that his voice would

not work. Fallon poured — oh, miracle! — a tiny amount of slightly salty water into his mouth. Rajiv swallowed. It was painful, yet pure bliss.

"Tell me, sahib," he managed to croak. "Are we dead, or just in another place?"

Fallon laughed and tousled Rajiv's hair, an affectionate gesture that Rajiv loved.

He saw now that the other sahib was also looking down at him. Sahib Hunter's face was filled with such profound relief that it brought tears to Rajiv's eyes. He was not used to having anyone care for him so deeply as these two men to whom he had attached himself.

"We're back on Earth, Rajiv," said Sahib Hunter gently. "And very glad to have you still with us. You had us frightened for a while."

"I had *me* frightened, sahib!" he replied, trying to grin, but not quite managing it. "More water, please?"

Again, Fallon poured a bit of water into his mouth.

"*Lots* more, sahib?"

Fallon shook his head. "Not too fast. Too much at once will make you sick."

With a sigh, the boy pushed himself to his elbows. "What is this place?" he asked, looking around. Before they could answer he cried, "The memsahib! Oh, you did it, sahibs! You brought her back with us."

Then he drew in a gasp of wonder and whispered, "But what is that next to her?"

"That is a unicorn," said Ian.

"But it is so beautiful!"

"It — he — is supposed to be," replied Fallon, his voice as soft as Rajiv's.

The boy turned to him. "I want to know more. But right now, sahib, I am starving!"

Placing a hand on his forehead, Ian said, "You'll have to be careful, Rajiv. Just as with the water, too much food too fast will make you ill."

"Sahib, right now *any* food will do!"

As Rajiv carefully nibbled the bits of fruit and cheese the men allowed him — he had no choice but to be careful, since they handed him the morsels very slowly — the mem-sahib came to join them.

"We looked for you for a long time, miss," said Rajiv. "It is nice to see you with your eyes open!"

Martha laughed and Rajiv, whose quick eyes did not miss much, noticed that her husband appeared first startled, then pleased.

"What are we to do next, sahibs?" Rajiv asked, when he had finished all the food they would give him.

"See that opening?" said Ian, pointing to the gate-within-the-gate.

"Ah, yes. More strangeness."

"It leads to another world."

"Are we going there? If so, I hope this one has food and water!"

"Yes, it does," said Ian. "And the land is real, not made of light. I have been there before."

"And is this where your friend is waiting, Sahib Fallon?"

"I believe so," said Fallon.

"And my daughter," said Ian.

"Then when shall we go?"

"There is . . . a complication," said Fallon. Quickly, he and Ian explained the problem with Lightfoot crossing back.

"Ah. Then we shall have to watch carefully."

"The first thing we have to do," said Ian, "is decide how to spend the night. Since we can be sure that Beloved will be sending some men through that gate to kill Lightfoot, the question is how to best be ready for them. Should we plan to meet them head-on? Should we prepare an ambush? How can we get some rest and still be ready for them — especially since we don't know how many men will be coming?"

"Surely it will be but one or two," said Fallon. "He is only one unicorn, after all."

Lightfoot, who was listening to this via his connection with Martha, whinnied his annoyance. Nodding, Fallon said, "No insult intended, Prince. But the point remains — it seems unlikely this Beloved would send through more than just a couple of men."

"You don't understand," said Ian. "She will be furious that Lightfoot escaped her, and even more furious that he did it by entering her castle, which she will consider a great violation. What we don't know is whether she recognized him. If she did, she may want to capture him alive — in which case she might send as many as twenty men. How do we prepare for that possibility?"

"Why don't we just hide?" asked Rajiv.

Ian looked at the boy in surprise. "What do you mean?"

"Sahib, fighting is what you do when you can't do anything else," said the boy, speaking with a wisdom born of the streets. "What *we* want to do is go through that gate. We can't do that until we know it is safe for Lightfoot. Since we know that when some men do come through it will mean it is also safe for the Prince to return, we have no need to fight them. We simply stay out of their sight and wait for a chance to slip through the gate and go to this Luster of yours. They will not be able to follow us!"

Fallon smiled. "I knew there was a reason we brought you along, Rajiv!"

It took several minutes for them to determine the best place to both rest and keep an eye on the gate. Ian hoisted Rajiv onto his back and carried him as they looked, partly so the boy could be part of the endeavor, but even more so that he would not be left alone in case the Hunters arrived. It was well he did, for it was the boy's quick eyes that found the best spot.

"Look, sahib," he said, pointing to the platform where Beloved had stood to rally her men just before their assault on Luster. "Perhaps we can wait behind there."

In short order they had carried the food, clothing, and

weapons they had taken from the castle to their hiding place, where they could distribute and pack them. Rajiv was delighted when Ian produced the short blade they had deemed would best suit him. "Oh, sahibs," he marveled. "I have always wanted a sword of my own!"

"And now," said Fallon, when the work was properly done, "I think we should get some rest. I'll take the first watch, if you wish. If we include Lightfoot, we'll only need to watch for two hours each."

"I can watch, too!" insisted Rajiv.

"I'm certain you can," said Fallon. "But for tonight, you sleep. There will be plenty of danger soon enough."

Ian and Martha returned to the castle. When they came back, Martha had changed from her white gown, and was now wearing a red plaid shirt, some formfitting jeans, and a pair of brown boots.

Fallon raised a questioning eyebrow.

"These are the clothes I was wearing when Beloved took me," she said.

She was also carrying blankets and pillows, with which she insisted on making a comfortable resting place for Rajiv.

"Memsahib," he protested, "I can sleep anywhere!"

"Nevertheless," she said, "tonight you shall have a decent bed. Who knows what the morning will bring?"

"Another world, most likely," he said contentedly. "And more adventures."

With that, and despite his protests, Rajiv drifted off to sleep.

DAY TWO OF THE INVASION

It is a pity that Earth has lost its dragons, for they
added immeasurably to the strangeness of our world.
This, it seemed to me, was a good thing.

Bellenmore the Magician,
Memoirs of a Mage (unpublished)

CHAPTER
XXI

FENG YUAN

Feng Yuan sat silently beneath the strange tree, enjoying its odd fragrance. She was not astonished to be in another world; astonishment had left her life the day the Hunter named Wu Chen had rescued her from the hillside where her father had abandoned her because the family could no longer feed a useless girl. She was five at the time and had expected to die in a few days. Given the pain that twisted both her heart and her stomach, death would have been a welcome relief. But then Wu Chen had appeared, seemingly from nowhere, to ask if she would like to go live with a woman named Beloved, who would feed, clothe, and educate her.

In return, all she had to do was help the sons of Beloved lure unicorns to their doom.

Better doom for a unicorn than for me, she had thought, with the cold practicality that comes from fear and hunger.

Bundled up, smuggled out of China in a small plane, Feng Yuan had found herself in an ancient castle, facing an even more ancient woman. The woman had terrified her at first — what child would not be terrified of the moon-white hair that shifted and lifted all on its own, much less the blazing red pupils of her eyes? But when Beloved had reached out a hand to stroke Feng Yuan's cheek and said in perfect Mandarin, "Welcome, child. Welcome to our great quest. I am glad to have you with us," something had melted in the girl's heart.

It was the first time in her life she had ever felt wanted.

That had been nine years ago. Now here she was in another world. Yet the change from Earth to Luster felt no stranger than had the shift from the hills of Shannxi to the castle of Beloved. Less strange, in fact, since she had been preparing for this during all the years in between. She was educated now — fluent in five languages and wise in the ways of science and history (not only the history known to most of the human race, but much of the secret history of the magical world as well).

You never knew, according to Beloved, when such things might come in handy.

During those same years, she had also received, from Wu Chen, a second education. The man who had fetched her to Beloved's castle was enamored of the great thinker Sun Tzu and gave her a copy of his classic book *The Art of War*. During her free hours he had trained her in its precepts.

She had been fascinated by Sun Tzu's clarity of thought and his wisdom, and used to murmur the passages about the movements of troops to herself in bed at night, in order to glide herself toward sleep.

Grateful for what she had received, it bothered the girl that despite her devotion to her training, she had yet to fulfill her purpose, much less repay her benefactor — something that could be done only by calling a unicorn to its well-deserved death. This was the great purpose for which she had been educated, the reason she had been saved from death herself when she was five.

Though Feng Yuan did not look behind her, or to her sides, she knew that the three Hunters she traveled with were there, waiting, hoping for her to do her job and draw a unicorn into the clearing. It was the second day since they had entered Luster, and though this was supposed to be the world of the unicorns, there had yet been no sign of the beasts. This did not worry her. She knew hunting could be a slow task, and she had been taught, by methods sometimes mild and sometimes cruel, to be patient.

Despite her keen awareness of the danger of her task, Feng Yuan tried not to tremble. It was not easy to stay calm; she knew the unicorns were fierce and wicked creatures, responsible for the death of Beloved's father, not to mention the terrible pain that the woman constantly suffered. But she had learned ways to still the pounding heart, to settle the fretful mind. *I have nothing to fear*, the girl told herself repeatedly. *My Hunters will protect me.*

And if they did not? If the unicorn she hoped to attract managed to savage her before they could stop him? Well, she had already had nine more years of life than she had expected. To die for Beloved now would be small payment in return for what she had been given.

The girl's thoughts stopped, her attention caught by a movement at the far side of the clearing. She saw a flash of white among the leaves, a white so pure it made her heart ache.

Then the branches parted, and a unicorn stepped into the clearing.

Terror clutched Feng Yuan's heart. But something else stirred in her as well, something unexpected — a longing so sharp it was like being stabbed. With it came a sudden, horrified awareness of how much more there was to know about this world than she had imagined.

The unicorn walked toward her, silent, beautiful, dangerous. She wanted to run. She wanted to scream to *him* to run. Before she could unclench her throat, an arrow hissed into the clearing from the dark of the surrounding trees, burying itself in the unicorn's neck.

The creature, glorious in a way she had never expected, reared back, bugling in astonishment and pain. His life's blood arced out in a spurt of silver and crimson, spattering hot against the girl's face, soaking into her hair, staining her pristine robe.

With a hideous cry of triumph, the Hunters rushed into the clearing, swords drawn, ready to slash and hack.

Feng Yuan could not watch. Filled with horror, wracked with confusion and guilt, she turned and fled.

CHAPTER
XXII

BEYOND THE MIST

It was on Martha's watch, just before dawn, that the Hunters arrived. She was peering over the edge of the platform, fretting about how soon they could pass through the gate and begin their search for Cara when the first of the men stepped through. Instantly she dropped down, shook her husband's shoulder, and hissed, "They're here!"

Ian sat up at once, moving from sleep to full wakefulness with a speed that had been drummed into him during his training to become a Hunter. Silently, he roused Fallon, Rajiv, and Lightfoot.

It was good, he decided, that they had chosen to hide rather than plan on a fight, since Beloved had sent back twenty Hunters. *All to catch one unicorn*, Ian thought, shaking his head.

Crouched together, scarcely daring to breathe, the little group waited until the Hunters had entered the castle. The moment they did, Ian gave the signal.

Moving as silently as possible, they bolted for the entry to Luster.

The five of them — Rajiv, Fallon, Ian, Martha, and Lightfoot — were walking side by side. The tunnel was smooth-sided, a wooden oval that extended for some twenty feet before coming to a shimmering curtain of mist.

Beyond that mist, dimly visible, was another world.

"Oh, sahibs," murmured Rajiv. "You promised me wonders. I did not also expect miracles!"

In appearance, the world that lay ahead was not radically different from Earth. There were trees, after all, and ground and grass and sky. Even so, it was clearly someplace else, as the blue leaves and silver bark of the trees made plain.

When they reached the mist, they paused.

"Once we pass this, there is no turning back, at least not for some time," said Fallon.

Ian nodded. "I think one of us should go ahead, to make sure there are no Hunters waiting on the other side."

"Do you think that's likely?" gasped Martha.

Ian shook his head. "Not really. Beloved won't be expecting anyone to come through from this side. And she'll want everyone out hunting unicorns as soon as possible. Even so, it would be foolish of us to just assume it's safe to move ahead."

"But we can't go back, sahib," said Rajiv. "Not with those men in the castle."

"We'll go whichever way is safest," said Fallon. "But we need to know what we're facing. Ian, I think I should go first. From what you've told me, it would go badly for you were you to be taken by the Hunters. If there *are* some there, they won't know me, which may give me time to get past them. With luck, there will be none. I'll check the far side of the tunnel, then give you the signal as soon as I know all is clear."

Reluctantly, Ian agreed.

Fallon stifled a gasp as he passed through the mist, for it sent tingles skittering across his skin. Moving silently, he approached the end of the tunnel. He glanced at the tunnel walls as he walked and did not like what he saw. On the Earth side of the misty curtain, the tunnel had been smooth, and it was not clear what it was made of. On this side, the tunnel walls were made of wood, living wood that was splintered and broken, with silvery sap oozing down its sides like slow running tears.

Ten feet from the tunnel's end, he dropped to his belly and crawled forward in order to be less obvious when he peered out to check for waiting Hunters.

He inched ahead, looked out cautiously, scanned in all directions, then breathed a sigh of relief. No one in sight. He scrambled to his feet and turned to wave the others on.

Side-by-side, Ian, Martha, Lightfoot, and Rajiv hurried forward, each emitting a small cry on passing through the tingling mist. When they were all on the Luster side, Fallon moved close to Ian and murmured, "I do not like this."

"What do you mean?"

"Look around. We are inside a tree."

"That's impossible. It's too big!"

"No, it's not. Just not something you might have seen before. I tell you, trees such as this are important. They should not be damaged."

The words struck Ian as being true, if somewhat odd. But he had long ago given up expecting to understand everything his tall friend said.

They continued to the end of the tunnel. It opened onto a broad meadow where the grass grew as evenly as if it had been mown.

"Oh, my god!" cried Martha.

She had turned and was looking up at the tree.

"Sahibs," breathed Rajiv, standing beside her and gazing up as well. "How is this possible?"

"There are more things in heaven and Earth, Horatio, than are dreamt of in your philosophy," replied Fallon.

"I beg your pardon, sahib?"

"It is a quote from the play *Hamlet*, Rajiv, but I think it applies to this tree."

"Well, it is certainly something I have never dreamt

of, sahib. I did not know a tree could be so ... so ... enormous!"

Fallon's response was interrupted by a tremor rippling through the ground. With a little cry, Martha staggered against Ian, who caught her in his arms. Lightfoot whinnied and reared up. Rajiv fell to his knees.

"What a greeting," said the boy, once the ground had stilled. "We come to a new world and five minutes later there is an earthquake. Do not worry, Memsahib Hunter. As long as you are not inside, or standing in the wrong place, tremors such as these are not so bad."

Fallon shook his head grimly.

"What is it?" asked Ian.

"I do not believe that was a mere earthquake."

"What else would it be?"

"Look at the tree," replied Fallon.

Ian turned to look more carefully at the tree through which they had just passed. He gaped in astonishment. With silver bark and blue leaves — that much, at least, he was used to, from his previous trip to Luster — it was even more vast than he had realized, its circumference greater than that of most houses. Moreover, he felt a sense — he could not say why, but the feeling was deep and powerful — of something ancient and sacred.

"It is awesome," he said slowly.

"Awesome — and damaged," replied Fallon. "Look at the space through which we just passed."

Ian turned his attention to the gap at the base of the tree. Though the opening through which they had entered the tunnel had been a smooth oval, its mouth on this side was more like a sprouting onion; rising from the oval base was a long crack that extended upward for well over a hundred feet.

"It appears the tree was badly damaged when Beloved forced her way through," said Fallon. "If it fails, I do not believe this world can survive."

Ian stared at his friend, stunned by this pronouncement.

"What do you mean, 'This world cannot survive'?" demanded Martha.

Fallon's face was grim. "I believe — no, I am certain — that this Luster we have just entered is not a 'world' as you would use that term. It was created, is in the process of *being* created, as an experiment, or an act of pride, or of love. Perhaps all three. But it is unfinished, and I suspect Beloved's violation of the tree through which we just passed has made it dangerously unstable."

Ian stared at Fallon. The big man was the closest thing he had had to a friend since he first dedicated his life to Beloved and the Hunt. Yet as he thought about it, he realized he still knew almost nothing about him. Finally he said, tersely, "Who are you, Fallon?"

This was a slight failure of nerve, since the question he really wanted to ask was '*What* are you?'"

The big man shook his head. "If we are lucky, there may be a time for me to answer that question. Right now, we have work to do — work, alas, that will lead us on different paths."

"Sahib! Will we not continue together?"

Fallon shook his head. "Our goals now pull us in different directions, Rajiv." Kneeling in front of the boy, he placed his huge hands on the slender shoulders and said softly, "You are solid and brave, and it has been a privilege to travel with you. You are everything I would have wished for in a son."

Rajiv's dark eyes welled with tears. But he had already done his pleading on this matter, back in the Rainbow Prison, before they even came to this strange new world. He knew no words would change the big man's mind. So he simply placed the palms of his hands together, bowed his head slightly, and whispered, "*Namaste*, Fallon."

Fallon repeated the gesture, murmuring, "*Namaste*, brave one." Rising, he turned to Martha. "I wish you luck in your quest for your daughter, Mrs. Hunter. I am sorry I did not have a chance to get to know you better. Your husband has been an excellent companion."

"We need your help," said Martha, her voice desperate.

"You have the best help you could ask for," replied Fallon firmly.

Martha nodded, but did not say more.

Fallon hesitated, then said, "Would you convey a message to the Prince for me?"

She nodded again.

"Please tell him I said it was a great pleasure to meet him. Then add this blessing: Travel safe, travel well. May those who have gone before be always with you."

Martha placed a hand on Lightfoot's neck. After a moment the Prince whickered in surprise.

"He wants to know where you learned that," explained Martha.

Fallon smiled. "Tell him I am a bit of a specialist in unicorns."

"He says you are also a bit of a mystery," replied Martha. "Even so, he is sorry you are leaving us, and returns the blessing."

Fallon nodded, then went to stand before Ian. He held out his hand, and Ian took it. The two men stared at each other then — as if some signal had passed between them — dropped their hands and embraced, the embrace of strong men who have become brothers by passing together through great peril.

"I pray we shall meet again," said Ian, his voice husky.

"I share that hope," replied Fallon.

He gazed at them all for a moment longer, then nodded, turned, and strode away.

Ian stood with his hands on Rajiv's shoulders, watching Fallon depart. He saw now that the great tree through which they had entered was surrounded by a wide greensward where the grass grew ankle deep, no higher. Some sixty or seventy yards away, as if holding a respectful distance, the forest began again. Though it was composed of trees that would have seemed enormous on Earth, here they were dwarfed by the great tree that grew in their center.

All too soon Fallon had disappeared into that mysterious woodland.

"I shall miss him, sahib," murmured Rajiv.

"I will, too," said Ian. Then he squeezed the boy's shoulders and said, "But you know you have a place with us, right?"

"Thank you, sahib. I do know that. Even so, it is nice to be told."

"Ian," said Martha urgently. "We have to get started."

Ian took a deep breath, nodded, then said fiercely, "Yes, my love. Let us find our daughter."

CHAPTER XXIII

ON THE WAY TO DARK MOUNTAIN

Shortly before noon of the second day of their journey Cara and Medafil came to an extended wetland.

"The Tamoran Marsh," said Medafil. He turned his head to speak over his shoulder rather than shouting to her as he usually did while flying. "If we weren't in such a hurry, I'd go around it instead of going over."

"Why?" called Cara.

"Bog-dappled place is filled with strange creatures. You never know what's going to come slithering out of that murky water."

With that he pumped his wings, shooting forward over the dismal landscape. It took nearly an hour to cross the swamp. Once clear of it, they flew on for another several minutes before Medafil called, "I'm going down to that clearing for a rest."

But as the gryphon glided toward the opening in the trees, Cara spotted something that filled her heart with fear. Leaning forward, she cried, "Not here, Medafil! Fly up, *fly up*!"

Without questioning her, the gryphon changed course. Beating his wings madly, he soared into the sky. When they were far enough from the clearing he turned his head and, panting from the exertion, demanded to know what was going on.

Cara's reply was simple. "I saw a man down there. I think he was a Hunter."

"Gaaaah! How do you know he's not just one of the humans who *live* in Luster?"

"I suppose that could be. But now that Beloved has made her gateway, we can't take any chances."

"Gad-dingled invaders! I ought to go back and eat him!"

"Don't! If he's not a Hunter, that would be rude. If he is a Hunter, he'll have a sword and maybe a bow and arrows."

"Yike!" cried the Squijum. "Stinky Hunters!"

They flew on. About fifteen minutes later Medafil spied another opening in the forest. This time they were able to land in peace.

After they had been resting for a bit and the gryphon had had time to catch his breath, Cara said, "All right, Medafil, it's time for the rest of that story."

"What story?"

"Medafil!"

"I don't know what you're talking about," said the gryphon, gazing at her innocently.

"Last night you were telling me about fleeing from your home. But you fell asleep before you could finish."

"Gaaah! I did no such thing!"

"Are you telling me you didn't flee from your home?"

"No, I'm saying I didn't fall asleep in the middle of telling a story! That's preposterous!"

Cara bit back a sharp retort. Deciding she was more interested in hearing the end of the story than in arguing, she said, "All right, *I* fell asleep! That was terrible of me, I know. But I really want to hear the end of the story."

"Well-l-l-l . . ." said the gryphon. He fanned out his left wing and inspected it as if he suddenly found it fascinating. After a maddening pause, he said, "Since you put it that way . . . where did we leave off?"

"You had just told me that you fell asleep while you were flying and made a crash landing."

"Gaaah! I did *not* crash. That bum-rumpled landing was just a bit . . . ungraceful."

"All right, you had an *ungraceful* landing. What happened next?"

"Well, at first I just lay there. I might have moaned a bit. I'm not saying I did, mind you! But I might have."

"And then?"

"I tried to get up. Only I couldn't. I was kind of . . . broken."

"That's terrible! What did you do?"

"Nothing, for a while. I told you, I couldn't get up."

"Well, you didn't die there, did you?" asked Cara in exasperation.

"Gaaah! What if I had? You probably wouldn't care, anyway!"

"Medafil, you're not making any sense. What happened?"

"Well, I lay there for maybe two days, getting weaker and weaker. I was hungry, thirsty, wracked with pain. Really, now that I think of it, it's a wonder I *didn't* die! Happily, your grandmother came along before I could pass from this world forever."

"Ah!" cried Cara. "So that's how you met her?"

"Of course. In fact, I've noticed that the two of you seem to have a shared habit of finding me when I'm in trouble. Must be family destiny or something."

"Was she a human or a unicorn when this happened?"

"Oh, I should have mentioned that, shouldn't I? She was still a unicorn at the time. Wandering, of course, as was her way. She came to me and healed me and did that thing with her horn that let us speak mind-to-mind."

"I didn't know you could speak mind-to-mind with my grandmother!"

"Well, you don't need to know everything, do you?" sniffed Medafil. "Anyway, that did more than let us speak mind-to-mind. Somehow it opened up the language in my heart. When I asked her how she found me, she said, 'I met a woman in the wood, tall and beautiful, with skin the color of wet sand and hair as golden as the sun. Her name was Allura. She told me you were here, and suffering, and asked me to come to you. So I did.'"

Medafil paused for a bit, obviously lost in memory. "Amalia and I traveled together for the next few weeks," he said at last. "But she was restless and eventually left me. The next time I saw her, she was in human form. I didn't recognize her, of course. And she didn't know me, either, because her memory was so fogged. Even so, it *felt* as if we knew each other. We had some ring-dingled good adventures together."

"Is that why you can speak English?" asked Cara.

"Actually, I learned it before I met her again. After she had opened my heart so we could speak mind-to-mind I became hungry for words. Ravenous. But I didn't have any way to learn until a year or so later, when I met a man called Armando de la Quintano —"

"I know Armando! I met him on the way to Ebillan's cave. That was before I found you caught in that delver trap."

"Gaaah! I don't like to talk about *that* little episode, if you don't mind! Anyway, as I was saying before I was so rudely interrupted, I met Armando — which, of course, meant meeting all of those crazy people who travel with him."

"The Queen's Players," said Cara.

"Yes." Medafil made a sound of approval in his throat. "I must say, I love show people. They're quite mad, but very sweet. Anyway, I traveled with Armando and the Players for several months, taking part in their acts. That was when I perfected my English. Unfortunately, it wasn't long after that I had to leave them."

"Why?"

Medafil put one wing over his eyes and muttered, "I'd rather not say."

"Medafil!"

The gryphon stood and stretched. "Don't pretend you don't have secrets of your own, my dear girl. Now come on — I need to get something to drink. Then we had better start moving again."

They made two more flights that day. As they traveled, the marshland gave way to drier terrain that sloped upward. By late afternoon Cara could see Dark Mountain rising in the distance.

As Alma Leonetti had described, it was shrouded in clouds. What the old woman had not mentioned were the constant streaks of lightning that lanced down from those clouds.

"Sizzle-splatting weather," muttered Medafil.

They flew on.

CHAPTER XXIV

ANOTHER DREAM WITHIN STONE

The stone wizard, Namza, dreamed his second dream.

In it he relived the pain that had consumed his body when he finally woke, bruised and broken, from his fall outside Bronzeclaw's cave. Even in his stony sleep he could feel, once more, the agony that had wracked him.

As the dream continued, he began the seemingly endless crawl across stone that had taken him the rest of the way down the mountainside. He moved in terror, always fearing that the dragon's eye might once again fall upon him. The trip was taken in stages, for he would often lapse into unconsciousness, waking he had no idea how much later.

He could not find food, for nothing grew on that stony slope. Even worse, there were many stretches where there was no shelter to be found from the wicked sun that beat upon his skin and tormented his eyes. After a while he removed his loincloth and wrapped it around his head, preferring to travel naked rather than endure the blinding rays. The precious sack of dragon stones he clutched always in one hand.

To his relief there was water; if he could not find a running stream he could at least, in the morning, lick the dew from the beloved stones.

His skin blistered. The blisters broke and oozed. And still he crawled on, hating the sun, hating the world, hating the unicorns, hating everything.

More and more often he would lapse into unconsciousness, only to begin crawling again once he woke, though what he was crawling toward, or why, he no longer remembered. Finally a dark haze overcame him, and he could crawl no more.

And then, a change. He roused to find himself not sprawled on the stone, but lying inside some sort of wooden structure. The walls seemed to be composed entirely of doors, fairly large at floor level, growing smaller and smaller as they went up. Even more startling was the realization that the structure was moving. He wanted to get to his feet, but found he was far too weak even to attempt it.

He checked for his dragon stones, was relieved to find he was still holding them, then fell back into a deep sleep.

The next time he woke, he saw someone — a human! — sitting nearby. The man wore a jacket patched together from mismatched pieces of brightly colored cloth. The jacket had numerous pockets, from each of which hung a gold chain. The man was bald as a delver, with a snub nose and eyes that radiated kindness, though Namza did not, at that time, understand what kindness was. Perched on his shoulder was a furry creature that was staring at Namza with curiosity. It chattered obnoxiously, then fell silent.

"Where am I?" growled Namza. "What am I doing here?"

He did not expect an answer, so was surprised when the human replied, in passable delvish, "I found you a few days back, lying on a patch of stone and nearly dead. My name is Thomas the Tinker, and my job is fixing things — though, alas, I am not nearly as good at fixing broken bodies as I am at mending broken pots."

"How could you have found me?" Namza had demanded.

The man raised his eyebrows and asked softly, "Why so angry?"

For this, Namza had no answer. He was a delver. Delvers were usually angry.

After a moment of silence, the man lifted his hand to stroke the creature perched on his shoulder. "My friend here led me to you."

"And how is it that you speak delvish?" asked Namza.

"I told you, I fix things for a living. I travel here and there to do so. The more folk I can speak with, the better the chance I have of finding work."

Namza wondered why he had never heard of this strange human, then realized that any delver who had actually done business with him would be unlikely to speak of it. Delvers and humans did not mix.

Because Namza was too weak to raise much of a protest,

they traveled together for the next month while he continued healing. Once he was able to go outside, Namza realized the moving structure was actually a cart, painted in ridiculously bright colors. To his surprise, he discovered that the man was able to pull the cart, which would seem to indicate that either he was far stronger than he looked or that the cart itself was enchanted.

Though Namza remained surly and suspicious, as tended to be the delver way, the human never lost patience with him. And as the weeks went on, an odd thing began to happen: Namza found his spirit growing quieter and his never-far-off anger beginning to dissipate.

"What are you doing to me, human?" he growled one night after he had climbed out of the cart, where he spent most of the daylight hours.

"What do you mean?" asked Thomas.

"I do not feel like myself anymore."

"Do you feel better, or worse?"

Namza hesitated for a long time, then said, "Better."

"Well, there you go," said Thomas. "My job is to fix things. I'm just trying to do my job."

Namza growled and stalked off into the woods. But at dawn of the next day he returned. He said nothing of his absence, just crawled into the cart to get out of the sun.

He traveled with Thomas for the remaining months of his *nakken-gar*.

Somewhat to his discomfort, he realized that he was continuing to change, slowly at first, and then — oddly —

more rapidly, as if the change were somehow building upon itself. This transition was difficult, and frightening, and many times he was still surly and resentful. But more often than not, he and Thomas were pleasant together, and the days passed in a way that he would not have thought possible before meeting the Tinker.

Yet even as his heart grew more at ease, another part of him was becoming nervous and fretful. To his horror — or at least to the horror of some scared, angry part inside of him — one night he found himself showing Thomas the dragon stones he had paid so dearly to gather and telling the story of what had happened to him.

Afterward, he berated himself fiercely. What would Metzram think of his student when he returned in such an undelvish state of mind?

The thought was so frightening his mind shut it out, ending, for a time, his dreaming.

CHAPTER
XXV

THOMAS

That same Thomas the Tinker who Namza dreamed of was even then returning from a mission he had undertaken for the Queen some weeks earlier. He whistled happily as he pulled his cart, which was currently expanded out to his favorite size in order to hold the successful result of his quest.

The trip had been a dangerous one, carrying him far into the mountains northwest of Autumngrove. The distance had not been great, but the terrain he had needed to traverse was some of the most rugged in Luster, and his quarry dangerous in the extreme.

"I am reluctant to ask this of you, old friend," Amalia had said, when she first made the request, "and you should feel free to say no."

"Well, that would be graceless of me, wouldn't it?" the Tinker had replied merrily. "Given that save for the gift of that drink from the Queen's Pool granted by your grandmother I would have been long ago moldering in my grave,

I figure I live on borrowed time, and that you unicorns were the source of the borrowing. So if you want to ask something potentially fatal of me, how can I deny you? The worst that can happen is that you get your time back!"

Thomas smiled ruefully as he remembered the moment. He had not been quite as lighthearted about the matter as he had tried to sound, since he loved his life here in Luster and very much wanted to keep on living it. On the other hand, a successful invasion and Hunt by Beloved would pretty much end that life anyway, or at least the part of it that he loved. So the risk of doing what the Queen had asked was no greater than would have been doing nothing.

"At least, I think it was no greater," he muttered, stopping to take out one of his numerous pocket watches and check the time. "I wonder if being turned to stone is worse than dying. Hard to say, I suppose, unless you've experienced them both." He returned the watch to a different pocket than the one from which he had taken it, grabbed a handkerchief from another, and wiped the sweat from his bald head.

He glanced back at his cart, hoping he had secured his cargo properly, then lifted the handles once more. Tightening his grip, he began to pick his way down a particularly difficult slope of rock.

It had been easier coming up, when he had folded the cart down so small that it could fit into his pocket. But that wouldn't do now. No, given what the cart now carried, that wouldn't do at all.

CHAPTER
XXVI

ON THE SLOPES OF DARK MOUNTAIN

It was growing late when Medafil, Cara, and the Squijum reached the line of clouds that marked the edge of Graumag's territory. No sooner had they flown past that line than a jagged streak of lightning split the sky to their left. Moments later its thunder rumbled past, so powerfully Cara felt as if she had been struck.

"Maybe we had better walk from here on," she called to Medafil.

"Ding-flibble it! We don't have time for that!"

"We won't have any time at all if we get fried by lightning!"

The words had barely passed her lips when another bolt of lightning sizzled down, terrifyingly close and filling their nostrils with the metallic smell of ozone.

"Gaaaah! All right, we'll grum-dingled walk!"

Cara hated the idea of a delay as much as the gryphon did. She also disliked having to be the grown-up on the matter. But she knew they could not continue to fly through that lightning and expect to reach Graumag's cave alive.

I suppose Medafil never had a science class, she told herself. *So I can't expect him to know how dangerous this is.*

Still, it was clear from the gryphon's attitude after he had circled down for a landing that he was glad she had talked him out of flying.

They trudged on for another two hours. As Alma Leonetti had foretold, the stony ground was bare of plant life. Cara was careful to weave a path between the numerous boulders and upthrust spars of rock, so there would always be something higher than them to attract the lightning strikes. Though she walked most of the time, once in a while she would ride on Medafil's back, usually with the Squijum perched on her shoulder.

During the times when she and the Squijum *were* walking, the little creature would often scamper off. Each time he did he would return in a few minutes muttering, "Hinky stinky no good rocky place."

"No bugs?" Cara would ask.

"Hotcha stupid place!" was all he would reply.

To Cara's relief, they did find an occasional stream where they could slake their thirst. As the evening wore on, she pointed out that although the thunder and lightning had continued unabated they had suffered only two bouts of rain, both of them brief and fairly gentle.

"Thank goodness for small favors," muttered Medafil.

By nightfall they were less than a third of the way up

the mountainside and it was getting cold. Cara hoped they weren't going to have to do any serious mountain climbing. It wasn't that she was afraid to try, simply that she had neither the skill nor the equipment for a major climb.

If it came to it, they would have to fly again.

No sooner had she accepted that idea than a zigzag of brilliant white lightning, followed closely by a deafening roar of thunder, made her dread the thought.

They slept that night as they had before, the Squijum snuggled against Cara's chest, Cara herself encircled within the giant catcurl of the gryphon. However, unlike the previous night, Medafil folded one great wing over her like a cover. It was delightfully warm, which helped make up for the hard ground. Though the constant crackle of lightning and boom of thunder made it difficult to fall asleep, a second day's exhaustion finally came to her aid, allowing her to drift off.

She didn't know how long she had been drowsing when a burst of warm wind woke her. She opened her eyes. At first she could see nothing. Then she noticed two glowing spots in the darkness. Without a sound, she reached behind her to nudge Medafil. As she heard him stirring, another jagged streak of lightning forked down.

What Cara saw in its brief glare caused her to abandon silence.

CHAPTER
XXVII

AMALIA'S DECISION

Amalia Flickerfoot was alone in her clearing, brooding both on the danger that had come to Luster and on Cara's words about using what she had learned as a human to help in their defense, when a husky voice said, "May I enter, O Queen?"

"You are always welcome here, Madame Leonetti."

The old woman stepped around the opening in the hedge that bordered the Queen's private space. She was dressed simply, in a tunic the color of wheat, sturdy brown pants, and high leather boots. Her long hair, silver as a unicorn's mane, was bound into a braid and coiled atop her head. Coming to Amalia, she laid a hand on her shoulder and asked, mind-to-mind, "How are you holding up?"

"Not well," admitted the Queen with a heavy sigh. "Madame Leonetti, I will say to you what I would say to no one else: I am sore troubled. I have had too little time to adjust to discovering who I really am — no time at all, really, given that the threat of Beloved's invasion has been hanging over me from the moment I recovered my true shape. And now we have not only Beloved to worry about, but also the matter of these shivers and tremblings in the ground, which surely must be related to what she has done. In addition, I am concerned about M'Gama. Her long silence is deeply troubling."

"Difficult times indeed," said Madame Leonetti.

"Cara said something interesting when she came to bid me farewell," continued the Queen, almost as if speaking to herself.

The old woman raised a questioning eyebrow.

"She said that perhaps my human experience could be useful in the struggle to come. Though unicorns are not used to deception and subterfuge, those are helpful things in time of war. And they are things that I learned, sometimes too well, in my human life."

"Nor are your people used to thinking in terms of battles and armies," replied Madame Leonetti.

"This is not a battle," replied the Queen wearily. "It is a Hunt."

"Must that be so?"

The Queen lifted her head.

"Yes, Beloved came for a Hunt," continued Alma Leonetti. "But why not give her a war instead? Even if unicorns don't think that way, you can, My Queen."

The idea made Amalia nod in grim satisfaction. Pursuit by Beloved's Hunters was what had driven her to the desperate act of becoming a human. Would it not be a delicious bit of revenge if the things she learned in that form could now help her defeat those same enemies? She sighed. "I wish I had paid more attention to the history lessons I was subjected to in my younger human years. More knowledge of the tactics and strategies used in great battles would be useful at this moment."

"Does that mean you're going to wait and let them hunt you down?"

The Queen snorted, a rather unqueenlike sound. "You have a rather sharp way of making your points, Madame Leonetti."

"Persuading Queens is my specialty. It was what first brought me to Luster."

Shaking her head, Amalia turned and called to a unicorn standing just outside the clearing. "Laughing Stream! Please gather the council. I wish to speak to them."

Laughing Stream, unusually solemn these days despite her name, whickered a reply, then trotted off to spread the word.

"Will you accompany me?" asked the Queen.

"I wouldn't miss it for anything," replied the old woman.

Together, they traveled the short distance to the Council Grove. Before long they had been joined by eleven other unicorns, all the council save Lightfoot, who was still missing.

"Why have you called us together, Amalia?" asked Moonheart, when the last of the group had arrived. "Is there news?"

"No news, brother, at least none from the outside. But I have been thinking, and I wish to hear what my council has to say about what is on my mind."

"What are your thoughts, Amalia?" asked Fire-Eye. Like Silvertail and Manda Seafoam, Fire-Eye was a close relative of the Queen. His time as a member of the council was supposed to be over, but because of her own lack of experience, Amalia had asked him to stay on.

She took her time before finally answering. "Beloved has come to Luster to hunt us and to kill us. She expects us to act like the beasts she believes us to be. I say let us defy that expectation."

"What do you mean?" asked Moonheart.

As she replied the Queen's voice rose, growing prouder and more firm with each sentence.

"I mean this: Let us not wait for Beloved. Let us instead take the fight to her. Let us plan for a great battle, on the field of our choosing. We may die if we do. But better to die on our own terms, bold and proud, than as victims of the Hunt. Shall we go quietly to our deaths? Shall we become victims who do not fight back? Or shall we rise and fight? I say we fight! I say we are not beasts to be hunted and herded! I say we are creatures of light, and fire, and strength. And I say we shall not quietly go to our graves! Who is with me?"

A moment of silence descended upon the clearing. Then Moonheart threw back his head and bugled a cry of defiance. An instant later Fire-Eye joined him, then gentle Cloudmane. Soon the entire council had reared, their silvery hooves pawing the air in sign of their readiness to fight, to defy the terror of Beloved.

Amalia felt a shiver of pride, of power, and of apprehension. They were with her. They were ready to fight.

But how?

I cannot do this on my own, she thought desperately. *But who is there to help me? Who is there in Luster who understands the ways of war and can help me channel my gifts for deception into a strategy for battle?*

The answer, when it finally came, would arrive from a most unexpected source.

CHAPTER
XXVIII

THE CALL IRRESISTIBLE

Belle wandered aimlessly for much of the day after the Whisperer first spoke to her, terrified that the voice would return even as she feared that it would not.

She had known fear before — she considered it a natural part of the life she led. However, what she felt now was something different, a fear not for her body, but for her deeper self, which she had thought was secret, but had clearly been seen by this strange, invisible being. Worse, what he had found in her was something she had been trying to deny, even to herself. But it was true — she did feel she was better suited to lead the unicorns than Amalia Flickerfoot, who had been absent for many tens of years and had returned to unicorn form only weeks ago.

Yet that very feeling was anathema to the part of her that valued loyalty and honored the chain of command.

Late in the day Belle felt a strange tug at her heart. It took her only a moment to recognize it as the call of a maiden alone in the wood, something almost irresistible to any unicorn.

She wondered, at first, if it might be Cara. The girl shouldn't be wandering out here now. On the other hand, it was quite possible that she and Medafil had not made it back to Autumngrove. The gryphon was a bit of a fool, after all. Anything could have happened to them.

Then she realized there was another possibility. The terrifying tremors that had begun shaking the ground had convinced her that it was likely Beloved had indeed opened a doorway into Luster. What if, when she came through that gate, she had brought along a group of maidens with which to entice unicorns to their deaths? The council had never even thought about that, never planned for it.

Belle cursed their inexperience, and even more their inability to think strategically. Had that wretched "Purification Ceremony" — if it really had occurred — robbed them of the fire and fight required to defend themselves?

She shook her head and forced herself to return to the immediate problem. The more she considered it, the more it made sense to her that Beloved would indeed have brought bait if she was planning a last great Hunt to exterminate the unicorns.

On another hoof, it was also possible that it *was* Cara she was sensing, in which case she should go to her.

So . . . how to determine if it was safe to respond to this urgent need to go to the maiden she was sensing? With a start, Belle realized she had already begun walking in the girl's direction. The ancient call — which had been driven into the heart of all unicorns on the horrible day when Beloved's father and Whiteling fought to the death — was that hard to resist. She stopped and shook herself. *I go on my own terms, or not at all*, she thought fiercely.

But the call was so strong . . .

No wonder this has lured so many of us to our deaths, she thought, feeling a sudden compassion for those lost unicorns who, until this moment, she had secretly considered weaklings and fools. Only now that she felt the call herself did she understand how truly compelling it was.

Not far ahead Belle saw a large tree with a split trunk, its two great boles diverging about four feet above the ground. She trotted to it, then thrust her head through the place where the trunk split, making the tree itself a barrier to going forward. She knew it was an artificial barrier, and she could back out of it at any time. But she prayed the action would give her a moment to gather her wits — and her strength.

Instead, it merely offered a different temptation a chance to present itself, as the warm, seductive voice she had hoped never to hear again whispered, "I know what you want."

Forced to silence, for fear of attracting the Hunters that might well be nearby, Belle thought fiercely, *Go away!*

To her horror, for it confirmed that the voice could indeed read her thoughts, it replied, "I could go a world away, and I would still know what you want. The question is, What would you do to have it?"

No, the question is, What would I do to be free of you?

With that, Belle dislodged herself from the tree and ran full speed in the direction of the girl. *Let the Hunters take me*, she thought. *I will not give in to the Whisperer!*

It took but moments for her to reach the clearing where the girl — the bait — was waiting. She galloped in and reared back, ready for the first arrow to strike, ready to die fighting.

CHAPTER
XXIX

IAN HUNTS

A slight breeze was playing through the leaves of the great tree. The ground trembled again. When it was still, Rajiv said, "How do we begin, sahib? We know nothing of this world."

"Actually, I do know a bit, Rajiv. As I told you, I've been here before. And Lightfoot has lived here all his life. The first thing we need to do is find our way to the entrance to the delver world."

"The main entry to Delvharken is said to be somewhere near the Axis Mundi," said Lightfoot, who was standing between Ian and Martha. In order to make the conversations more simple, Lightfoot had offered to make the same connection with Ian that he had made with Martha and Cara.

"I never thought I'd be talking this way with a Hunter," said the Prince after he had pierced Ian's chest.

"Nor I a unicorn," had been Ian's wondering reply.

"Have you been to this place?" asked Martha eagerly.

The question made Lightfoot shudder. "We prefer to stay as far from delvers as possible."

"They're nasty pieces of work," agreed Ian. "But they *can* be bargained with. I know, because I've done it. Right now, I'm hoping that Martha and I may be able to ransom Cara with the pair of rubies we're carrying."

"Possible," replied Lightfoot, though he didn't sound as if he thought it likely.

"How close are we to this entrance?" asked Ian.

Lightfoot made a sour face. "Just . . . close."

Martha closed her eyes in despair. Ian reached across Lightfoot's back to take her arm. "Don't worry, love. Simply knowing they are not halfway across the world is useful." Then, thinking the words to Lightfoot and at the same time speaking them aloud for Martha and Rajiv, he said, "I'm going to do some tracking."

"Tracking?" asked Lightfoot.

Ian smiled ruefully. "Do not forget, Prince — I was trained for the Great Hunt. Though I was taught for the sake of finding unicorns, I *can* track other things. Delvers, for example. Or my daughter." He took a quick look around, then said, "What's that? It doesn't look as if it belongs here."

He was pointing at a pile of stones not far ahead of them.

"You're right," said Lightfoot bitterly. "It doesn't belong. That's what's left of the place where the Dimblethum placed the wire sphere just before Beloved blasted her way through the tree."

"The Dimblethum?" thought Ian.

Lightfoot sighed. "He is . . . was! . . . a friend of mine. At least, I thought he was. Now, I do not know."

Ian went to examine the stones. Nearby was a spot where the grass had been burned to stubble. He knelt, ran his fingers over the scorched area, then shuddered. Though he was not particularly sensitive to magic, something about the blackened ground felt horrifying to him.

He stood and glanced around. Much of the surrounding grass had been trampled, presumably by Beloved's army of Hunters. Where were they now? He knew something of her plans — she had spoken of them often enough to her inner circle, of which he had once been a proud member. She would have established a camp by this time, probably not far from here. He would need to be cautious as he searched; he certainly did not want to run into a group of his "brothers" by accident.

He began a slow walk around the great tree. When the others started to follow, he glanced over his shoulder and said softly, "Stay where you are, please. I may need to do this several times. The less the ground is disturbed the better."

"As you request, sahib," said Rajiv.

Martha only nodded, then placed her hand on Lightfoot's neck to relay the message.

A moment later, Ian disappeared around the curve of the enormous trunk. He moved slowly, his eyes scanning constantly from side to side, seeking the tiniest hint that might lead him to the place where his daughter had been carried as captive. He passed a spot where a chunk of wood stuck out from the trunk at an odd angle. He wondered what it was. His curiosity was only increased when he noticed a similar piece about halfway around the trunk.

At that moment, he realized something else quite odd: The tunnel through which they had entered Luster did not extend all the way through the trunk. That must mean that the place where Earth and Luster intersected was *inside* the tree.

Marveling at the size of the thing, he continued his circuit. At what seemed to be about three-quarters of the way around he found two things: a third spot where a piece of wood stuck out at an odd angle and signs of a struggle. Kneeling, he examined the ground carefully. After a moment he lifted his head and called, "Martha!"

His wife was at his side almost instantly, as were Lightfoot and Rajiv. "What is it?" she cried.

Still kneeling, Ian pointed to various things around him. "There was a fight here. See, there's a blood spot. Here's another . . . and another over there."

"Excellent tracking, sahib," said Rajiv admiringly.

Ian smiled. "Thank you, Rajiv. Now, if you look closely you can see part of a footprint here — and another here. Notice how small they are, the bits of them that you can see? Delver size, I'd say. Would you agree, Lightfoot?"

Lightfoot, who was receiving this information through Martha, nodded his assent.

"But who were they fighting with?" asked Rajiv.

"I can't say, since I don't know what other humans are living in Luster. But I can see — from this mark, and this one — that it was someone much larger. And, see! Here's a shred of fabric, torn off during the fight, I assume."

He moved forward a bit. "The larger footprints disappear here. And now some of the small ones make more of an impression than would seem likely for their size. I think they were carrying off whoever they captured. If so, it's likely they were taking him — or her — back to their king."

"Then this is the trail to follow?" asked Martha.

"It's our best hope." Ian studied the ground for a bit longer, then said, "The trail looks to be about two days old."

"How can you tell that, sahib?"

"By the drying at the edge of some of the footprints. It's going to make it harder to follow — some of the signs will be lost by now — but I think I can manage it."

Without another word he started forward, as hot on the trail as a bloodhound with the scent in its nostrils.

CHAPTER
XXX

GRAUMAG

"Medafil!" hissed Cara. "Medafil, wake up! We've got company."

Cara felt the gryphon stir behind her, then heard him mutter, "What the rat-gaddled, burk-spiffled midnight nonsense —"

He broke off as another flash of lightning revealed the enormous form of a dragon crouching about twenty feet away.

The darkness returned. It didn't matter. The image had seared itself into Cara's brain.

When the thunder had faded to silence the dragon said, "What are you doing on my mountain?"

To Cara's surprise, the creature's voice was not huge and deep, as were the voices of Firethroat and Ebillan. It was smaller and somewhat feminine. Moreover, the question had been phrased in perfect English, though with a distinct Scottish accent.

Cara chose to answer in the language of the dragons,

hoping that in so doing she could stave off any thoughts that Graumag — she assumed this dragon must be Graumag — might have of eating them. Drawing in the deep breath she needed for this kind of speech, she said, "I come as messenger from Amalia Flickerfoot, Queen of the Unicorns, in search of Graumag, Lady of Dark Mountain."

The words rose from a place low in her belly, warming as they did until they almost scorched her tongue as she uttered them.

The dragon's eyes — all that Cara could see of her now — widened. Switching to dragonspeak, Graumag asked, "And how is it, little messenger, that you address me as if you were a wee dragon yourself? I have never heard such words pass human lips."

"I bear the gift of tongues from Lady Firethroat. She gave it to me as boon for a service I once did her."

The dragon smiled, her enormous fangs making it a terrifying sight despite the goodwill it seemed intended to convey. "Ah. Then, as I suspected, you must be Cara Diana Hunter. Rumor of your adventures has reached even here to Dark Mountain."

Cara felt a shiver to think that this great creature had heard of her, and wondered what kind of gossip network existed between the dragons of Luster. She waited for the next rumble of thunder to fade before saying, "I am indeed the one of whom you speak. I hope that what you have heard of me will dispose you to receive the Queen's message."

"I will listen, lass, but not out here. This mountainside

is no place for a conference of consequence. Let us go to my cave."

"Is it far?"

"Not far, but not easily walked. I will fly you there."

"What of my friend, the gryphon, who has carried me faithfully to this place?"

"He cannot join us. He must wait here."

Cara turned to translate this for Medafil, who cried, "Gaaah! I can't let you go to that monster's cave by yourself."

"It would not be the first time I have been alone with a dragon."

"She will be safe," said Graumag, speaking in English once again.

"How do I know that?" asked the gryphon.

"Is a dragon's word not sufficient?" replied Graumag, a dangerous tone in her voice.

Leaning close to Cara's ear, Medafil muttered, "Grub-dumble it, I don't want you to go with her on your own!"

"I'll be fine," Cara whispered back, patting his beak and speaking with more confidence than she actually felt. Though she knew very well that a dragon's word was considered as good as gold, knowing something and staking your life on it were two different things, and there was always the possibility that Graumag would be the exception to the rule.

Squelching the thought, she stepped forward. As she did, she was startled to hear a small voice chitter, "Hotcha stinky firenose dragon!"

She had been so focused on Graumag she had forgotten the Squijum was clinging to her neck. Reverting once more to dragonspeak, and hoping Graumag hadn't actually heard the Squijum, she said, "Do you mind if my smaller friend accompanies me?"

Graumag nodded. "That is acceptable. Now hold still so I can pick you up."

Bracing herself, Cara heard a flapping sound, then felt a rush of wind. Another burst of lightning erupted overhead, and the girl saw Graumag spread her batlike wings and launch herself into the air. As the thunder that had followed uncomfortably close to the lightning began to diminish, Cara felt another rush of air from the darkness. With no more warning than that, Graumag grabbed her by the waist and soared into the obsidian sky.

"Yike!" cried the Squijum, tightening his grip on Cara's neck.

They surged upward, gaining speed. The lightning that strobed around them made Cara flinch with each blinding flash. She knew the jolting shards of electricity were close, for thunder followed every flash almost instantly, the mighty sound waves pounding against her.

The storm did not seem to bother Graumag, who flapped her way without comment through the cold winds shrieking around them. Cara did not feel so calm and wrapped her arms tightly over the dragon's smooth claws, terrified that each new gust might sweep her into the darkness.

The world below — jagged rock faces slashed with deep valleys — appeared in brief fragments as the pitch black of the night surrendered every few moments to a new flash of vivid light.

Finally Cara could stand it no longer. "Graumag!" she screamed. "We have to get down or the lightning will strike us!"

Twisting her long neck so that her head was close to Cara's, the dragon replied, "Do not fear! We're shielded by magic."

Cara waited for the heat of the dragon's breath to pass before trying to reply. But by then Graumag had straightened her neck and obviously considered the topic closed.

They flew on, coming at last to an opening near the mountain's peak, which was revealed to Cara by another lightning flash. Graumag hovered in front of the cave, then opened her claws and let Cara drop. The girl did not have time to scream; the fall turned out to be less than two feet. She landed with a thump on the ledge that fronted the cave.

"Out of the way!" roared Graumag.

Cara flung herself down and crawled to the side of the ledge, the Squijum squawking and bounding along beside her. An instant later the dragon settled onto the rocky outthrust, then slithered into her cave. Turning about like a dog making its bed, she whispered, "You may enter my home, small one."

"Big lizard big bad," muttered the Squijum.

"Hush," whispered Cara. Fumbling in her pocket, she found her sphere, took it out, and twisted it until it was the size of a tangerine — providing just enough light for her to get her footing. Then she stood and walked into the cave, trying to look dignified. It was dry, warmer than she had expected, and smelled slightly of sulfur.

"An interesting device," commented Graumag, gesturing toward the sphere with a single, outstretched claw.

"My friend the gryphon gave it to me. If you don't mind, I'd like to make it glow a little more brightly. That way I can see you while we talk."

"I have no objection."

Cara twisted the sphere until it filled both her hands. As its gentle light grew stronger, she could see that Graumag was not as big as Firethroat. *Which doesn't mean she's not big enough to swallow me in a single bite,* the girl thought uneasily. *Two at the most.*

The bauble's light was steady. Even so, the dragon's scales seemed to shift in color, appearing now green, now bronze, then green again. She was long and sinuous, her body more snakelike than either Firethroat's or Ebillan's. A spiny crest ran along her neck from a spot just between her eyes — which gleamed with intelligence — to about five feet above the place where her wings erupted from her shoulders. Her front legs were long, and unexpectedly muscular. A series of long fleshy strands, twice the thickness of a man's thumb, hung from her neck.

Cara decided her hostess was both horrifying and elegantly beautiful.

The dragon gazed at Cara for several moments before saying, "I have been interested in meeting you since I first heard rumors of your exploits."

"Oh, well, rumors," said Cara, trying to sound casual. "Probably not very accurate."

"Precisely. Which is why I would rather hear the story from your own lips."

"I have come to seek your help," said Cara.

Scarlet flames danced around the edges of Graumag's nostrils, each of which was at least a foot wide. "You seek my help, but offer nothing in return?" she asked in tones of acid. "Not even a story?"

Realizing her error, Cara quickly bowed her head and said, "Forgive me, Mighty Graumag. I forget myself. Of course I ought to offer you something, and a story is a small price to ask."

The dragon raised a cautioning claw. "The story is not the price of my help. *That* will be given freely, should I decide to give it at all. The story is my price for *listening* to your request."

"I understand," said Cara humbly. She closed her eyes to gather her thoughts, then began to speak, telling all that had happened to her since that fateful night when a Hunter had pursued her and her grandmother into St. Christopher's church.

Graumag listened intently as Cara explained how, clutching the amulet her grandmother had given her, she had leaped from the tower of St. Christopher's and fallen into Luster.

The girl continued, telling of her first meeting with Lightfoot and the Dimblethum, and of how the two of them had helped her make her way across the wilderness to bring her grandmother's message, "The Wanderer is weary," to the old Queen, Arabella Skydancer.

She was especially detailed, for she thought it would interest her listener, when she recounted how she had met Firethroat and been given the gift of tongues.

Finally she told of her quest to fetch her grandmother back to Luster, of her confrontations with Beloved, and of the startling discovery that her grandmother was actually a unicorn who had been transformed into human shape.

She noticed that the dragon seemed to pay particular attention to this last part.

"Hmmm," said Graumag at last, gazing at the girl between half-closed eyes, "So you are actually one-quarter unicorn yourself."

"Yes, I am," said Cara.

The dragon stared at her for a long time. Finally she said, "Well! That was one of the strangest tales I have ever heard, and certainly worth the price I agreed to, which was to listen to your request. Therefore, you may now tell me what it is you came to ask."

Cara bowed low. Returning to the formal language of the dragons, she said, "I come with this plea from my grandmother, Amalia Flickerfoot, Queen of the Unicorns. She says: The Last Hunt is upon us. Beloved and her army of Hunters have invaded Luster, with the intent of slaying every last unicorn. We pray you will come to our assistance in this time of trial and danger. The bonds between dragon and unicorn have never been strong. Even so, we share this world and we both know that the invasion of humans will not be good for any of us, whether unicorn or dragon. Please, then, join with us, not only for our sake, but for the sake of Luster."

When she finished, Cara's throat felt scorched. She bowed once more, then held her breath as she awaited Graumag's reply.

CHAPTER
XXXI

GIRL IN THE WILDERNESS

Feng Yuan had rarely left the grounds of Beloved's castle after she had been brought there as a child. Even when she had left, it had been as part of a group, with strict supervision. So her first day on her own in Luster was also the first time in her life she had experienced real freedom.

She found it both delicious, and terrifying.

In the beginning, she had simply run, wanting to get as far as she could from the horrible crime she had helped commit. She expected the Hunters to pursue her. However, she also suspected that their first thoughts would be for the unicorn they had slain, which would give her time to get a fair distance from them.

Despite her terror, and the fact that as a Maiden of the Hunt she was in peak condition, she finally had to stop to catch her breath. That didn't take too long. What proved more difficult was gathering her wits. Once she managed that, she called to mind Sun Tzu's precept that all warfare is based on deception.

This wasn't war, really, but the idea was still sound.

So, how to deceive the Hunters?

She knew how they worked, knew that they would be after her, and knew how they would track her. With that in mind, she began to lay a false trail.

Her first act was to go about five feet into the brush, making sure to leave footprints and break a few twigs as she did. Hiking up her white dress, which was already stained with the blood of the unicorn and torn from her wild flight through the forest, she squatted and emptied her bowels. She cleaned herself with some leaves, hoping they were not the kind that would produce a rash, then returned to her path. She moved forward another hundred feet or so, not being too obvious, but not worrying about any marks she might leave. Then she removed her shoes and began to walk back the way she had come.

She had been careless in her first run and had surely left many signs to track. Now she moved cautiously, trying to avoid leaving any footprint pointing in the wrong direction, trying not to break any branches or twigs that would point opposite to the direction she wanted the Hunters to go.

After slowly and painstakingly covering some two hundred yards this way, she spotted, to her left, a large stone within jumping distance. She flung her shoes so that they landed on the far side of the stone, then leaped to it herself, managing to avoid landing on any of the mossy patches that might announce to a watchful eye that someone had passed this way.

She scrambled over the stone, slipped back into her shoes — blessing the fact that they were far more sensible than her white gown — and moved into the forest at a right angle to her previous path.

She had no destination in mind. How could she, knowing nothing of the world she had entered? All she wanted for now was to get away from the Hunters and their mad quest to kill more of the beautiful creatures that . . .

Feng Yuan turned her mind from the memory. She had participated in the death of one unicorn already, and she knew it would haunt her for the rest of her life.

For the remainder of the day, the girl traveled with a caution that was as extreme as had been the carelessness of her first wild flight. Whenever she came to a stream, she would remove her shoes, then leap into it from as far away as she could manage, in order to avoid leaving footprints in the soft soil at the water's edge. Then she would walk upstream for a hundred feet, where she would drink, if thirsty. These were the only times she would allow herself to urinate. That done, she would step out and leave a footprint, then turn and walk twice as far in the other direction.

Sometimes she would feel an overwhelming sense of being alone and lost in a world she did not understand, and her gut would tighten as panic threatened to seize her. In those moments she would stop and quiet herself with calming breaths, a technique Wu Chen had taught her.

Other times she found herself wrapped in wonder at the

beauty of this world. The streams through which she waded were crystal clear, and sparkled diamond bright when the sun's rays managed to pierce the blue and silver leaves that formed a canopy above her. Every once in a while she would catch a strange animal cry in the distance and find herself wondering what kind of creatures populated this forest. Occasionally she heard rustlings in the underbrush, and several times spotted brilliantly colored birds flashing among the leaves.

Having been taught self-discipline, she ignored her hunger until twilight. A child from another culture might have starved in the midst of plenty. Feng Yuan, remembering her early years in rural China, simply began to overturn such large stones as she could find. Though the soil held fewer grubs than she had expected, an hour's searching provided enough to quiet the sharp pangs that had been twisting her belly. She would have preferred to wash them, but she had nothing in which to hold them, and didn't want to risk making several trips back to the nearest stream.

Each rock was carefully replaced. If she could still see signs that it had been moved she would collect some of the blue and silver leaves that lay in profusion on the forest floor and use them to hide the evidence of the stone's movement. She continued this way until darkness forced her to cease her hunt for food.

The autumn chill, which she had ignored while traveling, made rest difficult until she decided she would take the risk of gathering enough of the fallen leaves to make a bed. Thus covered and warmed, she lay down to rest.

It was several hours before she slept.

She woke, stiff and uncomfortable, but glad to be free of the bloody dreams that had tormented her sleeping hours. But no sooner had she stretched and sat up than, to her horror, a unicorn came galloping into the clearing. It reared, pawing the air with its forelegs, and bugled a challenge.

Here, thought Feng Yuan, *is my punishment.* Clearly the unicorn had tracked her down and was going to kill her for what she had done.

Well, she could take that. She had it coming.

She spread her arms, inviting the unicorn to pierce her with its horn and end her sorry life.

CHAPTER
XXXII

FAMILY LINES

Ian, Martha, Rajiv, and Lightfoot had stopped to rest for the night. Martha, frustrated by the need to halt their search for even a moment, had cursed the darkness as it fell. She had suppressed her restlessness until Rajiv fell asleep, but once the boy was out she prowled the edges of the small clearing they had chosen for their camp. Finally she stopped and stared into the darkness, as if somewhere in its depths she could find a clue to her daughter's whereabouts.

"Martha," said Ian gently, "lie down. You should rest."

"I can't!"

"You'll need your strength for tomorrow. Lightfoot has first watch. Come and lie beside me."

She didn't move. Ian rose and went to her, but when he put his arms around her she pulled away, her body stiff and resisting.

"What is it?" he asked.

"What is it?" she echoed wonderingly. "Ian, have you thought for even a moment about what has happened to us? To *me*?"

"I try not to," he answered, deep sorrow coloring his voice.

She turned on him. Voice low but intent, she said, "Yes, that's just like you! Let's not think about it, Martha. Let's pretend it never happened. But while you were being trained by Beloved, I had plenty of time alone at home to do nothing *but* think."

"Martha —"

"Don't!" she said, putting up her hands. "Don't. I'm not done yet, Ian. I want my daughter, my daughter who was stolen from me by my mother. I want to find her, and I'll let you help me. But after that I never want to see you again."

Ian looked at her, stunned.

"You left me with Beloved!"

He shook his head. "That's not true. I left you in order to go train with Beloved, but you agreed to that. And I didn't leave you *with* her. She came and got you, something I was not aware of until Cara told me Beloved had placed your spirit in the Rainbow Prison." He sighed. "Martha, neither one of us knew, when this started, what we were being drawn into." Swallowing his pride, he said, "And I admit I got caught up in the Hunt. But we both believed the things Beloved told us when she came to recruit me."

Martha drew herself up as if her anger were surging, then seemed to collapse. "Ian, there's still so much I don't understand. But there is one thing I am clear on, and that is that there's a great deal that you're not telling me."

Ian bit his lower lip. He had been waiting, with both eagerness and dread, for the right moment to reveal to his wife all he had learned. But there had been so little time for quiet talk, and no privacy for the huge thing he needed to tell her.

Martha put her hands on the sides of his face. Her voice softer now, she said, "You're holding something back, Ian. I can see it in your eyes. What is it?"

And still he hesitated.

Martha clenched her jaw, and it was clear she was trying to control her temper. When she finally spoke, it was only to say, "Just tell me."

Ian had hoped to give his wife this information gently, to speak when they were linked in love, not locked in anger. He was glad he had been able to keep his own temper, which used to be such a problem, from blazing out, then remembered, with something approaching amusement, that he had learned this control as part of his training to become a Hunter. Glancing around, he spotted a tree from which a thick, low branch grew horizontal to the ground.

"Come," he said softly, taking Martha's hand.

She resisted at first, but when she saw where he was leading her, she relented and went with him. He gestured to the silver-barked branch in what he hoped was a gallant move. Martha sat.

As he stood gazing at his wife Ian Hunter felt his heart swell with love. The light of the moon, now two nights past its full, streamed into the clearing, its silver beams tinted blue by the leaves overhead. Perched there, her red hair tumbling over her shoulders, her fine features limned by the pale light, Martha reminded him fiercely, painfully of the young woman he had fallen in love with back when they were both teachers and neither one of them had imagined that unicorns really existed.

"What are you smiling at?" she asked sharply.

"I was thinking of when we met. And I thought to myself, 'So much has happened since then that it seems like it was another world.' Then I realized it really was another world."

The hint of a smile twitched at the corner of Martha's mouth. Perhaps to hide it, she looked away, studying the clearing. Some fifteen feet from them, curled on a pile of leaves, lay the sleeping form of a beggar boy from India. Standing protectively over him was a unicorn — a unicorn who had forged a connection with her so he could speak directly into her mind.

Martha scowled.

"What is it?" asked Ian.

"It's just . . . too much. You've moved into this slowly, Ian. I . . . I was a prisoner for a long time." Her voice quavered, and tears welled in her eyes. "I didn't even really understand that I was a prisoner until you freed me. It's as if I've been asleep for the last four years."

"If it's any consolation, I don't think those years were completely stolen," said Ian, taking her hands between his.

"What do you mean?"

"I mean I don't think you aged during that time. I suspect the spell had you in a kind of suspension."

She smiled wanly. "I'm glad to know that. But it doesn't give the *time* back. It doesn't give me what was happening *during* those years."

Ian thought about reminding her that they were bad years, but thought better of it.

"I knew when Beloved spirited me off to her castle four years ago that my world was spinning out of control."

"She came to get you herself?" asked Ian in surprise.

"No. It was that man, Kenneth."

Ian's face darkened.

"He told me that Beloved wanted me to come and join you at the castle."

She turned away, obviously pained by the memory.

He took her shoulders. "You realize I had no idea this was happening, don't you?" He tightened his grip. "You must believe me, Martha. *I did not know.*"

The tears that had been gathering in Martha's eyes now spilled over and began to roll down her cheeks. "Didn't you even wonder about me?" she asked bitterly.

He shook his head, puzzled. "What about the letters?"

"Letters?"

"Whenever I returned from a mission, Beloved would give me letters that she told me came from you."

Martha shuddered. "She's a horror, Ian. She'll do anything, say anything, to get what she wants. She lied to us about everything."

"I don't think all of it was lying," said Ian. "She truly believes that the unicorns are dangerous."

"All right, she's not a liar, she's insane! It's been just as bad for us either way." She paused, then said, "The thing is, after she took me there's just this big . . . blank. I didn't even know I was 'sleeping' or whatever you want to call it. And then I awoke to find that over four years had gone by. Do you wonder that I'm upset?"

Ian clasped his hands together, then pressed them to his face.

"What is it?" asked Martha. "Please, just tell me, Ian."

"There's more you need to know, sweetheart. A great deal more."

"How much more can there be?" she whispered, her voice thick with dread. She smacked her hand against his chest. *Just tell me!*"

And with that invitation, in the moonlight of an enchanted world, Ian Hunter began to unfold for his wife what he had learned of the strange tale of her own family.

"It starts with your mother," he said.

Martha's face hardened, but she nodded and said, "Go on."

"The reason she kidnapped Cara was to protect her."

"From what?" spat Martha.

"The Hunters."

"Why in the world would my mother have to protect Cara from the Hunters?"

And here they were, at the moment he had been dreading. Swallowing hard, he gathered his courage and said, "Your mother was born a unicorn princess."

Martha leaped to her feet and turned to walk away. Ian grabbed her arm. "Let go!" she hissed, trying to yank free. "I don't need a fairy tale. I need the truth."

He didn't let go. Taking her other arm, his own voice fierce now, he said, "Look around, Martha! We thought we knew the world, thought we knew the limits of reality, but our sense of it was just too small. You've been held prisoner in a world of light, put there by my ancestress who is more centuries old than we can imagine. Unless you let go of what you think is possible, you cannot understand your own life."

She sighed and seemed to collapse a bit. He led her back to the branch, lifted her to sit on it, held her hands while he gazed into her eyes and said once more, "Your mother was born a unicorn princess."

He went on, repeating the story he had learned from Cara in Ivy Morris's house, the night Cara had fended off Beloved's attack and he had left Beloved's service forever. "Your mother's true name was Amalia Flickerfoot. She was a wanderer, so obsessed with Earth that her own grandmother, the unicorn queen, had a spell prepared so that if her life were threatened by Hunters she could transform herself into a human."

He continued, explaining how using the spell had cost Amalia the memory of her unicorn life, and how she had gone on to live on Earth as Ivy Morris, human girl, then human woman, then mother, and then grandmother. But always haunted by the sense that there were people after her. She was told she was delusional, but she was not, for the Hunters were tracking her, always tracking her. She managed to stay one step ahead of them . . . until the night that he, her own son-in-law, finally caught up with her.

"Only I passed her by that night," he said, "because my true goal was Cara. I followed her here, into Luster. But in the end, she defeated me." He smiled ruefully. "That is one reason I am not in a state of pure terror for her, Martha. I know very well how resourceful that child of ours has become."

After her initial objections, Martha had listened without comment, as if the strangeness of the story had rendered her mute. But when he was all done, she said, "Where is my mother now?"

"Somewhere in Luster, I assume. The last time I saw her was that night in her house. She and Cara and Lightfoot returned here, and I set off on my quest to free you from the Rainbow Prison."

She reached out to stroke his cheek. "And for that gallant act," she said softly, "I am willing to forgive a great deal, my love."

He began to weep.

She stepped down from the branch, took him in her arms. "Ian, what is it?"

He shook his head. He wanted to tell her more, tell her of the price he had paid to the Blind Man in order to gain the information he needed to find her, but in the end all he could say was, "I've missed you so much."

Later, when they had both wept themselves dry and given up on talking, Martha lay nestled in Ian's arms, still unable to sleep. She stared at the moonlight filtering through the weave of silvery branches above her, trying to sort through it all.

The story about her mother was preposterous. She wanted — needed! — to believe it was a lie. Yet hearing it gave her own life — the strangely abrupt moves of her childhood, the odd and unexpected terrors, even the horror of having her own mother kidnap her daughter — a shape and pattern that, finally, began to make sense.

She held her hands crossed tightly over her chest, clasping her upper arms as if to keep herself from flying apart, as if to keep her heart in place.

"My mother was born a unicorn," she whispered to herself over and over again. "What does that make me?"

And then, even more desperately, *"What does it make my daughter?"*

STORIES ON DARK MOUNTAIN

Cara had expected Graumag to bargain or demand some price in return for her aid. But after a long silence the dragon simply nodded and said, "You are right, lass. Though I have been friendlier with humans than most of my kind —" She broke off and looked away, as if some memory had brought her sudden pain.

Cara waited respectfully, though it took all the self-control she possessed not to shout, "Yes, yes, go on!"

Finally Graumag shook her head and said, "*These* humans . . . these Hunters . . . do not belong here. I will help."

Cara could barely refrain from leaping forward to hug the dragon, though there was actually no good place on Graumag to deliver a hug. Instead, she said, "Shall we go, then?"

The dragon shook her massive head. "We'll wait until morning, lass. I've flown enough for one night."

Cara bit back her impatience. The dragon was doing her

an enormous favor, and she knew it would not be proper to push her to leave right this moment.

"You'll find some silks and furs in the second chamber behind us," said Graumag. "They should make your sleep more comfortable."

By the light of Medafil's sphere, Cara found her way to the chamber. Knowing that dragons were both treasure collectors and treasure guardians, she expected to find a vast trove, as she had in the caves of Ebillan and Firethroat. To her surprise, the chamber was almost empty; aside from the bedding Graumag had promised, she found a few golden cups and a scattering of religious relics. But that was it. Puzzled, Cara gathered the finest linens she had ever felt and returned to the front of the cave, where she arranged a cozy bed for herself. Before long, all three of them — girl, dragon, and Squijum — were asleep.

Cara was woken by a strange sound. Opening her eyes to darkness, at first she wasn't sure where she was. Then a sizzle of lightning illumined — briefly — the massive shape nearby, and she remembered that she was in Graumag's cave.

But what had woken her? The Squijum, who was snuggled next to her, stirred. "Shhh," she whispered. He patted her cheek to let her know he understood.

For several moments they lay silent, listening. Finally the sound came again, and this time Cara realized what it was: Graumag was weeping. She was tempted to offer the dragon comfort, but was not sure it was a good idea. What, after all, was proper under the circumstances? Dragons were proud beasts, and comfort from a human girl might not be welcome.

The question became more complicated when she realized the dragon was still sleeping. Would she want to be wakened, to be freed from whatever dream troubled her sleep? Or would her dragonly pride be affronted to know a mere girl had heard her in her sorrow?

The need to make a choice was removed by a shaking of the mountain that brought them all to full wakefulness. The Squijum leaped, shrieking, to Cara's shoulder. She stroked his fur, as much to calm herself as to calm him.

When the tremor — which lasted for moments but felt like hours — had passed, Graumag said softly, "It won't be much longer."

"What won't be much longer?" whispered Cara.

"Luster is starting to tear itself apart. I don't believe it will last more than another few days."

Cara's stomach twisted in horror. "What do you mean? Why do you say that?"

"I have been here for hundreds of years, lass. In all that time there has never been an earthquake — not here on Dark Mountain, not anywhere in Luster that I know of. Moreover, I happen to know a little of this world and where it came from. If this Beloved has violated its core in the way I suspect she has, then she has endangered the very thing that makes it solid."

"Yike," said the Squijum softly.

"Yes," said Graumag. "Yike."

Though no additional tremors troubled them, sleep was impossible. After a long silence Graumag said softly, "I was having an unhappy dream."

Something about the way she said this made Cara think it was an invitation and a question. Gathering her courage, she replied, "Yes, I heard you weeping."

"I was afraid of that."

"It's all right. I won't tell anyone."

Graumag laughed. "I do not live in such a state of pride that I care if anyone knows I weep, lass. I simply did not want to burden you with my sorrows."

"I know a fair amount when it comes to sorrow," said Cara, feeling oddly adult.

After another silence Graumag said, "Yes, I suspect you do."

The darkness of the cave seemed to invite a closeness, an intimacy. Gathering her courage, Cara said, "I already know that most of Earth's dragons went to a different world. How is it that you are one of the seven who came to Luster?"

Graumag sighed heavily, causing the flames at the edges of her nostrils to flare a bit. "That is a long story, Cara Hunter."

"We have time between now and morning," replied Cara softly. "And I'm not sure how much sleep we're going to get under the circumstances."

In the darkness all Cara could see were the circles of flame that lined Graumag's nostrils. They moved up and down; it took her a moment to realize that the dragon was nodding agreement. Despite this gesture, several minutes passed before the dragon said ruefully, "I did not fit into the dragon world."

"Why is that?" asked Cara, who was quite used to not fitting in.

Another long silence followed. When Graumag finally did begin to speak, her voice was soft, as if the memories were hard to pull up and painful to recount.

"My name, when I was born, was May Margret, of Arlesboro Castle. I was not a dragon at the time, of course. That did not happen until later."

"You were born a human?" asked Cara, fascinated.

Graumag sighed, causing the flames around her nostrils to flare again. "It began when my mother died and my father remarried."

"Oh, so you had a wicked stepmother!"

The circles of flame indicated that Graumag was shaking her head no. "Oh, I confess that I did *consider* her wicked for a while, especially after she transformed me into a dragon. But that was before I understood her part of the story."

Cara blinked, confused, and wondered if anything was ever as simple as it first seemed.

"You may know the bones of the tale," continued Graumag. "It's been told many times, though changed again and again in the telling, as these things usually are. The short version is, my stepmother changed me to a laidly worm."

"A worm? Just a worm?"

Graumag actually laughed. "In older times, dragons were often referred to as 'worms'."

"And what is *laidly*?"

"It meant ugly or loathsome. My stepmother put this transformation on me, and the only cure for it was for my brother, Childe Wynde, to come back from across the sea and kiss me three times before sunset on the day of his return."

"If he was a child, why was he across the sea?"

"That's 'Childe' with an 'e' at the end. It was a formal title in those days. It meant Wynde was the designated heir and would be lord of the castle after our father died."

"Ah, I see. And I do remember hearing something like this once. But didn't the brother in that story actually come back and turn the dragon — turn you — human again?"

"Exactly!"

Cara shook her head, more confused than ever. "Then why are you a dragon now?"

"Well, books and storytellers often like to stop at the happy ending. But there's more — quite a bit more — to my tale. However, if I am to tell it, I will have to ask you to stop interrupting and just let me do this in my own way."

"You heard the lady," said Cara to the Squijum. "No talking."

"Hotcha quiet!" agreed the Squijum. Climbing into her lap he clutched his tail and settled down to listen.

"After my transformation," began Graumag, "I coiled myself around the top of a high, narrow hill called the Spindlestone. From there I could watch the sea, aching and eager for my brother's return.

"Happily, Childe Wynde did indeed return, did indeed kiss me three times before the set of that day's sun. Once I had shifted back to human form, he wrapped me in his cloak and carried me to the castle. Together we climbed the stairs to the tower room where my stepmother had worked her magic. Holding my hand, Wynde struck my stepmother with a wand of rowan wood. The power that had turned me into a dragon — Transformational Magic, it's called, and it was still trapped inside me — flowed out of me and into Wynde, through Wynde and along the rowan wood, and finally into my stepmother.

"To my delight, she began to wither and shrink, finally turning into a large and loathsome toad. Then she hopped away down the tower stairs."

Cara had indeed heard this tale, in a slightly different form. It was one of the many her grandmother used to tell her.

"But that was not the end of my story," said Graumag. "In fact, it was only the beginning. . . ."

CHAPTER
XXXIV

A PAIR OF WARRIORS

Expecting sudden death, Belle was astonished to instead find that the maiden in the clearing sat wide-eyed and trembling, as if she were awaiting death herself. Puzzled, Belle walked toward the girl. Clearly she was one of Beloved's minions, here to draw unicorns to their doom. So why was there no attack from Hunters? Was the girl alone? If that were the case, why did she not flee? Surely if she had been brought to Luster by Beloved she must believe all unicorns were fearsome beasts, ready to savage maidens such as herself.

To Belle's surprise, not only did the girl not flee, she did not even rise, but simply spread her arms, almost as if inviting attack.

Now what do I do? thought Belle.

Knowing that the girl was not in real danger caused the compulsion that had pulled Belle toward her to fade. She could, if she wanted, simply turn and walk away. But the look on the girl's face — somehow defiant, defeated, pleading, angry, and heartbroken all at the same time — made the unicorn want to discover why she was here, what she was thinking.

Of course, there was only one way to do that.

Well, this will be the test, thought Belle, expecting the girl to leap to her feet and run when she stepped closer.

The girl confounded her by remaining stockstill.

Belle hesitated. Could this be a trap after all? But if so, what were the Hunters waiting for? Why did they not spring out and attack?

Belle stood in puzzlement for several breaths before taking another step forward. The girl was lovely, her jet-black hair and almond-shaped eyes reminding Belle somewhat of Li Yun, the tiny acrobat who was part of that ridiculous group called The Queen's Players.

Belle stepped closer. Still the girl made no effort to flee. However, her trembling grew worse, as if she were expecting some terrible punishment.

Belle whickered gently, trying to calm her.

The girl blinked, as if surprised, but did not cease her trembling.

Belle took one more step, then lowered her head. The girl flinched, but held her place. Setting the tip of her horn at the center of the girl's chest Belle pushed quickly, piercing the flesh. The girl's eyes widened and she cried out, not in pain, but — at first — in fear, then in astonishment.

Belle stepped back, withdrawing her horn. No blood stained the spot where she had pierced the girl's flesh, for it had healed in the moment she withdrew the horn. Only a small rip in the stained white garment indicated what had just happened.

The look on the girl's face turned to one of extreme confusion — a confusion that only grew when Belle slowly lifted a hoof then placed it on the girl's leg so she could send the thought, "I only did that so we could speak to each other."

Now the girl did shriek and leap to her feet. She backed away, staring at the unicorn in awe. Yet she still did not run.

Belle waited. After a moment the girl raised a tentative hand. It trembled as she laid it against Belle's neck.

"That's right," thought Belle. "We have to be in contact for this to work."

The girl said, "I thought you were going to kill me!"

"Don't speak! Just think. You have to *think* what you want me to understand."

The girl nodded and tried again. "I thought you were going to kill me."

Belle snorted angrily and replied mind-to-mind, "You've been lied to! That is not our way."

The girl stared at her for a long time before answering, "I believe you."

This was followed by a moment of blankness, as if they were not connected after all. Then, as if some wall had broken, a flood of memory poured out of her, horrible images of waiting in a clearing, knowing that she was being used as bait to draw a unicorn to its death and thinking it was the right thing to do. Then the arrival of the unicorn itself, then the first arrow . . .

Belle drew back, raging and furious. She was tempted to rear up and pummel the girl with her hooves, to slash and lacerate her for what she had been part of. *Stop!* she commanded herself. *She is little more than a child, and she has been lied to for who knows how long.* She stood for a moment, breathing deeply, trying to regain control — to convince herself of her own words. Finally she stepped forward again.

The girl, who was weeping, reached up to touch her neck. "I'm sorry!" she thought desperately. "I'm so sorry! I didn't know. I didn't understand."

"But why are you here now?"

More memories came flooding out — the girl's sudden horror when she saw the unicorn's death, her flight through the woods, her attempts to hide her trail from the Hunters. . . .

"I believe you," thought Belle.

"I didn't mean to let that first memory come out of me," continued the girl. "When you came into the clearing I thought you meant to kill me for what I had done. Or just for the sake of killing me. Either way, I felt I deserved it. But when you didn't . . ." Her thought trailed off, as if she could find no satisfactory conclusion for it.

"Piercing you was the only way I could establish communication," explained Belle. "But when you showed me what had happened . . ."

Here her own thought trailed off. Stepping away from the girl, she asked herself, *Why* did *I do that? I didn't need to talk to her. Now that I've done it, what do I do with her?*

The girl stepped forward. Touching Belle's neck again, she thought, "You're very beautiful."

Belle snorted. "I don't care about being beautiful. I am part of the queen's guard. I am a warrior."

"Oh, a warrior! I know a great deal about war."

"What would you know about war?"

The thought came out a bit more sharply than Belle had intended.

The girl's eyes flashed. Fiercely she replied, "If you know the enemy and know yourself, you need not fear the result of a hundred battles. If you know yourself, but not the enemy, for every victory gained, you will also suffer a defeat. If you know neither the enemy nor yourself, you will succumb in every battle."

Belle stepped back so she could look at the girl more carefully. The girl glared at her, as if daring a contradiction. Nudging the girl lightly with her nose, Belle sent, "That is not your own thought."

"Of course not. The words are from Sun Tzu."

"Who is Sun Tzu?"

"He is no longer. He lived over two thousand years ago. He was the wisest man of his age, perhaps of any age, regarding the waging of war. My teacher, Wu Chen, loved his book, *The Art of War*. He taught me from it endlessly. I can recite most of it by heart."

Again Belle backed away to study the girl. Finally she stepped forward once more and, placing her cheek next to the girl's, asked, "What is your name?"

"I am called Feng Yuan."

"And I am Belle. Would you like to come with me?"

"Where are you going?"

"To join the rest of the unicorns, in the hope that we can survive the Great Hunt that Beloved has launched against us."

Feng Yuan smiled. "Sun Tzu teaches us that one of the keys to victory is knowing the enemy's condition."

"And can you tell us something about that?"

"The enemy's condition? I can indeed. You are lucky to have found me, for Sun Tzu proclaims that knowledge such as this is best gained by the use of spies. Not only that, he says that the most useful of all spies is the converted one."

"The converted spy?"

"One who was part of the enemy, but now is on your side. That would be me." Feng Yuan smiled. "Of course, Sun Tzu also says that it is essential that converted spies be treated with the utmost liberality."

"What is 'utmost liberality'?"

"That means you should give me a lot of treasure." When Belle didn't answer right away, Feng Yuan said quickly, "I did not really mean it. Because of what I did, there was a death. I owe the unicorns a great debt, a debt I can never erase. Whatever I can do toward repaying it will be treasure enough."

"Then come with me, and I will give you your chance for treasure."

"Where are we going?" asked Feng Yuan again.

"To the Queen of the unicorns. She has need of the knowledge you say you can offer."

"Thank you," replied Feng Yuan. "I do not think I could go on living if I could not do something to atone for my crime."

As they left the clearing Belle could not help but wonder if finding Feng Yuan was a marvelous piece of luck, or if the Whisperer had led her to the girl in order to create more mischief.

CHAPTER
XXXV

ARKON'S CHOICE

Arkon the centaur stood just outside his cave, honing the edge of his sword. The metal of his blade glistened in the light of the bracket-mounted torches — as did the sweat that coated his muscular arms and chest. He was calm, despite what lay ahead. He was confident, too. The centaurs had not held a combat to choose a new Chiron in the hundreds of years since they came to Luster. Even so, Arkon had been studying the rules — and the necessary fighting skills — from before the time he could leave his mother's side. With his friend Basilikos, he had sparred and jousted and tussled through all the years of his youth, readying himself for this great event.

He was grateful the old Chiron hadn't died too soon; otherwise he, Arkon, could not have been ready for this moment.

Instantly he felt a flash of guilt for this thought. The old Chiron had been wise and good. Unfortunately he had also been tired. That was natural enough, given his oddly extended life, but it had meant that the centaurs, as a people, had been stagnant ever since they came to Luster. Now that the human girl, Cara, had provided the old Chiron with the death he so deeply desired, it was time for a new leader, with new ideas and fresh energy.

And, perhaps, thought Arkon, sliding the whetstone along his blade again, *time for us to move beyond the restrictions of this valley and take a larger place in Luster . . . no matter what the unicorns say.*

He extended his arm, raising the sword high enough to catch the moonlight instead of the torchlight. Though the Blood Moon was now two nights gone, in his mind the blade gleamed red, anyway.

He lowered the sword, then placed it carefully in the ornately decorated leather scabbard he had made himself from the hide of his first kill, one of the deerlike creatures that roamed the valley's sides.

The initial stages of tomorrow's test would not be dangerous — more like games, really. But the four centaurs who finally emerged as winners of those contests would face one another in a series of genuine battles, battles meant to determine who would be the new Chiron. Having studied past contests, Arkon knew it was unlikely all four of the final contenders would survive the day, at least not without severe wounds. This did not disturb him. Combat for the Chironate was an ancient tradition. He had longed to be part of it for many years.

The sound of hooves upon stone alerted him that

someone was coming. A moment later a familiar voice called softly from the darkness, "Arkon, I need to speak to you."

"Come closer, Arianna."

The centaur princess stepped around a boulder, entering the circle of torchlight at the front of his cave. Arkon was surprised to see that her face was serious, almost pained. He spread his arms, welcoming her to his embrace. She moved into it easily, sliding her own arms around his broad shoulders. Though Arkon was glad of her familiar touch, he felt uneasy, for he knew the Princess to be stoic of mind and not usually given to emotional displays. She had wept profusely after the death of her many-times great-grandfather, of course, both in public and then secretly, here in his cave, sobbing against his chest. But that was different. Rubbing his face against her thick, chestnut hair, he murmured, "What is it, my love?"

"I am leaving the valley tonight."

He pulled back, astonished. "Leaving? But why *now*?"

"Something has gone wrong," she said. "You must know that, Arkon. These tremors disturbing the land — there's never been anything like them. We already know, from what Cara told us, that Beloved has been trying to find a way into Luster. I cannot help but think these shakings are a sign she has done so."

"What does that have to do with us?"

"We live here, too!"

"But this . . . this *Beloved* is not after us. It's the unicorns she wants. And they are hardly friends of ours. So it doesn't matter to us."

Arianna's eyes widened, and he was startled by the anger he saw in her face. "Do you really believe that?"

"That they are not friends of ours? Of course!"

"No! That it doesn't matter to us. Arkon, this world — this *little* world — is all we have left to us. I don't know what, if anything, we can do about what now threatens it. But I feel we must go outside the valley and try to find out."

"Arianna, you know what tomorrow is."

She paused, then said, "That's exactly why I want to leave now. It will be easier while no one is in charge. The new Chiron will likely forbid such a trip. Better to go before that can happen."

"If that is what you truly want to do, once I am Chiron I will defy the ban on leaving and make it possible."

She sighed, and it was Arkon's turn to be angry. "Such faith!" he said sarcastically. "Do you not believe I will triumph tomorrow?"

"Of course I do. But I am not *sure* of it. And besides . . ." Her voice trailed off.

"Besides *what*? What is it, Arianna?"

"I do not want to see you fight. Maybe see you wounded. Maybe . . ." Her voice caught. "Maybe see you killed. Oh, I cannot watch it, Arkon. Come with me, dear one, come with me. This is more important. Please come with me!"

"But the Chironate . . ."

"*This* is more important!"

"Arianna, this is my chance — my only chance — to ascend to being Chiron. I have waited for this all my life."

"And dealing with whatever has caused Luster to begin this shaking may be the only chance for all of us. Think, Arkon. What good will the Chironate do you if our world itself is lost?"

He sighed and looked past her, out to the valley that had been both his home and his prison for as long as he could remember. Placing a hand upon his cheek, Arianna turned his head so he was once again looking into her eyes. "I'm leaving an hour before dawn," she whispered. "You know where to meet me if you want to join me."

Then she moved away, vanishing among the shadows.

When she was gone, Arkon pulled his sword from its scabbard once more. With a cry of frustration, he brandished it at the moon.

CHAPTER
XXXVI

JOURNEY TO AUTUMNGROVE

Feng Yuan was coming to a remarkable conclusion.

She was happy.

It was not a feeling she was used to.

The girl wasn't sure when the happiness had begun to creep over her. This was partly because traveling with Belle had been nerve-wracking at first. Despite the way her beliefs about the unicorns had changed, time and again she would experience either a sudden wash of fear or a sense that she was enacting some great betrayal. Both feelings, of course, were lingering effects of the hateful lies about unicorns that had been drilled into her head during her years in Beloved's castle. Such training does not fade easily. Yet she had only to place her hand on Belle's shoulder, only to sense the connection they shared, and the bad feelings would evaporate. She didn't even need to trade thoughts with the unicorn for this to happen; the connection itself was enough.

"What?" asked Belle, one time when Feng Yuan reached out to touch her. "What is it?"

"I just needed to be sure you are real and that I have not lost my mind."

"I'm fairly certain I'm real. I have no idea whether or not you have lost your mind." Startled at herself for making a joke, Belle hesitated, then added, "Would you like to ride on my back? We'll travel faster that way."

"Oh, yes, please!" cried Feng Yuan. She had been longing to do just that, but had been shy of asking.

"Climb on."

The girl scrambled onto the unicorn's back.

"Have you ridden before?"

"No."

"All right, we'll take this easy for a bit. Lock your knees against my sides. You can also use your hands to grip my mane. But try not to pull it! I might bite."

"Maybe I should walk."

"That was another joke. I guess I'm not very good at them."

"No, no, it is my fault," said Feng Yuan quickly, as she wound her fingers into Belle's silky mane. "We did not laugh much in Beloved's castle. I need to learn about jokes."

"Well, that makes two of us. Are you ready?"

"Yes."

"Then here we go!"

If Feng Yuan had been happy before, her heart now fairly burst with joy. The world around them was unutterably beautiful. The air was pure and sweet. And she was riding a unicorn.

They moved more swiftly now, which had been the real reason for Belle's invitation. She was anxious to get back to Autumngrove and join forces with the other unicorns. Even more, she was eager to present Feng Yuan and her odd wisdom regarding warfare to the Queen.

As the girl became more comfortable with riding, Belle picked up her pace. All unicorns could travel for great distances without tiring, and Belle was in better shape than most. Indeed, it was Feng Yuan who had to occasionally beg for a rest, as she was not used to using the muscles required for riding.

At one such stop, beside a narrow stream, she plucked a golden flower. Placing her free hand on Belle's shoulder she asked shyly, "May I put this in your mane?"

To her own surprise, Belle agreed, wondering to herself, *What is it about humans that can make the ones not trying to kill you so endearing?*

They traveled well into the night. When Belle finally decided to stop for a rest she chose a site well-situated to defend. "We'll have to watch for both Hunters and delvers," she explained to Feng Yuan.

"Delvers?"

"Vicious little creatures," Belle began with disgust. Then

she paused, recalling the Chiron's strange tale about where the delvers had come from. She sighed and said, "Let me tell you a story."

Later, standing between the roots of a large tree while the girl slept curled beneath her, Belle reflected on how odd it was that telling the tale of the Whisperer and the delvers had caused her to feel some sympathy for the delvers. What strange power did telling a story have, that it could open her heart like this?

"It's a lie," whispered a voice from somewhere in the darkness. "The Chiron just made it up so that foolish girl, Cara, would agree to kill him."

Belle shook her head. *The lies are all yours,* she thought fiercely. *I reject you. Go away.*

To her surprise, the Whisperer did.

In the middle of that same night, Belle — who was in the standing sleep preferred by most unicorns — cried out suddenly.

Feng Yuan woke instantly, scrambled to her feet, and put her hand on the unicorn's side. "What is it?" she thought. "Are you all right?"

"A unicorn has just been killed," answered Belle, who knew, as did all the unicorns, when one of their own had been slain.

Feng Yuan wailed and buried her face in Belle's side, awash with guilt even though she had had no part in this crime.

Sleep was impossible after that. In time, they decided to push on through the dark toward Autumngrove.

CHAPTER
XXXVII

WHAT THE STORYTELLERS
LEFT OUT

A massive bolt of lightning streaked down outside Graumag's cave. The dragon waited for the thunder that followed close on to fade before continuing her tale. When all was silent, she said into the darkness, "What the storytellers did not like to speak of was the courage it took for my brother to give me those kisses. Oh, they said it was brave because I was so hideous, which was true enough. But braver still was the way Wynde endured the heat that pulsed around me.

"What the storytellers chose to leave out was the ferocious pain my brother suffered as he tried to free me.

"And what the storytellers decided not to repeat at all, because they will have their princes handsome, is that in the moments it took for Wynde to give me those kisses, the heat of my breath scarred him dreadfully, in ways both plain and hidden."

"Plain *and* hidden?" asked Cara.

Graumag sighed. "After Wynde rescued me, his fair face was hideously scarred. But his scars were not only on the outside. As it turned out, he could no longer produce an heir."

Graumag fell silent for some time. At last she said, "And here is the final thing, the thing the storytellers never knew at all: Once you have been a dragon, it is very hard to be mere maiden once again. Though I was, at first, relieved to be back in my own skin, I soon found myself longing for the strength and power I had possessed when I was a dragon. I ached for the wings that had carried me high into the sky, and for the way hot blood tasted when it poured along my throat after I had swooped down to capture a sheep or a roe deer and killed it in one bite. There was a fire in my blood, and it would not go away. Finally I sought the advice of a wisewoman called Old Nell."

The dragon sighed, causing a gust of warm air to flow past Cara.

"It would be some time before I learned that 'Old Nell' was something far different from what she was pretending to be. So I took her seriously when she told me that if I truly desired to return to dragon form, I must fetch my stepmother, the toad queen, from her place of banishment in the depths beneath the castle. Her instructions were clear: I was to wrap my toadly stepmother in a cloth, being careful not to touch her. From that cloth, which would absorb some of the magic, the old woman claimed she could brew a potion that would return me to dragon form. She cautioned me again that if I were to touch the toad, it would muddy the magic, then sent me home.

"I did not go underground at once, for I was far from sure that this was really what I wanted — especially as the old woman made it clear that if I became dragon again, there would be no second chance at humanity. I might never have gone at all, if not for the dreams. But I *would* dream at night — dream of flying, dream of wings — and more and more often I would wake to find myself standing on the castle's parapet, as if I had been about to fling myself over in a fatal attempt to fly. So in time I did make the journey, descending far deeper into the earth than I had expected. It turned out there were strange things below Arlesboro Castle. Strange things indeed, strange and disquieting. One room in particular . . ."

Graumag's voice trailed off, and she shuddered, as if with a fearsome memory. After a brief silence she shook her head and said, "I returned to the world above, bearing my step-mother wrapped carefully in a cloth, just as I had been instructed.

"From that cloth the old wisewoman brewed the potion she had promised, which she gave to me in a little bottle of emerald green glass.

"Oddly, I found that simply having this potion gave me, for a time, the strength to resist the dragondesire. It was as if knowing that I *could* return to dragon form somehow soothed the burning in my heart. Yet the desire was always there, sometimes just an ember, sometimes a raging fire, but never totally extinguished.

"Now in this time something else very strange happened.

My stepmother, who I should have hated — who I *did* hate — convinced me to keep her in my room."

"How did she do that?" asked Cara, baffled by the thought.

Graumag chuckled. "She explained that it was better to have her close at hand, where I could keep an eye on her, than to dump her in the swamp, which had been my original plan. She told me that if I did *that*, she would soon be back, causing mischief that I could not keep track of. This made just enough sense — she was a master of persuasion — that I agreed to let her stay with me.

"To my surprise, she began to give me very good advice, claiming that all she had ever wanted was to protect the kingdom.

"Then, as if my life were not complicated enough already, Wynde — no longer 'Childe' Wynde, for our father had died and my brother now ruled the kingdom — announced he had chosen a husband for me." Graumag shifted restlessly, moving her great wings. "Though we did not speak of it, I knew one reason Wynde was eager for me to wed was that the fire of my breath had unmanned him and he could father no children of his own. This we later learned was also part of the plot against us, though we knew nothing of that at the time.

"Despite understanding Wynde's desire for me to produce an heir, I was angry at him for trying to push marriage on me. We fought bitterly. That ended when I finally met my proposed husband who turned out to be charming, handsome, and — worst of all — witty. In short, he was irresistible, and against my own will I fell in love with him. This was the last thing I needed — though, as it turned out, far from the last of the surprises in store for me.

"When the day of our wedding arrived, I went to be married in a state of hope, desire, and fear. Perhaps this is true of all brides. However, I do not believe any bride has ever brought to her wedding ceremony anything like what I carried hidden in my basket of flowers."

"What was it?" asked Cara breathlessly.

"Two things, actually. The first was the little green bottle holding the potion I had been told would turn me back into a dragon. I thought of this as my escape route, should I decide I could not go through with the wedding."

"Why would you not want to go through with it?" asked Cara.

"I was worried not only about my own divided heart, but about not being fair to my groom. He was a good man and did not know what he would have been marrying."

"And the second thing in the basket?"

"My toadly stepmother."

"You brought your wicked stepmother to your wedding?" asked Cara in astonishment.

"As I said, she had become a trusted advisor." Graumag paused for a long time. When she spoke again her voice was distant, as if she wanted to separate herself from what she was saying. "It was at the wedding that I finally learned the truth of how Wynde and I had been manipulated by my stepmother's family — including the 'old wisewoman,' who had brewed the potion and was neither old nor a woman."

"I don't understand!"

"'Old Nell' was actually my stepmother's father in disguise. His 'advice' had been designed to get me to bring his daughter back from the underground world, since the magic prevented her from returning on her own."

"What were they after? Money? The castle?"

Graumag shook her head. Noticeably uneasy, she said, "They wanted neither money nor land, but something deeper and more fierce. Their goal was to end our bloodline forever, and wipe our family from the face of the earth."

"That's horrible! Why would they want to do such a thing?"

The dragon sighed again. "The reason, when I learned it, was indeed horrible, more horrible than I could have guessed, though I had had a clue when I went underground. In truth, Cara, it broke my heart, for it turned out that my father, who I had loved, had done great wrong, great evil. . . ."

For a long time the only sound was the occasional boom of now-distant thunder and, once, the grinding of the stone from a slight tremor. Cara remained silent, too, though she was itching with curiosity. But she could sense that the dragon was not eager to speak of this next thing, whatever it was. And it hardly felt safe to ask her.

Finally Graumag said, "You are quiet."

Deciding to reply in the tongue of the dragons, Cara said, "A story like this must not be rushed."

"You are wise for one so young."

Cara continued her silence, which seemed the safest course. After some time, the dragon said, "I do not wish to speak in detail of what my father had done. I will tell you only that when I went to fetch my toadly stepmother from the depths beneath the castle I passed through a room that clearly had one purpose and one purpose only."

"Which was?"

"To cause pain."

"Torture?" asked Cara uneasily.

"Torture most vile. But then, all torture is vile. I had tried to tell myself, after that journey, that the implements of evil I had seen in that dreadful chamber were relics of a distant past, not anything that had been in use during my own lifetime. But that day in the chapel, I was forced to understand that the devices in that room had been applied to my stepmother's father." After a silence, Graumag said softly, "Which explains everything you need to know about why that family was bent on destroying us. You cannot commit such acts and not expect the wheel to turn against you."

Cara stroked the Squijum's fur as she waited for Graumag to continue, hoping that the attention would keep the chattery creature from breaking the spell of the dragon's story.

At last Graumag spoke again. "What happened next was . . . unexpected. Torn by sorrow, by anger, most of all by horror, I decided to flee my human shape. But when I

230

drank the potion that was supposed to return me to dragon form, it proved to be yet another deception."

"What do you mean?"

"Nothing happened, nothing at all. Our enemies did not want me to become a dragon again, for fear I would be too powerful. So they had lied to me about how it could be done. It was all false."

"Then how is it that you are a dragon now?"

"In my fury, I picked up my toadly stepmother, planning to shake the truth out of her. As you will remember, I had been warned not to touch her, and this was the first time I had done so since her entoadment. The moment I laid hands on her I understood the reason for that warning: It turned out that holding her in my hands was actually the secret. Once my skin was against hers the Transformational Magic that had first endragoned me, and that had later flowed from me, through Wynde, through the rowan wand, to cause her own metamorphosis, flowed *back* into my body. The pain was dreadful, for a change such as this rends muscle and bone and sinew, even as it re-creates them. But moments later I was once more a dragon."

"So did you devour them?"

"Oh, I wanted to. But something caught at my heart — my shame for my father's actions, perhaps. For whatever reason, in that moment of grace I understood that my stepmother's family were the first victims, and I could not blame them for wanting revenge. So instead of taking revenge myself, and continuing the cycle, I took a solemn vow, known only to myself. I swore that I would be the guardian of my country, and that in all my days we would never again do such evil as my father had perpetrated."

Cara pondered this for a time, thinking of her own strange family and the ties of blood that connected her not only to the unicorns, but through many generations to the tormented Beloved, who was never at peace from the pain in her heart. Keeping these things in her own heart, she finally said simply, "How is it that you are now here in Luster?"

Graumag's sigh this time was so heavy it caused a flow of heat to rush past Cara. "You do know that the dragons eventually had to leave Earth?"

"Yes, I have heard as much from Firethroat and Ebillan. They also told me there is a different world, not Luster, where most of the dragons now live. Ebillan explained that he had waited too long, because he did not want to leave Earth, and so ended up missing his chance to go there. Is that what happened to you?"

"Och, if only it were that simple. No, my story is different, lass. As the centuries wore on, the tale of how I had become a dragon was twisted and changed in the retelling. People no longer understood why I stayed coiled there on the Spindlestone, and more than one hero came to challenge me." After a long pause, she said, "I did not want to kill them, you know. It was just that they insisted. By then Arlesboro was not really my country anymore, for the small kingdoms had been merging into one, larger, realm. My mission was ending. At the same time the world was becoming hostile to magic. So when I received word that a pair of magicians named Aaron and Bellenmore were preparing a way for dragons to escape from Earth and go to a world where we would be safe, I was relieved. Truly, I did not want to have to kill another hero."

Cara recognized the name Bellenmore; he was the same magician Alma Leonetti had visited when she was trying to find her way into Luster.

"Of the exodus of the dragons there could be written a great book, for it was a long, dangerous, and complicated adventure. The world to which we traveled was indeed a fine place for dragons. At least, for most dragons . . ."

"But not for you," said Cara slowly, beginning to understand.

A silence followed, broken at last by a particularly ferocious clap of thunder that caused the Squijum to jump onto Cara's shoulder and clutch at her hair.

"Not for me," said Graumag at last.

"Why not?"

"Bellenmore believed it was because I was not dragon born, but rather a creature formed by magical intervention. The world he and Aaron had opened was, indeed, perfect for dragons . . . *too* perfect in my case. We don't know for sure what it was — something about the air, something about the water, maybe simply the world itself rejecting me. Whatever the reason, I did not thrive, and soon grew deathly ill. As I lay near to dying, a dragon named Heartflame found a way to get word to Bellenmore, who sent Aaron to fetch me back to Earth. It was a dangerous journey, and I owe my life to that young man's courage and daring.

"Once I had recovered my health, Bellenmore convinced me I should try making a home in Luster instead. With the Queen's approval, I came through one of the gates. It did not take me long to fall in love with this world, with its great forests and soaring mountains and — please do not be offended — its lack of people. Not only that, it was as if the world loved me back, for my health quickly returned, and I felt, if anything, stronger than ever. So I have plenty of reason to be willing to help the unicorns, Cara. Without their hospitality I would have perished long ago. I owe them, and this world, my life."

DAY THREE OF
THE INVASION

All warfare is based on deception.

Sun Tzu, *The Art of War*

CHAPTER XXXVIII

ARIANNA DEPARTS

Princess Arianna stood halfway up a low mountain. Ahead of her was a little-used path that led to the top of the southwestern rim of the Valley of the Centaurs. She placed a tentative hoof on the path, then turned to look back. In the dim, pearly light that precedes sunrise, the valley below was painted in shades of gray. She gazed at it lovingly, trying to make herself believe she was studying the land and not looking for Arkon. As her eye traced the outline of the familiar hills something twisted in her heart. She had been happy here and knew that leaving would pierce her to the soul.

The air was still; no breath of wind stirred the thick, chestnut hair that flowed nearly to the place where her human form merged with the horse portion of her body. That stillness seemed right. In this hour before dawn, all the world should have been quiet and unmoving. Alas, it was not; though there was no wind, the very ground beneath her hooves was troubled and the occasional tremors that shivered through the stone made Arianna shiver as well.

She turned to look at the path ahead. She would have to start, and soon, if she wanted to pass over the valley's rim before the sun rose. Oh, where was Arkon? Was he really not going to come?

Tears trembling in her eyes, she thought, *Do love and duty always have to be in conflict?* Her love for her grandfather had kept her from doing what should have been her duty, relieving him of the unbearable burden of his life. And, in the end, she had lost him, anyway, when Cara had done what she could not.

"Arkon?" she called softly, hoping, *longing* for an answer.

No sound at all, save for the first song of an early-waking bird.

Love and duty. Was it truly duty that kept Arkon from joining her, his sense of duty to the centaurs, a genuine belief that he was indeed the best to lead them now that the old Chiron was gone? Or was it mere ambition? A different kind of love, she guessed bitterly . . . a love of power.

And what of her? Why could *she* not surrender to love and stay with Arkon? Was it really only her sense of duty that was calling her to abandon the safety of their home? Or was she, too, following another wish, a long-held desire to see the world that lay beyond their valley?

Oh, why did Arkon not join her?

The blazing rim of the sun poked above the tops of the mountains that formed the valley's eastern wall.

Arianna sighed. He was not coming. Brushing aside the

tear that trickled down her cheek, the centaur princess turned and trotted up the trail.

An hour later she had passed through a gap in the low mountains and stood on the downward slope.

As she started forward, the world again trembled beneath her. But that disruption felt as nothing compared to the trembling of her own divided heart.

CHAPTER
XXXIX

ELIHU

Morning on Dark Mountain took forever to arrive. When it finally did begin to brighten the eastern sky — a brightness that stretched forward from beneath a shadow, for heavy clouds still blanketed the mountain itself — Cara, the Squijum, and Graumag stood at the mouth of the dragon's cave.

Thunder continued to rumble in the distance.

"Do dragons always live in such high and desolate places?" Cara asked, gazing nervously at the enormous void yawning before her.

"We learned to inhabit them back on Earth, as humans drove us ever more deeply into seclusion. By the time the seven of us reached Luster, we were so used to such terrain that it seemed natural to seek it for our homes here as well. Besides, we did not want to intrude on the unicorns. After all, we are — to some extent — their guests in this world." Graumag crouched and lowered her head. "Now, lass, climb up. It's time we returned to your friend, the gryphon. I believe you will find the best spot for riding is at the base of my neck, just above my wings."

Thankful that she could ride this time, rather then be carried in the dragon's claws, Cara took her place. She realized that even as she was clinging to the dragon's neck, the Squijum was clinging to hers.

"Now I am going to let you do something very rare."

"What?" asked Cara, feeling slightly nervous.

"Reach under my neck. Feel those thick tendrils?"

"Yes."

"All right, take one in each hand. You can use them to hold on."

"Won't I hurt you?"

Graumag chuckled. "I'm fairly tough. Besides, if you hurt me too much, I'll just eat you."

"Maybe I should just hold your neck!"

Graumag sighed. "It was a joke, lass."

"Oh. Sorry. I haven't had much experience with dragon humor."

"Not many people have," said Graumag dryly. "Now get yourself settled in."

Cara reached under the dragon's neck and took one of the strands in each hand. Except for the fact that they were hot to the touch they felt so much like snakes that she almost expected them to writhe in her hands.

"Ready?" asked Graumag.

"Ready!" replied Cara, tightening the grip of her legs against the dragon's neck.

With no more warning than that, Graumag leaped into the air.

"Yike!" cried the Squijum, tightening his grip on Cara's neck.

She had to repress a scream of her own as they hurtled into the yawning abyss. After a moment, Graumag snapped out her great wings, almost like a ship unfurling its sails. The leathery appendages caught and cupped the air, slowing their descent. At the same time the crest on her neck rose to its full height. Flexing it like a rudder, Graumag tipped slightly to the left, swinging in a graceful circle. Cara looked down. The mountain below was carved and rutted with cliffs and gorges, and marked by shadows that looked like the openings to caves. She had a sudden sense that it contained many secret places. *How many secrets,* she wondered, *are there in Luster?*

Occasional bolts of lightning still seared down from the darkened sky. Cara watched them nervously. Despite the fact that Graumag had assured her the lightning was not a danger, the girl could not help thinking, *I hope she's right that it really is magic that keeps the lightning away and not simply centuries of good luck that might run out at any moment.*

They had almost reached the spot where they had left Medafil, and Graumag was gliding down for a landing, when an arrow whizzed past Cara's ear.

"You fool!" cried a nearby voice. "Put down your bow! That's not the way to get her!"

Twisting her neck, Graumag banked so sharply that Cara nearly fell off. With a cry, she leaned forward. At the same time she tightened her legs, gripping the dragon's sinuous neck so tightly she could feel the shift and play of Graumag's muscles beneath her thighs.

"Bad men!" cried the Squijum. "Bad men! Bad men! Fly, dragon. Fly!"

Graumag did fly, her great wings beating the air as she pivoted, then hurtled back in the direction from which they had come.

They landed a fair distance up the mountain. "Well, lass," the dragon said softly, "it appears you have some enemies."

"Hunters," replied Cara. "They have to be."

"Certainly. But why are they hunting for *you*?"

"Are you sure they aren't just here looking for unicorns?" Cara replied nervously.

"If they are, their hunting skills are not as good as you have led me to believe, since there are no unicorns on Dark Mountain. Besides, you heard that shout, 'That's not the way to get her!' I suppose they could have been referring to me, or that Squijum thing of yours, but I highly doubt it. So, again: Why are they hunting for you? I thought it was only unicorns they were after."

"I don't know. Beloved did want me before, but that was to get my amulet so she could open a gate into Luster.

She's here now, so I don't know why she would still be after me."

"Perhaps she simply wants to get to know her descendant a little better," said Graumag darkly.

Cara flinched at the thought, then gasped as she remembered who they had been planning to join. "What about Medafil?"

"If he was alert, he may have managed to fly away before they could take him. I hope so. I suppose it depends on how skilled these Hunters really are."

"You don't think they would hurt him, do you?" asked Cara in terror.

The dragon tipped her enormous head, as if thinking. Finally she said, "It's hard to tell. Their stated task is to hunt and kill unicorns, so I guess it depends on whether Beloved has decided she wants to destroy *all* magical beasts while she's at it. And, I suppose, how deep is their taste for blood." The dragon looked at her intently. "How quiet can you be? We need to do some spying. I would go myself, but I'm too big for such a task."

"Squijum go!" cried the Squijum, leaping down from Cara's neck. "Squijum good quiet sneak! Squijum look. Squijum listen. No one see brave Squijum!"

Before either Cara or Graumag could respond, the little creature scampered into the underbrush.

"Can that wee bouncy beastie really be quiet?" asked Graumag.

"I think so. He hunts bugs and other little things, so he

must be quiet enough to sneak up on them. And he managed to trail me into Delvharken without being caught."

"All right, we'll give him a chance."

Despite her assurances that the Squijum could spy in silence, Cara worried. Her concern grew to near panic as the minutes, and then the hours, dragged by. After a while, mostly to distract herself, she said to Graumag, "How is it that you know the Hunters' stated task?"

"Back in Arlesboro I was friends with one of those unicorns you call 'Guardians of Memory.' In fact, I twice managed to save him from Hunters."

This comforted Cara somehow, and she settled back into her waiting. But she soon became fretful again. She was about to suggest she should go look for the Squijum when he bounded out of the gloom crying, "Squijum lookded! Squijum *finded*! Hotcha good Squijum!"

"Squijum, what did you see?"

"Many men."

"How many?"

"One, two, many! Many manies!"

Cara sighed. She had tried several times to teach the Squijum to count, but two was as high as he could get. Anything after that was "many" — which meant there could be three men on the slopes below or three hundred.

"What about Medafil?" asked Graumag.

"Beakface wingcat all tied up!"

"Oh, no!" cried Cara. "Graumag, we have to do something!"

"Squijum didded do something! Good Squijum, quiet Squijum, sneakied into camp. Good Squijum, quiet Squijum bited bad ropes. *Bite bite bite bite bite!* Bite right through!" Hugging his tail in delight he crooned, "Hotcha good Squijum!"

"You *are* good, Squijum!" said Cara.

"*Hotcha* good!" corrected the Squijum smugly.

"Hotcha good," agreed Cara. "What did Medafil do after you freed him?"

"Beakface wingcat wait till stinky men not looking. Then he fly away!"

"If Medafil has any sense, he'll fly *far* away," said Graumag. "Which is what we should do now, too. Climb on my neck, Cara. We'll detour around them and head straight for Autumngrove."

"Shouldn't we look for Medafil?"

"Right now it's more important to get you out of here. If he's thinking clearly, he'll head for Autumngrove himself, anyway."

"He won't. He'll search for me."

Graumag sighed. "All right, we'll see if we can spot him as we travel. If he's not hiding I should be able to see him once we're in the air. But he is *not* my first concern right now."

As Graumag began to lower her head a deep voice from the gloom said, "There's something you should know before you go."

Cara gasped and reached for her sword, terrified that one of the Hunters had found them. Yet those words didn't seem like anything a Hunter would say. She looked around, but could see no one. Clutching her sword's hilt, she hissed, "Who are you? *Where* are you?"

"Right here," said a man, as he stepped from between two trees. He was very tall, with brown skin and golden hair that almost seemed to cast its own light. Oddly, he wore nothing save an animal skin that had been fashioned into a kind of tunic. Cara felt her heart lurch; even in the deep shade of Dark Mountain's heavy clouds it was clear he was the most beautiful man she had ever seen.

"Who are you?" she asked again.

"My name is Elihu."

Cara blinked, remembering that a man named Elihu had been present at the Purification Ceremony that led to the birth of the Whisperer.

It couldn't be the same man, she told herself. *Even people who have extra-long lives because they've drunk from the Queen's Pool age as time goes on. Just look at Thomas and Alma Leonetti!*

"Where did you come from?" asked Graumag, a dangerous edge in her voice.

"That is not important," replied the man. "At least, not right now. What matters *now* is that there are some things you must know."

"And what would they be, exactly?"

Elihu took a step closer. Graumag stirred and hissed, and her spiny crest rose to nearly its full height, clearly warning the man not to try anything. Taking the dragon's message, Elihu stopped. Looking at Cara, he said, "You wear one of the Queen's amulets, do you not?"

Cara reached toward her neck. As soon as she realized what she was doing she cursed herself for giving up the information so easily. "How did you know that?" she asked.

A sad smile curved the man's lips. "Because I made them."

"But they're hundreds of years old!"

He shrugged. "What's to say that I am not?"

Cara wondered if this might be the same Elihu after all. Before she could ask, the man said, "I know you have it, because the amulets call out to their maker."

"What do you mean?" asked Cara, puzzled by this response.

Elihu tipped his head in an odd way and said, almost shyly, "All things call out to the one who made them."

"Do you really want to take credit for the Queen's amulets?" asked Graumag, her voice threateningly soft. "That's a powerful claim."

The man sighed. Turning to Cara, he said, "Take out the amulet, please." When Cara hesitated, he said, a bit gruffly, "It's not as if I don't know that you have one."

Blushing a little, she pulled the amulet from her shirt. Closing his eyes, Elihu lifted his right hand so that his large palm was facing her. At once the amulet began to glow. A moment later it floated up from Cara's own hand to hover in the air about three inches above it.

"That proves nothing," said Graumag sharply. "I have known more than one wizard who could lift something from a distance. Let's stop the blather and get to the point. I want to get the girl off the mountain *before* those men below us figure out where she is. Unless," she added dangerously, "you're trying give them time to get up here."

The tall man shook his head. "Those people are no friends of mine," he said bitterly.

"You said there was something I should know," prodded Cara.

"Those men are hunting you —"

"I know *that* already!" The words sounded ruder than Cara had intended, but she was still not comfortable with the big man, not sure of how to react to him.

"And how many of them do you think there are?"

Cara shrugged. "Three or four, I would guess."

Elihu shook his head. "By my count there are two groups, of twenty each."

Cara gasped. "They can't be here just to catch me. How would they have known where to find me?"

"Beloved has given them something she called 'tracking packets.' I don't know how they work, but it is clear from what I heard the men say that they were created specifically to help them find you."

"Look at me, human," said Graumag, her voice low and intense.

Elihu complied, gazing directly into the dragon's golden eyes.

After a moment the dragon nodded and said, "He speaks the truth, Cara."

"You have excellent protection," continued Elihu, gesturing toward Graumag. "But even she is vulnerable, are you not, good lady?"

The dragon sighed and said, "The right arrow in the right place, a well-aimed spear, yes, one of these things could end my life."

Cara felt new alarm course through her. "You said there was something I should know," she repeated to Elihu.

His muscles rippled as he pushed back a strand of golden hair that had fallen over his high, brown forehead. "The amulet can —"

He broke off and pressed a finger to his lips.

Cara held her breath.

"Don't make a sound!" hissed Elihu. "Dragon, hold them off!"

Lunging forward, he snatched Cara into his arms, then bolted into the gloom.

CHAPTER
X L

COUSIN-CONFERENCE

Each delver that entered the cave after Razka and Gratz first settled into their designated places took one look at the situation — with their huge eyes they could see it all, despite the darkness — then sought the stone to which his name had been attached. Some moved quickly, boldly. Others trembled with fear. Yet each, finally, claimed his stone, held it close, and took his place, sitting cross-legged with hands folded over his chest.

It was many hours before Gergga, the seventh to respond, came into the cave. "Broken boulders!" he muttered, when he saw what was going on. But he found his stone and joined the others, who sat in a half circle facing the one who had summoned them.

The seven delvers remained this way for many hours, silently calling to their cousin with all the power of their connection. They were not trying to pull him from some great physical distance, as he had them. Rather, they were trying to draw him back from the edge of the oblivion to which his spirit had wandered as he let himself sink back into the Stone from which he had come. The effort was so fierce that several of the delvers had grains of sand popping out on their foreheads, much as beads of sweat would have formed on the brow of a human.

At last they heard a cracking sound. Opening their eyes, they saw their cousin begin to straighten his back. Slowly — very slowly — the traces of stone began to fade from his flesh. The fissures that had opened in his skin began to seal themselves shut. Yet they all knew that the dark lines where those cracks had been would remain with their cousin for so long as he lived, a set of tattoos that would mark him as one who had gone deep into the Stone. Were he not an exile and a traitor, those lines would earn him great respect.

Suddenly his teeth began to chatter. Moments later he was trembling violently.

"He's got Stonechill!" cried Gratz. "Quick, we have to warm him!"

Three of the delvers leaped to their feet and caught their cousin up in their arms, pressing against him and holding him tight.

Slowly — painfully slowly — the shivering diminished. At last he drew a deep breath, opened his eyes, and whispered, "Thank you, my cousins, for answering my call. Thank you for pulling me back from the Stone."

It fell to Zagrat, oldest of the seven who had responded, and therefore now the cove's leader, to reply. "Nedzik, do you realize what you have done?"

He flinched. "Do not call me that! It is no longer my name."

"Well, it is the name *we* had to use to call you back from the Stone!" flared Zagrat. "Do you not understand that in doing so we have cast ourselves out from Delvharken? Do you not understand what we have sacrificed to redeem you? Do you not understand that in order to save your miserable life, we have had to make ourselves exiles, too?"

"When the King is mad, it is an honor to be an exile," he replied, causing the others to gasp.

Zagrat was so infuriated he could not speak and seemed on the verge of exploding instead.

Razka, who was sitting to Zagrat's left, put a hand on his arm and murmured, "Let me." Turning to their troublesome cousin, he said, "For what reason have you called us together, after the King ordered us sundered? Why do you once again put us, your cousins, whom you should protect, at risk?"

Rocky did not answer at first. Instead he extended his arms, then flexed his fingers, looking surprised that they still worked. Finally he said, "I believe the King is wrong in helping the Hunters."

"We already know what you believe," snapped Zagrat. "It was listening to you yammer on about that idea that started all the trouble for us to begin with. Besides, it does not make any difference. The help the Hunters sought has already been given."

Rocky stared at Zagrat in horror. "What do you mean?"

"Someone provided a way for the human female called Beloved to open a gate from Earth to this world. She has entered with her army of Hunters."

Rocky shuddered. "This news is worse than I had expected."

Zagrat sighed in exasperation. "Why should this news trouble *us*? The Hunters are after the unicorns, who are our enemies. They will not bother delvers."

"Pray to the Great One that you are right, cousin. But my worry is not so much that the Hunters will bother us. It is what their entry will do to our world."

"You still have not answered the main question," insisted Zagrat. "*Why* did you call us here?"

"Because I have learned something new, something so important that I felt you, my beloved cousins, must hear it, too."

"How important can it be? Do you realize how you have endangered us for this?"

"Do you realize how the King has endangered Luster?"

Against protocol during a cousin-conference, there was a murmur among the other six delvers. It was Razka who finally said, a bit of awe in his voice, "After what you have already suffered, you still dare question the King?"

"Gnurflax's ability to make me suffer does not prove him right," snapped the rebel cousin. "It merely proves

253

him . . ." He hesitated over the word, but decided no other would fit. "It merely proves him a tyrant." He paused, then swallowing his anger said more calmly, "Do you think the King was right to sunder our cove, Razka?"

Razka hesitated. He did not at all believe the King had been right in that action. But to admit that was to admit that the King was fallible, something he could not bring himself to say aloud. He was still wrestling with his response when Gratz shouted, "Of course the King was not right! Cousins belong together!"

His words generated a mutter of agreement from the other delvers. Finally even Zagrat nodded in assent.

The rebel seized the moment. "If Gnurflax was wrong in that, he can be wrong in other things as well."

Zagrat scowled. "Be careful how you speak!"

"It is too late for caution! I have already been accused of treason, and punished for it, and survived." He paused, then said softly, "Cousins, I do not wish to bring you into danger. If any of you wish to go, I release you from the Call. But if so, go now, at once, for I have important things to say, and if you cannot join me you may prefer never to have heard them."

A long silence followed. The cousins glanced at one another and shifted uneasily. But none of them, not even Zagrat, rose to leave.

The rebel nodded. "All right. Now I will tell you what happened after the King had me thrown into that cell."

The reunited cove listened in rapt attention as their

cousin regaled them with his story of meeting Cara. They were near breathless when he told how the two of them — with the help of a strange creature called "the Squijum" — escaped from the delver dungeons and, accompanied by a dwarf and a gryphon, traveled to the Valley of the Centaurs. Their fascination grew to startled indignation when he recounted the tale of the Whisperer, a force born from an ill-advised attempt of the unicorns to purge themselves of all darkness. But it was not until he claimed that this strange entity had seduced a tribe of dwarves and from them created the delvers that they erupted in anger.

Above their cries of denial, the rebel shouted, "And thus it is that we are locked in this endless struggle with the unicorns! Our roots are tangled in their own darkness."

"Now, at last, you truly go too far!" roared Zagrat. "Delvers have *nothing* to do with unicorns. We were in Delvharken first. Everyone knows that."

"Were we?" asked their cousin. "Are you sure?"

"That's what 'The Story' tells us," said Wurtza, sounding a little confused.

The others muttered their agreement. They had all been raised on "The Story." It was the first tale a delver learned, sung in simple form to the youngest delvlings as soon as they were able to listen, then repeated endlessly, with ever more detail, as they grew older, until it was embedded in their heads and hearts as absolute truth. "The Story" told that the delvers, the one true people of the Stone, had been pulled from the harsh and hurtful light by the Great One and given all the deeps of Delvharken to be their own forever and ever. In this world, which was made from a fallen star, they lived in peace — until the unicorns invaded and spread themselves across the land above them, calling it "Luster" and acting as if they owned it.

"All right, then who is the Great One?" asked the rebel. "Where did he come from? Does he really exist? If so, why has he been silent all these years?"

"Those are deep mysteries and not meant for the likes of us," said Zagrat gruffly.

"Well, there are other mysteries unraveling as we speak, mysteries that may indeed be meant for us. You know as well as I that King Gnurflax has changed in recent years. Why? What happened to him? The delver-guard gossip that they have seen him listening in secret to someone, then speaking as if to the air. Is the King mad? If not, who is he talking to? The Great One? If so, why does he not share the prophecies? And if not the Great One, then who? *Who?* What mischief might be brewing from these secret conversations?"

The cousins stirred uneasily.

"Do you not feel the changes in the stone around us?" pleaded the rebel. "Something is happening, and I do not think it good. Oh, my cousins, I did not wish to challenge the King! I did not wish to break from delver law. But what is this uneasiness I feel in the secret stone of my heart?"

Zagrat snorted. "Madness, most likely — not the King's, but yours."

He shrugged. "That may be. Yet you agreed with me,

Zagrat, that it was also madness when Gnurflax let the human, Ian Hunter, into our caves."

"There have always been humans prowling around on the surface," said Gergga.

"But they always arrived here by ones and twos. Now a flood of them has poured through! And though the unicorns have always been our enemies, we have never been involved in killing them, as these Hunters wish to do. You were uneasy about it, but you all joined me when I first spoke to the unicorn prince in the forest. You joined me because you knew something strange, something frightening was happening. Well, now it has gotten worse."

As if to punctuate his words, the ground beneath them shuddered and rolled.

The cove of delvers shuddered, too. This was *not* how the world was supposed to act.

"What do you propose to do, genius?" asked Zagrat, when the temblor had passed.

"I want to discover if the unicorn prince, Lightfoot, still lives. He is the only one who will listen to me." The rebel paused, took a breath, then said something that made his cousins gasp. "I want to see if, together, we can find a way to heal this wound."

"You *are* mad!" cried Zagrat, as if this were the final proof.

"How can you hope to find one unicorn in all of this annoyingly bright upper world?" asked Rendzi, somewhat more helpfully.

"We did it before!"

"Yes, but you had your teacher's help that time," said Gratz.

Every delver had a teacher, assigned to them in a secret ceremony at the end of their eighth year — a ceremony that marked their transition from delvling to full-fledged delver. The teacher remained secret, always, and there were terrible stories of what happened when a delver did reveal the name of his or her teacher. For the rebel cousin, this secret had been more joyful, and a greater burden, than for most delvers, because his teacher was someone of great power. Now he pondered for some time before replying, "I had not thought of that. You are correct, Gratz. Therefore, I must seek my teacher."

Zagrat rolled his eyes. "Your know very well your teacher will not talk to you. You have no name! You do not even exist as far as he is concerned."

"I have a nickname!"

"A *what?*" asked Zagrat, sounding truly puzzled.

"It is a name given by a friend, to be used in place of your true name. I am now called 'Rocky.'"

"You grow more demented by the moment!"

"Maybe so. On the other hand, while I have a nickname, you — having used my real name to call me back — have no name at all! So I think you need a nickname as well."

It was all the others could do to keep Zagrat from leaping onto their cousin and throttling him.

CHAPTER
XLI

SEPARATION ANXIETY

Rajiv watched in silence as Ian Hunter, who was cursing softly to himself, stared at the ground. The sahib had lost the trail, and Rajiv could see that he was struggling to hold in his frustration.

The boy longed to help, but knew the sahib did not like interference. Besides, it was clear he really was very good at this tracking business.

Rajiv looked to the memsahib. Her face was creased with worry. Next to her stood Lightfoot. Rajiv wished mightily that the unicorn had seen fit to pierce *his* chest, so he could also talk with the Prince mind-to-mind.

He settled to his haunches to wait. He had done a great deal of waiting during his years as a street boy in Delhi and was quite good at it by this time.

The problem for Sahib Hunter was simple. They had come to a swath of smooth rock that was a good ten yards wide and did not take a footprint. If the creatures they were trying to track had gone straight across, he should have been able to pick up their trail on the far side. But he had been unable to find any sign of them directly opposite the place they had stepped onto the rock. Rajiv knew, without being told, that this indicated they had turned to walk along the stone. Unfortunately, the broad ribbon of rock stretched both right and left for as far as the eye could see. The delvers could have followed it for a long way in either direction without leaving a sign before finally entering the forest again. Rajiv put his hand to the wonderful sword that the sahibs had given him back in the castle. He was looking forward to meeting one of these delvers.

The sahib came back to them. "This may take a while," he said.

The memsahib closed her eyes, but said nothing. Rajiv sensed she was trying not to interfere, but he also knew the sahib was constantly aware of the way she watched him. The boy wished he could give the woman some of his patience. It would help Sahib Hunter if she could be calmer.

Rajiv was very fond of Sahib Hunter. True, he, Rajiv, had nearly died as a result of their adventure in the Rainbow Prison. Still, he found this new life an interesting change from begging for a living.

He watched as the sahib paced the edge of the stone, going some fifty yards to the right, then crossing over and returning along the opposite side. He walked past them and went the same distance in the other direction, again coming back on the opposite side. When he stood in front of them once more he looked grim. "We have to split up," he said.

Rajiv could not help himself. "Sahib!" he cried in alarm.

The man raised his hands in a gesture for silence. "Just until we can find the trail again, Rajiv. Or until nightfall, if it comes to that." Pointing to his right, he said, "I am going to head that way. I want you three to go in the other direction. Walk as close to the edge of the stone as you can and scan the ground on both sides for the kind of footprint we've been following."

"Why are you going alone?" asked the memsahib. "Why don't we go two and two?"

"For two reasons. First, if your group finds something, I want Lightfoot to come at a gallop to get me. That will cost us the least time. If we were traveling in pairs, that would leave whoever had been with Lightfoot alone, which I would rather not do."

"If I went with the Prince, I could just ride him back," said Rajiv.

Despite their situation, the trace of a smile curved the sahib's lips. "I am sure that is something you have been dying to do, you scamp. But as I said, I have two reasons for wanting to work this way. The second is that tracking like this is what I'm trained for, what I've spent years studying and practicing. None of you have had that training, and it's possible any one of you might miss an important sign. With three of you working, there's a better chance of your spotting the trail if it does lie in that direction."

"And what if *you* find the trail?" asked the memsahib. "Will you come back for us?"

For a moment, no one spoke. Rajiv watched Sahib Hunter's lean face carefully. Finally the man said, "If I find something in the next hour or so I will come and get you. You'll be moving slowly, so I should be able to catch up to you with no problem." He paused, then said reluctantly, "If more time than that has passed, I think I should just keep moving."

Rajiv could hold his peace no longer. "Sahib! How will we then reconnect?"

"If you have not found something by tomorrow night come back to this spot and wait for me. If I am not back within a day after that you should return to the Axis Mundi and be ready to pass through it should this world become too unstable. I will try to meet you there."

"But, sahib —"

The memsahib interrupted him. "Ian is right, Rajiv. If we find the trail we will have to fetch him, as he is the only one who can speak with the delvers. But if he finds the trail, he *must* go on as quickly as possible. Getting Cara is the most important thing right now."

She paused, and Rajiv could tell she was communicating with the unicorn again. Oh, how he wished he could do the same!

"What was that about?" asked Sahib Hunter, when it was clear she had finished.

"Lightfoot said that he could speak a bit of delvish as well. I asked him if he could also go underground, and he replied that, given the tunnel entrances he had seen, that

262

was unlikely. So I told him we would still need you, even if we found the trail."

The memsahib put her hands on her husband's shoulders. Looking directly into his eyes, she said, "If we find something, we will send for you at once. If *you* find something, just keep going. *Find our daughter!*"

The sahib placed his hands over hers. "I don't like this, Martha, don't like it at all. But I do think it is the wisest course." He sighed and broke the contact. Looking at the others, he said, "We need to mark this spot firmly in our minds."

Rajiv spread his hands. "The trees all look the same, sahib. How can we tell this spot after we spend two days looking at more and more of them?"

"Look more carefully, Rajiv. Surely if you could travel the streets of Delhi without getting lost, you can find this spot again."

Rajiv thought about that for a second, then began to gaze around with intent focus. "Aha!" he exclaimed after a moment. "Look there — that tree is very crooked, not like the others at all. And right in front of it is a fallen tree that almost touches the stone path. And see? On the stone itself is a dark spot as big as my head. Yes, sahib, I understand. Those three things will mark the place for us."

He began to walk away.

"Rajiv! It's not time to start!"

"I know that, sahib. But I must see this from the other side, too. As you know, it will look different coming back."

The memsahib stared at him in surprise. Rajiv continued what he was doing, but listened carefully and was happy to hear Sahib Hunter say, "The boy is an excellent traveling companion, brave and true of heart." He walked a little farther than he had intended, so that he could pretend he had not heard. When he returned, he said simply, "Yes, I can find this again, sahib."

"I knew I could count on you."

Then the sahib and the memsahib went off to talk on their own for a bit. It was not long, though they did take a moment to kiss. Rajiv rolled his eyes and turned to the Prince. Feeling daring, he reached out to place his hand on the unicorn's neck, something he had been longing to do. The beautiful creature did not shy away, and even though they could not communicate — he *did* hope that would happen sometime soon — the boy felt a flow of peaceful energy. It was very nice.

Then the sahib came and took him aside. "I hope to see you soon, Rajiv. Very soon. I do not need to tell you to be wise and cautious — sometimes I think you are better at that than I am. But, please . . . take care of the memsahib for me."

The boy smiled, white teeth flashing in his dark face. "Do not worry, sahib. We went to great trouble to fetch her from that terrible red place. I do not want to lose track of her now!" Then he placed the palms of his hands together, bowed slightly, and said, "*Namaste,* Sahib Hunter."

The sahib returned the blessing. A moment later he was

gone. A moment after that, Rajiv, Lightfoot, and the mem-sahib were moving in the opposite direction.

Rajiv glanced back once or twice, hoping that it would be only a matter of moments before the sahib stood and hailed them, shouting that he had found the trail once more.

Or, even better, he might find it himself.

With that happy thought, he turned all his attention to the task at hand, eager to bring the time of separation from his friend the sahib to a quick and happy conclusion.

CHAPTER
XLII

THE THIRD DREAM

Namza's third dream was the strangest one so far, for it was of the strangest thing that ever happened to him.

As the dream began he had left Thomas and was returning to Delvharken after his *nakken-gar*. He was eager to return home, yet nervous about how he would present himself to his teacher.

At least I have the stones, he thought, patting the pouch that rattled at his side.

He entered the world below through a secret tunnel, known only to the court wizard and his apprentice. Trotting along the stone passageways, moving easily through the transit points, he felt happy to be back, yet aware — in a way he never had been before — of how troubled his home really was. Why was everyone in Delvharken always so suspicious, so quick to anger?

He passed into Metzram's cave, where he found the old wizard sitting on the floor, legs crossed, hands on his knees. Namza entered as silently as a lizard crawls along a wall.

Metzram did not open his eyes. Even so, he said, softly, "Welcome back, my student. Sit, please."

Namza did as he was asked. For a long time there was nothing but silence in the cave. Yet Namza could tell — and it was terrifying to him — that though his eyes remained closed, Metzram was studying him. Finally the old wizard said, "I am well pleased."

"Because I have returned with the dragon stones?"

His teacher chuckled. "No, though I am glad to have them. I am pleased because I can tell that you have learned what I really sent you into the world to discover."

"What was that?"

"That there is another way for us to be."

Awash with relief, Namza said, "Then you are not angry that I have grown . . . softer?"

To be "soft" was considered almost a crime among delvers.

"We would all do well to be softer," answered Metzram, a reply that shocked his student to the core.

And then he told a story, which Namza, in his stony dream, experienced as if it were happening to him, as if it were a dream within a dream. . . .

Metzram, in his youth, had been sent into the upper world to do his own *nakken-gar*. One day, as he was walking in the twilight forest, which was dark enough to be comfortable, he came upon a woman dressed in white robes, with long golden hair flowing down her back. This was all he could see of her, for she sat on a stone at the edge of a stream, gazing into the water and sighing heavily.

Because he was curious, and because the *nakken-gar* is meant for learning, Metzram approached. He certainly did not expect to feel compassion for the woman or to comfort her in any way. But when she turned toward him, he gasped, astonished at the beauty of her lustrous brown skin and enormous eyes. The beauty was an alien thing to him and something he might normally have found repulsive. Yet it was undeniable in its power.

"Greetings, delver," she said in a voice like the sweet sound of water flowing over stones.

Without realizing what he was doing, he fell to his knees. Without realizing that he was speaking, he said, "Lady, you are sad. What troubles you?"

She smiled a wan smile. "I came to this world to look in on a friend who is lost to me."

"Lady, what is his name?"

"I called him Elihu."

"Lady, I would help if I could, but I know of no Elihu."

"No, nor should you."

"Lady, what are you?"

"That I do not wish to say. But I can tell that you are sore troubled. If you come to me, I can ease your heart, for I know of a bad thing that was done to you and your people."

Entranced, Metzram approached her. She placed her

268

hands upon his head and said softly, "Delver, you can choose to be different. You can choose to let go of the darkness inside. It is not easy. It is never easy. But you are not doomed to carry this forever."

Metzram felt an odd stirring in his heart, uncomfortable and frightening, yet also sweet and exciting.

"I would assign you a task," said the lady.

"I have a task already," replied Metzram, not thinking to wonder why she could speak to him. "I am on my *nakken-gar* and must return to my teacher with a prize."

"If you have a year, you have time for this, too," she said softly. "In a cavern not far from here there is a great library. It is called the Unicorn Chronicles —"

"We hate the unicorns!" spat Metzram, and was at once ashamed because it felt bad to say such a thing in front of this lady, who was like . . . who was like . . .

Words failed him, and he began to weep, which he had never, until now, done from the heart, only when he was in pain, usually from being beaten.

"I know you hate them. But you do not have to, and your spirit will be easier when you stop. Now, here is what I ask of you. Seek out this cavern, which is occupied by a dwarf called the Chronicle Keeper. Watch carefully, enter secretly. Find your way to the great library. In one of the oldest of the books you will find a story, the story of the Whisperer." She paused, and the look of pain that creased her face nearly made him weep. "I want you to remove those pages."

"Shall I destroy them, lady?"

She shuddered. "No! I am not a destroyer, nor should you be. To destroy knowledge is a great sin. But for the sake of my friend, who I have loved, I would hide this story away for now."

"You are powerful and beautiful, lady. Why not do this yourself?"

She smiled, another sad smile. "It is bad enough that I ask it of you. I am stretching ancient law even to do that, for I should not interfere." With a sigh she added, "But love makes fools of us all, even those of us among the Great Powers."

"Lady, you could never be a fool!"

Her laugh was also like water over stones, but now the light, tinkling sound of water flowing rapidly. "You would be amazed at how foolishness pervades the world, young Metzram."

"I did not tell you my name!"

"Nonetheless, I knew it, and I have been waiting for you. Now listen. It is indeed possible I could do this, though I might pay a very dear price. I may pay, anyway. But I have another hope, and that is that if you do this for me, you will discover something about yourself, as you are beginning to already. That may help ameliorate my crime in asking you."

She paused for a long time, then said, "Change is often hard, young delver, hard and slow. To change the great wrong done to you and your kind will take many, many years."

"What was this great wrong?"

"It is in the pages I have asked you to recover."

"How will I know them? I cannot read dwarvish writing."

"You may be surprised."

All through this conversation she had kept her hands on the sides of his head. Now she leaned closer, looked directly into his eyes, and whispered, "Go. Go and do this, Metzram." She kissed him on the forehead. "And when you have the pages, take them to the Valley of the Centaurs and say that Allura asks the Chiron to keep them in safety. Will you do this for me?"

Unable to resist the plea in her eyes, he nodded and said, "I will."

As the dream ended, and the images of his teacher's strange experience faded, Namza would have shifted uneasily in his sleep. But, of course, he was held tight by the Stone, and could not move at all.

CHAPTER
XLIII

THE FIRE IN THE BLOOD

"Stop struggling!" whispered Elihu. "I got you away from there just in time."

From the distance, Cara heard a cry of rage, followed by a deep-throated roar and the screams of men in pain.

"It sounds as if your dragon friend didn't appreciate having those men try to take you," said Elihu, not slowing his pace. He tightened his grip, pulling her closer to his broad chest. His body was warm in the moist, chilly air. "Now, no more talk. There were a lot of them, more than even your dragon friend could keep from following us, though she'll doubtless do some serious damage while she's trying. Nonetheless, it's a certainty that some are still after us even now."

As if to prove his words, moments later Cara heard someone crashing through the bushes behind them.

Elihu picked up his pace. Despite his bare feet, he ran swiftly and silently through the misty gloom, dodging between trees, leaping roots and stones, never slowing until the sound of pursuit finally faded. Only when he stopped to let Cara slide to the ground did he begin to pant for breath.

"Thank you," she whispered. "But what about —"

He pressed a finger to her lips for silence.

She nodded.

Elihu took her hand. Wrapped in his enormous grip, it suddenly felt tiny to her. Moving in perfect silence, he led her farther up the mountainside. Cara herself did not attain complete silence, though she managed without making too much noise, mostly because he carefully guided her around brush and rocks. At last they came to a cave. Cara followed Elihu inside.

The darkness was even greater here. "Wait," she pleaded. Fishing Medafil's sphere from her pocket, she twisted it between her hands.

At the first glow of light, Elihu whispered urgently, "Turn that off! Do you want to bring them right to us?"

"But I can't see!"

"I'll carry you if need be, but turn it off!"

She did as he asked, and he picked her up once more. However, this time it was only a few minutes before he set her down again, saying softly, "All right, we've turned a few corners. It should be safe now."

Cara twisted the sphere until it filled her hands, then cupped her fingers around it. Its glow, tinted rose by her flesh and blood, was just enough to see by. "Thank you," she whispered. "I feel better this way."

"Good."

"Who are you?" she asked again.

The big man shook his head, causing his golden hair to slide across his broad, brown shoulders. "I didn't search you out to talk about me. And we don't have a lot of time. Now listen carefully. The men who are hunting you won't stop for anything. Hunting is what they do, they're obsessed by it, and you are their quarry. But there is a way for you to escape them. It's not without danger of its own, but it should baffle them for now."

"What is it?" asked Cara, half afraid to hear the answer.

Elihu held out his hand. "May I hold the amulet?"

Cara shook her head.

Elihu sighed. "In case you've forgotten, I did just save you from those Hunters."

"Yes, but I don't know why. Maybe it was so you could steal the amulet yourself."

She felt ungrateful saying it and was painfully aware that the man could simply take the amulet from her if he wanted. But she couldn't bring herself to hand it over to him. And she clung to a memory of something she had heard from both Beloved and the delvers: If they were forced to *take* the amulet, rather than having Cara give it to them freely, it would somehow damage its magic. She hoped Elihu knew this, too, then wondered if perhaps the rules were different for him, assuming he really had made the amulets.

The tall man stared at her for a few moments. Finally he said, "The crafting of those five amulets took great power, and much of that power remains locked within them. You

274

already know the amulet can move you from one world to another. I suspect you are not aware that it can also unleash that which is hidden within you."

"What is hidden within me?" asked Cara.

She suspected the answer even as she asked the question and found that simply suspecting it filled her with both fear and longing.

"*That*, I am quite sure, you do already know."

Closing her eyes, she whispered, "I'm part unicorn."

"Follow the thought," said Elihu gently.

Cara opened her eyes, her heart pounding with both joy and fear. "Are you telling me I can *become* a unicorn?"

A flicker of pain twisted Elihu's beautiful features. It vanished as quickly as it had appeared, so fleeting she wasn't certain she had actually seen it. He took a deep breath, then replied solemnly, "Yes, that's what I am saying."

"Will I be able to turn back?"

His face hardened. "That I cannot guarantee. Such transformations are . . . difficult. They require a great deal of energy."

Though her mind thrilled at the thought of becoming a unicorn, Cara also felt a shudder of fear. It was only her body that would change. She would still be herself inside, right? She would still be Cara.

Or would she? Her mind turned to her grandmother, so different now that she was Amalia Flickerfoot. Had becoming a unicorn done that to her? Or had she simply returned to a truer self that had been lost during her years as a human?

She remembered, too, Graumag's tale of how endragonment had changed her not only in form, but in spirit.

How would being a unicorn make me *different?* she wondered. Remembering the rest of Graumag's story, she also thought, *And how much will the transformation hurt?*

But her mind was also bubbling with eager ideas of what such a metamorphosis would mean. How often had she tried to imagine the joy of running with Lightfoot's grace and freedom, of leaping nimbly over the hillsides, of feeling her silvery mane flow in the wind? Had those thoughts been mere pleasant fantasies? Or had they come from something inside her, something that was crying out to be set free?

Cara stretched her arms in front of her and frowned. What would it be to live without hands? She recalled Finder saying that having hands was the one thing he envied about humans. The pang of loss she felt at remembering the big, gentle unicorn brought to mind the other great loss of her life. What about her parents? If . . . *When!* she corrected herself fiercely . . . *when* she found them again, what would they think of her if she had become a unicorn?

Would they still love her?

The question was frightening. Yet Elihu's offer had woken a desperate yearning inside her. She resisted, forcing her mind to a more practical question: "I don't understand. What good will it do me to become a unicorn? The Hunters are after them, too."

"True enough. But this group, which is large and fierce, is clearly after *you*."

"How do you know that?"

"I have been following them since shortly after they entered Luster and have listened in on their conversations."

"Why were you following them?"

"I didn't intend to, at first. I was actually looking for you."

"Why?" asked Cara, startled.

"Well, not you, specifically. When I sensed the amulet you carry, I grew curious and wanted to see where it was. Following my sense of the amulet brought me to the Hunters, which eventually led me to you." He paused, looked back toward the mouth of the cave. "I'm sorry, Cara —"

"How do you know my name?"

"I heard it from the Hunters, of course."

"Of course," she murmured, wondering whether to believe him.

"What I was going to say was that if Beloved has diverted a group of her men from the Hunt strictly to seek you out, she must want you very badly. Whatever the reason for that, it cannot be good."

"How do you know all this?"

"I have been aware of Beloved and her Hunters for a very long time. Now listen. Here is the reason I suggest this. The men following you cannot outrun a unicorn. No man can. They can lure unicorns — lure and entrap them — but they *cannot* outrun them. So if you are smart enough to avoid being taken by surprise, and strong enough to ignore their enticements, you should be safe. Do not mistake me. This is not without risk. It is simply . . . a chance to keep you from the clutches of Beloved."

"I need to think about it."

"I understand. But every moment you spend thinking brings them closer."

"What about you?"

"They are not after me. However, I will try to create a diversion to give you more time to flee." He spread his hands. "I don't want to pressure you, Cara. But your pursuers will be here soon and we need to get you out of this cave, or you will be trapped. If you go as a girl, you may escape for now, but they will continue to trail you. To outrun them in your present form is impossible, and there are too many for me to fight. But if you go as a unicorn . . . well, the whole game changes, doesn't it?"

She considered the alternatives. Both were frightening, but when she recalled her last terrifying confrontation with Beloved, one fear quickly became overwhelming. She needed only to imagine herself caught and taken before her horrible ancestress once more and the choice was made. In a voice barely above a whisper, she said, "Transform me."

"You're certain?"

Cara only nodded.

"I need you to say it."

She swallowed, but the words rose freely, almost unbidden. "I want to become a unicorn."

Elihu closed his eyes. "This is the last time I will see you in this form," he whispered. "Now, take my hand."

She did as he asked.

Clasping her hand firmly in his, he raised his other hand and smashed the amulet against the cave wall.

CHAPTER
XLIV

NICKNAMES

"Our cousin is right, you know," said Gratz. "In bringing him back we have given up our names. We must find a new way to speak to one another."

"I say we use our old names, anyway!" cried Razka.

The others looked to Rocky, as they had so often when they were young. It was Rocky — Nedzik then, of course — who always had the best ideas for games and pranks, the best ways to annoy the adults, the best suggestions for satisfying mischief.

Rocky looked at them for a moment, then said, "My name is gone, taken by the King. Yet in my heart I know that I am still myself and he had no right to do this. So I say, if the King thinks your names give him power over you, then take new ones to spite the tyrant!"

"But you said the name must be *given* to you," protested Razka.

"Then I give you the name Diamond," replied Rocky

instantly. "For you are hard and sharp, and you have secret fire in your depths."

"Diamond," murmured his cousin. "*Diamond*. I like that!"

"What shall I be?" cried Erkza, the elder of the twins.

Rocky smiled. "That is easy. You were born first, so that should be your nickname. Greetings, First."

"If he's First then I want to be Smartest!" cried Rendzi, his younger-by-ten-minutes brother.

"No, no. Rocky has to choose your name for you," repeated Razka, now known as Diamond. "The nickname must be *given* to you."

"Well, I don't want to be called Second! Or Last, either."

"You shall be called Hammer," said Rocky, after a moment's consideration. "For you are strong and useful."

"Hammer," said Rendzi contentedly. "Good. I like that!"

"And me?" asked Zagrat.

"I know!" cried Gergga. "You should be Lizard!" When the others looked at him in puzzlement, he said, "Because of his tongue!"

Zagrat stuck out his tongue, which was famous for being the longest in all of Delvharken, and the others laughed. "All right," he said, grinning. "I accept this . . . this . . . what is the word, Rocky?"

"Nickname."

"I accept this nickname."

"Now me!" cried Gergga.

"Waterfall," said Rocky at once. "Because of the way you always won our pissing contests."

"Waterfall!" said Gergga proudly. "Yes, I like that."

That left only Gratz, who was soon named Pebble, because his smooth skin made him seem so young, and Wurtza, who was dubbed Wart, because of an unfortunate problem he had had as a delvling.

"Now we are outlaws together," said Rocky when all the names had been properly bestowed.

A sudden somberness came over the group. Sensing their concerns, Rocky said, "To be an outlaw in the realm of a tyrant is an honorable thing! We are a free band of cousins, and that is an honorable thing as well!"

"Honorable," murmured the others, though it was clear they were not quite convinced.

"Now that we are honorable exiles, what is it that we must do?" asked Waterfall.

"I told you, I want to seek my teacher."

"And I told you he won't speak to you, nickname or not," said the delver now called Lizard.

"But he will!"

"What makes you so certain?"

"Because he, too, knows that the King is mad."

Lizard narrowed his eyes. "Just who *is* your teacher?"

"You know I cannot tell you that!" cried Rocky, appalled at the question.

Lizard hooted derisively. "You call the King a tyrant. You scorn his punishment. You summon your cousins to rebellion and give each of us a new name and say it is an honor to be an outlaw. And yet *you* will not name your teacher? Are you a rebel . . . or just a big-talking coward with worms where your guts should be?"

The others gasped. A long, uncomfortable silence filled the cave. Finally Rocky nodded and said, "You are right, Lizard. The world is changing, and we must be free to change, too. It was my teacher's wisdom that set me on this path. He will understand if I do this."

"All right then, I ask it again: Who is your teacher?"

Rocky took a deep breath, then said softly, "Namza."

"The king's wizard?" whispered Diamond in awe.

"There is only one Namza," said Rocky.

"Not even one," said Lizard, his anger shifting to gloom. "Namza has disappeared."

Rocky looked from face to face, hoping to see a sign that this was a joke, an attempt to tease him. But in his cousins' eyes he saw only sad confirmation that it was true.

"Oh, my teacher," he wailed. *"My teacher!"*

Falling to his knees, he buried his face in his hands and began to weep.

CHAPTER
XLV

FENG YUAN AND THE QUEEN

Late in the afternoon of their second day together, Belle the warrior and Feng Yuan the Hunters' girl arrived at Autumngrove.

"Belle!" cried the sentry who met her at the forest's edge. "The Queen will be glad to see you. You have been much on her mind. But who is that you carry on your back?"

Belle hesitated, thinking of why she had brought Feng Yuan with her. Finally she replied, "She is a gift to the Queen."

When they were taken to Amalia Flickerfoot, Belle explained how she had met Feng Yuan and outlined the unusual knowledge that she possessed. The Queen gazed at the slender, dark-haired girl for a long time before saying, "So, you came here with Beloved to lure unicorns to their deaths."

Feng Yuan, who had her hand on Belle's shoulder so she could understand the Queen, nodded.

"Yet now you want me to believe that you are ready to work with us for Beloved's defeat?"

Again the girl nodded.

"Why should I trust you on this? It seems to me there is little that would please Beloved more than to have someone like you in our midst."

Now it was not Feng Yuan who answered, but Belle who said, "The girl and I are in close contact. I have detected no deceit within her."

"Yet one of our kind is dead because of her."

"That is why I turned against them!" thought Feng Yuan passionately. "It was not until I saw the unicorn — and saw what the Hunters did to him — that I began to understand all this. It was not until I offered to let Belle slay me, but she instead forged a connection so we could speak mind-to-mind, that I knew I had been lied to all these years. Yes, I was raised to the Hunt. That does not mean I must remain its prisoner!"

Slightly embarrassed, Belle translated this for the Queen, who continued to gaze quizzically at the girl. Finally Amalia said, "Belle, would you mind if I established my own connection with her?"

Belle hesitated, feeling, to her own surprise, a flash of jealousy, of possessiveness. However, she was well aware that "She is *my* girl!" would have been a foolish answer. So she simply nodded and said, "As you wish, My Queen — assuming it is all right with Feng Yuan."

When the girl had agreed and the Queen had pierced

her chest to make it possible for them to talk directly, Amalia thought to her, "What is it you believe you can offer us?"

"Information, first. While I do not know everything about Beloved and her plans, what I do know I can share."

"Belle seemed to think there is more you can do."

Feng Yuan nodded modestly. "I understand war craft."

Setting aside, for the moment, her own previous thoughts on the matter, Amalia responded, "This is not war, it is a Hunt."

"That is what Beloved wants it to be. But why must you play by her rules? Are you born to be victims?"

Amalia's eyes widened, and Feng Yuan thought quickly, "Excuse me! That was rude, and I apologize."

"No, it was a question well asked. And, in truth, exactly what I have been contemplating. The answer, by the way, is 'No, we were *not* born to be victims.' But we have surrendered some of our fire, and we need to find a way to regain it. Worse, we are not schooled in the ways of war. These are not things we know, not skills we possess."

"Happily, that is exactly what I can offer," replied Feng Yuan. "Well, I cannot tell you how to regain lost fire. But I can assist with the preparation and the strategy for what is to come, for these things are what I have long studied."

"Why have you studied them?" asked the Queen. "Who was your teacher?"

With this invitation, Feng Yuan explained how Wu Chen had taught her from *The Art of War* and how much of it was engraved on her memory. She told the Queen, too, how they had run simulations, where Wu Chen had asked her to apply what he had taught her to understanding great battles of the past and then, as her understanding grew, to new scenarios he created especially to test her.

"Have you ever tried this in real life?" asked the Queen.

"No," answered Feng Yuan. "Have you?"

The Queen laughed. Turning to Belle, she said, "She'll do."

Amalia's first act after accepting Feng Yuan's help was to gather the council so that the girl could share with all of them what she knew. This was accomplished by Feng Yuan standing beside Belle, with one hand on her shoulder, and thinking what she wanted to say, which Belle would then translate for her.

"Beloved has come here with nearly five hundred men, all of them highly trained in ways to hunt and kill unicorns. I say 'nearly' five hundred because one Hunter has gone renegade and is now siding with the unicorns."

Feng Yuan paused while Belle repeated this for the others, who were listening with rapt attention. She heard a sharp intake of breath from the Queen at the number five hundred, but when she turned toward Amalia, the Queen had composed her features and showed no sign of her shock.

"There are also two dozen Maidens of the Hunt, girls such as myself, who were brought along to help the Hunters. Our job is to lure a unicorn to our side so that a Hunter can slaughter it." She closed her eyes, took a deep breath, then continued. "A maiden usually travels with a small group of Hunters. The first thing Beloved did when we came through was to send all these groups out, hoping for an early kill." She hesitated again, swallowed, then said, "To my shame, I was part of one of them. As a result, a unicorn died."

She trembled with grief and shame as she confessed this, but she managed not to weep.

"For that death, I am deeply sorry. But seeing it happen was what opened my eyes and made me flee the Hunt. Now I want to try to atone for my crime."

"How do you intend to do that?" asked Moonheart.

Receiving the question through Belle, Feng Yuan replied, "First, by telling you what I know. Beloved's entry to Luster passes through the center of a vast tree, which is greater than any I have ever seen, or could even imagine."

"The Axis Mundi!" cried the Queen. "I was certain these tremors were caused by what Beloved has done. But it never occurred to me that she had attacked the world tree itself."

"I guessed that you must know of this tree," said Feng Yuan through Belle. "You will find Beloved encamped in a meadow less than a mile southwest of that place. She expects you to be fleeing, disorganized, scattered. This is all right, for Sun Tzu tells us if we feign disorder we can crush the enemy."

"Deception is not our way," said Cloudmane gently.

"All warfare is based on deception!" cried Feng Yuan,

quoting Sun Tzu directly. "These people are trying to destroy you! Do you not understand that?"

In her vexation, she had forgotten to think the words to Belle while she spoke, and had to repeat what she had said mind-to-mind. She caught her breath and tried to calm herself while Belle translated.

When Feng Yuan had herself under control, she thought to Belle, "Beloved believes you are fierce and dangerous, but foolish and disorganized."

"Which, alas, is true," replied Belle privately, before speaking the words out loud.

"To have her think this is not all bad," continued Feng Yuan. "Let them continue to believe it. Encourage them in their error. Then you can trample them beneath your hooves."

"They won't like that trampling part," thought Belle, before translating.

"They won't like the dying part, either!" replied Feng Yuan fiercely.

"What do you advise?" asked Amalia, sensing that Belle and Feng Yuan were having a private conversation.

Feng Yuan thought to Belle, "Tell the Queen that Beloved will not expect you to march on her and attack her where she waits, and by this surprise you may gain victory."

Belle translated. A long, uncomfortable silence fell over the clearing. Feng Yuan could feel Belle shifting impatiently and sensed that her friend wanted to speak out, but must wait for the Queen.

As for Amalia, she was gazing at her council, trying to judge them. She did not know them well enough, had not been Queen long enough, to feel she could truly read their faces, their hearts. At least three of them were trembling. But each of those three also, when she looked straight at them, nodded his or her assent.

"Of course we can do it," said Amalia — hoping, even as she did, that Feng Yuan really was true of heart and not simply leading them into a trap.

CHAPTER
XLVI

UNICORN

The blaze of silver light that exploded from the amulet when Elihu shattered it so dazzled Cara that she could not see. But she could *feel* — feel the light swirl around her before it flowed into her, feel it fill her veins, feel it invade her heart. Her body began to twist and stretch. She wanted to scream with the pain, but something deep in her brain remembered there were Hunters nearby and that to make any sound at all would be dangerous.

Nor was what she felt *all* pain. She had a sense, too, of joyous release, as if something long imprisoned within her was being set free.

"Elihu!" she whispered urgently, still unable to see. *"Elihu!"*

He did not answer. Instead she heard something that sounded like a moan of despair. Before she could call to him again she felt her fingers cleave together and was lost once more in the astonishment of her transformation. Her nails grew broad and thick, merged, began to flow up and back across her fingers. As they did, they became the silvery material of unicorn hoof.

She heard the rending of fabric as her clothing split and tore away from her. At the same time, a vigor and power she had never known flowered within her.

Now a sudden flare of pain, more intense than any she had ever experienced, did cause her to make a sound — not a cry, for what came from her throat was neither the voice of a human nor, yet, that of a unicorn.

The pain increased. Fire blossomed in her brow and her head felt as if it were about to split wide open. She would have grabbed at it and tried to tear it open herself, but she no longer had arms or hands, only long, slender forelegs that ended in cloven hooves.

Just as the pain passed the limit of what Cara thought she could endure, the source of it burst free as a pearly horn erupted from her forehead — the unmistakable mark and seal that the transformation was complete and she was now a unicorn.

Yet, still the light flowered around her, so thick and bright she felt as if she were breathing it.

"Elihu!" she tried to call again. But rather than human words, she uttered a cry that rang like silver as it echoed from the stone walls. She stopped, concentrated, and managed to speak his name. The word felt strange in her mouth and twisted her throat oddly. Her voice was deeper and so changed that she hardly recognized it as her own. That was oddly frightening in itself. Even so, she was relieved to find that the gift of tongues remained intact. It made no difference; there was still no answer from Elihu.

Her vision began to clear.

She looked around frantically.

Elihu was nowhere in sight — and she realized she had just made a possibly deadly mistake. Had the Hunters heard her?

Cara shook her head and was at once distracted by the feel of her newly sprouted mane flowing over her shoulders. She twisted her neck to survey the length of her body, then whisked her moon-white tail, just to make sure she could.

Part of her was quivering with delight.

Another part — a small, terrified voice deep inside — was wailing, *What have I done?*

And a third part, wiser and more alert, was urgently warning that whatever she had done, she was not safe yet, because Hunters still roamed the slopes of Dark Mountain, and even if they had been seeking a red-haired girl, they would gladly slay a unicorn if they happened across one.

Where is Elihu?

She started toward the mouth of the cave and quickly discovered that walking with four legs was considerably more complicated than moving with only two. After a few stumbles — something she would have thought she could avoid now that she was a unicorn — she began to get a feel for it. Part of the trick, she realized, was to *not* think about it too much and just let her body do the work.

Cautiously, wobbly as a newborn colt, Cara made her way to the cave's entrance. As she neared it, she heard a shout and a roar down the mountainside and realized Elihu must have gone to distract the Hunters.

Cara's first urge was to race to his assistance. But that would bring her in direct contact with the Hunters — exactly what Elihu had been trying to avoid when he went to face them.

Moving more cautiously, she stepped forward to peer out.

Immediately she realized something that hadn't been obvious to her while still in the cave: As a unicorn, her vision was more clear and far sharper than when she had been human.

It was also disturbingly different. Though it took her a moment to figure out why, she soon understood there were two major changes in how she was seeing, one exciting, one unnerving.

The first, the exciting thing, was that she could see much farther to each side than she ever had in her human form. Balanced against this, and very distressing, was the fact that there was a spot directly in front of her where her vision failed completely. Turning her head, she realized the changes were due to the way her eyes were now placed — not centered in her face, as when she had been a human, but at the sides of her head, just as with any unicorn.

Though the blind spot was annoying, she quickly decided that her expanded field of vision — she could see so far to each side it was as if she had been given extra eyes — made the trade worth it.

She took a moment to look, and listen — which was when she realized her hearing had improved as well.

Rising from the mountainside came the sounds of pitched battle — almost certainly Elihu fighting with the Hunters. She longed to go help him, but fiercely reminded herself that the whole reason he was fighting them was to give her a chance to escape.

What of Graumag? She had also been battling Hunters. How had that fight gone? Surely not well for the Hunters. But it was all too possible that the dragon could have been wounded, perhaps even killed, by their spears and arrows. Then another thought struck her.

Even if Graumag did escape, she would have no way of finding me now — or recognizing me if she did find me!

Making a quick, regretful decision, Cara headed *away* from the fighting. Glancing down at her legs again, she thought, *I'm so white! I'll be incredibly easy to spot.*

She decided it would be best to keep a screen of bushes between herself and the sounds of the fight. She tried to move faster than a walk, stumbled twice, and realized she wasn't anywhere near ready to run.

I'd better learn fast if I'm going to escape the Hunters! she thought nervously.

She continued to pick her way down Dark Mountain, making a long arc around the sound of fighting, until it finally faded behind her. When the cries of the men had vanished altogether, Cara tried to figure out her next move.

It was simple, actually. She had to make her way back to

her grandmother and the unicorn court at Autumngrove. But which way was Autumngrove? With all that had happened, she had completely lost her sense of place and direction.

Of course, that assumed the unicorns were still at Autumngrove. Which brought on another thought: *Do the Hunters know where they are? If so, how quickly will they be there?*

As she fretted about this, Cara discovered a new sense — not an improvement on an old sense, as with her vision and hearing, but one that she had not even guessed at: She *knew* where the unicorns were! Not every one of them; it was nowhere near that specific. But she could sense the mass of them, with her grandmother, Amalia Flickerfoot, at the center. It was almost as if her heart were a compass and the great glory of unicorns true north.

Pointing herself in the direction her heart had given her, Cara began to move a little more rapidly.

High above, the clouds of Dark Mountain still loured and loomed. Lightning flashed and crackled, revealing a world that seemed at once horrifying and unbelievably beautiful.

Though her new body was graceful, Cara was still awkward within it, uncertain of how to use it, of how much space it took up. She had to learn her shape all over again — learn which branches she could duck under, which trees slip between. Yet her nimbling feet seemed already to have become almost immune to tripping, and while she more than once banged herself against a low-growing bough with a very un-unicorn-like clumsiness, she was soon trotting down the rocky slope with no fear at all of stumbling or sliding.

The strange reality of her transformation was still sinking in.

I'm a unicorn, she thought, over and over again. *A unicorn!*

It was a joyous feeling. Even so, troubling questions continued to run through her mind: *Will I ever be able to turn back? Do I even want to?* And, most compelling of all, *What will my mother and father think?*

That last question made her particularly uneasy. But she also took a bit of assurance from it, since it seemed to assume that she would indeed see them again.

Then she found herself asking a question that truly startled her, because it mattered more than she would have guessed: *What will Lightfoot think?*

This time she did not feel the comfort that had come from asking the same question about her parents, but she was not sure whether that was because the question had some deeper meaning or because she was afraid her dear friend was lost to her forever. The horrid memory of that cove of delvers swarming over Lightfoot as he battled to protect her shot like acid through her brain. She shook her head, trying to force the images to the farthest recesses of her mind.

Delvers, she thought unhappily. *One more thing I'll have to look out for.*

But she also found herself thinking of Rocky, who — though a delver — had become such a good friend. She wondered where he was now and if he would dare return to the Delverking's court to tell what he had learned about the Whisperer.

A little while later, Cara realized that though she was sure she was heading toward her grandmother and the unicorns, there were many things she did *not* know. What lay *between* her and her destination? Traveling in a straight line would be well enough, but what if she came to some river or gorge or mountain range she could not cross? How would she know the best path then? She could waste days — weeks! — trying to get around something like that.

How long would the journey take? Which raised a more important question: How much time did the unicorns have?

No more than a moment after that frightening query crossed her mind, she felt a sudden stabbing in her heart and was overcome with a sorrow so intense that it made her stagger. For a moment she was confused. Where had this feeling come from? What did it mean?

All too quickly she realized the answer.

Somewhere a unicorn had just died.

Half-blinded by tears she had not known she could shed — did other unicorns weep, or was this an artifact of her human side? — Cara continued down the mountainside.

CHAPTER
XLVII

THE MISSING TEACHER

It took the newly nicknamed delvers a long time to calm their weeping cousin. This was not surprising. The relationship between a delver and his teacher is intense, almost sacred, and the news of Namza's disappearance was naturally disturbing, though even Rocky's cousins did not understand how deeply.

When Rocky had been chosen by the old stone wizard, he knew it had been a great honor. As the years rolled on, as he grew to treasure Namza's strength, power, and wisdom, his appreciation had turned to awe and then to love. With a few sad exceptions, all delvers love their teachers, but Rocky's feeling for Namza came close to worship.

However, it was not only this that had devastated Rocky when he learned Namza was missing. In all that had happened, all through his imprisonment in the dungeon of Delvharken, through his journey to the Valley of the Centaurs, through learning the appalling story of the birth of the Whisperer and how that dark force had shaped the delvers, Rocky had always believed he would eventually reconnect with Namza, and that his teacher would somehow make sense of it for him.

Now the world made no sense at all.

"I have to find him," he said at last.

"And how do you expect to do that?" asked Lizard scornfully. "Gnurflax has had a dozen coves scouring Delvharken for Namza."

"And the world above as well," put in Waterfall.

"Without a pebble of luck," added First.

"So why should you fare any better?" finished Wart.

"I'll have to go back to Delvharken," said Rocky stubbornly.

"You really *are* insane!" yelped Hammer.

Rocky flicked his left hand three times, a delver sign of rejecting a sentence. "As student and teacher, Namza and I are bound. You know very well that I am able to sense him in a way no one else can. Something has happened to him. He is missing, but that does not mean he is dead. I must try to find him."

"But how do you expect to get into Delvharken without being arrested?" asked Pebble nervously.

"I don't know yet. I'll work that out when we get there. I had other plans for us, but this is what we must do now. We need Namza's wisdom — not to mention his power."

"But he is a servant of the King," said Diamond. "What good will it do to find him? Will he not betray us?"

"It was Namza who first brought me to awareness of the King's madness," replied Rocky. "Why do you think I became a rebel? I did not work these things out on my own. It was my teacher who helped me see the world more clearly and gave me the strength to say no to the tyrant."

"But he continued to serve that same tyrant!" protested First.

"Only so he could try to rein him in," said Rocky. "I tell you truly, the tyranny would have been even worse without Namza pulling Gnurflax back from the greatest of his excesses." He paused, then said, "Sit, my cousins. I will tell you more."

The cove gathered around him, hideous faces looking up. "I am convinced that for some time now, the King has been in thrall to this voice that I told you of. It is a formless presence that speaks to him out of the darkness."

The cove murmured nervously. Finally Lizard said, grudgingly, "That would explain his passage from wise ruler — well, somewhat wise — to the tyrant he has become."

"Exactly," said Rocky. "For a long time my teacher could not understand what was happening to Gnurflax and despaired of changing his course. When we met for learning sessions, Namza would speak to me of this, bemoaning that he no longer had the power to soften the King's impulses.

"Finally he informed me of the rumors he had heard from the delver-guard, rumors of a voice speaking to the King from the darkness. He was reluctant to tell me much about it, but I am convinced that the story I learned from the Chiron, the story of the Whisperer tells us all we need to know. *That* is who is advising the King!"

Pebble moaned in despair.

"I know that Namza was spying on Gnurflax," continued Rocky, "trying to learn more about this voice. And I know this had to be dangerous. Perhaps the Whisperer, who I am sure has powers we do not understand, caught him at it! Whatever happened, I tell you this: We *need* Namza."

Lizard sighed. "So it's back to Delvharken?"

"Yes," said Rocky. "It is back to Delvharken. Once there, we will decide what to do."

"Well, that's about the most brilliant plan I ever heard," muttered Waterfall.

Rocky ignored him.

CHAPTER
XLVIII

THE TAINTED CROWN

A hush had fallen over the assembled centaurs, who stood on a hillside overlooking the arena where the combat for the Chironate had been going on all day. Now the shadows were lengthening, the day and the combat both drawing to a close.

In the center of the arena the remaining combatants, Arkon and Basilikos, stood about ten feet apart, facing each other warily. These two alone had survived the earlier trials and tests, which started simply with races and leaping contests, but had grown ever more dangerous as the day went on.

The final stage was simple but potentially deadly: hand-to-hand combat with sword and shield.

Arkon nodded to his opponent. They had been friends since shortly after the time they were foaled. Basilikos nodded back. His broad chest was heaving, but Arkon was sure he was far from exhausted. They were, in fact, almost evenly matched, something they both knew from years of friendly sparring with much less at stake. Indeed, in all those years they had never been able to determine who was the better. Now, at last, the matter would be decided for good. Arkon's own arms ached, and his legs were weary. He took solace only in the thought that, though not yet exhausted, Basilikos must be equally weary.

Even so, Basilikos had an advantage Arkon now lacked. In the throng that surrounded them stood Kallista, a golden beauty who loved him deeply. Basilikos fought in the warmth of her approving eye, and Arkon knew it gave him strength — just as it seemed to deaden his own soul that Arianna was nowhere in sight.

Foolishly, he took a moment to glance at the crowd, hoping, yet again, to see her face.

It was a mistake, a mistake he had repeated more than once through that long, difficult day. Basilikos, spotting his opponent's momentary distraction, rushed forward.

Alerted by the hoofbeats, Arkon raised his shield just in time to fend off Basilikos's sword, which descended in a sideswipe that would have ended the contest and, quite likely, Arkon's life. Basilikos thundered past, wheeled, raced back. Their swords clanged against each other, then rang out again and again as they struggled at close quarters in the rays of the lowering sun.

At an impasse, each took a step back to gain new position. In the moment of quiet Basilikos said softly, "It should be me, Arkon. I will have a queen, as befits a Chiron. Yours has disappeared."

A fury surged in Arkon's heart. Yet he was too well trained, too disciplined, to let it lead him into foolish action.

"That was cruel of you, Basilikos."

"I do not mean to be cruel. I am simply speaking the truth."

The two continued to circle each other as they spoke, giving the appearance — which was accurate — that each was seeking an opening in the other's guard.

"Strike!" cried a voice from the hillside. "Strike, Basilikos!"

"Strike, Arkon!" cried another. And suddenly the silence ended as the hillside erupted in a cacophony of voices, all calling for the battle to rage anew.

And still the two warriors circled each other.

"I do not mean to be cruel," repeated Basilikos, loud enough to be heard above the clamor, but not loud enough for any but Arkon to hear. "We are equally matched, old friend. And each of us would make a fine Chiron. But whoever *is* Chiron should have his lady at his side. I do not know what has happened and it is not my business. But I do know that your lady is not here."

"We will not speak of that," said Arkon. Then he launched himself forward.

Once again their blades rang out and the hillside erupted with cheers. Strike, strike, and strike again, their swords flashed red in the sun, their shields rose and fell, faultlessly blocking each slash and thrust. They locked shields, broke from each other, then circled for a new rush. Basilikos bellowed a challenge, rearing on his hind legs. Arkon replied in kind.

And in that moment, disaster.

Without warning, the ground beneath them shook, then split. Basilikos, his front hooves plunging toward what had, but instants before, been solid earth, felt both feet continue downward into the narrow opening. Overbalanced, he toppled forward, carried by the force of his charge. The ghastly snap of his front legs as they broke was lost in the horrified cries of the crowd. In the next instant silence fell, broken only by Arkon's cry of grief and Basilikos's wail of agony.

Flinging aside his blade, shaking off his shield, Arkon dropped to his knees beside his old friend.

"Basilikos," he cried. *"Basilikos!"*

Eyes glazed with pain, his beloved opponent shuddered, then murmured, "The combat goes to you, Arkon. Now, please . . . do what you know you must."

Tears streaming down his face, Arkon nodded. Shaking in his agony, Basilikos passed to his old friend the blade he had so recently raised against him. Their hands lingered for a moment, fingers intertwining, as Arkon took it from his grasp.

"Do not delay," pleaded Basilikos.

Arkon raised the blade. But before he could strike, another hand was on his arm.

"Arkon!" cried Kallista. "Arkon, do not do this!"

Basilikos looked up at her. "Please, Kallista, do not make this harder than it must be. You know I cannot go on."

"We are not beasts! You do not have to end like this!"

"There is no life for me after this, you know that. Kiss me once, my love. Then let Arkon do what he must."

Sobbing, golden-haired Kallista dropped to her knees. Taking Basilikos's head between her hands, she kissed him full and fierce upon his paling lips. Then, with a sob, she cradled his head against her chest. "Do it now," she said to Arkon, "now, while I am holding him."

Arkon raised the blade and did what was necessary.

Later that night, the new Chiron stood alone in the caves that came with his high office. In his hands, he held his crown, the mark of his triumph. But he could not bring himself to place it on his head. The victory had been forever tainted.

Arkon's mouth twisted bitterly. He was about to fling the crown aside when he heard a noise at the mouth of the cave. Turning, he saw Kallista. Her eyes were red, her face ravished with weeping, but her hair gleamed like burnished gold in the flickering light of the torches.

He tried to speak, but could find no words.

"By custom and by law, I am yours now, Arkon," she said, her voice low and husky. "And if I must submit, I will. But I tell you truly, if you have an ounce of sense you will go and find Arianna."

"I grant you release, Kallista, for that is not a custom I will enforce. And I long to go and do just as you say. But how can I leave when there is such danger here? I am Chiron now. I must stay with my people."

"Stay and protect your little kingdom?" she cried scornfully. "How long do you think this valley is going to last? Something has gone wrong with the world, Arkon. Don't you understand that? If you want to do something for the centaurs, go and find out what it is." She paused, drew a heavy breath, then said slowly, "If you want to honor your friend, and perhaps even redeem your crown, go and find out what is happening." Her eyes narrowing, she added fiercely, "I want to know why Basilikos had to die."

CHAPTER
XLIX

RUDE AWAKENING

Ian's search for a trail was greatly complicated by having to scan both sides of the stone highway for signs of where the delvers might have left it. The constant retracing of his steps across that broad swath of rock, only to start again on the opposite side, was maddening. The task was complicated by the frequent rippling of the stone's surface, which made it hard to keep his footing.

Hours later, frustrated and exhausted, Ian paused for the night. He stopped not because he was tired, though he was. He could work past fatigue, could follow a trail in spite of deep weariness. It wasn't his body that had failed him, it was the light.

Leaving the stone, he gathered some fallen leaves and made a bed for himself on the floor of the adjoining forest. His makeshift mattress rustled beneath him, releasing a pleasantly spicy odor, part cinnamon, part something he had never sensed before, but somehow comforting.

Even so, sleep did not come easily. He was consumed with worry over Martha, Rajiv, and Lightfoot. Interlaced with these thoughts were his questions about Fallon, and who — or what — he really was. And, of course, underneath it all was his desperation to find Cara. Finally, with the help of some breathing techniques he had learned during his training, he drifted off to sleep.

Yet Hunters, especially those on the Hunt, never sleep too deeply. So when some part of him, some never-resting part that stayed always alert and aware, detected danger, Ian gasped and sat up.

As it turned out, he didn't need to find the delvers.

They had found him.

CHAPTER
L

NIGHT IN THE FOREST

Cara traveled on well past nightfall, pleased to discover that as a unicorn she possessed more strength and stamina than she had ever known as a human. Of course, the travel was made easier by the fact that her new eyes could see so much better in the darkness. That happy understanding was undercut by a brief but piercing sorrow. Thinking of darkness and light had brought her to the sudden realization that she had left Medafil's sphere, which had lit her way through so many dark times, in the cave where her transformation had taken place. She didn't need it now, of course — and couldn't have carried it with her even had she wanted to. Yet she still felt a great sadness at leaving it behind.

She was tempted to try to make her horn glow, as if to replace the sphere, but knew it would be foolish to do anything that might attract attention. Her main goal at the moment was stealth and secrecy. It was not merely Hunters she might encounter here in the nighttime forest. If there was one thing she now knew about Luster, it was that there was an enormous amount she didn't know — including what dangers might be lurking in the darkness. Had she not had the heart connection to the unicorns to assure her she was heading the right way, she might have succumbed to sheer terror. As it was, she barely kept her fears at bay.

Despite her newfound strength, exhaustion finally set in, forcing Cara to look for a place where she could rest. She settled on a sheltered spot against a sheer rock wall, made more attractive by a nearby waterfall with a little pool at its base. Another rock wall towered on the far side of the pool.

No one can come up behind me this way, she told herself, trying to ignore the fact that the rock also reduced the directions in which she could run if she suddenly needed to escape some attack.

The night was cool, but that did not bother her as much as it would have were she still human. Thunder still rumbled over Dark Mountain, but she had come far enough down the slope that the sound was more distant. A light breeze playing through the trees brought a medley of smells to her broad nostrils which, like her eyes and ears, were far more sensitive now that she was a unicorn. Flickering bugs danced among the branches. They were larger than the fireflies she knew at home and glowed blue rather than yellow. Even so, she found them comforting.

The world is so beautiful, she thought drowsily. *Why do people put such badness into it?*

She remembered asking gentle Finder the same question and immediately felt a new wave of grief at the memoy of his death.

Would the killing never end?

She was still trying — pointlessly, it seemed — to fall asleep, when a nearby sound roused her to instant alertness. Heart pounding in terror, she scrambled to her feet, ready to bolt into the darkness. But before she could move a small, furry figure bounded into the clearing.

"Stinky unicorn girl run too fast!" cried the Squijum, leaping to her shoulder. "Hotcha bad stinky girl leave good Squijum behind. Stinky, *stinky* unicorn girl!"

Cara heaved an enormous sigh, then laughed in spite of herself. "Squijum, you nearly gave me a heart attack!"

Instantly she felt a new flash of fear as she realized that with her own words she might have revealed her presence to anyone still hunting her.

"Shhhh!" she cautioned the Squijum. "Hunters may be after us!"

"Hotcha stinky no good Hunters," replied the Squijum, his own voice hushed now.

"I'm glad you found me, Squijum," said Cara softly.

She was amazed at how true the statement was. Small and silly as the creature was, her heart felt easier for having him with her. She tried to reach up to stroke his fur and realized with fresh shock that it was a move she could no longer make.

"How did you find me, anyway? How did you know it was *me*?"

"Smart Squijum know friends!" he chittered, as if answering the most foolish question imaginable. "Squijum hotcha good friend! Squijum hotcha good hunter!"

"Don't say that," she whispered with a shudder.

"Not all hunters bad," muttered the Squijum sulkily.

"No," she agreed. "Some, like you, are very, very good."

"Hotcha smart girl," he said, curling up on her shoulder.

"Wait. Let me lie down first. I have to rest."

Settling on her side, Cara gazed at her front hooves once more, and was surprised to see that the right one had a small but distinct lump. This puzzled her, until she realized that — unlike her clothing — M'Gama's ring was still with her. Something about that seemed comforting — as did the presence of the Squijum, who had nestled inside the arch of her long, graceful neck. He was no real protection, of course. Even so, she felt better for his being there.

Despite Cara's nagging fears about the Hunters and the strangeness of her new body, she began to drift toward sleep. The bubbling plash of the little waterfall — oddly peaceful for a world tilting into chaos — helped soothe her way.

She was not sure how long she had been sleeping when the first tremor woke her. It was brief and not too bad. But as she was trying to fall back into slumber, a second tremor, much stronger, dislodged an enormous boulder from the rock wall on the far side of the stream. Twice the height of the Dimblethum, the rock landed with a crash that sent an explosion of muddy water slamming against Cara and the Squijum.

She leaped to her feet, her heart thudding. The Squijum clung to her mane, trembling and scolding, though he couldn't seem to determine where to direct his wrath.

Completely filthy, she longed to plunge into the pool, which was starting to grow larger as water collected behind the fallen boulder. But given what had happened, the idea seemed terrifying. Wet and miserable, she decided to move on, despite the fact that it was still dark. She knew there was no chance of falling asleep again, and their place near the rocky scarp suddenly seemed not a safe haven, but a deadly trap.

CHAPTER
LI

A MESSAGE FOR BELOVED

The greatest glory of unicorns ever assembled flowed like a tide of moonlit water through the forests of Luster.

At the front of the glory strode Amalia Flickerfoot, head high, senses alert. She was flanked on the right by her brother, Moonheart, on the left by Belle, who was being ridden by Feng Yuan. Other members of the council, including Fire-Eye and Cloudmane — the latter often ridden by Alma Leonetti — stayed close by as well.

Though the Queen did not show it, did not *allow* herself to show it, she was weary.

Her weariness came not from traveling. In fact she reveled in the strength and endurance of her unicorn form, which was such a change from the body of the old woman she had grown to be as a human! But as tired as her human body had sometimes become, the fatigue the Queen felt now was far deeper — an exhaustion of heart and spirit that came from the relentless responsibility of being the one all the others turned to in this time of danger. It was a kind of responsibility she had never thought to shoulder, a responsibility that did not lift for a single moment, waking or sleeping. The unicorns of Luster — even Moonheart, grumble though he might — had put their faith and trust in her, and it was a fearsome burden. No matter what else she was doing, what else she was thinking, a ribbon of worry ran constantly through the back of her mind: Was she leading her people into triumph — or catastrophe?

Though she was relying on Feng Yuan for strategy, the Queen's chief confidante during this time was Alma Leonetti, whose calm wisdom was something she needed and appreciated. Even so, she would have been happier still to have M'Gama with her. One of the many threads of worry tugging constantly at her heart was the disappearance of the Geomancer.

It was not till well after darkness fell on their first day of travel that Amalia ordered the glory to halt for the night's rest. They were in a forested area, bordering a large meadow. She was just lowering her head to drink from a stream that ran through the center of their gathering place when the guards set up a cry of, "Dragon above! Dragon above!"

Amalia felt a lift of hope. Perhaps Cara's mission had been successful! Moving with unicorn silence, she turned and headed eagerly in the direction of the commotion. The Gathered Glory was large, and though all stood aside for her when they realized who she was, it took several minutes to pass through it. Along the way she was joined by Moonheart, as well as Belle and Feng Yuan.

As they emerged from beneath the towering trees, Amalia saw, by the light of the rising moon, a dragon crouching about a hundred feet away. She was fairly small for her kind, though frighteningly large nonetheless. Her batlike wings were folded at her sides, the points of the largest joint nearly meeting above her shoulders. Her burnished scales shimmered bronze and green in the moonlight, and a hint of scarlet flame flickered about her nostrils.

She would have been quite beautiful, if not so terrifying.

Despite her initial relief at the creature's arrival, Amalia's heart clenched. Where was Cara?

The unicorns who had gathered at the edge of the forest — they were keeping a respectful distance from their visitor — parted to make way for the Queen. Moonheart, Belle, and Feng Yuan continued beside her as she approached the dragon.

"I'll be fine on my own," she murmured.

"All well and good, Amalia," responded her brother. "Even so, we will stay beside you."

She decided not to fight about it. Stopping in front of the dragon, she said, "Greetings, Graumag. It is good to see you again." Despite her words of welcome she looked past the dragon, as if searching for something, then said in worried tones, "You come alone. I had hoped you would bear a rider."

"You mean your granddaughter."

"Ah, then you *have* met Cara! But why is she not with you? Has something happened?"

Graumag answered softly. "Yes, Amalia, something has happened."

Only the briefest flicker in the Queen's eyes betrayed her reaction to these words, but Graumag caught it and said quickly, "I would speak to you in private."

The Queen hesitated, then turned to the unicorns still gathered at the edge of the wood and called, "No need to be concerned! The Lady Graumag has come at my request. I must have a conference with her. Please leave us in peace."

She heard a reluctant murmuring, but the unicorns turned and drifted slowly back among the trees. Shifting uneasily, Moonheart said, "Are you sure it's a good idea to send them away?"

"It will be all right, brother. Graumag is an old friend. We met in the days when I was known as the Wanderer." She returned her attention to the dragon. "May I assume my granddaughter told you the story of my return to my true shape?"

Graumag merely nodded.

Fighting to control her voice, Amalia said, "What is it that you want to tell me about her?"

"As I said, I would prefer to speak to you in private."

"Those with me are trusted advisors. Anything you tell me I will soon share with them, anyway."

"All right then. In short, your granddaughter has disappeared."

The Queen felt her knees buckle, almost as if there had been another tremor. But this time the disturbance was in her heart, not the surface of the world. "What do you mean?" she whispered.

"This morning your granddaughter and I were flying from Dark Mountain to join you when an attack by a group of Hunters forced us to backtrack. Shortly after I had landed in what seemed like a safe place, a man named Elihu joined us. He claimed to be the one who forged the Queen's Five and gave some proof that he had indeed done so."

"What kind of proof?" demanded Moonheart.

Graumag recounted how Elihu had made Cara's amulet respond to his commands.

Moonheart scowled. "Moving things that way is not beyond the skill of even a minor wizard. Even so, the amulets have considerable power of their own. It is unlikely any but the most skilled of magic makers could do such a thing. I don't like this, Amalia, but the man may have been telling the truth." He paused, then added, "There's probably some story about the forging of the amulets, but I certainly can't recall it. For once I actually wish that annoying Grimwold was with us."

The Queen merely nodded, then said, "What happened next?"

"Moments later we heard Hunters approaching. Elihu snatched Cara into his arms and disappeared into the forest. I chose to stay and ward off the Hunters. There were a surprising number of them, by the way, which seemed to confirm what I had suspected and Elihu had claimed: that they were specifically looking for Cara. I managed to deal with a fair number of them. Indeed, some of them will never hunt again, though this victory was not without cost."

Here she shifted a wing, revealing a long wound scored along her right side.

"Fight though I would, there were more than I could handle, and some managed to get past me. By the time the others had fled, Elihu and Cara had disappeared as well. I searched for them for hours, but it was as if they had both vanished into thin air. Finally I gave up that quest, deciding I should seek you out instead."

The Queen closed her eyes, struggling to contain her feelings. At last she said, "What was your sense of this Elihu?"

"My contact with him was brief, but I will say that I did not sense any malice or evil. If I caught anything, it was a profound sadness. I am troubled that I was not able to locate either him or Cara after I had dealt with the Hunters. Some Hunters did get past me, so it's possible they were taken, but somehow that seems unlikely. In truth, regarding those two I am more mystified than worried."

Amalia breathed deeply. "Thank you. That is good to know." She paused for a moment, then said, "When I sent Cara to you it was to seek your help in the struggle against the Hunters. Did she deliver that request?"

"She did, and I have agreed to do so."

The Queen nodded. "For that, my thanks as well." She paused, then continued quietly, "My intent had been to ask you to help us defend ourselves. However, I now have an additional request."

"Which is?"

"Beloved is encamped in an open field not far from the Axis Mundi. Would you be willing to deliver a message to her?"

The dragon looked startled. "If her Hunters feel the same way about dragons as they do about unicorns, I am not sure I will survive long enough to get the words out. But I am willing to try."

"Again, I thank you."

"Amalia," said Moonheart. "What do you have in mind?"

The Queen managed a wan smile. "Strategy, dear brother. Strategy."

"And what is this message you would like me to deliver?" asked Graumag.

"Tell Beloved that Amalia Flickerfoot, Queen of the Unicorns, asks if she and her Hunters have the courage to meet the unicorns at noon three days hence. If she agrees, we will face them in the field northeast of the great tree, where all shall finally be decided."

Graumag looked at her in astonishment.

Feng Yuan, however, smiled.

"Will you deliver this message?" asked the Queen.

"I think it is madness, but I am willing to do as you request," replied the dragon.

When Graumag had departed, Feng Yuan said, "Well done, O Queen."

"Well done?" demanded Moonheart furiously. "I agree

with Graumag! This is madness. Why tell Beloved when and where we intend to meet her?"

"What makes you think that is what I have done, brother mine? As Feng Yuan has been teaching me, 'All warfare is based on deception.'"

In her heart, the Queen felt some sorrow at having deceived the dragon. But dragons do not lie, and the only way Graumag could tell Beloved what Amalia wanted her to hear was if the dragon had no idea of her true plan.

CHAPTER
LII

THE DELVER AND THE HUNTER

It was full night, and Rocky and his band of rebels were making good progress toward the underground world. Fear had been their primary companion on their journey, a fear that escalated every time another tremor disturbed the surface of Luster. Even so, the delver found himself taking a strange comfort in the tremors. Oh, the quakes were terrifying — probably more terrifying for the delvers than anyone else, given that they lived underground. But they also provided useful proof that something horrible was happening, proof that kept his still-nervous cousins from growing mutinous.

What baffled Rocky now was that they had not passed any unicorns. It wasn't that the things were so numerous you ran across them in every grove and clearing; happily, a delver could travel for days without actually *seeing* one of the silvery beasts. But delvers could *sense* the creatures from several hundred feet away, and neither he nor any of his cousins had ever been on the surface this long without at least knowing they had passed near one.

Where had they all gone?

Rocky was pondering this question when they came to the familiar swath of stone called by delvers "the Great One's Highway."

Delvharkonians always thought it was odd that the parts of the world they liked best — the areas where the surface was, sensibly, covered with stone — were also the least comfortable, because there was nothing to shield them from the big sky and the terrible sun. They loved the Great One's Highway, but only traveled it at night.

To their horror, when they stepped onto it they discovered that the highway's surface, once so smooth it looked as if it had been crafted by delvers rather than risen naturally, was now cracked and broken.

The delver who used to be called Gergga began to weep.

"Oh, stop!" snapped Zagrat, now known as Lizard. "Your nickname may be Waterfall but that doesn't mean you have to snivel all over the place."

"But . . . but the highway," moaned Waterfall, drawing his arm across his nearly nonexistent nose.

"I know," said Lizard, his voice softening. "It's terrifying."

"Shhh!" hissed Rocky. "Listen — there's someone ahead of us!"

They froze, each straining his oversized ears to catch any

sound that might indicate danger. What they soon heard was not something that most humans would have caught — the sound of someone not far ahead breathing, deep and slow and still.

"Asleep," whispered Diamond.

"On the highway?" asked First.

"No, off to the side," replied his twin, Hammer.

The delvers crept forward, prisoners of curiosity. When they reached the place the sound was coming from, they glanced at one another, then stepped off the stone to surround the sleeping man. Despite their ability to move with near perfect silence, he somehow sensed them. Sitting up with a shout, he put his hand to the sword strapped to his waist.

Rocky suspected that the sounds that came from the man's mouth were supposed to mean something, but not knowing the human tongue — actually, Cara had told him they had many languages, which must be wildly confusing — he had no idea what that meaning might be.

To his amazement, the man paused, then said to them in perfect delvish, "Stay back!"

The cousins glanced from one to the other, but left it to Rocky to answer. Raising his hands, he said, "We do not want to fight. Do you see us rushing at you, weapons raised and ready?"

"I see that you surrounded me while I was sleeping."

Hand still on the hilt of his sword, the man got to his knees, which put him at about eye level with the delvers.

Rocky gasped, and it was all he could do to keep from blurting out, "We have met before!" This was the same Hunter Lightfoot and Cara had been fleeing a few months back — the Hunter that Rocky and his cove had misdirected, so the Prince and Cara might escape his attention.

For a moment Rocky was offended that the man did not recognize him as well, taking it as yet another sign that in the eyes of humans all delvers looked alike. On second thought, though, he was just as glad. He had a sense that things had shifted, and he was not yet sure in what way.

"If you do not want to fight, why did you surround me?" demanded the man, drawing Rocky's attention once more.

"We were curious, that is all. But a far more curious matter than why a human was sleeping next to the Great One's Highway is this: How is it that you speak our tongue? This is not a common thing among humans."

The hint of a smile twitched at the corners of the man's mouth. "It is an enchantment, one that served me well the night I entered the delver world and spoke to your King."

Cautiously Rocky said, "And are you a friend of King Gnurflax?"

The man appeared startled by the delver's response. "Would friendship with the King be a bad thing?" he asked, clearly avoiding a direct answer.

Rocky cursed himself for having been obvious. Speaking aloud, he said evasively, "It is always good to be on good terms with those in power."

"I am seeking to meet with Gnurflax once more," replied the man, again without declaring allegiance. "Alas, I am having a harder time finding my way underground than I did before."

Still probing, Rocky asked, "Why is it you wish to meet with our honored King?"

"He has something I want. I am hoping to bargain with him for its return."

"What would that be?" asked Rocky.

The man hesitated, apparently trying to decide how much to reveal. Finally — and from the desperate look in his eye Rocky could tell the man was taking a gamble, hoping to learn something in return — he said, "I believe he has my daughter."

And suddenly all the pieces connected as Rocky remembered the things Cara had told him while they were traveling together. "You are Cara's father!" he cried.

Ian Hunter looked at him in surprise. "How do you know that?"

"Cara is my friend! We have been imprisoned together, traveled together, saved each other's lives."

The man scrambled to his feet. "Do you know where she is now?"

Rocky, noticing the eager look in the man's eyes, chose his words carefully. "We parted company some time ago. She was fine when I left her —"

"But do you mean she escaped the delver dungeon?"

Rocky patted his left shoulder, a delver sign of affirmation. "We escaped together! She is a brave girl."

The man repeated his earlier question: "Where is she now?"

"The last time I saw her, the gryphon Medafil was about to fly her to the unicorn court. I cannot say for sure that they arrived, but the gryphon is, for all his foolishness, brave and faithful."

"Thank you," said Ian, his words carried on an enormous sigh. "This is a great relief to me."

Rocky looked at him appraisingly. Finally he said, "For this information, I would ask a boon."

"And what would that boon be?" asked Ian, too wary to grant such an open request.

"I must return to Delvharken. Because I am seen as a traitor, this will be a difficult thing. However, if you were to escort me, taking me as if I were a prisoner you intended to return to the King, we could pass without a problem. Once we are far enough underground, you can release me to do my business and return to the surface."

Ian shook his head. "I'm sorry. I would like to help you in this, but I must return to my friends. I need to tell my wife that Cara is safe!"

Rocky lunged forward and took Ian's hand, pressing it to his forehead. "I have given you information you desire. For that you owe me. Set that aside, and consider this: I go to seek one who may be able to stop the doom that is overtaking this world. Can he save us? I do not know. What I do know is that terrible things are happening. Think how many will die — delvers, dragons, centaurs, unicorns, so many others — should this world collapse."

"But my wife . . ."

"There is a world at stake. Your daughter is *in* this world!"

Ian froze. If Cara was no longer a prisoner in Delvharken, he would have to begin his hunt for her all over again. That could take weeks, months even. But according to Fallon he didn't have months. Luster was unlikely to last for more than a few days.

And if Luster died, Cara died as well.

"Can this person —"

"Not person. Delver."

Ian sighed. "Can this delver you seek really save Luster?"

Rocky shook his head. "I told you, I cannot guarantee that. I know only that he is the single hope I can think of."

Ian turned to look back along the broken and fissured path. "Forgive me, Martha," he whispered. Returning his gaze to Rocky, he said, "All right, I will go with you. But let us start now. I have no time to waste."

"None of us do," replied Rocky grimly.

As if to prove his point, another tremor shook the ground beneath them, opening a foot-wide fissure in the stone highway.

The delvers cried out in horror.

Seeing the look on Ian's face, Rocky said, "We are not cowards. But it hurts us to see the stone torn this way." He turned to his cousins. "You have heard what I intend to do. This saves you from having to go below with me. I ask Lizard to be your leader until I return. Do you accept this?"

The cousins nodded their assent.

"But what shall we do while you are gone?" asked Lizard. "Where shall we look for you?"

Rocky hesitated. While he was thinking, Ian said, "Do you know what has caused the world to shake this way?"

"Yes. The woman called Beloved has opened a gate between your world and ours."

"And do you know where that gate is?"

Rocky turned to his cousins. They shook their heads.

"There is a great tree," began Ian.

"The tree?" wailed Rocky in horror. "She damaged the great tree?"

"She came straight through it."

The delvers groaned.

Rocky turned to them. "If I can find Namza, I am certain that is where he will want to go. You should go there now and wait in the forest beyond the meadow that surrounds the tree. When I arrive, I will make another cousin-call —"

"Have you lost your mind?" interrupted Pebble. "It took all we had to bring you back the last time you did that!"

"You will be close by, and you will be expecting the call. It will not be nearly so difficult. And if I have Namza with me, he can keep me from going too far.

"Waterfall, will you lend me your rope?"

"What for?"

"I will need the human to bind me before we go underground. Otherwise they will not believe I am a prisoner."

Though he shuddered at the idea, Waterfall stepped forward and handed the coil of rope to Rocky. Then he crossed his arms over his chest and bowed.

The other cousins repeated the gesture.

Rocky returned the farewell, then prodded Ian and said, "You should do the same. It would be courteous."

When Ian had complied, Rocky said, "All right, follow me."

Without another word, the two unlikely companions began to trot along the fractured, stony highway.

CHAPTER
LIII

FALLON ON HIS OWN

Fallon loped easily through the darkness. He missed Ian and Rajiv. Even so, it was a relief to no longer be constrained by hiding the extent of his strength and abilities. It would have been too much to try to explain why he could move through the forest as swiftly and silently as a cat, despite the near pitch-blackness. And well past too much to try explaining why he had been able to run for several hours now without taking a rest.

He was enjoying the world around him. Though this place should not exist, and though the *fact* of its existence had cost him dearly, it was clearly a masterwork. Yet seething beneath the pleasure was an uneasy confusion. Though he could sense that the one he had sought for so long was indeed here in Luster, the connection he should have felt was oddly muffled, like clear water that had become unexpectedly muddy. Could his *alahim* — the friend who was more than a friend, more than a brother — have changed that much?

Fallon paused, closed his eyes, once more let his senses reach out. There! Though the feeling of connection was still strangely indistinct, he had found the direction at last. Relieved and delighted, he veered slightly to the right and picked up his pace.

A few minutes later he stopped, more puzzled than ever. His sense of where Elihu should be had divided, as if his friend were in two places at once. How was that possible?

Fallon stood for a long time, reaching out with all his heart for the one he sought. One strand of connection was definitely stronger than the other.

Puzzled, deeply troubled, he began to move toward it.

As he did, another tremor shook the ground beneath his feet.

He sighed, wondering how much time this world had left, and hoping he could find his *alahim* before it was too late.

CHAPTER
LIV

"TO THE SURFACE!"

Delvharken was in chaos. Each new tremor that shook the underground world drove increased fear into the hearts of those who made their home far beneath the surface of Luster.

In his terror, King Gnurflax spent hours in the private cave where he went to listen to his secret friend, calling on him for help, for advice.

But the Whisperer never came.

Where can he be? wondered the delver king. *What could have happened to him?* And in his stony heart rose another question, a question he tried desperately to ignore: *Has he betrayed me after all?*

Gnurflax's worries were made worse by that fact that his second most trusted advisor was also missing. The wizard Namza had been with him from the time he, Gnurflax, was but a delvling. Since it was impossible for Gnurflax to imagine that the old magician had abandoned him, he believed something worse must have happened. Namza often ventured into the deepest areas of Delvharken, seeking the great secrets he believed to be hidden there; all too likely the old wizard had roused one of the terrible beasts that lived down there and had paid the price for it.

The King's frettings were interrupted by a guard standing at the mouth of the cave, shouting, "King Gnurflax! King Gnurflax!"

Spinning about in a rage, the King screeched, "Have I not given orders that I must not be disturbed here?"

The guard looked terrified, but Gnurflax had the uneasy feeling that he himself was not the one who had instilled that terror. "You have indeed, O King. But there is a mob in the throne room calling for you. If you do not come, we fear . . . we fear . . ."

"You fear *what*, you fool?"

The guard looked helpless. "I don't know what. We just fear."

As he spoke, another tremor rocked the ground where they stood. An enormous boulder fell from the ceiling of the cave, barely missing Gnurflax.

"Come, My King," cried the guard. "This place is not safe!"

What he did not say, but they both knew, was that there were no longer *any* safe places in Delvharken.

The King flinched when they reached the great cavern that housed the Stone Throne. They approached through a secret passage known only to the royal family and their guards. It led to an entry behind the throne. Even before he stepped inside, Gnurflax could see that the chamber was full, more full than it had ever been, filled not just by delvers, but by terror — a terror so thick he felt as if it were choking him, filling his lungs where the air should be.

"The King!" chanted the crowd. "Where is the King?"

Swallowing hard, Gnurflax stepped around the throne. At once a cry went up from the closest delvers. "The King! The King!"

The chant was picked up by the ones behind them. It rolled toward the far side of the cavern like a wave, echoing from the stone walls, then rolled forward again. Gnurflax, realizing he could not be seen by those in the rear, made a quick decision and climbed onto the Stone Throne, standing on the seat to make himself more visible.

"The King!" cried the delvers again.

Gnurflax raised his hands for silence, which came, though very slowly. When all had at last fallen still, when the final echoes had died, the King spoke. His voice was weak at first, and he was uncertain of what to say. Faltering, hesitant, he felt a secondary fear, a fear of losing the crowd.

And then, like a miracle, a soothing voice whispered in his ear, "Be brave, and speak as I tell you."

Filled with unexpected courage, Gnurflax threw back his shoulders. His voice rolled out over the assembled delvers as he repeated the words the Whisperer gave to him.

"O my people, terror is indeed upon us! But are we not delvers? Are we not made of stone and sinew, with hearts too hard for fear? Yes, the world shakes. But whose fault is that? The blame can only lie in one place. It must be the unicorns!"

"The unicorns!" responded the delvers, as if they suddenly understood.

"They have betrayed us somehow," roared Gnurflax, feeling his own courage return as he tried to pump bravery into his subjects. "It is *their* fault Delvharken trembles, *their* fault that stone shakes, walls crumble, boulders fall. For too long have we allowed these parasites to live on the surface of our world. We must repent our weakness and destroy our foes."

"Destroy our foes!" echoed the delvers.

"O my delvers, will you follow me to the surface? The air may be hot and dry. The light may blind and pain us. But it is there that we will find the enemy. It is there that we will engage the enemy. It is there that we will, at last, *destroy* the enemy. Whatever the unicorns have done, it will end once we end their reign over the surface. To save Delvharken, will you follow me above, even into the accursed light?"

"We will!"

"Then it is war at last!" cried Gnurflax.

Another temblor shook the cavern. Stalactites broke loose, plummeting from the ceiling like spears of stone, then shattering as they hit the floor. Screams of pain sounded from three or four places where delvers had been struck.

"See to the wounded!" cried Gnurflax. Then he grabbed his own spear and leaped from the Stone Throne. Amid screams and cheers, he pushed his way to the far side of the cavern, on into the tunnels that led to the surface. Despair gone, his heart pumped with fierce energy and growing pride.

Behind him streamed his delvers, some powered by fear, some by anger, all ready to invade the surface and destroy the ancient enemy — an enemy to whom they were bound by a history more puzzling than any of them could imagine.

DAY FOUR OF
THE INVASION

Change will come, whether we wish it to or not. To
fight it is like fighting the sunrise. Better to say, "Ah,
welcome old friend. Here you are again."

Edgecomb the Eccentric
Second Chronicle Keeper of Luster, Seventh Scroll

CHAPTER
LV

THE DIMBLETHUM

Cara and the Squijum were walking through the mist of the early morning forest, which swirled silvery around Cara's silver hooves. She was slowly growing used to her new body and continued to delight in the ways that it was stronger and had so much more endurance than the human form she was used to. That, combined with her sharpened senses — especially her eyesight — had made night travel fairly easy. It hadn't actually lasted very long, since it turned out it had been fairly close to morning when that second tremor had made sleep impossible.

Being wet and filthy from the great mud splash had made the first hour of travel extremely uncomfortable. But then they had come to another stream — this one with no cliffs nearby — and had managed to clean themselves up.

Now both she and the Squijum were wet and bedraggled, but the exertions of travel kept them from being too cold.

* * *

Almost before there was a hint of light in the sky, the Squijum went bounding off in search of something to eat. Cara decided to do the same, without the bounding part, and realized to her dismay that she didn't know what was safe to eat and what was not.

I wish I'd paid more attention to what Lightfoot and the others ate, she thought, spitting out some particularly distasteful leaves. After several unhappy experiments she found some sprouts that tasted fairly good. She was nibbling at them — hoping they wouldn't make her sick and wishing that sunberries were still in season — when she heard a soft groan.

She looked around, but could see nothing. Then she realized that her newly sharpened senses had deceived her again; the sound was coming from much farther off than she had realized.

She listened again and heard another moan.

Certain now of the direction, she moved cautiously down the slope toward a pair of large trees. Despite the moans, she was not prepared for what she found when she stepped around them.

It was the Dimblethum. He was slumped on the ground, cradled between the thick roots of a quilpum tree.

Cara stared at the great creature in horror. Her reaction came not from his shockingly strange form, for she was long used to his looking like a bear who had started to turn into a man. It was what had happened to him that chilled her blood now. For this friend — so frightening in size and appearance, yet so gentle in his dealings with her — had clearly been in a terrible fight. His eyes were closed, his head lolled back, and his thick fur was matted with blood. Cara hoped, at first, that it was the blood of his foes. Alas, it didn't take her long to see that the blood was flowing from his own wounds — from more wounds than she could quickly count.

He had fallen silent. Despite the moans that had drawn her to him, she suddenly feared he must be dead. She panicked, but a moment later he shifted slightly, and she felt a lift of hope. She moved closer, stumbling as she did, not because of her new body, but because the tears welling in her eyes made it hard to see.

She found herself wishing, oddly, that the Squijum would return from his hunting so she would not face this horrible moment alone.

Her approach was so quiet that her friend did not notice she was there until she said softly, "Dimblethum, what has happened to you?"

The Dimblethum twitched, then slowly opened his eyes. "Unicorn," he muttered in that low, rumbling voice she had come to love. "Dimblethum is sorry, unicorn."

Cara realized what she should have understood at once: Though the Squijum had managed to recognize her in her new form, it was unlikely anyone else would know who she really was.

"Dimblethum," she said gently. "It's me. *Cara!*"

The great creature's eyes widened. Then he nodded, too weak to do more. His head lolled again, and she wondered whether he had really heard her.

"What has happened to you?" she repeated.

"Dimblethum fought Hunters," he growled slowly, not opening his eyes. "Dimblethum crunch Hunters. Hunters cut Dimblethum."

"What were you doing on Dark Mountain to begin with?"

He moaned, then murmured, "Looking for Cara."

"I'm Cara," she repeated softly.

The Dimblethum nodded, and his eyelids slowly closed again. "Yes. You told Dimblethum."

It was only then that Cara realized the second thing she should have known at once. She possessed — or, at least, *might* possess — the ability to heal him. Was there enough of the unicorn in her to do that? Did it take special training? She didn't know, knew only that she had to try.

She paused, remembering how such a healing always drained Lightfoot. Were there still Hunters in the area? If so, it would be dangerous — possibly fatal — for her to lose consciousness. She shook her head, irritated at herself. The Dimblethum had saved her life when she first entered Luster and saved it more than once since then. What did it matter if doing this would endanger her? How could she not try to help her friend if she had the ability to do so?

"Listen, Dimblethum, I'm going to try to heal you."

His eyes flew open. "No!" he growled, "No! Do not do that!"

"But you are so badly wounded."

"Cara must not do this."

"Why? I want to help you."

To her astonishment, he managed to stagger to his feet, roaring, "Do not touch the Dimblethum!"

She drew back, frightened of him, which was a terrible feeling.

With a cry of despair the Dimblethum stumbled away from her, leaving the unicorn girl wondering and heartbroken.

CHAPTER
LVI

A SPLIT IN THE ROAD

Ian and his unexpected companion had been trotting along the stone highway for an hour or so when Ian asked, "How long will it take to reach Delvharken?"

"Not long," replied the delver in his rasping voice. "At this pace we should be there in less time than it takes for true dark to fall after the wretched sun has finally set."

It took Ian a moment to realize that the delver was describing the period of dusk. It was a vague measure of time, but clear enough to let him know they were within another hour of reaching Delvharken. Closer than he had dared hope!

They continued in silence for a time, though Ian kept glancing down at the delver, trying to comprehend that his daughter had actually befriended the hideous creature. Wondering if he could do the same, he asked, "What is your name?"

"I have no name."

Ian made a sound of disbelief.

"No, truly. The King took my name as punishment for my being a rebel. However I do have a nickname! Cara gave it to me. It was a great gift, because I had never known about nicknames until she explained them to me." He glanced up at Ian, "Is it true that you used to call her 'Pookie'?"

Ian's chuckle was cut short by an unexpected wave of grief as the question brought back full force the loss of so many years of his daughter's childhood. "It's true," he said at last, past the lump in his throat.

"It is an interesting nickname. I thought, at first, that she was going to call *me* Pookie. But she decided to call me Rocky instead. I like this nickname. It makes me proud." He paused, then added, "What shall I call you?"

"Ian."

"All right . . . Ian."

They continued to trot in a surprisingly companionable silence, the delver easily keeping pace with Ian's longer legs. As they passed a large boulder, Rocky said, "That is a marker. We are not far now."

The words had barely left his lips when a tremor — the most powerful one Ian had felt so far — shook the rock. With a horrible grinding sound the ribbon of stone split, opening a crevice that ran the full width of the stone highway.

"Rocky, watch out!" cried Ian. He managed to leap over the gap himself, but his warning was too late. Rocky, with his shorter legs, tumbled in.

Turning at the delver's cry, Ian dropped to his belly and

peered into the crevice. The opening was frighteningly deep. Even worse, he could see no sign of his delver companion.

"Rocky!" he called. "Rocky, are you all right?"

After a nerve-wracking silence, a quavering voice responded, "I'm here. I am in pain, but I do not think I am broken."

"Can you climb out?"

"I don't think so. The walls are smooth and they slope inward. I am on a ledge. I fear falling again. And . . . Ian, I don't think there is a bottom!"

Ian rolled his eyes at this, then suddenly found himself wondering if it might be true. He thought for a moment, then called, "Do you still have your rope?"

"Yes! Yes, I do!"

"Can you throw it up to me?"

"I can't see you! I don't know how far it is!"

"Well, try!"

"All right. Just a moment."

After a brief silence, Ian heard a cry of, "Here it comes!" He lay on his belly and stared intently into the crevice, readying himself to try to catch the rope. But he saw nothing.

A moment later he heard a delvish curse.

"Try again!" he cried.

Rocky did try again, with no more success than the first time. He tried again, and again, and again. After what seemed hours he called, "My arm is getting tired!"

"You'll be more than tired if we can't get you out of there," replied Ian. "Keep trying!"

The delver continued his efforts. Several times Ian caught a hint of the rope snaking upward. More than once it came within inches of his outstretched hand — close, but not close enough.

"I almost had it that time! Do it again!"

With a cry of despair, Rocky hurled the end of the rope upward once more. Leaning perilously far over the crevice, Ian snatched at it. "Got it!" he cried, and at once began to pull.

"Don't!" shouted Rocky. "Don't pull. Just hold it steady and let me climb."

Ian slid back to a more solid position. The delver was light enough that Ian did not need to brace himself against anything. Wrapping his end of the rope twice around his forearm, he called, "All right, go ahead!" Then he stared intently into the crevice, ready to stretch down a helping hand as soon as Rocky was close enough.

The delver had just reached a place where he was visible when Ian heard a sudden clamor from behind. He glanced over his shoulder, but could see nothing.

"Climb!" he hissed down to Rocky. "Climb! Something is coming, and it doesn't sound good."

"I'm moving as fast as I can!" wheezed Rocky.

Ian looked over his shoulder once more, and his heart nearly froze. A horde of delvers was racing toward him.

"Rocky!" he called. "Rocky, there are delvers heading our way. A lot of them."

"If they catch me all is lost!" cried the delver.

Ian could see his companion's eyes now, staring up at him. He glanced over his shoulder again. The delvers, moving faster then he would have thought possible, were appallingly close. From the sounds of their shouting, they were in no mood to parley.

Ian was relatively certain he was about to be captured. If Rocky were captured, too, he would not be able to go forward to find the delver he believed might know how to save Luster.

He had but an instant to make a decision.

"Can you make it out from where you are without the rope?" he called down.

"Yes, I think so!"

"Then grab some stone and hold on. Wait until the horde has passed. Then climb out and continue the mission!"

Dropping the rope, Ian turned to face the oncoming delvers.

CHAPTER
LVII

STILL HUNTED

Cara stood without moving, replaying over and over in her mind the moment when the Dimblethum had fled from her.

Why had he rejected her offer to heal him?

She was so upset she had no idea how long she had stood watching after him, well past the point when he had vanished in the distance. Only when a rustling overhead alerted her that the Squijum was returning did she sigh and turn away.

"Yum!" he cried happily, leaping from a branch to land on her white shoulder. "Good bugs! Good Squijum!"

Though she was glad of his return, her reply was less than joyful. "Hello, Squijum."

"Unicorn girl sad?" he had asked, instantly sounding sad himself, and reminding her how amazingly alert he was to her moods.

"Yes, I'm sad."

"Why?"

"The Dimblethum was here. He was hurt, and I wanted

to heal him, but he refused and ran away. Why would he do that, Squijum? Why wouldn't he let me heal him?"

"Dimblethum crazy," replied the Squijum, tugging at her mane. "Dimblethum always been crazy."

"Thanks, that explains everything."

"Squijum good explainer," he replied contentedly.

They lingered by the tree for a while longer, Cara telling the Squijum she needed to rest. Though Cara *was* tired, her main reason for delaying was her hope that the Dimblethum might return. Finally, reluctantly, she abandoned the thought and they resumed their journey. But she had not gone more than a few feet when she halted. Her sense of the direction she must travel in order to join the great glory had changed. It took her a moment to work it out — directions had never been her specialty — but she finally decided they had moved eastward.

Uneasiness crept over her. Did this mean that her grandmother had led the unicorns out of Autumngrove? Why would she do that? Had some disaster struck? Were they even now fleeing the Hunters?

Whatever had happened, she wanted to join them. Her place was with the unicorns. So she started out again, the Squijum still clinging to her mane.

It was about midday when Cara heard the voices of men nearby. She froze in place, hoping desperately that if she didn't move she would not attract their attention.

"What is it about this girl that's so all-fired important, anyway?" asked one of them, his voice uncomfortably close.

"Beloved hasn't seen fit to tell us," replied another. "Though given the way the kid so completely disappeared, I'm guessing she must have some kind of magic. Where can she have gotten to, anyway?"

"I know where I'd like to get to," said a third voice. "Away from this godforsaken mission and back to the main event. I didn't come here to hunt for Ian's whelp. I came to kill unicorns!"

"We'll hunt what Beloved tells us to hunt," snapped the first voice.

"Well, I can't promise what we'll find," replied the third voice, sounding surly. "These blood trackers Beloved gave us were fine in the beginning, but the stupid things seem to have stopped working altogether now."

Cara silently thanked Elihu for her transformation as the Hunters passed on, moving as silently as if they were unicorns themselves. That silence frightened her, making her realize she could not count on hearing a Hunter if he was nearby, not even with her unicorn ears.

But even worse than their silent passage was the conversation that preceded it, which made it plain that she was indeed the one they were seeking. Clearly, Elihu had been right about her being safer in unicorn form — a thought that made her wonder where he was now. Had the Hunters he was fighting captured him? Killed him?

She shuddered at the thought and continued down the

mountainside. She did not always head in a downward direction to do so, since the sides of the mountain were rumpled; and even here in the forested section, there were rocky clefts through which she had to make her way, heading down one slope then up the opposite side. She was pleased to discover in doing this that her cloven hooves let her negotiate these places with a nimbleness she had not expected.

She wasn't sure how many miles she had covered when a sudden, sharp ache in her heart told her that another unicorn had been killed. Though her vision was once more blurred by tears, she walked on.

The Squijum, riding on her back, patted her neck, as if, again, sensing her sorrow.

CHAPTER
LVIII

THE DELVER HORDE

Ian's mind raced as he watched the delver horde draw near. His first instinct was to flee, but despite their short legs, he was not at all sure he could outrun them. Besides, if they continued along this stony road they must eventually come upon Martha and the others. So even if he did flee, the only direction he would want to go would be parallel to the road so he could try to reach them first. It was unlikely he could do that and escape detection. Moreover, it was vital he divert the delvers from discovering Rocky, who still clung to the wall of the crevice. If his new companion's search for his teacher really could lead to an end to the increasingly violent tremors ripping at Luster, he had to hold on to that chance.

With all that in mind, Ian decided to walk *toward* the delvers. His original plan had been to enter Delvharken and speak to the King. Perhaps he could bluff it out here, instead.

The horde came to a halt several feet in front of him. Now that they were closer, Ian was appalled to see how many there were, standing so tightly packed that their hairless scalps made it look as if the road before him was paved with cobblestones. The hideous faces of the closest ones almost made Ian reconsider his decision to stand rather than flee. But it was too late now to change his mind.

After a mumble of activity, five of them stepped forward. He soon recognized the large delver in the center of the group as the King. Taking the initiative, he raised a hand in salute and said in delvish, "Greetings, Mighty Gnurflax. It is good to see you again."

The King scowled at him for a moment, then cried, "*You!* What are you doing here, Hunter?"

"Returning to Delvharken, as I promised after my first visit."

The King's scowl deepened. "That promise has long since passed the time when it should have been redeemed."

"I would have been back sooner, but one of your own delvers pointed me in the wrong direction when I was in pursuit of the girl and her amulet. That detour cost a great deal of time."

"The nameless *skwarmint* who did that has been punished!" shrieked Gnurflax, his face twisting with sudden rage. Just as quickly he caught his breath. After a moment he nodded. Staring at Ian shrewdly he said, "Do you have the amulet now?"

Ian spread his hands. "Alas, the delay had its effect. I lost track of the amulet."

He saw at once that it was the wrong answer and his gut twisted as the King screeched, "Then you are no longer of any use to me!" Turning to the delvers beside him, Gnurflax cried, "Seize the human!"

Ian realized at once that to fight was useless. There were hundreds of them. Even if he managed to slay the first twenty — or even the first fifty — that came at him, they would eventually overwhelm him. The more havoc he wrought now, the greater would be their wrath when he finally did fall to their attack. If he angered them too greatly, they might kill him on the spot. And his main goal, right now, was to stay alive in the hope that he might escape later and somehow find Cara and then rejoin Martha and the others.

So he simply stood his ground and let the delver horde take him.

He had to use every trick at his command to keep himself calm as they bore him to the ground, then trussed him up. After binding his hands and feet the delvers slid him onto a pole, then hoisted him as if he were a slain deer.

Once he was safely dangling that way, Gnurflax stood at his head, smirking. Gazing at Ian with his bulging eyes, the Delverking rubbed his chin and said, "You may prove to be a wonderful bargaining chip." He spat on the ground beside him, then turned away.

A moment later the horde started forward, the sound of their bare feet slapping against the stone like that of applause celebrating his capture.

It was only two or three yards before they came to the crevice where Rocky was hiding. The four delvers carrying Ian — two in front, two behind — simply leaped over it.

It took less than a heartbeat, but with his head tipped back, Ian could see Rocky staring up at him in terror. Then his carriers were on the far side of the crevice, trotting forward.

Ian had no way of telling if the delvers that followed had spotted his last hope or if Rocky remained free to continue his mission.

CHAPTER
LIX

RETURN OF A FRIEND

The forest on the lowest part of the mountain was dense, and Cara realized that without the clear guidance provided by her heart, she would be deathly afraid of being lost. Here in Luster there would be no road to eventually stumble across, no city, not even some small town that might surprise her. She had a new sense of the great wilderness of much of this world, and it was slightly terrifying.

By midafternoon she and the Squijum were off the mountain and far enough from its clouds that the brightness of the day lifted her heart. They had entered an open area, a wide meadow bordered by a tumbling stream.

The Squijum had just flounced off to hunt for bugs when a winged shadow sliding over the ground caught Cara's attention. Looking up, she was delighted to see Medafil circling toward them. Yet despite her relief at seeing him, she also felt a sudden, strong impulse to flee.

Why do I want to run? she wondered as she forced herself

to stand steady. *Medafil is a friend. Is it the unicorn in me that reacts this way?*

The final flutter of the gryphon's wings as he slowed his descent caused the meadow grass to bend around Cara's hooves.

"Unicorn!" he said, keeping his voice low. "Do you know the danger here? There are Hunters about!" Then he sighed and muttered, "Oh, drat. The flick-spickled creature probably can't understand me."

Cara realized that, unlike the Squijum, the gryphon had not realized who he was speaking to. "I know of the Hunters," she replied in English. "I have been dodging them all day."

Medafil started back. "How do you know that tongue?"

She hesitated, then said, "I studied it with a friend."

Medafil nodded. "Well, in all that dodging you've been doing, did you by any chance see a human girl? She was in my care, but yesterday I lost her while fending off some Hunters. I have been seeking her ever since, but can find no sign of her."

Cara hesitated. Should she reveal herself? Or would it be better to keep her true identity secret? Medafil was a trusted friend, so her hesitation didn't come from fear. And it would be good to have someone to confide in when she was feeling so lost and uncertain. Yet something held her back. Shame? No, it was not that. Fear of his disapproval? To her surprise, that rang true. Yet it was not reason enough to avoid telling him.

Taking a deep breath, she lifted her head and said softly, "I am the one you seek, Medafil."

"Gaaah! What kind of fig-dingled fool do you think I am?"

"You and I first met by a rock in the moonlight, when I freed you from a delver trap," she said softly. "You went with me to Ebillan's cave, and later we traveled together through delver caverns to reach the Valley of the Centaurs."

The gryphon blinked in surprise, then asked slyly, "How was I injured on that journey?"

"We were fleeing the skwartz, and in the last moments you had to pass through a space that was too small, tearing your wing. We thought you might never fly again, but Belle healed you."

"Gaaah! It is you! But what in the frim-dibbled, dat-splangled, frak-frumpussed world have you done to yourself? Even your voice has changed!"

Feeling safer with Medafil at her side, Cara took her time explaining all that had happened since she and Graumag had left him on the mountainside. When she was finished, the gryphon shook his wings as if he had felt a chill and said, "Cara, strangeness seems to follow you around like a lovesick boy. Who is this Elihu? What is his game? Where does he fit into all this?"

"I have no idea. Nor do I have much idea what I should do next, except try to rejoin the unicorns."

"That will not be a safe place for you."

"No place is safe for me now! But at least that will be the *right* place. I am part of the unicorns, Medafil. I must stand with them in their time of danger."

The gryphon regarded her seriously. Finally, in tones more gentle than usual, he said, "Grim-bobble it, you may be dressed as a unicorn, but you are still just a child. You do not need to face this danger, Cara. I do know places where you can hide until this is over."

"If I hide, what would be left for me if the Hunters win? My people slain, I would be the last of my kind. And even then Beloved will hunt me. I cannot hide forever."

She took a breath, then uttered the words she had not been willing to speak to anyone for some time now, not even to herself, for fear the truth of them would freeze her in her tracks and prevent her from doing what she must. "Medafil, I'm terrified. But being young didn't save me from being pulled into this, and it doesn't excuse me from doing my part now." She hesitated, then added sadly, "The hard thing is, I don't even know what my part *is*. I just know that I am woven into this in ways I cannot understand."

The gryphon sighed. "It is no small burden to be a child of destiny, Cara. Well, what do you wish to do now?"

"Besides hide?" she asked with a laugh. "I must get back to the unicorns. Except even that has gotten complicated, because I thought they were at Autumngrove. But now I sense that they are moving."

Medafil frowned. "I hope they are not fleeing in panic."

"I don't think they would do that. My grandmother is not the kind to panic. Nor is Moonheart, for that matter."

"Sudden death can change things. You know I love your grandmother, Cara, but dank-fribble it, she is not ready for this. Nor are the unicorns. They've had this world as a haven so long that they are not hardened to the kind of challenge facing them now. I fear for them, each and every one."

The words, unusually serious for the gryphon, made Cara nervous.

"You said you can sense them," continued Medafil. "In which direction?"

When Cara pointed with her horn, Medafil said, "Had I not lost you, I would have been heading back to Autumngrove. But I hardly dared return to Amalia Flickerfoot with the news that I had misplaced her grand-daughter. So I have been searching for you all this time. I will fly in that direction now and see what I can learn. Will you wait here until I return?"

"Are you going to tell them what has happened to me?"

"Do you want me to hide it from them? And if so, how am I to explain why I have spoken with you, but returned without you?"

Cara thought about that for a moment. Because of the way she and her grandmother had lived, she had a tendency toward secrecy, toward keeping things to herself. But in truth, she could see no reason to hide this from her grandmother.

"No, you can tell them," she said, feeling oddly uneasy even as she made the decision. "As to waiting here, I would prefer to continue moving toward them. In truth, I can still use some practice in this new body. I wouldn't want to be too awkward when I join my kin."

"Beware of vanity!" said Medafil in what Cara hoped were joking tones.

"I promise," she said.

Medafil stretched his head forward, and she longed to stroke his feathered neck as she would have in the past. Except, of course, she had no hands. His voice low and urgent, he said, "Listen, unicorn girl. There is danger all about and I am uneasy at leaving you. Even so, I think it best for now. I wish I could carry you, but that is not possible given your new form. So here is my advice: You have the gift of tongues. If the Hunters catch you, tell them at once who you are. Otherwise, they will slay you without a second thought."

"But if I do that they will take me to Beloved. Avoiding that was the whole point of turning into a unicorn to begin with."

"Bib-dribble it, if they keep you alive and take you to Beloved, you have hope! If they slay you, all is finished."

Remembering how her grandmother always said that if you were alive you had a chance, Cara swallowed hard and whispered, "Yes, I understand."

"Good." The gryphon turned, ran across the meadow, then leaped and stretched his wings. A few minutes later he was out of sight.

As Cara watched him go she heard a rustling in the grass. Glancing to her side, she cried, "Squijum! I'm glad you're back."

"Good Squijum always come back," he crooned, hugging his fluffy tail.

"Yes," she replied. "Good Squijum always come back."

"Keep moving now?" he asked, leaping to her shoulder.

"Yes, keep moving," she said as he settled into his favorite perch.

She began trotting across the meadow, moving in the same direction Medafil had flown: toward her grandmother, toward the unicorns, who were themselves moving, she sensed, toward the place where the Hunt must finally end, whatever that end might be.

CHAPTER
LX

SKY TALK

Medafil had been flying in the direction Cara pointed him for about an hour when he saw a something moving through the air in his direction. "Prat-spakkle it," he muttered to himself. "Can't be alone even in the sky!"

Preparing himself to take evasive action if necessary, the gryphon continued on his way.

It wasn't much longer before his sharp eyes identified the approaching figure as that of a dragon. Within another few minutes he saw that it was, as he had hoped, Graumag. "And thank the poot-doodled powers it's not Ebillan," he murmured.

The two beasts continued toward each other. When they were within hailing distance Graumag called, "Greetings, Air Brother!"

"Greetings, Sky Sister!" replied Medafil. "It is good to see you again." He actually meant this, mostly.

"And good to see you. However the truth is I would be

even happier to see young Cara. I was separated from her and have not been able to find her."

"I have found her," replied Medafil proudly. "In fact, I am on the way to tell her grandmother that she is well."

The gryphon wondered, briefly, if he should inform the dragon of Cara's transformation, but decided that since she had not authorized him to tell anyone but her grandmother he would not mention it.

"I have but recently come from the Queen," replied Graumag. "The Gathered Glory is on the move."

"I have been told that this is so," replied Medafil.

Having come close enough for easy conversation, the dragon and the gryphon began to circle each other, as neither was built to hover.

"Who told you this?" asked Graumag.

The gryphon cursed himself for being a loose-beaked fool. Finally he said, vaguely, "I met a unicorn."

He was flapping hard to keep up with Graumag.

"And did this unicorn say where they were going?" asked Graumag.

"It did not."

"They are heading for the Axis Mundi. I am flying now to deliver a challenge to Beloved to meet the unicorns for a final battle."

Medafil was so startled he momentarily forgot to flap. "Gaaaah!" he cried, dropping several yards. "You can't be serious."

"Serious as death," replied Graumag. "Which seems to me is the inevitable outcome, though how many deaths, and whose, it is hard to say."

For a time Medafil flew in silence alongside the dragon. At last he said, "I think that rather than going to the unicorns, I should return to Cara to tell her which direction they are moving. I know she wants to join them."

"I consider that foolishness on her part, but I would guess that you are correct," replied the dragon.

"Good luck in your mission, Sky Sister."

"Give my greetings to Cara, Air Brother."

"I will," promised the gryphon.

And with that, the two great creatures parted, Graumag to carry her message to Beloved, Medafil reversing course to return to Cara.

CHAPTER
LXI

THE CHRONICLE KEEPER

Aside from the horrifying tremors that began on Blood Moon night and had been slowly escalating ever since, Grimwold had had an uneventful journey from the Valley of the Centaurs back to his underground quarters at the great library known as the Unicorn Chronicles. After the arduous trip, the old dwarf took great pleasure in being once more in the caves that he called home and ran his fingers along the wood-paneled walls, as if savoring the very feel of them.

He did not rest long, though. Within a few hours of his return he went to the Story Room, where he took out paper, ink, and quill. He had an enormous amount to record, considering all that had happened during their travels to the valley. "Crusty inkwells!" he muttered to himself, using one of his favorite expletives. "I hate it when I end up being part of the story!" He much preferred simply waiting in his caves for the unicorns to come to him with tales of their adventures.

He was in his second day of writing, and deeply absorbed in recording the tale the Chiron had told about the birth of the Whisperer, when a bell rang, informing him that the Queen wished to speak with him.

"Drat," he muttered. "Can't a fellow ever be left alone to do his work?"

But a summons from the Queen was not something to be ignored, especially since, as Chronicle Keeper, he was a pledged servant and also received a nice living. So he left his work and made his way to the place in his complex of caves where the scrying pool was always ready to reveal the Queen's messages.

Unlike many of the caves in his home, this one had been left in its natural form. Three small cauldrons, each suspended from a tripod, lit the cave with a soft orange glow. Centered amidst the tripods was a stone basin. Usually the water it held was dark and cold looking, but now, with a message coming in, it, too, emitted a soft glow.

After the surprises and shocks of his recent journey, Grimwold did not think he could be startled by whatever this message might be. Yet when he went to the edge of the basin and saw that the image in the water was not a messenger, but Amalia Flickerfoot herself, he felt a shiver of apprehension.

Of course, it was a bit of a surprise simply to see Amalia in her true form, since he had known her for so long as Ivy Morris. She was heartbreakingly beautiful. The unicorns all were, of course, though Grimwold would never tell them that. But Amalia was more so than most, a quiet beauty made more real and solid by the strange life she had led.

"Greetings, old friend," she said.

"Greetings, My Queen."

"I must be brief. In two days time, the Gathered Glory will meet Beloved for a final battle at the field northeast of the Axis Mundi. As you are the Keeper of the Chronicles, it would be good if you could be there to observe, whether it be our downfall or the beginning of our true freedom." She turned her head slightly and — was he imagining it? — winked at him before adding, "By the way, you might want to bring some friends."

He stared at her in astonishment. Before he could think of any reasonable response, she said, "That's all for now." At once the pool rippled and her image disappeared.

Grimwold blinked. What in the world was she thinking of? What did she mean by "You might want to bring some friends"? He didn't even have any friends. And had she really winked at him?

Then he remembered that the last time he had tried to communicate with the Queen of the unicorns through this pool — it had been the old Queen, Arabella Skydancer — the message had been intercepted by Beloved. Did Amalia know about that? Was she tipping her hand, or playing some mysterious game of her own?

Whatever the answer, Grimwold's duty was now clear. The coming battle was the most significant thing to happen in Luster since he became Chronicle Keeper, and it was important for him to be there.

Returning to his living quarters, the old dwarf packed ink, paper, and quills, as well as a couple of spare robes, some waybread, and a packet of dried mushrooms. He had nearly finished this task when he suddenly stopped working and stood bolt upright.

"Oh, no," he said. "No, she wouldn't ask me to do *that*."

But now that the idea had come to him, he knew he was right and who the "friends" the Queen had been referring to must be.

Shaking his head in disgust, he got out a stack of maps and studied them until he was confident he had spotted the most likely location to connect with the Queen's "friends." Happily, it was not too far out of his way. Shouldering his pack, he set off.

He would have preferred to travel underground, but given the worsening tremors that no longer seemed safe. Before he closed the door to his subterranean realm, he took one last, loving look back. "I hope you'll still be here when I return," he whispered to his home. Then, feeling foolishly sentimental, he closed the door and set out on the Queen's mission.

CHAPTER
LXII

NEWS FROM THE QUEEN

Cara and the Squijum were crossing a wide grassland when they heard a familiar squawk from above. A moment later Medafil glided down in front of them.

"Back already?" asked Cara.

The gryphon ruffled his feathers. "Well, I like that! No 'Glad to see you, Medafil.' No 'My, you performed your mission with amazing speed, Medafil.' Just, 'What are you doing back already?' Hmmph. If I wanted to be insulted I could have stayed at home with the other gryphons."

He sniffed and turned away.

"Don't sulk," said Cara. "I didn't mean it that way! I was just pleasantly surprised you made it back so quickly." She hesitated, then asked, "Did you tell my grandmother of my transformation?"

"Gaaah! Um, no. I didn't actually make it all the way to the unicorns. I came upon Graumag along the way. She told me that your grandmother has issued a challenge to Beloved, asking for a single great battle. According to Graumag,

Amalia says this is no longer a Hunt, it's a war. I thought it best to bring you this information as quickly as possible."

"That was probably a good idea," agreed Cara, actually feeling a bit of relief that her secret had not been delivered.

"I figured you should know where the Gathered Glory is headed, since if you want to connect with them sooner you should alter your path."

Cara tilted her head, puzzled. "What do you mean?"

"If you keep following your sense of where they are at any given moment you'll reach them eventually, but do it by making a long curve. Turn to the southeast. You'll shorten your route a good deal by cutting directly toward the place they are heading."

"But how will I know I'm going in the right direction? Right now I'm following my sense of where they are. It's the only guide I have. I wouldn't know how to find my way to the center on my own. It's not as if I have a compass."

"Dimblethum's cave near big, tree," said the Squijum. "Squijum know where. Squijum find way."

"Well, it's good to know that drak-splattled little beast is good for something," said Medafil. He paused, then said softly, "Are you all right, Cara?"

"As well as can be expected." She thought for a moment, then said, "What are you going to do now, Medafil?"

"I plan to rejoin your grandmother. You don't think I would let the Wanderer go into this without me at her side, do you?"

"Of course not! I know you are a good and faithful friend."

Medafil ruffled his feathers. "I should say so. But I also thought it might be well for me to travel with you. I can't fly you now, of course. But it doesn't feel right to leave you alone. So we can walk together, if that's all right with you. It will take a bit longer, but I'll still end up in the same place."

Cara had been hoping for this, but had feared to ask it. "Thank you," she said. "Your company would be most welcome."

"Move, move!" cried the Squijum. "Let's move, unicorn girl!"

Cara laughed. "You're right. Except I don't know the way so you'll have to be the guide now."

"This way!" he cried, leaping down and scampering ahead of her. "This way to Dimblethum's cave!"

Cara wondered, with both hope and some apprehension, if there were any chance the Dimblethum might be there.

Cara found it difficult to follow Medafil's advice to not move directly toward the unicorns, for her sense of them had become overpowering, and her heart longed to join them. Even so, she forced herself to heed the gryphon's words, and as the afternoon wore on she could tell that the glory's position was indeed shifting, just as the gryphon had said would happen. After that, she was glad to let the Squijum guide their path.

For most of the day, the sun was warm above them, the air so still it was as if the world was holding its breath, waiting for something. Twice more the ground shook beneath them, nearly knocking Cara off her feet. The third tremor, early in the evening, did send her sprawling. Medafil took to the air. The Squijum, who had been clinging to her mane, shrieked, "Hotcha silly world! *Hold still!*"

"Frik-doobled earthquakes," muttered the gryphon, once the ground had settled and he had landed again.

An hour or so later Cara sensed something new, something that called to her with an amazing power. It took her a moment to realize that it was a girl, a human girl such as she had been just a short time ago. She found she had to steel her heart against that call. Resisting the urge to seek the girl took more effort than she would have guessed. No wonder the unicorns were so vulnerable to the traps the Hunters placed for them!

Another time Cara thought she saw the Dimblethum in the distance. But when she called out, the shaggy form turned and ran. She was hurt at first, but then remembered that, other than Lightfoot, the Dimblethum really did not care for unicorns. Besides, maybe it hadn't been him. Who knew what other creatures prowled the wilds of Luster?

*   *   *

"Hotcha gotcha not far now!" cried the Squijum, who had been riding on Cara's neck without taking a break to hunt for food for some hours. Cara was still astonished at how much territory she had been able to cover.

Not that I know how many miles it actually was, she thought. *But I could never have traveled so long without stopping when I was human.*

It had taken her a while to trust the Squijum to be her guide. Still, she was glad to have him. The forest was so vast and unmarked that it would have been easy to fall into raw panic had she not had the Squijum and the gryphon traveling with her. Silly as they might sometimes seem, without their company the overwhelming wilderness would have been crushing to her.

They had just crossed a stream, its water clear and sparkling, when the Squijum gripped her mane with sudden tightness. Before she could complain, he hissed, "Shhhhh, unicorn girl! *Shhhhh!*"

It was so unusual for the Squijum to be the one to caution silence that Cara felt a quick shiver of fright. "What is it?" she whispered.

"Listen!" he replied in the softest voice she had ever heard him use.

CHAPTER
LXIII

TALKING TO THE ENEMY

Graumag loved to fly. It was her greatest joy in a life that had otherwise been marked by loss and tragedy. As she soared through the skies above Luster she could not help but think how intensely she cared for this world that had accepted her when she was most in need of succor. Gazing down at its rolling hills and silvery-blue forests, its clear lakes and towering mountains, the thought of losing it pierced her with a sorrow more profound than she could have imagined.

To her surprise, she found herself weeping — fiery tears that would have scorched the grass had they not had time to cool in their long fall to the ground. She had a fearful sense that the unicorns had not yet grasped how great was their peril, didn't yet realize that even if they defeated Beloved and her troops, the whole of Luster was tottering at the edge of doom.

And how could they, really? That the very world they had lived in for these many centuries might actually fall apart was almost beyond imagination.

Immersed in these thoughts, Graumag had lost track of how long she had been flying when she spotted the Axis Mundi. Though she had seen the great tree many times, its gargantuan size never ceased to astonish her. It reared above the forest that grew beyond its surrounding meadow, tall though those trees were, like a giant among pygmies.

With her predator's eyes, sharper by far than a mere hawk's, it was not hard to spot Beloved's encampment, which consisted of a small village of tents, as well as two wooden watchtowers. It lay a good half mile from the Axis Mundi — Graumag still had a keen feel for distance from her centuries on Earth, where such measurements mattered more than they did here in Luster. Another three meadows of equal size lay the same distance from the tree. Equally spaced, they formed the corners of a large square.

As Graumag drew closer to Beloved's encampment, she found herself hoping, again, that Hunters did not feel about dragons as they did about unicorns. Her earlier battle with that group on the mountain had been all about trying to hold them off while Cara and Elihu escaped. She didn't know whether they would have fought her so fiercely otherwise.

She felt her vulnerability acutely. Though she was well armored, it would not be impossible for an arrow that found the right spot in her throat to do her in. Her wings, too, were at risk; while the leathery membranes that stretched between the bone structure did not feel much pain, a sufficient number of arrows tearing through them could bring her plummeting down.

She reviewed the details of the challenge Amalia had requested her to deliver. As she did, she wondered if the Queen had really understood the risk she was asking her friend to undertake. But then, under the circumstances, perhaps all risks were considered reasonable.

Graumag noticed that some of the men had now spotted her. Standing in the open, they had gathered in a knot and were gazing up. She saw no weapons yet, but she would have to be careful.

Men continued to join the group, many of the newcomers clutching bows or spears. Then, from a brightly colored tent much larger than the others that filled the camp, there emerged a woman who could only be Beloved. Knowing that this was the person who had brought such trouble on Luster, Graumag felt an urge to swoop down and simply eat the woman. Except the dragon was fairly certain she would be dead before she could get anywhere near Beloved.

When Graumag had accepted Amalia's request to deliver this challenge, she hadn't fully considered how tricky the process might be. She was still trying to figure out the best way to open negotiations when Beloved stepped to the front of the group and cupped her hands to her mouth. Graumag gazed down in surprise. Did the silly woman really think she could be heard from that far away? But a moment later, and much to the dragon's surprise, Beloved spoke so clearly it was as if she were standing right next to her ear.

"Dragon! Why have you come to our encampment?"

"How are you able to speak to me?" replied Graumag. "And can you hear me now?"

"Don't be foolish! Of course I can hear you. And the how is of no importance. It's a minor magic, that's all. The question stands: Why have you come here?"

"I bring a message from the unicorns. May I land in safety to deliver it?"

"I see no reason why you should not repeat it from exactly where you are."

Having expected all this time to have a parley on the ground, Graumag was startled to realize there was, indeed, no reason not to continue speaking exactly as they were. "All right, here is the message: Amalia Flickerfoot, Queen of the Unicorns, asks if you and your Hunters have the courage to meet the unicorns on field of battle, where all shall finally be decided."

"When and where?"

"Two days hence, at noon, in the great meadow northeast of the tree where you entered."

"Tell the Queen that if she is fool enough to face us directly, we welcome the challenge."

That was all Graumag needed to hear. "I will deliver the message," she said. Then she banked in a graceful arc and headed back toward the Gathered Glory.

CHAPTER
LXIV

SILVERHOOF

Cara held still as stone, then slowly swiveled her ears — another trick that had not been possible in her human form. After a moment she heard it, too: a man, singing. She wondered, briefly, whether the Squijum's ears were even more sensitive than hers, or if she simply hadn't learned to listen well enough yet.

"I hear it, too," murmured Medafil.

For the next several minutes, unicorn, gryphon, and Squijum remained silent and waiting, so still they might have been carved from stone. Soon it became obvious that the singer was moving in their direction. Was he a Hunter? Cara hesitated, uncertain whether to flee, but in doing so possibly draw attention to herself, or to hold still, hoping that the path of whoever she was hearing would not bring him close enough to spot them.

As the voice drew nearer, she realized it was one of uncommon beauty. She realized, too, that the haunting words of the man's song were unlike anything that would come from a Hunter:

> *Beautiful creatures of fire and light,*
> *Shimmer like moonbeams cascading through night,*
> *Crafted from starshine, fire, and air,*
> *The Hunt has awoken, beware, friends, beware!*

Cara felt a strong desire to move toward the singer, so she could see the owner of this beautiful voice.

Don't be ridiculous! she chided herself. *Just because a man can sing like an angel doesn't mean he's not also ready to drive a spear through your heart.*

But in another moment she recognized the voice and relaxed a bit. It was Elihu! With a sigh of relief, she started toward the singer.

"What are you doing?" whispered Medafil, clearly alarmed.

"It's all right," she said. "I know him."

She moved silently, not out of fear, but simply because she was a unicorn and silence came naturally to her. Soon enough she saw the flash of the man's golden hair through the leaves. A little closer and she could see that he was now fully dressed. A little closer and, despite her silence, he sensed her presence and turned.

Cara gasped. The singer was not Elihu after all, though

he looked enough like him to be his brother. She stood, trembling, trying to decide whether to run.

The man lifted his hands and moved them away from his body. When Cara continued to tremble, he unstrapped the scabbard at his waist and let his sword fall to the ground. In a voice so much like Elihu's that it both confused and comforted her, he said softly, "It's all right, unicorn, I won't hurt you. Nor you, gryphon," he added, nodding toward Medafil who stood slightly behind her.

"Turn around," she said. "I want to make sure you don't have any weapons at your back."

He looked startled to hear her speak, but did as she asked, still holding his hands out at his sides. When he had gone full circle he asked gently, "Satisfied?"

"Who are you?" she replied, not really answering his question.

"I am called Fallon."

"And what are you doing in Luster?" demanded Medafil.

Fallon did not seem surprised to hear the gryphon speak, causing Cara to wonder how much experience he might have had with legendary beasts. Without hesitation, he said, "I seek a friend. His name is Elihu."

Now Cara did relax a bit. "I've met Elihu."

"Do you know where he is now?"

The eagerness in the man's eyes was so like a hunger it frightened her.

"It was early yesterday," she stammered. "He . . . he did me a favor. Then he sort of . . . disappeared."

Fallon's disappointment showed only in his eyes. "Do you mean he vanished?" he asked, as if he considered fading into thin air a perfectly likely action.

Cara shook her head. "No. While I . . . slept, he slipped away. Or something. I don't know why. He was nearby when I went to sleep, but gone when I awoke."

Fallon rubbed his hands over his face in a weary gesture. "What was the favor he did you?"

"I'd rather not say."

"As you wish." He looked at her more closely. "I didn't expect you to be able to speak to me. At least, not without first establishing some sort of connection."

Cara cursed herself for behaving in a way so clearly unlike a unicorn. To recover, she asked quickly, challengingly, "How do you know about that?"

"You're not the first unicorn I've met."

Trying to keep her voice from trembling, hoping against hope, reminding herself that there were hundreds and hundreds of unicorns, Cara said, "What was this other unicorn's name?"

"He called himself Lightfoot."

A sob of relief burst from her throat.

"I take it you know him," said Fallon.

"He's . . . a dear friend. The last time I saw him he was in great danger. I can't tell you how happy I am to learn that he survived. Do you know where he is now?"

"I left him the day before yesterday." The man took a breath, as if he were about to say more, then stopped.

At first Cara was annoyed. Then she remembered that she, too, was not about to tell all she knew to someone she had just met. She couldn't just go galloping off in search of Lightfoot right now, anyway. And just knowing he was alive lifted her heart, as if she had suddenly shed some dark and horrible weight she had been carrying ever since that horrible last moment when she had seen him being swarmed by delvers. "You still haven't explained why you can speak to me in human tongue," said the man.

"It's a gift from a dragon."

"Well, *that's interesting*," he murmured, speaking as much to himself as to her. He straightened his shoulders, and she realized again how amazingly tall he was. "Look . . . uh, you didn't tell me your name yet. Can you do that? I mean, I understand about magic and names, so I'm not asking for your truest name. But what do other unicorns call you?"

The question brought the reality of her situation back to her. She didn't have a unicorn name yet! Before she could answer — and before her pause became too suspicious — Medafil said, "Silverhoof. They call her Silverhoof."

She breathed an inward sigh of relief. She would have to remember to thank him for that.

"All right, Silverhoof"— she could tell by Fallon's voice that he knew this wasn't really her name — "it seems likely to me that we're on the same side of things here. So just in case, let me give you some information. Are you aware that a woman named Beloved has opened a door from Earth into this world?"

"Yes, I know."

"And are you aware that she has brought a small army of men called Hunters with her and that their goal is to kill the unicorns, every last one of them?"

Cara nodded.

"All right, I just wanted to be sure you knew. Now, having freely given you that information, may I ask a question?"

"You can ask," she said cautiously.

"Good. I know about gryphons. But what in the name of all the stars above is that thing clinging to your neck?"

Cara laughed. "He's called the Squijum."

From behind she heard, "Good Squijum! Squijum hotcha good critter!"

A look of surprise passed over Fallon's face, but vanished almost as quickly as it had appeared. Cara decided it must have been caused by hearing the Squijum talk. Of course, the man couldn't have understood the little creature.

Or could he?

She looked at him with new puzzlement.

"Another question," he said, his voice intent and serious. "One far closer to my heart. You say you met Elihu and he slipped away. Do you have even the slightest idea where he might have gone?"

Again, she was startled at the note of desperation in the big man's voice and sorry that she had to shake her head no.

Fallon sighed. "Can you at least tell me where this happened?"

"We were on the slopes of Dark Mountain. I can't tell

you the exact direction, because I've been —" Again she hesitated, not wanting to reveal that she had been following her sense of the unicorns. She wasn't ready to trust him that much yet.

"You've been what?"

She shook her head and said simply, "I haven't been moving in a straight line."

"Where are you going now?"

Medafil made a warning sound, and she paused before answering. She wanted to trust the man, indeed *felt* that she could trust him. But she knew far too much about betrayal to do that easily. She was surprised to realize she was also resisting because he was so beautiful that he seemed too easy to trust, as if his beauty itself was a kind of trap.

He smiled into her silence. "Why should you tell me that, eh? Is that what you're wondering? No reason, and I'm sorry I asked." He paused, then said, "If I tell you something about what I'm up to myself perhaps you'll feel more comfortable. Unless you're in a terrible hurry?"

"We do need to keep traveling."

"May I walk with you? I don't have a specific direction, and you're the closest thing to a clue to Elihu's whereabouts that I have."

"Frim-dangle it," muttered Medafil, which Cara knew meant that the gryphon disapproved. Even so, she once again found herself wanting to trust this man. She recognized that the feeling was a weird tangle of wanting human company, of welcoming another guardian as they traveled through this wilderness, and also of desire, since her girl's heart, trapped in her unicorn body, was longing toward Fallon's beauty.

Stop it, she told herself fiercely. *Don't feel, think!*

But in the end, it was feelings that guided her, since she had nothing else to go on.

"Yes," she said softly. "Please walk with me."

"I'm going to pick up my sword. Are you all right with that?"

Ignoring Medafil's soft growl, she said, "You're not a Hunter. You wouldn't have waited this long to try to kill me if you were."

He smiled ruefully and retrieved his sword. As he was buckling it on, the ground rippled beneath them.

"Yikes!" cried the Squijum, clutching Cara's mane. She staggered, but didn't fall. She saw Fallon do the same.

When the quake had passed, he said grimly, "We don't have much time."

"Before what?"

He studied her for a long moment, as if somehow testing her. Finally he said, "Before this world falls apart."

Cara nodded, unhappy to have this confirmation of Graumag's dire prediction. But she was also surprised that this stranger would understand the peril Luster was in. "Why do you believe that?" she asked.

"Let's walk. While we travel, I will tell you a story. Part of it will be what I know. Part of it will be guesswork. But all of it, I promise, will come straight from my heart."

CHAPTER
LXV

FOUND, YET STILL LOST

Rocky clung to the wall of the crevice while the delver horde passed overhead, each of them crying out as he or she made the leap. He was terrified that they would spot him and even more terrified that the world might shift again before he could climb out, crushing him between the walls. So he pressed himself against the stone, trying to make himself invisible while he prayed to the Great One that the delvers would not look down and that the world would hold its peace.

It had been agonizing not to be able to help Ian, but against those overwhelming numbers there was nothing he could have done. And given his current status with Gnurflax, the only result of trying would have been his own capture, which would not do any of them any good. Right now the main thing was that he try to find Namza.

He waited until the sound of the horde had passed, then climbed the remaining distance, about twice his own height, back to the highway. He gazed in the direction they had carried Ian, unable to forget the heartrending look on the man's face as his bearers had leaped across the crevice with him bound to that pole. Rocky hoped his own cove would hear the horde coming in time to get off the highway and avoid capture. He felt a flash of guilt for having called them from their coves, knowing they would *all* be marked as deserters now.

He glanced up. The sky was turning gray with the coming dawn. He wondered if the horde would continue to travel once the sun had risen or if they would seek shelter against the wretched light.

Though it was troubling to see what appeared to be the entire population of Delvharken out in the open, it was not hard to guess why they had swarmed to the surface: Given the near-constant shaking of the world, their underground home, so solid for so long, must have suddenly seemed unsafe. But where were they heading? Did they have a plan, or was it mindless flight?

With a sigh, Rocky turned and continued his own journey, back to the world his people had just fled.

Many paths led from the surface world to Delvharken. Most were small tunnels, easily hidden and accessible only to delvers. The main entrance was different. It was sealed with a pair of stone doors, crafted so carefully as to be all but invisible to an unpracticed eye. Yet to one who knew their secret, they opened easily to reveal a beautifully carved tunnel, broad enough for four large humans to walk abreast.

As Rocky approached he felt a pang. Knowing the secret to opening the doors was no longer necessary. They gaped wide, half torn from their frames. He passed through them boldly, expecting no challenge and finding none. What he *did* want to find was a sense of his old teacher.

He followed the tunnel downward, his heart aching as he climbed over the rubble of collapsed ceilings and shattered walls, astonished at the destruction of what he had thought indestructible.

Finally he came to the great chamber of the throne room. Here, too, the doors had been left wide open. He entered, chilled to see the vast space empty, the floor littered with the shards of fallen stalactites. Among these shards lay the bodies of delvers who had been killed by the falling stone.

Standing still, Rocky closed his eyes and opened his heart, hoping to catch a sense of his old teacher.

Nothing.

Namza, where are you? he thought desperately.

No answer.

He went to the Stone Throne. Feeling more rebellious than ever, he climbed into the raised seat and looked out on the empty hall, imagining it filled with delvers.

Stop! he ordered himself, shaking his head. *Concentrate!*

Closing his eyes once more, he tried to still all thoughts, all fears. Another tremor shook the hall, and he could hear the crash of a falling stalactite as it shattered on the cavern floor. When the disturbance was over, he took several calming breaths, as Namza had taught him, and tried to regain his focus.

After a time Rocky had cleared everything from his mind but thoughts of his old teacher — memories of how Namza had chosen him; memories of the wizard's aged face and bent body; memories of his lessons, his occasional flashes of anger, but also of his unexpected gentleness; memories of how he had slowly, cautiously begun to speak of his concerns about the King and his sanity, and of how the delvers might someday be different, more peaceful of heart.

And as Rocky thought these things slowly — so slowly he had no idea when it had actually begun — the sense of Namza began to creep into his brain. It was slight, and odd, as if something had changed. Yet it was definitely real.

Rising from the throne, scarcely breathing lest he lose the connection, Rocky descended to the cavern floor. He circled behind the throne and entered a tunnel he had never known about.

As he walked, his sense of Namza began to grow stronger, even though still oddly muffled. That sense drew him on into the king's quarters. This was forbidden territory for a mere delver such as himself, but he was long past caring about such things. The thread of connection he was following led him through the chamber, down a narrow tunnel. The connection grew stronger with each step. Yet he still felt that troubling sense of it being muted by some barrier.

And then something even more troubling: His sense of Namza's presence began to diminish, as if he had somehow passed his teacher. But how could that be? Even if Namza were unconscious, he would still have seen him.

Rocky turned and walked back in the other direction. His sense of Namza grew stronger and then, again, began to diminish.

Frustrated, he turned back once more.

And then he spotted it: a shelf of stone at the base of the tunnel wall, just outside the opening to a chamber. With a cry of horror he raced to the stone and flung himself against it.

"Teacher!" he cried. "Teacher, it is I, your student! Oh, can you hear me? Can you feel me? I need you. Delvharken needs you. Doom is falling, and I don't know what to do!"

From the stone to which he clung came no answer.

But the stone surrounding them shivered once more, opening new cracks in the tunnel walls, as if to mock his pleas for help.

CHAPTER
LXVI

"A WORLD OF HIS OWN"

Though Cara was eager for Fallon to speak, she did not press him. So the four of them — she, Fallon, Medafil, and the Squijum — walked for two or three miles before he finally said, "This story begins several thousand of what you call years ago, back when Elihu and I were fairly young."

Before coming to Luster, Cara would have found such a statement absurd. Now she managed to take it in stride, saying only, "That's an awfully long time."

"There are levels of existence," the big man continued. "Levels of power. Elihu and I were of the Great Powers, and lived in a place that you might call Paradise. But even there, things are much as they are among humans."

"What do you mean?"

Fallon sighed. "I mean that even in that realm pride, anger, jealousy, desire, and ambition all exist. A little more controlled, perhaps, a little more refined. But ever ready to erupt ... and to *dis*rupt, for these things are always disruptive when they arise, Silverhoof. Fortunately, as in the human world, there is love to temper matters.

"Now, Elihu and I were alike in many ways, especially in that we were both possessed of a powerful desire to create. However, his urge in that regard far surpassed anything I felt. The problem for Elihu was that there are limits on what is allowed to beings of our level. He, alas, refused to recognize those limits and insisted on experimenting, playing, pushing forward with the project that engaged his deepest passion."

Fallon lapsed into silence. They walked on for a time, the only sound that of the silvery-blue leaves rustling about their feet. When Cara could stand it no longer she asked, "What was this project?"

Fallon shook his head, causing his burnished hair to shimmer over his shoulders almost like a unicorn's mane. "He wanted to make a world of his own."

Medafil squawked. Cara stopped cold, causing the Squijum to chitter at her in vexation. *"What?"*

"Elihu wanted to make a world." Seeing her reaction, he added quickly, "Oh, that desire is hardly unheard of. But to actually do so is a privilege reserved to powers of a level far greater than mine and Elihu's. It is, in a word, forbidden. This chafed at Elihu, who did not believe in such limitations — who, in fact, considered them a kind of tyranny. When he urged me to join him in his experiments, I refused — out of wisdom, I claimed, though I sometimes wonder if it was simply out of fear.

"Anyway, one day Elihu came to me and said, *'Alahim'* —"

"Alahim?" asked Cara. Before Fallon could respond she realized that though the word was not of any language known on either Earth or Luster, her gift of tongues had supplied the meaning, anyway. "Ah, it's a special kind of friend, right?"

Fallon smiled. "Your ability with language is indeed impressive, Silverhoof. 'Heart-brother' might be the closest translation. It is the greatest kind of friendship, a bond of love and affection that requires no explanation, no promises, no forgiveness, though those things may all be freely given and often are. Having an *alahim* is like having another self, even if your goals and dreams are not all the same. And Elihu's dreams were certainly not the same as mine. So the pride in his voice when he said *'Alahim,* I want you to come see what I have done,' made me nervous."

"Why?"

Fallon sighed. "I suspected — correctly — that he had succeeded in doing that which he should not."

Medafil muttered something to himself. Cara shook her head. The idea was too bizarre to settle in easily. "He really made a world?" she asked at last.

Fallon considered, then said, "Perhaps I should say that he had created the *beginnings* of a world. He led me to a place of emptiness. Floating within it was something like an island. Rising from the center of that 'island' was a small tree, which I knew at once must be an Axis Mundi.

" 'Where did you get the seed?' I asked.

" 'I stole it,' he replied without a shred of remorse.

" 'And the blood to quicken it?'

" 'My own.' "

Fallon shuddered at the memory. "It is hard to explain to you the nature of this crime, Silverhoof," he said grimly. "I will only tell you that my heart grew cold with fear at what would happen should it be discovered. Elihu was too enraptured with what he had done to share my dread. 'It is not much now,' he said. 'But it will grow, *alahim*. As the tree's roots spread, my world will spread with it, growing bigger and bigger, until it is a true world all its own. *My world!*'

"I stared at him in horror. '*Alahim*,' I whispered, 'the Higher Powers will surely punish you for this.'

" 'Not if they don't find out,' he replied, knowing that he had bound me to secrecy.

"I was furious, for he had put me in an impossible situation. He knew I would not breathe a word of his secret; no *alahim* would do that. But he also knew that if what he had done was discovered — and, further, if it was discovered that I had known and had said nothing — there would be severe punishment for both of us."

"Was it discovered?" asked Medafil.

"Naturally."

"And what was the punishment?" asked Cara.

"The first punishment was to separate us. This was like

tearing a heart in two, for *alahim* are meant to be together. What made this worse — far worse — was that *I* had already separated us, for I had not spoken to Elihu from the day he showed me what he had done."

Fallon sighed again, then said, "We both knew my wrath would cool in time and we would be together again. What we did not know was that Elihu's rebellious act would be discovered *before* we could reaffirm our bond — which meant our last words to each other were spoken in anger, not love. Before we could heal the wound, I was sent to live on a lower plane of existence."

After a long silence, Cara asked, "What do you mean?"

Fallon smiled ruefully. "I was plucked from Paradise and exiled to Earth."

Deciding she didn't want to think about the idea of Earth being a "lower plane of existence," Cara said, "And what did they do to Elihu?"

"Of that I am not certain. In fact, that was part of our punishment — that neither of us would know what had been done to the other.

"Now, though no word was spoken by my judges, I knew that the only way for me to return to Paradise would be to do enough good in the world to *earn* my way back. I have spent millennia trying to do exactly that. But at the same time I have been undercutting myself. For even as I sought to do good, I sought something else."

"Elihu," whispered Cara.

"Of course. He is the other half of my heart, and I will not be complete until I find him again."

Cara, thinking of her grandmother's Earth friends Kevin and Phil, could not help asking, "Was he your . . . were you two . . ."

Fallon laughed, a kind and comforting sound. "Were we a couple? No. To be *alahim* is something different. Not better or worse, simply . . . different."

Though Cara was fairly certain she knew the answer to her next question, she wanted to hear Fallon actually speak it out loud. So she asked, "If you were exiled to Earth, how is it that you are here in Luster?"

The big man smiled and moved his arm in a sweeping gesture, indicating everything around them. "I am here because *this* is the world Elihu created all those years ago. I had heard whispers of Luster during my millennia on Earth, for I sometimes traveled in strange circles, and I suspected it must be Elihu's world. But I wasn't certain until I actually arrived. Then I knew, instantly, that this was the place he had created, for I can sense him in every part of it, feel his presence in every leaf and every pebble." He paused, and his face grew troubled. "Yet I cannot sense Elihu himself, save but dimly. Where can he be? His world has grown enormously since he first showed it to me, grown beautifully, just as he dreamed. But now it is in mortal danger."

"Why is that?" asked Cara. "I mean, I assume it has to do with Beloved opening her gate, but how could a new gate have caused what is happening now? There were seven gates already, and they didn't have such an effect."

"I suspect those gates were opened with a great deal more care than this one. The kind of magic involved is disruptive by nature, but can be controlled. However, Beloved did not merely do this carelessly. Whether through malice or ignorance I do not know, but the fact is she chose to blast her opening through the exact center of this world."

"Gaaah!" cried Medafil. "She came *through* the Axis Mundi?"

Fallon nodded. "I'm afraid so, friend gryphon. And in doing so, she pierced the living heart of Luster. The results, as we have all been feeling, were catastrophic. I know how these things work, and I am certain that the roots of that tree extend to the very edges of this still-growing world, however large it has become. Now that the tree is in mortal danger, so is the world that is defined and held together by its roots." He paused, then said cautiously, "It is almost too much to imagine Beloved chose that place at random. But if she simply wanted to destroy Luster, why come through with all her men? Merely opening that tunnel would have been sufficient. It's possible she doesn't even realize what she has done. If so, I fear there is some other force at work here, some power of malicious intent."

Cara shivered at these words and thought of the Whisperer, even as another tremor rippled the ground beneath their feet.

"Feel that?" asked Fallon. "It was the roots of the tree, writhing in pain. That pain, that writhing, is the source of the tremors and quakes. They are the spasms of a dying world and, if the tree is not healed soon, Luster will tear itself apart."

"*Can* it be healed?" asked Cara, sick with horror.

Fallon shook his head. "In truth, I do not know. Even if it is possible, it's likely Elihu is the only one who could do it. But where is he? Why would he leave his world at the time of its greatest crisis?"

For this Cara had no answer, of course, and so they traveled for a while in silence. Finally Fallon said, "Do you mind telling me where you are heading?"

Cara paused. Deciding to trust him, she said, "I'm going to the Axis Mundi."

Fallon smiled. "I have just come from there. However, I begin to believe it is the proper place for me to be right now, after all. Do you mind if I journey back with you? It's not very far. We may even be able to connect with my former traveling companions."

"Was Lightfoot one of them?" she asked, nearly unable to contain her joy.

"Yes."

"Who else were you traveling with?"

"A man named Ian Hunter —"

Now she could not contain herself, and a most un-unicorn-like cry broke from her throat.

Fallon looked at her in concern. "Are you all right, Silverhoof? Oh, that was foolish of me! I'm sorry, I should have realized the name of Hunter would have a fearful quality for you. But this man is not an enemy of the unicorns. He came through with *me*, not as part of Beloved's army."

Cara's mind was racing, wild with happiness that her father was back in Luster, desperate to see him again, but also terrified of how — or if — she could tell him what she had done. And looming beyond all that was the greater question of whether he had been successful in his latest hunt, the quest to find her mother.

"Silverhoof?" asked Fallon.

She shook her head again. "I'm fine, just a little startled. I have met the man you were traveling with. I wasn't expecting to see him again so soon."

"Do you know anything of his story?" asked Fallon.

Cara wondered if he was testing her in some way. "I do," she said. Then, tentatively, filled with hope and fear at what the answer might be, she added, "He was on a mission when last I saw him. Do you know anything of that?"

"When I met him he was seeking his wife, Martha, who was being held captive in the Rainbow Prison. Is that what you mean?"

Cara nodded, unable to speak.

"Yes, he was successful. His wife is here with him, and he is now seeking his daughter. He is very intent upon his quest."

It was all Cara could do to keep from crying out again. Her trembling grew greater.

"Peace, Silverhoof," whispered Fallon, placing a hand on her shoulder. "It will be —"

With a cry he pulled back, almost as if he had been burned. At the same time Cara's knees buckled as an unexpected feeling of connection surged through her.

Man and unicorn stared at each other, astonishment writ large on both their faces.

Fallon was the first to speak. "What is this about?" His voice was firm, just this side of anger.

"What do you mean?" she asked, trying to not let the quaver in her own voice betray her.

"I can sense something of Elihu in you, some essential part of him. How can that be?"

"I might be able to answer that if I understood what you and Elihu really are," she responded. "Why did I feel such a start of recognition when you touched me? What is your connection with unicorns?"

Fallon smiled. "I'd rather start with you. What in heaven's name *are* you?"

"Why would you say I am anything other than what you see?" countered Cara, trying to hide her alarm.

Fallon looked away. He was silent for a time, but finally said, "I know a great deal about unicorns."

"That's no answer."

He turned back. His expression was not angry, exactly,

but she could see that he had made a decision about which he was not entirely happy.

"Why do you know a great deal about unicorns?" she pressed.

Fallon took a deep breath, let it out slowly, then said, "Because I am the one who created them."

CHAPTER
LXVII

A BARGAINING CHIP

Ian was in considerable pain. Yet all he could think about was the fact that the horde was continuing in the direction he had sent Martha and the others. He was wracked with fear that the delvers might capture them, too. So his relief was considerable when, after another hour or so, they left the stone highway.

His sense of direction was good, even dangling upside down, and it didn't take him long to realize that they were heading toward the great tree. His feelings were mixed. If they went to the tree, it might prove easier for him to reconnect with Martha, assuming he could manage to escape. But it also meant the delvers might find Martha and the others after all, since they were supposed to return to that very spot the next day.

Accepting that he could do nothing about it under the current circumstances, Ian concentrated on staying calm, which was the only way he had of preserving his strength. The bonds chafed, and he felt a growing agony in his shoulders and hips. So he was relieved when Gnurflax called for a rest and the delvers lowered him to the ground. He was still uncomfortable, and he had lost feeling in his hands and feet, but at least the pain began to ease.

The horde had been resting for perhaps an hour when a group of delvers came trotting up. It didn't take long for Ian to discern that they were scouts, sent by Gnurflax to determine what lay ahead.

"There is a camp in the meadow southwest of the great tree," said the first.

"Many tents, many men, many weapons," said the second.

"We spied, sneakily, skillfully, and learned that it belongs to the woman Beloved," said the third.

Though their news was disturbing, it was Gnurflax's response that struck true terror into Ian's heart. Rubbing his hands together, he said, "Excellent news. We have captured one of her men, who I am sure she would like to have returned. He will make an excellent bargaining chip." Turning to his commanders he said, "Rouse the horde! We continue our journey."

Before long Ian was once again hoisted off the ground. With two delvers before him and two behind, sagging from the pole with his back occasionally scraping against the ground, he was carried toward the last place in either of two worlds that he wanted to find himself: Beloved's camp.

CHAPTER
LXVIII

DRAGON TALK

Graumag approached Firethroat's cave cautiously. Other than a dragonmoot once every five years, the dragons of Luster did not usually visit each other. Territory was territory, after all, and not to be transgressed upon lightly. She was glad it was Firethroat Amalia had asked her to call upon; that venerable dragon was the closest thing Graumag had to a friend among Luster's great beasts. Though she never, these days, thought of herself as anything other than dragon, Graumag took some pleasure in this semi-friendship. There remained a human element of her heart that longed for companionship in the way dragon hearts did not.

Once she reached Firethroat's mountain, she flew back and forth in front of the cave, waiting to be invited in, though in truth she could not be sure that the lady was even at home. But at last a voice boomed out, "What is it, Graumag? Why do you come uninvited to my lair?"

"Uninvited, but not unsent," replied Graumag. "The unicorn queen has asked me to speak to you."

"Then I guess I must hear what it is she has to say. You may approach."

This was not actually an invitation to enter, but it was a first step. Graumag threw back her head and blew out a gust of flame, as was proper. Then she dropped to the ledge that fronted the cave. She perched there, her great tail dangling down, until Firethroat said, "How is it with you, Flame Sister?"

"I am affrighted by what is happening to the land. And you, Flame Sister?"

Firethroat scowled. "I, too, am gravely concerned." She paused, then said, "You may enter."

Graumag crawled into the cave, which was pleasantly warm with the older dragon's presence, even here in the thin mountain air. As always, she was admiring of Firethroat's burnished red scales and in awe of her size.

The two beasts stared at each other for a time — it was never entirely comfortable for dragons to share a cave. Finally Firethroat stretched her head forward. Graumag did the same, and they pressed their necks against each other, the dragon version of an embrace.

"Though I do not often wish for visitors, I am glad you have come," said Firethroat, drawing her neck back. "I have been sore troubled these last days, for I have been in Luster hundreds of years and never felt anything like this." She cocked her head. "May I hope that you bring news?"

"I do. The woman Beloved has invaded Luster. To do so, she blasted an opening through the trunk of the Axis Mundi. That great violation is what troubles the world."

Firethroat groaned. "I feared it must be something of this nature. But what you have told me exceeds my worst imaginings. Does the Queen wish us to fix the tree? That does not seem possible to me."

"No, she asks for help in another way. Beloved has come with nearly five hundred men to hunt and kill the unicorns. Amalia Flickerfoot has decided rather than wait passively, she will go on the attack. She has challenged Beloved to meet on the field of battle near the Axis Mundi. She wants to know if you will join in this endeavor and fight on the side of the unicorns."

Firethroat smiled. "Now this I consider good news! It is time that the unicorns showed some fire and spirit. And long past time since I have had man to eat."

Graumag winced a bit at this. The dragons had, mostly, given up eating humans some time ago. But, for Firethroat at least, the appetite had never entirely gone away.

CHAPTER
LXIX

THE CREATOR

Fallon's claim that he had created the unicorns struck Cara almost as powerfully as the energy that had transformed her into this shape to begin with. Taking a few steps back so that she could look at him straight on, she whispered, "What do you mean?"

The big man spread his hands as if the answer were simplicity itself. "I created the unicorns. They did not exist, and then I made the first pair. Pairs, actually. There were eight unicorns when I was done."

The jumble of questions pressing for attention — "How? When? *Why?*" — seemed to clog her brain, making it almost impossible to speak. Finally she managed to whisper what seemed the most important of them: "Why?"

Fallon was silent for a moment. Finally he said, "It's what we do, those of us at my level. But, really, why does anyone create? You feel a . . . a restlessness inside, a need to make something new, something no one has ever seen before. You want to add to the beauty and the richness of the world with a gift, an offering that is uniquely yours. It's an act of selfishness and generosity, all rolled into one."

Cara pondered this for a few moments, then said, "Does that mean you're the god of the unicorns?"

Fallon uttered a most ungodlike hoot of laughter. "No, it does not. And if it did, I would decline the position. I didn't make the unicorns out of a desire to control or to be worshipped. I made them . . ." He paused, as if searching for the right words, then finally said softly, "It was an expression of joy. Joy and thanks. I wanted to give something wonderful to Earth, as a way of thanking the world for sheltering me after I was cast out of the Higher Realms."

"How did you do it?" she asked, genuinely curious.

Fallon shook his head. Smiling gently, he said, "That, my dear Silverhoof, would fall under the category of 'professional secrets.' "

Cara stamped a hoof in agitation. "Why did you tell me any of this if you're not going to explain?"

Fallon looked startled, then nodded and said, "I'm sorry. It's not that I want to be vague. But I've already explained more than I should. I would prefer not to invite additional punishment by spilling ancient secrets. I will say only this: I told you because my blood flows through your veins and because, though you and I are connected, there is something mysterious about you that I had hoped to learn in return. You are most clearly not just any unicorn."

Trying to sidestep his implied question, she said, "If you

made us, why haven't you been taking better care of us? We're in pretty big trouble, you know."

Fallon sighed. "You do have a gift for going straight to the heart of things, Silverhoof. Among the Powers, little is debated with greater ferocity than the question of what the creator owes the creation. Some feel you must hover over it, guarding it every moment. Others believe the highest, hardest, and most important task is to let go. They say that just as the parent must at some point release the child to the world, the creator must release the creation. Otherwise you stop it in its tracks, strangle its growth. Then you become not only its creator, but its executioner."

Cara did not answer right away. What Fallon was saying made sense, but at the same time troubled her, making her think of struggles she had had with her grandmother back on Earth, the fight between wanting to be independent and wanting to be taken care of. And the fact that Fallon was claiming, in a way, to be her own creator was far more than she could begin to think about at the moment.

"Now you, Silverhoof," said Fallon, his voice breaking into her thoughts. "I have told you my most treasured secrets. So, in fair trade, I ask: What is your secret? For I say it again: You are like no other unicorn."

Cara hesitated. Part of her ached to tell Fallon the truth. Another part of her thought that to do so would be insanity. She had not known him long enough to trust him with her secret.

413

"How do I know what you told me is true?" she asked. This was no answer, but it did put the burden back on him, where she was glad to have it.

Fallon smiled ruefully. "I didn't expect my unicorns to be quite so cynical. Alas, what can I offer as proof?" He shook his head. "It's an ancient question, you know. For what do we require proof, and what must we take on faith? I myself am not wildly faithful. In fact, I am a bit of a cynic when it comes to how worshipful those at my level are supposed to be of the Powers above us. I suppose that's one reason I ended up in so much trouble." He smiled. "Maybe cynicism runs in the family. If so, I can hardly blame you for wanting more proof. But, truly, Silverhoof, I have nothing else to give you. Is what I have told you not enough to receive your secret in return?"

It was Cara's turn to sigh. How much proof *did* she require? Fallon claimed a connection to Elihu, who had actually managed her transformation to her unicorn self. She could think of no test — what test could there be for such a claim? And she was weary of being alone.

Yet her own secret was too heavy and made her too vulnerable. She could not offer it to him.

"I'm sorry," she said softly, "I cannot tell you."

Fallon looked as if she had broken his heart. But he only nodded and said simply, "I hope someday you will trust me more."

With that, they resumed their journey.

CHAPTER
LXX

CONFUSION

The shaking of the ground, more violent than ever, knocked the Dimblethum to his knees. The great creature groaned. It was not a sound of pain, or even fear, but of deepest despair.

What was happening to Luster?

He had been heading back toward the Axis Mundi, but moving slowly, deliberately. This was partly because of his wounds, which still pained him. It was partly because he could no longer trust the ground beneath his feet. But most of all it was because of the fog in his mind, which seemed denser than ever.

At least he had heard no more from the wretched tempter who had whispered him into putting . . . the Dimblethum's mind drew back in horror.

He had done something bad. Something very, *very* bad. But what? *What?*

He slapped at his head, trying to dislodge the half-formed memory. Or perhaps simply to punish himself.

What had he done?

What had he done?

Beneath him, the world groaned and the ground rolled once again. Though he staggered, the Dimblethum managed to stay on his feet this time.

It would be easier if there was something to fight. Why couldn't he find some delvers to crunch?

No! Delvers were not important right now. It was Luster that mattered.

He had to get back to the tree.

But why?

And why had he ever left it?

CHAPTER
LXXI

RIFT

Rajiv stood in front of Lightfoot. The boy spread his arms and stared at the unicorn prince, his large, dark eyes filled with an urgent plea.

The three of them — Lightfoot, Rajiv, and Cara's mother — had stopped for a brief rest. It was their second day of tracking, and the work had proved more tedious than Lightfoot would have guessed. It was made even harder by the worsening tremors, by his own growing sense of impending doom, and — smaller, but inescapable — by Martha's desperation about finding Cara, which only fed and fueled his own dark fears on that matter.

And now, again, the boy was asking to be brought into communication. As if to reinforce the request, Rajiv tapped himself on the chest urgently, insistently, then spread his arms once more. He looked both puzzled and hurt.

Lightfoot sighed. Why had he been resisting this?

Because I'm already connected with more humans than I ever wanted to be, was his first thought. That felt true, but he knew there was more to it, so he pursued the idea. It wasn't, he quickly realized, just the number of connections. It was that the ones he had made already were so deep and intimate that they could be frightening and — in the case of Martha, who was filled with so much fear and anxiety — exhausting.

But the boy was sincere, and Ian had clearly thought highly of him, as had the strangely disturbing Fallon. Wearily, Lightfoot nodded his assent.

Rajiv returned a smile of dazzling brightness.

The Prince lowered his head so that the tip of his horn was directly in front of the boy's chest, then pressed forward.

Rajiv had been prepared for the intense pain, but was surprised by how briefly it lasted, replaced almost instantly by a strange tingling that spread across his skin until he felt as if he had been kissed by a star. The feeling was disturbing, yet also warm and comforting.

The unicorn pulled back. Rajiv, slightly dazed, placed his hand over the bloodless wound, then bowed his head as a sign of thanks.

In response, Lightfoot extended his neck until the left side of his muzzle lay against Rajiv's cheek. Speaking mind-to-mind, he said, "You don't have to use sign language now. You can communicate with me this way."

The unicorn's thoughts came directly into the boy's consciousness as a mixture of images, sounds, and emotions that somehow carried a meaning even more clear than words. The sensation was so strange that Rajiv felt a brief desire to flee. But he held his ground and said, "Thank you, Prince."

"No, no. Do not speak. *Think* what you want to tell me."

Rajiv tried again. "Thank you, Prince."

"Much better. Now, why were you so eager for us to be able to talk?"

"Why would I not be? It is very hard not to be able to speak to someone you are traveling with."

He did not mention the envy he had felt of Martha and Ian for being able to communicate with the Prince, nor his simple longing to be in closer contact with this strange and beautiful creature. Nor did he ask why the Prince had resisted, something he was not sure he wanted to know. Instead, he added, "Besides, I am worried about the memsahib and thought we should speak about her."

"Why are you worried?"

"She seems as if she might . . . I don't know. Explode?"

Lightfoot chuckled grimly. "I know what you mean."

They both glanced at Martha, who had been pacing — she did not do well with their brief resting periods — while all this went on.

"But she has reason," continued the Prince. "She is worried about finding her daughter."

Rajiv was glad to know from having listened to Martha and Ian discuss the matter that, while he could now communicate with Lightfoot, the unicorn could not simply read

419

his mind. He did not want to reveal the depth of his own longing and loss when it came to parents.

Martha started toward them. "We need to get moving," she said.

Rajiv translated this for Lightfoot, who winked and nodded. The boy smiled, happy in the connection. "Yes, we should," he agreed.

Despite her gnawing fears, despite her concerns for her daughter and her husband, Martha Hunter felt alive in a way she had not for many years — not just the years of her captivity in the Rainbow Prison, but the years she had spent home alone, waiting, while Ian trained for the Hunt and then went searching for Cara. At last she was *part* of what was happening, no longer simply a passive victim.

She gazed ahead. The wide band of stone she, Lightfoot, and Rajiv were following was obviously a natural formation. Even so, she could not help but think of it as a road. *The road to my daughter?* she wondered wistfully.

As they scanned the stone highway's edges for any sign of where the delvers might have veered off into the soft soil at the sides, she had to keep reminding herself that the search might be in vain, that their quarry might as easily have gone in the direction that Ian was now traveling.

She felt a deep urge to communicate with both of her companions. From Lightfoot, she wanted to know more, much more, of his experiences with Cara. From Rajiv, she wanted details of his travels with Ian. But the intensity of their search for any sign of where the delvers might have passed made it difficult to talk. It was only when they were crossing from one side of the stone to the other to resume the search that there was really an opportunity. Frustratingly, those times were too brief for any serious conversation.

Despite her eagerness, her desperation, to spot something that might lead them to the underground world, Martha found it hard to maintain her focus on the task at hand. Too much had happened in the last few days, and her mind was swirling with strange revelations clamoring for her attention.

She kept glancing at Lightfoot, trying to take in the fact that they were, to some degree, cousins.

The boy, Rajiv, was another matter. He was so down-to-earth in his approach to things that despite the fact that he was a homeless, parentless child her husband had taken from the streets of India, at the moment he seemed the most solid and grounded thing in her life. She was charmed by his courtesy and concern, and the way he addressed her as "memsahib," and sometimes found herself wondering if, when all this was over, they should try to adopt him. Whenever this thought arose she would immediately chastise herself for, yet again, letting her mind wander from the immediate goal.

Focus, Martha! she thought fiercely. *Focus!*

She wasn't sure how long they had been traveling, criss-crossing the stone as they desperately sought any sign of the delvers, when Lightfoot suggested they take a break to eat.

Martha, who had her hand on the unicorn's shoulder at that point, repeated this out loud for Rajiv.

"An excellent idea!" said the boy enthusiastically. "I am near to perishing of hunger!"

They had the food they had carried with them, of course, but Lightfoot showed them some other things they could eat, and as it seemed wise to preserve their rations, they were more than happy to try them. Rajiv was particularly delighted by the root called *skug*, which looked unpromising with its wrinkled brown skin, but popped open to reveal a white interior that was crisp and tasty.

When they resumed their quest, Martha found it a bit easier to focus and realized that hunger had been affecting her more than she had been willing to admit. Still, she looked up occasionally and was soon frowning as she saw how low the sun was growing. Before long they would have to stop for the night. They had agreed that if they had not found the trail by the end of this day they would return to the tree to await Ian. Even so, she found it hard to think of turning back.

She put her hand on Lightfoot's shoulder to discuss the matter and at once realized the Prince was also in deep distress. "What is it?" she thought.

"I walk with fear as my companion."

Martha, who could think of many things to fear at that moment, replied simply, "Of what?"

"The death of my world. If Luster should fail — and how such a thing can be I do not understand, but it is clear that we are in danger of that happening — then what is to become of the unicorns? Many will die with the world, I know that. Even if some of us manage to escape to Earth, what then? It is no longer a place where unicorns would be . . . understood."

"It will help if you have friends with you," thought Martha, instantly trying to be comforting, which was a life-long impulse. Then, because she could not stop herself, she thought, "My own fear is of not finding my daughter."

"I know. I see it in your every move and gesture, sense it in your every thought. But I tell you again, Cara is brave and strong and will surprise you with what she can do."

This calmed Martha, at least a bit. Even so, she thought, "I am not sure we should turn back."

Before Lightfoot could respond, she saw that Rajiv had joined them and motioned that it was all right for him to enter the conversation. As soon as the boy had put his hand on Lightfoot's other shoulder the unicorn thought, "Martha is not sure we should turn back tomorrow morning."

"But we told the sahib we would await him at the great tree!"

Martha, in contact with Lightfoot from the other side, could sense not only Rajiv's message, but the intensity of the boy's devotion to her husband, and was moved by it.

"Dark is drawing on," she thought to them. "We should wait to discuss this and continue to search as long as we still have light."

The others agreed. However, they had gone on only five minutes when the strongest tremor yet rumbled through the stone. Terrifyingly, it did not cease, but grew in intensity, finally knocking both Rajiv and Martha to the ground.

"Memsahib!" cried the boy, scrambling back the way they had come. "This way! This way!"

Martha screamed as the stone highway split beneath her.

Immediately Rajiv reversed course, lurching toward Martha. She had twisted around, but not fast enough, and half of her body had disappeared into the rift. Now visible to Rajiv only from the waist up, she clutched at the surface, desperately seeking any small hold.

And still the tremor intensified, the sound becoming deafening as the ground writhed and bucked and the gap in the stone opened ever wider. One twist flung Martha forward. Just as it looked as if she might be safe, the stone tipped again and she slid backward.

Rajiv flung himself flat and scuttled closer. Screaming to be heard above the roar of the quake he cried, "My hands, memsahib! Take my hands!"

Martha stretched forward and grasped Rajiv's wrists. The stone shivered again. She began to slide backward, into the widening abyss, pulling the boy with her. She tried to let go, crying out for him to save himself, but he clung to her, shrieking, "Hang on, memsahib. HANG ON!"

Suddenly Lightfoot, legs splayed over the boy, bent and snatched the back of Rajiv's shirt in his teeth. The muscles in his neck bulging, fighting desperately to keep his balance against the still-twisting stone, the unicorn halted their slide into the void.

"Hold on," he thought desperately, echoing Rajiv's plea to Martha. *"Hold on!"*

A moment later it was over and the stone ceased its tormented shaking. Rajiv, aided by Lightfoot, began to move backward, pulling Martha with him. It only took a few inches before she was able to pull herself back onto solid stone. Flinging herself forward, she swept the boy into her arms and began to sob against his neck.

CHAPTER LXXII

SHAKEN LOOSE

By the fifth day of M'Gama's underground imprisonment, she was filled with deep frustration and an even deeper terror.

The reason for the frustration was simple: She continued — though only occasionally — to catch hints of the hidden power she had felt when the delvers first chained her in this cave. She now had a sense of where that power was radiating from, at least the general direction. But she still had no idea who it might be, much less why it was only intermittently present.

The source of her terror was also simple: The tremors wracking the stone that surrounded her were growing both more frequent and more intense.

She feared for herself — how could she not, chained to a wall far underground with the very rocks shifting and shaking on all sides? But she feared even more for Luster and every creature that inhabited this increasingly unstable world, whether aboveground or below.

The delvers had brought her food only once since she

had been bound here. The Geomancer was not surprised. She had not anticipated the best of treatment, and she suspected that by now they were trapped in their own fear and she was the least of their worries. As much as she disliked the little monsters, she knew they were as tied to the stone and soil of Luster as she was.

That had been yesterday. At least, she thought it was a day ago. As she had been finishing the meal — it was revolting, but hunger could make eating almost anything possible — another tremor, the worst yet, made the walls around her bulge. From the distance, in sound carried by stone, which her magic made more intense, M'Gama had heard a terrified clamor. Puzzled, she had finally understood the sound to be that of a huge number of delvers crying out. At first she had thought they were cries of fear, but in time they turned to something far more chilling, shouts that sounded almost like triumph.

Then the cries had faded.

Now, a day later, the only disturbance came from the occasional grinding movement in the rock around her. M'Gama was slowly realizing that though Delvharken had seemed silent to her before, there had always been a low murmur of activity that she could sense. That was gone.

What had happened? Where were the delvers?

She blessed the fact that her chains let her reach the water that continued to collect in the small pool on her left. But for the first time, she began to wonder if she might actually die of starvation down here.

Wouldn't that be a sorry end to a glorious career? she asked herself mockingly.

Though the Geomancer did not want to die, she refused to panic at the thought. That was not her way.

And then something happened that did cause her to panic, at least momentarily. The rock chamber shook and shifted more violently than at any point so far. With a grinding rumble, the wall beside her split. A huge chunk of stone fell from the ceiling, missing her by inches. Other pieces of stone clattered around her, bouncing off her neck and shoulders. One large shard struck her arm and for a painful moment M'Gama feared the bone was broken. Before she could think about that, the tremor grew worse. With a deafening roar, half the chamber collapsed. The choking dust made it impossible to see. Coughing and gasping, expecting the rest of the chamber to fall in at any moment, the Geomancer prepared herself to die.

And then . . . silence. The shaking had stopped. At least, the *world* had stopped shaking. M'Gama discovered, to her disgust, that her own body was still trembling violently. *Stop it!* she ordered herself. She pressed tight to the wall behind her, hoping to gather some calming strength from the rock. As she did, she heard a loud clank. The metal ring to which the chain holding her arm was fastened had come loose from the wall and fallen to the floor.

Feeling a sudden surge of hope, M'Gama kicked outward, pulling against her leg chain. It remained tight in the wall, and for a moment hope faded. But she gave another kick, and then another, and then a stubborn fourth, and at last was rewarded with a second delicious clanking sound.

She was free!

Yes, she was still underground, in the realm of the enemy, with the stone itself no longer to be depended on. But she was free nonetheless. Dragging her chains behind her like a ghost, the Geomancer crawled over the debris that clogged the mouth of the cave.

Common sense demanded she head for the surface as quickly as possible. She could find the right direction easily enough — she was the Geomancer, after all. But when she was about halfway up, something else, something even stronger, began to pull her in another direction.

Fighting instincts that screamed for her to flee these crumbling tunnels, M'Gama turned. Despite the danger, she was determined to find the strange power that had been calling to her, off and on, ever since she was first chained to the wall of Gnurflax's dungeon.

CHAPTER LXXIII

PASSING IN THE NIGHT

Cara, Fallon, and Medafil traveled mostly in silence, each wrapped in his or her own thoughts. Even the Squijum was quiet for much of the time. Occasionally a tremor would cause them to cry out. More than once they fell against each other trying to get their footing.

Each time that happened, each time she brushed against Fallon, Cara felt that same odd thrill of recognition. Somewhat against her will, she found she was beginning to believe the big man's mad claim to have been the one who created the unicorns.

A few times, Cara asked Fallon to tell her about the Higher Powers, but he was unwilling to provide much information. Other times he was the questioner, asking about life among the unicorns. She remained equally vague, partly because she was annoyed at his own reluctance to speak, but more because she had not been in Luster — much less been a unicorn — long enough to answer most of his questions and feared him catching her out. For that same reason, she dared not ask much about her father and mother, though the questions throbbed within her heart. It was enough, for now, to know that her parents were well and here in Luster.

As the hours passed, her sense of the unicorns grew continually stronger. She became certain it would not be long before her group reached the Gathered Glory. Though she had been looking forward to that, she found herself becoming anxious. What would she tell her grandmother when she finally saw her again?

Night fell. They continued to travel, coming to a broad stretch of stone that extended as far as they could see in either direction. Its surface was broken, and great gaps yawned where the tremors that shook Luster had pulled it asunder. They had traveled this road for perhaps an hour when Fallon placed a hand on her shoulder and whispered, "Back up — step off the road."

She did as he ordered, moving in perfect silence. The Squijum, clinging to her shoulder, remained silent as well, as did Medafil.

A moment later she heard what had alerted Fallon: the sound of delver voices — a lot of delver voices. She wondered if the fact that he had heard them first meant his ears were even more sensitive than hers.

Peering from their hiding place at the edge of the road, they watched a horde of delvers flow by. Cara tried to count, but lost track. There were hundreds and hundreds of the little monsters. They were so thick upon the road that she did not see, carried at shoulder level in the midst of them, the pole from which her father hung suspended. So she had no idea they were bearing him right past her.

"Those, I take it, are the delvers you spoke of?" asked Fallon, once the horde was safely beyond them.

"Yes, those are delvers," whispered Cara.

"Never saw so many of the frat-spickled creatures in one place," muttered Medafil. "Kind of terrifying to see them all together like that."

"I wonder where they're heading," said Fallon.

"As near as I can make out, it's pretty much the same direction we're going," replied Cara nervously.

"Well, it looks as if everything will be decided at the center after all," said Fallon.

Medafil groaned.

They began to walk again. Prompted by the sight of the delvers, Cara decided to tell Fallon the story of the Whisperer. This was partly because she wanted to find how he would react, but even more because she thought it might be important for him to know what the unicorns had done.

The big man listened intently, and it was obvious that he found the story deeply disturbing. When Cara had finished her telling, he stopped and turned away. She couldn't be sure, but she thought his shoulders trembled, as if he were suppressing a sob. She wondered if it was for the unicorns, and their foolish pride, or because Elihu had been part of the dark event that led to the existence of not only the Whisperer, but the delvers as well.

After several minutes he turned back to her. His face was grim and hard, his eyes clear. But all he said was, "Thank you. This is something I needed to know."

"So it makes sense to you that this could have happened?" As she asked the question, she realized she had been hoping he would tell her it was impossible.

"It makes all too much sense. And I fear it explains something that has been troubling me."

"What is that?"

But he merely shook his head and said, "Let us continue our journey."

"Secrets," muttered Medafil. "I hate secrets. Grukpingled things."

Cara felt the same way.

She would have been angrier about it were she not holding a secret of her own from Fallon.

CHAPTER LXXIV

SIGNED, SEALED, AND DELIVERED

A cluster of delvers surrounded the bound form of Ian Hunter, which had been placed upon a long, low rock. Gnurflax, King of the delvers, leaned over his prisoner. Using a twig dipped in a pot of dark liquid, he scrawled some words across Ian's forehead.

Ian would have protested, but his captors had sealed his lips with a thick, foul-tasting paste, and he could not open his mouth.

"With regards from King Gnurflax," read the delver standing next to the King. "She should like that," he added approvingly.

"But why do we wish to curry favor with the invader to begin with?" asked another of the delvers.

The King smacked him in the back of the head. "Because, you fool, she has one of the Queen's Five. She could not have entered Luster without it. I want that amulet so we can create our own passageway. And the best way to get it is to be friendly enough to find where it is hidden so we can steal it."

"As always, your wisdom exceeds all bounds," growled a third delver.

Gnurflax snorted, then said, "All right, he's ready. Take him to the camp of the humans."

Ian did his best to ignore the hoots and catcalls that erupted from his former comrades as he was carried into Beloved's camp. He wanted to reserve his wits, and his strength, for whatever was to come next, and he couldn't afford to waste energy in reacting to mere mockery. His primary task now was to remain calm and hold himself ready for the smallest opportunity should it present itself.

Escorted by a group of Hunters, the delvers carried him directly to Beloved's pavilion, easily identified as the focal point of the encampment. Once there, they dropped him unceremoniously in front of the entrance flap, between the two Hunters who stood guard. Both of them looked down at Ian with scorn.

"We wish to see Beloved," announced the lead delver. Since they spoke in delvish, the only word that could be understood was "Beloved." That was enough. One of the guards nodded and went into the tent.

A moment later Beloved emerged, dressed in a scarlet robe, her moon-white hair swirling about her shoulders. When she saw the "gift" the delvers had brought for her, she cried out with malicious delight. Staring down at Ian, her eyes glittering, she said sweetly, "So, the prodigal has returned! You didn't really think you could get away from Grandmother Beloved, did you, Ian?"

When he said nothing, she bent and pinched his face between her fingers, puckering his mouth, which caused the paste to tear at his lips. "Poor Ian," she purred. "Captured by delvers, and now the cat has his tongue." Then, with a quick, sudden move, she slapped him. It was almost playful, yet hard enough to sting.

Rising, Beloved looked down at the delvers, who stood about waist high to her. She reached into the pocket of her robe and withdrew a stone. Ian guessed it was a speaking stone, similar to the one he had carried on his first trip to Luster. Her next words emerged from deep in her throat, sounding harsh and guttural. "To what do I owe the honor of this gift?" she asked in perfect delvish.

The lead delver bowed, then in grating tones replied, "King Gnurflax sends this man as a reminder that the delvers are not to be toyed with. This Hunter made promises to the delvers that he did not keep." He kicked Ian in the side. "Thus do we deal with any who do not properly respect us. That the man lives at all is a sign of Gnurflax's mercy. He is delivered to you as pledge of the King's desire to maintain good relations between us, since our people and yours are both enemies of the wretched unicorns."

"This man has betrayed me as well," replied Beloved smoothly. "I have little use for him, save as a lesson to my other men that it is wisest to remain faithful. Still, I will accept him, as a mark of my ongoing friendship with the delver king. Should Gnurflax wish to speak with me about what is to come, I will be glad to host him and two of his closest in command."

The delver hesitated, then said, "Gnurflax wishes to know, lady, what has happened to so vex the world that it now shakes and quivers."

Beloved smiled and in a voice close to a croon said, "Tell your King that Luster quakes at my power and that he should do so as well."

The delvers looked at her in terror.

"Now go!" she cried.

The delvers turned and fled.

Once they were gone, Beloved crouched beside Ian. Staring into his eyes, she said, "I do not take betrayal lightly." Her voice was so soft that only he could hear her. "I poured a lot into you, Ian. Trust and love and training. Was simple loyalty too much to expect in return?"

Ian said nothing, could not have spoken even if he did have anything to say

Beloved sighed, as if his silence were one more betrayal. "You could have had everything," she murmured. "Now, you will have nothing but a world of pain." Standing, she said contemptuously, "Put him inside. I will deal with him later."

As she strode away, two of the Hunters lifted Ian's still-bound body and carried him into Beloved's pavilion, where they dumped him on the floor.

"Hard to have much sympathy for a traitor," said one of them, giving Ian a kick in the same spot the delver had.

The other simply spat on him.

Then they turned, leaving him bound and alone.

The world shook again.

Were it not for the fact that he could not, would not, surrender as long as there was the slightest chance of finding his daughter, of connecting again with his wife, Ian would have been just as happy for the ground to open and swallow him.

As if to make his misery complete, the Blind Man chose that moment to take his sight again.

Let him, thought Ian wearily. *It's a good time for it, actually, as there is nothing for me to see right now.*

He concentrated on trying to free himself from his bonds. But delver ropes are strong, and delver fingers are skilled, and he made no progress on loosening them.

Blind and bound, the best thing Ian could do was try to relax and save his strength. Who knew what chance might arise an hour from now? But even as he was trying to steady his breathing, he felt something new and unexpected and wildly frustrating.

Beloved was summoning the Hunters. It was an "all call" — something Ian could feel because even though he had rebelled, there still existed a bond between himself and Beloved. He knew that all the Hunters, no matter where they were, or what they were doing, would sense her command to return and begin making their way back.

For himself, being so close, the feeling was overwhelming. And it was flat-out maddening to be drawn to a woman he so thoroughly loathed, even as the delver ropes held him bound in place.

But *why* was she calling her men back from the Hunt that she had so long desired?

What was she up to now?

CHAPTER
LXXV

SEDUCTION

When they had gathered their wits, Martha, Rajiv, and Lightfoot stood gazing at the newly opened rift. The gap was several feet across — far too wide to jump — and stretched as far as they could see in either direction, well beyond the edges of the road.

No point in debating, now, whether to go on. Moving forward was flat-out impossible.

"I hope we won't find another gap like this behind us," thought Lightfoot to the two humans.

"It would be like being trapped on an island, Sahib Lightfoot," agreed Rajiv. "Only with shores made of empty air instead of water."

Which, as it turned out, was exactly what they did find only twenty minutes later. Wearily they turned from the abyss, agreeing they would, instead, try to make their way directly to the Axis Mundi come morning.

It was not hard to find a place to rest for the night in the surrounding forest. Managing to fall asleep, however, was another matter. It was difficult to relax when you were aware that the ground might open beneath you at any moment.

So it was that Martha was awake, staring morosely at the fat but waning moon, when a seductive voice whispered from the darkness, "I know what you want. . . ."

Martha's eyes flew open. "Who are you?" she whispered in terror. "*Where* are you?"

"I am someone who can make wishes come true."

The words were uttered in tones so sweetly soothing that she found her fear fading. Calmer, she asked, "What do you want of me?"

"It's not what I want that matters. It is what *you* want that concerns me. And I *know* what you want."

"How can you know that?"

"To me your heart is as an open book."

Martha shuddered and crossed her hands over her chest, as if to close that book. "Why can't I see you?"

"I am . . . a friend. You don't need to see me to know that. And I can help you, because I know what you want."

"I don't believe you!"

"You want your daughter. . . ."

Martha caught her breath, then said slowly, scornfully, "That doesn't take a genius."

"Maybe not. It might not take a genius to know where she is, either."

Martha sat up. "You *know* where Cara is? Will you take me to her?"

"Certainly. But you must understand that nothing is free. If I take you to her, I will need something from you in return."

"What?"

"Not much."

"What?"

"Why so distrustful?"

"I've had my fill of magic and have little reason to trust it."

"Do not be so cynical. You have no idea what wonders I can work."

"What is it you want?" she demanded.

"Just a little thing. Not much at all. Will you help me?"

"How can I answer unless you tell me what it is you want?"

"Can you keep it between us?" asked the voice caressingly. "I would not like the others to know."

"Why? Will I be doing something wrong?"

"No, no! Of course not! Of course not. You will be a boundary breaker and a peacemaker. Think of how proud your husband will be."

"Please, just tell me what is it you want me to do."

"How would you feel about helping me to capture your mother?"

Silence.

"I know what she did to you."

"How can you know that?"

"I have my ways. I know many things that are hidden in human hearts."

"Why do you want to capture my mother?"

"You do not need to know that. You only need to know that I can lead you to your daughter."

"Will you hurt my mother?"

"Do you care?"

"Yes!" said Martha, surprising herself.

"Then I will not hurt her. Now will you help me capture her?"

Martha hesitated, then said slowly, "What must I do?"

DAY FIVE:
THE AXIS MUNDI

Things fall apart; the center cannot hold . . .

William Butler Yeats
"The Second Coming"

CHAPTER
LXXVI

THE WIZARD IN THE STONE

M'Gama was surprised — and impressed — to see that despite several days of shaking and destruction, the glowing orange lines that ran along the walls of Delvharken's tunnels were still working.

She continued to follow her sense of the power that had been beckoning to her since her imprisonment began. She had no idea of how much time had passed, when she heard a voice in the distance. It was the first sound, other than the groans of shifting stone, to reach her ears since the strange silence had descended on Delvharken. And it came from the same direction as the power she was seeking. She paused to gather up her chains so they would not clink against the stone. Then, moving more cautiously than before, she continued onward.

Rounding a corner she saw, several paces ahead of her, a lone delver crouched next to a lump of stone. He was wailing in despair.

M'Gama stepped forward cautiously. She did not particularly want to feel sympathy for a delver, but this creature's distress was so obvious and so deep it was difficult not to.

Trying to remember how her captors had shaped their words, she said awkwardly, "What is it, delver? Why do you weep over that piece of stone?"

The delver gasped — he clearly had not heard her approach — and drew away in fright. He stared at her for a moment, then cried, "I know who you are!"

M'Gama merely inclined her head, wondering at the dark, wavy lines that marked his face. However, his next words caused her to gasp. Spreading his large, knobby hands, he said, "I am sorry about what happened to your servant, Flensa."

Her immediate response was anger. It was delvers who had killed Flensa. Yet this one was apologizing. Why? Had he taken part in the attack on her home and now, facing her, begun to think better of it? If so, no mercy for that! After an uncomfortable silence she said stiffly, "How do you know about Flensa?"

"Cara told me."

Now M'Gama was doubly startled. "You know Cara? You've seen her since she left my home?" The Geomancer squatted so that she was close to the delver and said, "We need to talk."

He nodded miserably, then drew an arm across his horribly upturned nose, wiping away the unpleasant result of his recent spasm of weeping.

Averting her gaze, M'Gama said, "Since you know who I am, why don't you begin by telling me your name?"

The delver gave a dark chuckle and said, "I have lost my name." When the Geomancer looked at him skeptically, he continued, "King Gnurflax stripped it from me as punishment. I do, however, have a *nickname*. In fact, it was a gift from Cara. She decided to call me Rocky. That is the name I go by now."

"Rocky will be fine," said M'Gama tartly. Despite this delver's seeming friendliness, she was not inclined to trust him too easily — nor to forgive him, whether he'd had anything to do with the attack on her home or not. From her point of view, all the delvers were equally blameworthy.

Another tremor shook the tunnel walls, causing them to both glance up in fear. "Is that why you were wailing just now?" asked M'Gama.

Rocky shook his head, then looked around as if seeking some means of escape.

In the silence M'Gama realized that the strange power she had been sensing was close by. Yet she was certain it did not come from this "Rocky."

"Where have all the other delvers gone?" she demanded.

"They fled to the surface."

"Then why are you still here?"

Again he glanced around. M'Gama wondered what he was looking for, then realized that he wanted to be sure there was no one near to listen. When he was satisfied they were truly alone, he said, "I was seeking this one."

The Geomancer was more puzzled than ever. "What one?"

Stroking the stone outcropping upon which he had been sobbing, he said mournfully, "*This* was once a delver. He was very important to me."

"Was he a relative?"

"Closer than that. He was my teacher."

"What happened to him?"

Looking at her as if she were a slow child, Rocky said, "He turned to stone."

"You make it sound as if he did it to himself."

"Most likely he did. Few there are who could do this *to* him."

"He was powerful, then?"

The delver hesitated, then said, "Very."

"Can you think of why he would have done this to himself?"

Rocky was silent for a moment, then said slowly, "If he had been trying to hide, and tried too hard, it's possible this could have happened. There is a danger zone, when you're hovering between flesh and stone. If you fall into it . . . well, I almost went there myself a while ago. I would have, if my cousins hadn't pulled me back."

M'Gama took a moment to absorb this piece of information, realizing as she did that the delvers were more complicated than she had suspected. "You say he was powerful," she said at last. "Who could have frightened him enough to cause him to do this?"

"The King, perhaps."

"Did he fear the King?"

The delver burst out in a harsh laugh. "The King is a fool and a madman, and this one" — here he patted the stone again — "this one saw his madness and helped me to see it as well."

Stranger and stranger, thought M'Gama. Aloud, she said, "You claim you came down here seeking him. Why?"

"He is the wisest delver I know. The wisest delver there is, probably. We're in a world of trouble right now. We could use some of that wisdom."

As if to punctuate Rocky's statement, the tunnel walls shook again.

"We can't stay here any longer," said M'Gama, getting to her feet. "Let's head for the surface."

"I can't! Not until I bring him back."

M'Gama looked at the delver in astonishment. "Bring him back? From being stone?"

"I told you, my cousins did the same for me."

"Yes, but you said you had *nearly* fallen into that state, not that you had become stone altogether."

"This one is much more powerful than I. It is possible he could become stone and still return."

Intrigued despite herself, M'Gama knelt beside Rocky. The chains that still dangled from her wrists clanked as she put her hands on the stone. "He *is* strong," she said after a moment. "I've been sensing him for days now. It's been driving me slightly mad trying to figure out where that pulse of magic was coming from." She hesitated, then added with a bit of wonder, "His power is much like mine."

Rocky looked at her eagerly. "Of course it is. You are the Geomancer. Help me bring him back!"

Her face hardened. "Bring back a delver?" she said scornfully. "After what they did to Flensa?"

The delver renewed his plea. "You have to help! You understand these things. He is a stone magician. *You* are a stone magician. You can call to him."

Still M'Gama hesitated, as the part of her that had hated delvers for years struggled with the part of her that was seeing this delver not as an enemy but as . . . what?

Something almost human?

"I can get you jewels!"

M'Gama laughed, sounding crueler than she intended. "You cannot buy my help that way."

"Then what *do* you want, you horrible woman? I have helped your Prince Lightfoot! I have helped the girl Cara! I have sacrificed my name and my place in Delvharken to try to fight the King in his madness. What do you want? *Why are you so cruel?*"

He turned from her and flung himself back onto the stone, his shoulders wracked by fresh sobs.

M'Gama stepped back, startled. *Who is this creature to call* me *cruel?* she thought angrily. Then she caught herself. Closing her eyes, she took several deep breaths. As she gained control of her anger, as it lost its hold on her, allowing her to truly hear what the delver had been saying, the hardness in her heart began to melt. She took one more deep breath, then knelt beside the delver. "What must we do?"

He looked at her in shock. "You're the stone magician! Don't you know?"

M'Gama paused, then realized that she did, indeed, know what to do. The question was whether she could bring herself to do it. . . .

CHAPTER LXXVII

CENTAURS

The morning after he became Chiron, Arkon had thundered over the rim of the valley and into the larger world, followed by fifty of the finest archers and sword-wielders the centaurs had to offer. Some of the band Arkon had chosen to accompany him had been his teachers; some had trained side by side with him when they were young together; and some he himself had taught the ways of sword and spear and arrow.

Each he would have trusted with his life.

Though the new Chiron had accepted that his duty lay beyond the valley's borders, in the secret places of his heart he also hoped that in pursuing this duty he would find Arianna. She was little more than a day ahead of them, after all. Yet now, at the start of their third day, he was beginning to despair. On an open plain you might spot someone from a distance, but in the deep forest you could pass within thirty paces of the one you sought and not realize he or she was there. There would be so many ways to miss her.

Trying not to despair, he forced his thoughts back to the

task at hand. *How do you find out what is causing a world to shake?* he asked himself. *That is a mystery that was never addressed in our training!*

The best plan seemed to be to seek out the unicorns. It was their world, after all. They ought to know something about this.

He was hoping Arianna had made a similar decision. With that in mind, he had gathered some of the maps collected by the old Chiron. He carried them now in the quiver slung over his shoulder — a quiver that was, of course, also filled with arrows. . . .

The Chiron was jolted out of his thoughts by another tremor shaking the ground beneath his hooves.

"Arkon, look out!"

The call came from Danbos, the muscular centaur he had selected to be his second-in-command. The warning was well-timed. Though Arkon leaped the rift that had opened in the ground ahead of him nimbly enough once he saw it, without the call from Danbos he would likely have plunged in a foreleg. Glancing back, he shuddered, painfully reminded of what had happened to Basilikos and how dangerous the world had become.

They were crossing a broad grassland when Arkon spotted a pair of dragons in flight some way ahead of them.

"Look," he said to Danbos, who was cantering alongside him.

"That's strange," replied the other centaur. "I thought dragons were solitary beasts. Never heard of two of them traveling together!"

"There's a lot we don't know about this world," said Arkon bitterly. "Too much. I loved the old Chiron, but his letting the unicorns restrict us to our valley has left us in a state of ignorance. Worlds are for exploring, not hiding from."

As he spoke, the larger of the two dragons changed direction and began flying toward them. Did it want to talk — or was it planning to attack? Because it was still some distance away, and because he did not want it to seem that the centaurs were afraid, Arkon continued forward. As they cantered across the grassland, it became clear that the dragons were farther off than he had thought — and, consequently, were also *bigger* than he had thought.

When the one approaching was close enough, Arkon raised an arm to halt his band. "Draw bows, but hold fire," he shouted. Alone, he trotted forward another fifty yards. Once he was far enough from the others, he spread his hands to show he was weaponless and it was safe should the dragon want to parley.

"Tell your men to lower their weapons," called the dragon in a deep but clearly female voice. "We have no quarrel with each other."

"How can I be sure of that?"

"Because I have said so! Do you not know that dragons cannot lie?"

"How do I know that *that* is not a lie?"

"I cannot be responsible for your lack of education, centaur. I have information that may be of use to you. If you wish to speak with me civilly, I will impart it. Otherwise, I have my own work to do."

Arkon paused, then bowed stiffly from the waist and said, "I did not mean to be rude, friend dragon. Alas, we have not been much out in the world."

"It shows," replied the dragon tartly. "Now, shall we speak?"

Arkon turned and called, "Put down your bows."

The centaurs did as he asked.

The dragon, whose scales were the color of fresh blood, settled to the ground, sending small gusts of wind past Arkon. Coiling her tail around her — really, she was astonishingly large — she said, "My name is Firethroat."

"And I am Arkon."

"Good. May I ask, Arkon, why you have left your valley after all these centuries?"

"Is it not obvious? The world is crumbling beneath us. We seek to know the cause."

"That I can explain easily enough," replied Firethroat. Quickly she told Arkon what Beloved had done.

The centaur groaned. "Is there no hope for the world?"

"It seems unlikely. Still, if there is no hope, there may at least be vengeance. My companion and I are heading toward the meadow northeast of the Axis Mundi, to join the unicorns in their battle with the invaders tomorrow morning."

"Then that is where we shall go as well," declared Arkon. He paused for a moment, then said, almost shyly, "In your flight, have you seen any other centaurs?"

The dragon shook her head.

He sighed, then asked, "How far is it to the center?"

"If you mark the distance from your own valley, you have traveled about two thirds of the way."

"Then we shall be there by nightfall."

"I think I can speak for the unicorns when I say that you will be most welcome. I predict a day bathed in blood. If we do not live through it, at least we will have left our mark."

With that, Firethroat spread her batlike wings and took to the sky. She circled once above them, then called, "We will meet you at the center. May it all be settled there." She shot forth a burst of flame as a kind of seal on the pledge, then turned to rejoin her companion.

Arkon watched as she flew back toward the other dragon. Only once she was gone did he allow his hands a moment of trembling. Though he was no coward, it had been all he could do to control himself while face-to-face with the awesome beast.

He returned to his band and told them what he had learned. Then he consulted his maps — he spread them across Danbos's broad back to do so — and made a slight correction in their course.

Pointing, he called, "That way lies the center of the

world. We meet the invaders there. If we cannot save Luster, we can at least exact a price upon those who have destroyed it. Are you with me?"

The centaurs roared their approval.

With their new Chiron in the lead, they galloped forward . . . not having any idea that Firethroat had directed them to the wrong meadow.

After all, dragons cannot lie and that was where she herself believed the battle would take place.

CHAPTER
LXXVIII

NAMZA'S LAST DREAM

Namza's final dream was of what happened the night his teacher, Metzram, returned to the Stone for good.

Drifting into this new dream, Namza saw himself as he had been that night, still young, his heart breaking at the thought of losing his teacher.

As if inhabiting his own story, he found himself kneeling once more beside Metzram, who lay on a stone pallet, shivering under a coarsely woven blanket.

"It will not be long now, my student," Metzram had whispered, reaching out to take Namza's hand. "Soon I must return to the Stone from which I came." His voice was feeble. His breathing sounded like pebbles being rattled in a tube.

"Teacher, do not go! I am not ready to take your place."

"Nor was I when the time came for me to let go of my own teacher. We are never ready, young Namza. We simply do what we can. And what we must." Metzram broke off, caught by a spasm of coughing, and tightened his grip on

458

his student's hand. When the fit had passed, he said, "Namza. Student. It is harder for you and me than it is for others, for we know things the others don't, things it is not yet safe to tell."

Namza had nodded, knowing that to speak what they had learned, what they believed, could cost them their lives.

"It's not just the danger," Metzram had wheezed, as if he had read his mind. "The greater fear is that if we do speak these things the denial will be so strong that the truth will be lost altogether. And it must not be lost! The changes we need to bring must come, but they can only come slowly, as slowly as the change that comes to stone when water wears against it, making its shape something new."

Metzram coughed again, a terrible sound that struck fear into Namza's heart. The older delver smiled wanly. "Not long now," he whispered.

"Teacher, stay with me!"

"I am ready, Namza. I —"

Metzram's eyes widened as he saw something — clearly something unexpected — behind Namza. Puzzled, his student turned to see what could have drawn the dying delver's attention. He gasped. Standing near the entrance of the cave was a beautiful woman, with skin as brown as *zakram* leather and hair as yellow as the dreaded sun.

"Lady Allura!" gasped Metzram. "You came!"

"I owe you that much," said the woman who was, from a delver's point of view, absurdly tall. She walked to the stone pallet where the old delver lay, knelt on the side opposite

Namza, and placed her hand upon Metzram's high, domed forehead.

"Your touch is cool, lady."

"It is meant to soothe," replied Allura.

"It does," murmured Metzram.

"It will not be long, venerable one," she said softly.

"I know," he replied, heaving a sigh that changed to a sharp, shuddering gasp.

"Teacher!"

But the moment had come. Metzram's body had stiffened, the flesh begun to gray, the cracks to appear, as he returned to the Stone.

Namza lay his head upon that rocky breast and began to weep.

He wept for so long that he was surprised to see, when he raised his head once more, that the woman was still there.

"There is another story you need to know, young delver," she said softly. "I do not know when, but I am certain that the time will come when someone must bear witness. The tale I want to tell you is not in the pages your teacher stole for me so long ago. Rather, it is etched in my heart. Will you listen to me tell it? Will you remember the story and hold it in your own heart until the time is right?"

If Namza could have shifted in his sleep he would have, for he knew what was coming. But he could not move, any more than he could stop the dream. Yet a moment later the dream ended, anyway, interrupted before Allura could tell her story.

Someone was calling him through the Stone.

Who was it? What did they want?

Namza resisted. Sleep was good. Dreaming was good.

But the voice would not let him be, insisting that he wake and respond.

CHAPTER
LXXIX

THE CREATOR VIEWS HIS CREATION

Fallon was fascinated, and slightly troubled, by his new companions. Not so much the gryphon and the chattery little creature; unusual beasts were well within his range of experience, though something about the Squijum seemed oddly familiar. No, it was the unicorn, Silverhoof — there was something strange about her that he could not identify. She knew so much about some things and so little about others. And that bit of Elihu he sensed in her — her claim of having simply met him once was not enough to explain that!

Of course, he was well aware that there were things she was not telling him, sometimes under the guise of not knowing them. But most of his confusion came from what he felt when they were in contact. Even as he sensed the connection of blood and magic he had with all unicorns, the feeling was muddled somehow with her, as if there was something else inside her. He might have thought it was simply a sign of how unicorns had changed in the centuries since he had last been in contact with them, save that he had felt no such oddness from Prince Lightfoot. He could not figure out what it meant, and it was maddening.

Even so, Silverhoof was really the least of his concerns. It was the strange tale she had told about the Whisperer that occupied most of his thoughts. Could Elihu really have done something so mad as to assist at that Purification Ceremony? What could have possessed him?

And how might he have been punished? That was the truly soul-twisting question. It was possible the Higher Powers might not have noticed and thus would not have interceded. But Fallon's instincts told him this was highly unlikely.

He sighed.

"What is it?" asked Silverhoof, who was walking a few feet away.

Fallon shook his head, then smiled. "That is usually my question. It is rare for someone to feel concern on my behalf."

The unicorn looked at him curiously. "Don't you have friends?"

Her words pierced him, and he thought for a time before saying, "I have people I have helped. They would consider themselves friends, and I have a strong fondness for many of them. But my path is, mostly, a solitary one."

"You need to relax," said the unicorn.

Fallon actually laughed.

"What?"

"As I said, I am usually the one who tries to help. I'm just not used to such concern. It is most welcome."

"I see," said the unicorn. Then she asked a question that completely startled him. "What are you going to do about the Whisperer?"

"Why do you ask that?"

She shook her mane in irritation. "Because you've been brooding ever since I told you the story. Because I watched your jaw clench and your hands tighten as I was telling it. Because for some reason, I can tell that the idea of it really got under your skin. So, are you going to fight him. It?"

Fallon stopped in his tracks. Several moments passed before he said, "Yes, I think I'm going to have to."

He started to say something else, but stopped, his heart lifting with an unexpected joy at what he sensed ahead of them.

"What is it?" asked Cara.

"Unicorns," whispered Fallon. "Hundreds of them! Not far from here."

"They're heading for the Axis Mundi to do battle with Beloved," replied Cara.

"How do you know that?" asked Fallon.

"A dragon told me."

He chuckled. "Silverhoof, you continue to amaze me. And given how old I am, and how much I have seen, that is no small thing. What do you think — shall we join them or stay separate for now?"

Cara felt an unanticipated burst of shyness. How well did the unicorns know one another? Could she simply lose herself in the Gathered Glory, or would she be taken to her grandmother? Certainly Fallon would be expected to meet the Queen if he were to try to join them. The likelihood was she would be taken along with him. If so, what would she do then?

"I don't know," she said nervously.

To her surprise, Fallon said, "Neither do I. Perhaps we should simply observe for a bit."

"Gad-fingle it!" said Medafil, shaking his wings. "What are you two afraid of?"

"Caution is not the same thing as fear, friend gryphon," replied Fallon gently.

"Well, fear or caution, I intend to go to the Queen."

"I'd rather you didn't just yet," said Fallon.

"Actually, Medafil, I don't know that I'm ready to join them, either," said Cara.

"Stig-fraggle it, what's wrong with . . . oh!" He stopped his sputtering and turned his eagle's head to stare at Cara with one gleaming black eye. She could tell he realized she was uncertain about what to tell her grandmother. "All right," he sighed. "I'll stay with the two of you."

"Not two, *many*!" complained the Squijum, which actually made Fallon laugh.

They began to move in a loop, circling around the unicorns. At one point they mounted a low rise and could, by standing behind a row of dense bushes, look down and see the Gathered Glory, which gleamed among the trees. Cara could hardly bear the longing, the urge to rush down and become part of that great and beautiful wave. She turned to Fallon to say that maybe it was time after all and saw that he had fallen to his knees. He was gazing at the unicorns, tears streaming down his face.

"I didn't know," he murmured after a moment. "I just didn't know. . . ."

"Let's move on," said Cara softly, feeling an unexpected tenderness for Fallon. "Since they're heading toward the Axis Mundi we can join them there if we want."

In this, of course, she was mistaken. When Graumag had told Medafil that the unicorns were heading for the Axis Mundi, she had been speaking generally. In reality, Amalia Flickerfoot had no intention of going to the Axis Mundi at this time. Her plans involved heading for somewhere close to it, somewhere far more dangerous.

CHAPTER LXXX

TO FREE A WIZARD

"Do you have a knife?" asked M'Gama.

Rocky looked at her, puzzled. "What for?"

"Never mind what for! Do you have one? If not, help me find a sharp stone."

Without another word, she began searching for such a stone herself. The dim glow of the orange lines that ran along the corridor was sufficient for her eyes, which were long accustomed to low light. As she searched, she realized something she had previously noticed, but that hadn't completely registered because she had been focused on so many other things: The delver tunnels were beautifully crafted. She would have found no sharp edges, or even any loose stones, if the tremors had not done so much damage. As it was, she crossed to a pile of rubble where part of the ceiling had collapsed and quickly located a shard about a foot long. Running a finger over it, she murmured, "Perfect."

Returning to the outcropping over which she had found

Rocky weeping, the Geomancer knelt in front of it. She held out her left arm and drew the edge of the shard across her flesh. Blood welled out, scarlet against her ebony skin. She turned her arm so the blood would drip onto the stone outcropping, then closed her hand into a fist and clenched it. She repeated the action, the blood flow increasing each time she did. When she was satisfied she had enough, she relaxed her fingers. Then she used her right hand to pinch the divided flesh together, chanting in a low voice until the wound had sealed itself shut. It was not healed, and would not be for some time, but the bleeding had ceased.

She took a deep breath, then placed her hands upon the bloodied stone. Turning to Rocky, she said, "What is his name?" When the delver hesitated, she snapped, "If you want me to bring him back, I need his name! You must know that much."

Rocky swallowed hard, then whispered, "He is called Namza."

"Ah," said M'Gama. "The King's wizard." Rocky nodded.

M'Gama closed her eyes and pressed her forehead to the stone. She began to chant in a low voice, *"Amma kreymos petra. Amma kreymos petra vivat!"*

She felt the stone open to her, felt her magic begin to weave its way between its very atoms.

Hear me, O Namza, she thought. *Hear me! I am M'Gama, come to call you forth.*

No answer.

Hear me, O Namza, she thought again, more fiercely

468

this time. *If you are still here, if there is any part of you left that can answer, then I bid you do so. I have sensed your power for days now, and it is akin to my own. Though you are delver and I am human, we have much in common. Wake, O Namza! Wake from this stony sleep and return to your living shape. Your student has need of you. I have need of you. Lus . . . Delvharken has need of you.*

No answer.

The tunnel walls shivered around them once more, but M'Gama did not notice. Again she called, and yet again, forcing her voice, her mind, her very self, into the Stone.

At last she sighed and began to withdraw. As she did, she felt something stir. And in her head a voice — faint, as if from a great distance, but clear nonetheless — whispered, *Wait. I will come with you.*

Rocky watched in horror as the Geomancer gasped and rolled off the stone she had been trying to call back to life, now seemingly lifeless herself. Scrambling to her side, the delver pressed his ear to her chest. To his relief, she was still breathing. Before he could check on her further, a sound caught his attention. He looked back, then cried out in joy.

Namza was returning from the Stone!

With a lunge, Rocky threw himself against the outcropping that had once been his teacher. He remembered, too well, the terrible cold he had experienced as he returned from his own near-Stone experience. Because Namza was

469

older, and had gone much deeper, he feared the old wizard would be that much the worse upon reviving.

M'Gama groaned behind him, but Rocky's focus was entirely on his teacher now. Slowly, very slowly, as if some invisible sculptor were carving him, Namza was returning to delver form. First a broad outline appeared, crude shapes that *might* be seen as arms and legs, as a delverling sometimes imagines he sees the shapes of delvers in the walls of a cave. Heartbeat by heartbeat the lines grew deeper, the shape more distinct, until it was obviously the form of a delver. Just a delver, though — any delver, not one with a name and a personality. Yet on the process went, the features becoming ever more pronounced, the brow high, the chin wide, the age lines deep, until at last it was clearly Namza and no other.

Then, as silent, clear, and swift as when the moon emerges from behind a cloud, came the moment when Namza's form shifted from stone to flesh and he lay shivering in his pupil's arms.

Rocky held the old wizard close, muttering soothing words and feeling strange that he was the one now doing the comforting, after all the times his teacher had comforted him.

"Dear student," whispered Namza, lifting a trembling hand. "Is that you?"

"It is I, master. I have come for you."

"But who was it that brought me back? It was a great power that called me, a great power indeed."

"It was M'Gama, the Geomancer," replied Rocky, feeling regret and shame that he had not been able to work the magic himself.

"Is she well? She put forth a mighty effort."

Rocky turned to glance at M'Gama and stifled a cry. The Geomancer remained still and unmoving upon the tunnel floor. "I must check on her. Will you be all right?"

"The cold is fierce," said Namza, still shivering. "But it will pass. Look to the lady."

Scuttling back across the stone floor, Rocky knelt beside M'Gama and asked urgently, "Lady, are you well?"

She moaned and her eyes fluttered open. "Not yet," she whispered. "But I will be. I simply need to rest."

As if to contradict her words, to say there was no time for rest, the walls of the tunnel shivered and they heard stones falling somewhere behind them.

"What was that?" cried Namza in alarm. "What is happening to Delvharken?"

"The world is wounded," replied M'Gama, her voice still weak.

"How can this be?" gasped Namza.

"Delver, help me to your teacher's side," said the Geomancer. She pushed herself to her knees. Leaning on Rocky, but not rising to her feet, she scuffled across the floor, then collapsed beside Namza. She looked at the old wizard, shook her head as if she could not believe what she was about to do, then lifted herself enough to press her brow to his.

A moment later he cried out in fresh horror. "Oh, this is what I have feared! How long do you think we have before it is too late?"

"A day or two at the most," replied M'Gama. "After that, this world, Luster or Delvharken, whichever you choose to call it, will shake itself to pieces."

"Is there no way to heal the tree?" asked Namza with a groan.

"None that I know of."

"That is why I came searching for you, teacher," whispered Rocky. "I hoped you would have the answer."

Namza closed his eyes. "I wish I had as much faith in myself as you have in me, my student."

Even as he spoke the world shook again, causing a boulder to crash down just feet away.

"We must leave!" cried Rocky. "We must go to the surface!"

Before M'Gama and Namza could struggle to their feet, another tremor rippled through the walls of their tunnel. With a roar, most of the ceiling collapsed, boulders thundering down on either side of them.

CHAPTER
LXXXI

MERRY FOOLS, DESPERATE TASK

Grimwold was both annoyed and relieved to find that his calculations about where to go had been correct. Relieved because he knew this was what the Queen wanted. Annoyed because . . . well, this was going to be bouncier than he liked and ridiculously exuberant.

He heard them first, of course, which was almost always the way. They were, after all, a noisy lot.

With a sigh, he hurried forward.

"Grimwold!" cried a dozen voices as he stepped into the clearing. Immediately three men grabbed instruments — a flute, a trumpet, and a drum, which Grimwold considered an absurd combination — and played a minor fanfare.

Four brightly colored wagons were arrayed around the clearing. The back door of the largest flew open and out sprang a short, chubby man who completely ignored the steps attached to the back of the wagon. Bounding over them, he landed deftly on his feet, took another leap forward, did three somersaults, and ended up standing, smiling broadly, right in front of Grimwold.

"Greetings!" he cried merrily. "Greetings, O Chronicle Keeper, Master of Stories and therefore Source of Inspiration. Armando de la Quintano and The Queen's Players welcome you!"

"Greetings, Armando," replied Grimwold, somewhat wearily. "I'm glad to find you here, since I had to do quite a bit of guesswork."

"Where else would we be, my friend?" cried Armando. "Are we not The Queen's Players? Jacques sought us out with the lady's request that we bring ourselves here to wait, so here we brought, and here we waited. I must say it's been a bit dull with no one to perform for, so we are glad to see you!"

"This is likely not the time for a performance," said a gloomy voice as two men stepped down from the last wagon on the left side. The face of the one who had spoken was worn and weary. Grimwold thought it odd that, to look at him, with his dour face and slumped shoulders, you would never know that he carried more jokes and riddles in his brain than there were stories in the Unicorn Chronicles.

The other man — bald, snub-nosed, and dressed in an absurdly colorful patchwork coat — appeared equally serious. This was unusual, since Grimwold knew, from many previous meetings, that he was generally as cheerful as Jacques was solemn.

"Greetings, Jacques," said the Chronicle Keeper to the

solemn man. "And greetings, Thomas." This was to the man in the patchwork coat.

Both men returned the greeting.

Speaking to Thomas, Grimwold said, "Have you succeeded in your quest?"

"I have indeed," replied Thomas, with a slight shudder.

"I'm impressed. After Amalia told me what she had asked of you I did not expect I would ever see you again — or at least not see you both alive and successful, since it seemed your quest must end in either death or failure!"

"Thomas is a continuing source of amazement," said Armando happily. "He really should have been an actor!"

This led to another fanfare and a round of cheers from the Players. Nine of them built a human pyramid in Thomas's honor. When they finally calmed down, Jacques said to Grimwold, "Can we assume that you bring new instructions from my former bride?"

Grimwold winced. Jacques had been married, briefly, to Amalia Flickerfoot during the time she was trapped in human form and known as Ivy Morris, the Wanderer. He believed — hoped — himself to be Cara's grandfather. However, the Queen had not confirmed that, and Jacques had not yet found the courage to ask her directly.

"I do indeed," said Grimwold. "She asks her Players to join her and the unicorns of Luster, for the Gathered Glory is traveling to the center of the world to battle Beloved and the Hunters."

An odd smile creased Jacques's face, pulling up at the deep-etched lines. Turning to Armando he said, "Well, old friend, the time has come. Are you ready to perform for the enemy?"

Armando turned to the Players, who had gathered in a half circle around them. They were a motley crew, arrayed in everything from rags to spangles, but alive with joyful energy. "Are you ready for what we have discussed?" he cried.

The response was a mixture of cheers, headstands, flips, and drumrolls.

With a grin, Armando said, "I think we're ready."

"Good," said Jacques. "Then it will soon be time for the performance of our lives. With an astonishing amount of luck, we may even live through it."

CHAPTER
LXXXII

MERGING MAGICS

Namza, who was very old and very wise — though perhaps not as wise as his student liked to think — had been terrified when the tunnel roof collapsed. Such fear was a sensation he had not felt in more years than he could remember. But for all his long life he had believed Delvharken unshakable, and in the few moments since he had returned from the Stonesleep, that belief had been shattered.

The orange lines had finally failed, making the darkness complete. Even had the lines still been glowing, the air was filled with so much dust from the collapse of the ceiling that they would likely have been visible as no more than dim orange smears.

Where were Nedzik and M'Gama? Had they survived the stonefall? Namza tried to call out, but the choking dust made it hard to breathe, and he began to cough instead.

"Teacher, is that you?"

Warm relief flooded Namza's heart. His student, at least, was still alive. With that thought came a question: How had

Nedzik found him down here? The old delver scowled. He wasn't supposed to call the boy by his real name anymore. On the other hand, what was that cruel ruling but additional proof of Gnurflax's tyranny? Not only that, it was his — Namza's — fault the lad was such a rebel to begin with. The old wizard corrected himself. No, it was not his fault; it was his success!

"Teacher?"

"Yes, I'm here and unhurt. But what of the Geomancer? M'Gama, are you with us?"

"I'm here," she called, then began to cough from the effort.

"Well, we all survived," grunted Namza. "That's one thing. Now all we have to do is find a way out."

He sounded more positive than he felt.

"Any ideas?" asked M'Gama.

Namza tried to read her voice, seeking tones of challenge or despair. But she had kept it marvelously neutral. He was impressed.

"Well," he replied, "the first thing we need is light. Can you call it from stone?"

"Not unless I know the stone. Can you?"

"With the same limitation. Which means we'll have to start by learning the stone that surrounds us." He hesitated, then said, "It will be faster if we work together."

Silence.

"Come," he said sharply, "do not be shy. Our magics

have already touched and mingled or you could not have called me back to begin with."

The Geomancer's reply was indirect. "Why are you so different from other delvers?"

"Age has its benefits."

"This is not a time for jesting! You are not like the others and I want to know why."

Namza sighed. "If that is what is required for your cooperation then I agree to tell you." Thinking of his recent dreams, he added, "Indeed, I believe you will find it interesting when I do. But surely there will be a better time for such a tale!"

"True enough," said the Geomancer grudgingly. "All right, how do you suggest we begin?"

"Let us join hands. This will be easier if we are in contact."

Namza heard M'Gama moving toward him. A moment later her outstretched hand grazed the back of his head. He reached up. A brief period of awkward fumbling followed as the two wizards tried to find each other's hands in the darkness. Once their fingers were linked, Namza said, "All right, let us enter the stone."

He could feel the Geomancer's magic twine around his as they moved their power into the stone. Another tremor rippled through Delvharken. It was painful to experience, as if it were their own bodies being shaken and disturbed.

Once the tremor passed, M'Gama thought, *I did not expect our powers to merge so easily.*

Perhaps we are not as different as you have wanted to believe, replied Namza.

When the Geomancer did not respond to this, Namza felt a brief flash of anger, then reminded himself that delvers were prickly as well. Perhaps he was expecting too much of her. Opening his mind, he thought, *I am ready to work.*

As am I.

Their first task was to learn the stone, which proved to be fairly simple, partly because the stone here was basic, partly because their magics were combining more easily than either of them had anticipated. Once they had studied the form and structure of the stone and examined a bit of its history, Namza thought, *Ready?*

Ready.

Together they began to coax out the energy hidden within the stone, teasing it loose, freeing it. Slowly at first, then at an increasing pace, the stone began to warm around them.

"The walls are beginning to shine!" cried Rocky.

By common consent, without speaking a word, Namza and M'Gama set the magic so it would hold, then retreated to their bodies. When they opened their eyes, it was to a space permeated by a soft glow, though the light came as if through a fog because of the choking dust that still filled the air.

"The light should last long enough for us to find a way out," said Namza.

"Or make one," replied the Geomancer.

"That will require merging magics again," said Namza.

M'Gama closed her eyes, then said, "I am ready to do that, ancient one. But if we do live through this, when it is over I will expect you to answer my questions. I think there are things we can teach each other."

"Of that I have no doubt," replied Namza. "I have long wished that you and I could be in contact, for I agree there is much to be learned. But now is not the time for that discussion. Let us try to find a way out while we have light. If that does not work, we can try to move, if not mountains, at least a few stones."

His words proved prophetic; several minutes of searching showed the space in which they were trapped to be sealed on all sides.

"Well," said Namza glumly, "it appears that shifting some stone is our only option."

"The problem is," said M'Gama, "we don't know where to start. There's no point in trying to burrow our way through a tunnel clogged for a half mile ahead of us."

"Then we must return to the stone to find the best place to do this," said Namza.

Now that they had twice merged magics, reentering the stone was easily accomplished. Finding the best place to work, however, was difficult, and the answer, once located, was distressing.

That barrier is almost impossibly thick, thought M'Gama in despair.

It would be easier if we could attack it from both sides, replied Namza.

Yes, and if stone were made of sugar we could just eat our way through.

Tut! Are you always so gloomy?

This is hardly a situation to inspire mirth, replied the Geomancer, as another tremor shook the rock around them. *If you have a suggestion, just tell me.*

I do. Let us return to our bodies, and I will explain.

A few minutes later M'Gama was looking at Namza with astonishment and new respect. "You can really do this?"

The stone wizard patted his left shoulder. Realizing the Geomancer might not recognize the sign of affirmation, he said, "Yes, I can. It is not easy, nor is it done without pain. But it seems the best tactic at the moment. I spotted a tiny channel through the stone. As you correctly noted, if we place one of us on each side of the barrier it will be easier to open a complete passage."

"Teacher!" cried Rocky. "You know this will pain you!"

"So will dying before my time, though I suppose if I attempt this, that is possible as well. Now be still and let me concentrate."

The dusty air was still illumined by the spells they had placed in the stone walls, allowing M'Gama to watch in admiration as the old wizard began a magic she knew was possible, but had never dared attempt herself. He sat cross-legged on the cave floor. Resting his hands on his knees and closing his eyes, he began to chant. The Geomancer followed as much of the magic as she could, but too many of the words were unknown to her. She would not be able to repeat this spell — not that she was likely to want to try!

An acrid odor permeated their small space. Soon after that, Namza's skin began to grow scales. His body trembled with the pain of the coming transformation, and then he loosed a horrible cry of agony as he began to shrink.

Rocky clapped his hands to his ears and threw himself facedown.

The old wizard's robes sank in, then collapsed.

A moment later, a small, brown lizard wriggled out of one sleeve. It looked at M'Gama, flicked out its tongue, then scampered up the wall and disappeared into a tiny crack.

Trying to ignore the pain that had accompanied his transformation, Namza entered the thumb-wide opening he had spotted when he and M'Gama had been exploring the stone-fall from inside.

"Be careful, teacher!" he heard his pupil call from behind him.

Namza did not reply, mostly because being careful would have prevented someone of his age from trying this to begin with. As he slithered though the tiny opening, he hoped he had been correct that it extended all the way to the other side of the stonefall, no matter how far that might be. He also hoped, even more intensely, that the world would not shift again until he had made it through.

In this latter hope he was disappointed. He had crawled about ten feet along the narrow opening when a low rumble set his tiny heart racing with terror.

The stone was moving again.

He knew that not far ahead was a larger space — a kind of pocket in the stone at least five inches across.

Namza crawled toward it as fast as he could, hoping to reach it before the walls closed around him and smashed his tiny body to a lizardly pulp.

CHAPTER LXXXIII

BATTLE PLANS

Amalia Flickerfoot gazed out on the Gathered Glory with a mixture of pride and terror. That her gentle people were now ready to fight for their home was a source of inspiration to her. At the same time, her heart was pierced by the blood-certainty that many of them would be dead before the night was over. What made it hurt even more was that she knew her unicorns did not really understand war and its horrible toll. Despite the Hunt, their deaths had been scattered, random. They had never experienced anything like what was coming.

Of course, that was assuming Luster even lasted until nightfall. She had begun to fear that the plans she had worked out with Feng Yuan and Belle were pointless. What if Beloved had accomplished her goal of destroying the unicorns simply by entering this world? How much more of this quaking and shaking could Luster endure before it just . . . fell apart?

Feng Yuan placed a hand on her side. "You seem troubled, My Queen."

"How could I not be troubled, given what we face this night?"

"Let us call together your leaders and review the plans one more time. It may ease your spirits."

As the Queen's Council was gathering, a unicorn — one Amalia did not know by sight, though that was not unusual now that the unicorns had converged from all corners of Luster — came trotting up and said, "We have a visitor."

"Thank you, um . . ."

Not knowing his name, she let the sentence hang. After a moment the messenger ducked his head and said shyly, "My name is Seeker. I believe you knew my second cousin, Finder."

The Queen felt another lance of sorrow. "He was very dear to me, Seeker. Now, who is this visitor?"

"A centaur, My Queen. She does not speak our language, but I was able to determine that her name is Arianna and that she wishes to meet you."

"How did she find us?"

"She didn't. One of the outrunners found *her*."

Feng Yuan, who had remained in contact with Amalia through this conversation, smiled. The outrunners, or scouts, had been her suggestion.

"Bring her to me, please."

"As you wish."

It was not long before the centaur was standing before them. Her horse's body was larger than that of all but the biggest unicorns; her human portion, rising from the front shoulders, added more height, with the effect that she towered over the Queen. She spoke a few words, but they were incomprehensible to Amalia.

"That sounds like a form of Greek," Feng Yuan told the Queen. "I know only a bit of it, and what I did learn is differently spoken from what she has said. Even so, I may be able to communicate with her enough to explain how she can be opened to mind speech."

"Go ahead and try," replied Amalia.

Feng Yuan began a halting conversation, carried on partly in broken Greek, partly in sign language, that finally led to Arianna nodding and spreading her arms. At this invitation Amalia stretched her neck and, straining upward, pierced the centaur's chest. After a brief cry of surprise, Arianna smiled. Following Feng Yuan's example, she placed her hand upon Amalia's shoulder. As with most, it took a few tries before the Princess grew accustomed to speaking mind-to-mind, but she got the knack of it soon enough.

"What brings you to our camp?" asked the Queen.

"I was traveling toward the Axis Mundi, eager to learn what is troubling the world, when one of your people spotted me. I had hoped to find the unicorns, anyway, thinking perhaps you might know what has disturbed Luster, so I was happy to follow him to your side."

Quickly Amalia explained to the Princess what Beloved had done, then said, "We are about to discuss the plans for our final confrontation with the enemy. Do you wish to fight at our side?"

"With all my heart! I have met your granddaughter, you know. She did something . . . difficult for us."

"She has told me of it," said the Queen solemnly. "I was proud of her, and I offer you my condolences on your loss."

Arianna nodded. "In granting my ancestor's deepest wish, Cara earned my eternal gratitude. It would be my honor to fight at her grandmother's side."

"Then you may join with us. From what I know of centaurs, you are somewhat more warlike than we and may have much to contribute."

Feng Yuan agreed, despite the flash of jealousy she felt at this statement.

The council had been gathering while the Queen and the Princess spoke. Now Moonheart stepped forward and said, "Let us begin."

"Agreed, brother," said the Queen. "Let us begin."

The plan was simple, really, and relied largely on their hope that Beloved, believing them to be brutish, would not think them capable of the deception they had been plotting.

"Let me understand," said Arianna at one point. "Beloved believes you will meet her in the field northeast of the tree tomorrow morning. But you plan instead a surprise attack on her own camp this very night?"

"That's the basic idea," replied Feng Yuan.

"It will help," added the Queen, "if Beloved is aware that dragons cannot lie."

Arianna wrinkled her brow. "Why will that help?"

"Because I sent a dragon to deliver this challenge."

"I'm confused. If a dragon cannot lie, how could it deliver a false challenge?"

The Queen grimaced. "Because I lied to the dragon. She will be annoyed with me when she finds out. I am not looking forward to telling her. It is far better to stay in a dragon's good graces."

"Are the dragons with you now?"

"Nearby. They will join us later in the evening, which is when I will tell them. It will be on their signal that we attack. We do not have a horn to announce the charge and do not want to provide such a warning, anyway. Instead the dragons will be positioned at either end of our flanks. When the time comes, they will shoot two columns of flame into the air. That will be the signal for the charge."

"And how will they know when to do this?" asked Arianna, intrigued by what the unicorns had planned.

"We have arranged for a diversion in the camp," said Feng Yuan with a smile. "When the Hunters are sufficiently distracted, two humans, members of a group called The Queen's Players, will alert Graumag and Firethroat that it is time. And then . . ."

"Yes?" asked Arianna.

The Queen's face was grim. "Then we end the Hunt — or die trying."

CHAPTER LXXXIV

TUNNELING

When the stone walls began to shift once more Rocky embarrassed himself by screaming. He could not help himself. But his terror was not on his own behalf; it was for his teacher.

The movement of the stone lasted only a few moments. When it was done he turned to M'Gama and cried, "Is he alive? Surely you can tell if Namza still lives!"

Some ten feet away, Rocky's teacher did indeed find himself, much to his own astonishment, still alive. Though the stone had sealed the narrow shaft through which he had been crawling, he had managed to reach the air pocket. Unfortunately, during the temblor the space had been compressed so that it was now barely bigger than his own tiny body. His relief at being alive was so great it took a moment for him to realize that his right foot was trapped.

Ignoring the pain, which was intense and growing worse, Namza stretched out his mind to contact the Geomancer.

M'Gama's eyes flew open. "He lives!"

Rocky gasped in relief.

"Be still," ordered the Geomancer. "Your teacher and I have work to do." Closing her eyes, she relaxed into herself, then entered the Stone once more. When she and Namza were in solid contact, she thought, *Shall we begin?*

I see no point in delay. And I am rather eager to leave this space if I can.

He did not mention the trapped foot.

Once more they linked their magics, straining to force the stone to their will. But though they exercised all their power, nothing happened.

We need my student to join us, thought Namza at last.

Is he ready for this?

Not at all. In fact, it may well destroy him. But the three of us — not to mention the world itself — are already at the edge of destruction.

I will see what I can do, replied M'Gama.

Namza sighed and settled in to wait, which was not easy, given that tons of rock seemed ready to crush his finger-sized body.

* * *

"We need your help," M'Gama said to Rocky.

"Of course! I'll do anything!"

M'Gama made a sound of exasperation. "I wish people would think before they say such things. Oh, trust me," she added quickly, "you're not the only one. But I need you to understand that we are asking you to take part in a magic for which you are not ready. It may well be more than you can bear."

"What I cannot bear is to lose my teacher! What must I do?"

M'Gama sighed. The rate at which she was becoming connected to these delvers was alarming! To Rocky she said, "Take my hands. I will pull you into the magic. Your biggest task will be to let go — let go of your body, and then let go of your fear, for both will block what we are trying to do. Mostly we need to draw on your energy. Have you practiced this at all with your teacher?"

"Only once, and it was . . . not a success."

"Well, it had better succeed now. Otherwise this will be our permanent resting place." To herself, she added, *At least, I think it will be our permanent resting place.* The truth was, she had no idea what would happen if Luster actually disintegrated, which was beginning to seem more and more likely. . . .

Rocky reached forward and took her hands.

"Ready?" she asked.

"Ready."

She drew him into the magic.

Rocky felt as if his soul were being plucked from his body. This was different from when he had nearly fallen into the Stonesleep. Then he was, in a way, returning to where he belonged, or at least his body was. Now he felt as if part of him were going somewhere it did not belong at all. Panic seized him, and he began to fight the magic.

Stop struggling! ordered M'Gama. *You will do yourself no good and in fact will make things worse for all of us.*

Rocky wanted to take a deep breath to calm himself, but since he was no longer in his body that was not possible.

Do you trust your teacher? demanded M'Gama.

Yes. YES!

Then please, trust me as his partner in this magic. You will be with him soon, I promise.

That did the trick. Thinking of Namza, Rocky was able to hold himself together just long enough for M'Gama to finish the linking. Once secure in the presence of his teacher, he let go of his fear and began to observe.

His first thought was that it was beautiful to see what M'Gama and Namza were doing, which was weaving their very selves into the Stone. Soon he began to understand how it worked. After several minutes he relaxed and joined them.

At first they simply pulled parts of him along with them, but after a little while he was able to participate in the work.

Despite all this, he was shocked when they actually

began to shift the stone. For a moment he nearly lost consciousness. But he held on, held on, held on. . . .

A terrible grinding sound began, the sound of stone reluctantly moving at their command, compacting itself, opening a way for them to pass.

The work took hours. Namza and M'Gama set things in motion, but it was Rocky's youthful strength that let them finish the job, though they pulled so much energy from him to do so that when it was done he was nearly drained.

After the Geomancer and the delver returned to their bodies, they crawled — dragged themselves, really — through the tunnel the three of them had opened. Rocky went first, taking a moment to gather up Namza's robes before he began. He was about halfway through when something dropped onto his bald scalp. He barely stopped himself from brushing it away before he realized it must be Namza. "Teacher?" he asked softly.

"Yes, it's me," replied Namza, crawling past his student's ear and onto his shoulder. "I do not have the strength to return to my normal shape right now, so I must ask you to carry me."

"It will be my honor."

"Will you please keep moving?" snapped M'Gama from behind them. "I do *not* want to be in this tunnel when the next tremor hits!"

Rocky scurried forward. When he climbed down from the far side of the tunnel, he was delighted to find that the orange lines on this side were still glowing. M'Gama emerged shortly afterward. Accepting Namza's continuing lizardhood without comment, she said simply, "Which way to the surface?"

Rocky wept as they made their way out of Delvharken.

He wept not because the journey was hard, though it was, for there were great rifts in the floors of the tunnels, as well as massive stonefalls that were nearly impossible to pass and several places where they feared the ceiling was but moments from collapsing onto their heads.

No, it was the destruction, which was even worse now than when he had made his way underground not long before, that drew his tears. He wept, too, for the work itself, for the craft and the care that had gone into creating the tunnels and gateways, the smooth floors and the perfect angles of Delvharken. Those passageways were the work of generations of delvers, and it had taken but days for all that labor to be swept away. Most of all he wept because if stone itself was not solid and safe, then nothing was.

Namza was more resigned, but seemed to understand what Rocky was feeling, for he often muttered soothing words into his pupil's ear from his perch right next to it.

M'Gama did not speak much for the first part of the journey, but finally she stopped and turned to Rocky. When the delver stopped, too, she got on her knees so she could be face-to-face with Namza, who, still in lizard form, remained on Rocky's shoulder.

"When your student asked me to pull you back from the Stone he told me he believed you were the only one who could halt this destruction. Yet you claim you know no way of doing so. Were your student's words just a ruse to gain my help?"

Namza took a long time to answer, and M'Gama had to lean close to hear when he finally did speak. "I can do nothing to stop this myself. However, I do know of one who might accomplish it. Unfortunately, he has not been heard from in hundreds of years."

"Who is it?" asked Rocky eagerly.

"You have known of him as 'the Great One.'"

M'Gama snorted in disgust. "A delver myth is not going to help us now."

"He is not a myth," insisted Namza, though he did not seem offended. "There truly was . . . *is* . . . a Great One. He may seem to have disappeared, but I tell you truly he is still a part of Luster."

"What are you talking about?" asked M'Gama.

Before Namza could answer, they heard a roar behind them — not the sound of falling rock, but the cry of some great beast.

"What is that?" asked the Geomancer.

"Hard to say," replied Namza, his forked tongue flicking out with each word. "Any number of strange creatures haunt the deeper parts of Delvharken. It would make sense that they, too, are making their way to the surface. You and I might be able to battle such a beast, lady. Even so, I suspect it would be wiser to flee."

M'Gama glanced behind her and quickly agreed.

"This reminds me of the time I was fleeing the skwartz," panted Rocky, after they had run up a long, sloping tunnel and turned a tight corner.

"You attracted a *skwartz* and lived to tell of it?" asked Namza in astonishment.

"I had help. I was with a human girl, a gryphon, and an old dwarf named Grimwold."

"Student," said Namza, "it is clear you have a great deal to tell me when the time is right. Even so, for the moment I would suggest we talk less and move faster."

Another roar from behind, clearly closer now than the last time they had heard it, underlined his point.

They quickened their pace and soon came to a wide corridor, partially blocked by rubble. With a glad cry of "There's the way out!" Rocky turned into it.

"Not there!" said Namza urgently.

"But we want to go to the surface. This is the main exit."

"If we're planning to go to the Axis Mundi, I know a better way. There's a transit point not far off. Follow my directions."

Soon they turned into a side tunnel that, after about a hundred feet, ended at a solid wall.

"What treachery is this?" demanded M'Gama.

"Any treachery lies in our sharing this with you," replied Rocky sharply. "This is a transit point. It is one of the great secrets of the delvers. Look more closely, Geomancer."

Barely visible in the dim light was the outline of an arch in the wall. Even harder to see were the odd symbols carved around it. Tracing them with his fingertip, Rocky began to chant.

Another bellow from the beast pursuing them overpowered his voice.

"Whatever you're doing, you'd better do it fast," cried M'Gama. "That thing is at the mouth of the tunnel!"

Fingers trembling, still chanting, Rocky finished tracing the symbols.

The space within the arch began to glow.

"Hurry!" cried the delver.

Stepping through the arch, he disappeared.

M'Gama followed, crying out at the cascade of tingles that flowed over her skin. As soon as she was through, Rocky turned and, again, began tracing symbols.

"The transit point would seal by itself in a little while," explained Rocky. "But we don't want to take a chance of that thing following us."

"What just happened?" asked M'Gama, shuddering with the aftereffects of passing through a transit point. "I felt a similar tingling several times when I was carried into Delvharken, but I was blindfolded and could never tell what was going on."

"The transit points are . . . shortcuts," said Rocky, who had finished his chanting. "You go through in one place and come out in another."

"How do they work?"

"That is deep magic," said Namza. "As is the fact that we are now quite close to the Axis Mundi."

As if to underscore where they now stood, the tunnel shook violently.

"The disruption is greatest here, closest to the tree," said M'Gama, her face grim. "We must get aboveground as quickly as possible."

"The exit is not far," said Namza. "May I suggest that we run?"

It was just as well that they did, since the tunnel collapsed behind them as they emerged onto the surface.

Dusk had fallen, so although there was some light, it was not painful to Rocky's eyes. They were in a forest, which made things even darker, but not far ahead they could see a lighter area, indicating that the forest thinned. Pointing that way, M'Gama said, "That must be the edge of the meadow that surrounds the tree."

She began to stride forward.

"Wait, please," said Rocky. "I need to call my cousins. They were expecting to meet me here should I manage to return from Delvharken. They may have news for us."

M'Gama turned back and watched as Rocky lowered himself to the ground. He set Namza's robes beside him, then crossed his hands over his chest. Having done this recently, it did not take him long to move into the trance-like state that let him make the call.

As Rocky sat, Namza limped down his student's arm, then over his abdomen. He made his way to the ground, then crawled a few feet away. M'Gama watched in fascination as he slowly returned to his delver form. When the transformation was finished, he fell backward, panting, his eyes closed in anguish.

Concerned, the Geomancer went to his side.

"I'll be all right," he said. "I just need time to recover. Those changes are . . . painful." He paused, then said, "Would you hand me my robes? And if you know any spells for stanching the flow of blood, you might apply one to my foot."

She glanced down and gasped at the sight of his torn and twisted toe.

"It was caught in the movement of rock while I was in the tunnel," he explained. "I managed to stay the bleeding then, but the transformation has opened it again."

M'Gama hesitated, then pulled one of the jeweled rings from the fingers of her left hand. Murmuring a low chant, she slipped the ring over Namza's big toe. After a moment, the pulse of blood stopped.

"Keep that on for now," she said. "Not only will it help with the bleeding, it will hold some of the pain at bay."

She handed him his robes.

"Thank you," replied Namza, managing to get to his feet. "I welcome the relief from the pain, which was making it hard to think."

As Rocky had predicted, it did not take long for the first of his cousins — again, it was Gratz, now known as Pebble — to sense the call.

Knowing the connection had been made, Rocky moved back to full wakefulness. He smiled to see his teacher in his true form again, then said proudly, "The rest of my cove will be here soon."

Indeed, ten minutes and two tremors later, a group of seven delvers came trotting into view.

CHAPTER
LXXXV

CONVERGENCE

It didn't make any difference what you had been told in advance, the first time you saw the Axis Mundi, you could not help but gasp in awe.

At least, that was Cara's reaction when she, Fallon, Medafil, and the Squijum reached the edge of the meadow that surrounded the great tree. Until that moment, the true height and width of the Axis Mundi had been hidden by the lesser trees through which she and her companions were walking. Seen suddenly in its full glory, the tree was . . . awesome.

Except it was also heartbreaking, because at its base gaped a ragged opening that had to be where Beloved had blasted her way into Luster. Even more appalling, it was clear that the wound was growing, extending upward, splitting the massive trunk like a spreading infection.

Cara started to take a step forward, then cried out and pulled back in shock. The meadow was *rippling*, the ground rolling and humping as if massive snakes, yards wide and hundreds of feet long, squirmed and twisted just beneath its surface.

The Squijum chattered in alarm and tightened his grip on Cara's mane. At the same time Medafil spread his wings, crying, "Gaaah! What in the froomp-dingled world is happening?"

"The roots of the tree are in pain," replied Fallon softly.

Cara turned away, sickened. In that turning, she spotted a cove of delvers standing not far away. They, too, had stopped at the edge of the meadow and, like her own group, were staring at it with clear dismay. Their presence would have been yet one more reason for concern, if not for the fact that in their midst stood the Geomancer.

Cara blinked, startled. What was M'Gama doing with a group of delvers? She had always hated the creatures.

Of course, Cara admitted to herself, her own feelings about delvers had changed drastically, at least in regard to Rocky. So it was certainly possible M'Gama might have befriended some as well. Even so, Cara's first reaction was to fade back into the forest, hoping Fallon and Medafil would follow her lead. But an instant later — thanks to her improved eyesight — she realized one of the delvers was her own dear Rocky. At least, she thought it was Rocky. What had happened to his face? It was scored with a series of wavy marks that looked like dark tattoos.

Leaning toward Fallon, she murmured, "A cove of delvers stands to our right. Normally I would suggest we retreat, but one of them is a friend of mine, as is the tall woman in their midst."

"Then let us join them," said Fallon.

No sooner had the words passed his lips than Cara cursed herself for not thinking more quickly. Neither Rocky nor M'Gama would be able to recognize her now that she was a unicorn. So how was she going to explain to Fallon that she had just claimed them as friends?

Well, Lightfoot spoke passable delvish, she reminded herself. *So it's not as if Rocky hasn't spoken to a unicorn before. And Fallon won't understand what I say when I speak delvish. Maybe I can pull this off.*

Taking a deep breath, she called, "Rocky!"

Instantly she felt more a fool than ever. Her grandmother had always said truth was the simplest thing, and that was certainly true right now. What was *not* simple was that there was no way, as a unicorn, that she should have known her delver friend now went by the nickname she herself had given him. Well, at least he wouldn't recognize her voice. She braced for his questions, desperately hoping she could get her story straight.

The delvers turned toward the call and immediately began to chatter. Rocky said something — Cara couldn't hear what — and the others fell silent.

Apparently he was now their leader.

The two groups walked toward each other until they were about twenty feet apart. Staring at her curiously, Rocky said, "How is it, unicorn, that you know my nickname?"

Medafil, seeing that Cara was fumbling for an answer, asked softly, "What did he say?"

When she had translated for him the gryphon stepped forward and said, "I told her, of course, you silly delver!"

Cara shot him a grateful look, then translated his comment for Rocky.

The delver nodded. "It is good to see you again, Medafil. Though it has not been that long since we traveled together, the world is changing rapidly."

Cara translated, as she continued to do throughout the conversation.

"Too rapidly, sot-groggle it," agreed the gryphon.

"Who are your friends?" asked Rocky.

Gesturing with his wing, Medafil said, "The unicorn goes by the name of Silverhoof."

As she translated this, Cara admired the way the gryphon had shaped the sentence to make it both deceptive — and absolutely true.

"The Squijum you know, of course," continued Medafil. "The tall gentleman goes by the name of Fallon."

"And how is it, Silverhoof, that you speak delvish?" Rocky asked, addressing her directly.

"I . . . learned it from my friend, Prince Lightfoot."

"Ah. And I see that you have the Squijum on your back. As far as I know, he is the only one of his kind. He used to travel with a friend of mine called Cara. Seeing him without her makes me fear she has suffered some mishap."

Cara translated this for Medafil, partly as a way to give herself time to think. To her relief, he again answered for her, saying, "I saw Cara not long ago. She was fine at the time. As to the Squijum — well, you know as well as I that he's a flighty little creature. You're apt to find him anywhere."

The Squijum made a rude sound and pinched Cara's neck, but said nothing.

Rocky nodded. Seeing that he had accepted this explanation, Medafil asked, "In return, and remembering that you are an exile from Delvharken, I am wondering who travels with you and how it is that you are here at the Axis Mundi."

"These are my cousins," said Rocky, gesturing toward the cove. "They are known as Lizard, Waterfall, First, Hammer, Diamond, Pebble, and Wart."

Looking at the delvers, each of whom bowed as introduced, Cara could not help but think, *They're sort of like the Seven Dwarfs, except half naked and really ugly.*

Gesturing to his right, Rocky continued, "And this is Namza. He is my teacher and the wisest of all delvers who live. The tall human is someone you must certainly have heard of, if not actually met — M'Gama, the Geomancer."

M'Gama stepped forward. Speaking in the language of the unicorns, she said, "What brings us here is the troubling of the tree. I would ask the same of you, as well as wondering who the human is who travels with you."

"As Medafil said, his name is Fallon," replied Cara.

"Not his name. Where did he come from and why are you all here?"

Cara turned to Fallon to translate this, then stopped cold. From the corner of her eye she had caught something she would never have noticed if not for the extended field of vision that had come with her transformation — something that set her heart pounding with joy.

The clearing that surrounded the tree was no longer empty. Approaching it from the far side were two humans and a unicorn. One was a brown-skinned boy she guessed must be the "Rajiv" Fallon had spoken of.

Fallon, who had followed her gaze, hailed them.

"Sahib Fallon!" cried the boy. He raced ahead of the others, flinging himself into Fallon's arms. "Sahib Fallon! I feared we would never see you again!"

Fallon caught the boy up — he seemed absurdly small next to the towering man — and swung him into the air. "I feared the same, Rajiv! I am glad the world has brought us together once more." He set Rajiv down beside him and rested his huge hand on the boy's jet-black hair as they awaited the arrival of the others.

Their reunion gave Cara time to still her beating heart, which her chest could barely contain, for the unicorn was none other than her beloved Lightfoot, alive and well. Oh, how she longed to act just as Rajiv had and to run to him! She might have, if not for the fact that the woman . . . the slender, graceful woman with the long red hair . . . was her mother.

Even without the improved vision that had come with Cara's transformation, she would have recognized her;

with that vision she could clearly discern, despite the distance between them, the features of a face that — other than a brief time in an enchanted dream — she had seen only in photographs for the last nine years. It was all she could do to hold in a sob of joy, and her impulse was to race forward. In fact, she started to do just that, then caught herself, torn between longing and fear. What was she to say? How was she to explain to her mother that she, her long-lost daughter, was now a unicorn?

Then another question seized her, this one far more frightening: Fallon had said her parents were together when he left them. *So where was her father?*

Lightfoot uttered a cry of greeting, a sound that made Cara's heart leap with responding joy, even though it was Fallon the Prince was calling to, not her. But an instant later the same concern she had had regarding her mother overwhelmed her again.

What would her dear friend think of what she had done?

To her surprise, she realized she was hoping he would welcome the change, even be delighted by it.

Their approach was made slower by the fact that after a few steps they backed away from the rippling meadow, choosing to walk around its perimeter instead. When they were finally within speaking distance, Fallon bowed gravely and said, "Greetings, Prince. And greetings, Mrs. Hunter. I am pleased to see you, but somewhat concerned that your husband is not with you."

"We are hoping he will be here soon," said Martha. Quickly she explained what had happened since they had last seen each other.

Cara's heart sank as she listened, and it was all she could do to keep from wailing in her despair. Had she found her mother only to lose her father? The thought that he might have entered Delvharken in search of her not only terrified her, it filled her with a wrenching guilt. How would they ever get him back? What if that underground world collapsed on him while he was down there looking for her?

Her bleak thoughts were interrupted by M'Gama stepping forward again. At her side was the old delver Rocky had introduced as "Namza."

Cara, who had grown used to the hideousness of the creatures during her time with Rocky — indeed, had come to accept it as just part of who they were — was momentarily startled by the way her mother recoiled at the sight of the aged delver.

Namza was staring at Fallon intently. Finally he said, "I have met someone like you before, tall one. Who are you, and what brings you to this world?"

Cara began to translate this from delvish, but Fallon startled her by saying, "Never mind, Silverhoof. I can understand him." Turning to the delver, his eyes more intense than Cara had ever seen them, he said, "Who was it that you met, venerable one?"

Though Fallon did not speak in delvish, it was clear the old delver understood him. She wondered if the big man had some version of the gift of tongues. If so, had he understood all her conversations with Rocky?

"Her name was Allura," said Namza.

Fallon closed his eyes and heaved a great sigh. "And what was the story she told?"

"You are of the same race as she, are you not?"

"Race is not the word I would use. However, you are correct that we are different from humans. We can discuss that later — assuming there is a later. For now, the story?"

"Let us move away from the meadow," replied Namza. "I mislike looking on that heaving ground."

This met with quick agreement from everyone, so the entire group — counting the Squijum there were now sixteen of them in all — moved into the forest until they found a space large enough to hold them. Everyone sat, save Lightfoot and Cara, unicorns generally preferring to stand. To Cara's mingled delight and concern, her mother — who she noticed had been looking at her oddly, as if she sensed something strange about her but could not figure out exactly what it was — took a place right next to her. Cara found herself leaning toward her, drinking in her scent and the sound of her every breath.

Namza began to speak again. As she had in the Chiron's cave, Cara served as translator, so that her mother, Rajiv, and Medafil could understand the tale that Namza unfolded.

"It is a sad story," began the old delver. "I know it only

510

because this woman, Allura, appeared to me on the night of my teacher's death. She had come to honor him, which moved me. After he returned to the Stone, she told me this story. She said she thought the day would come when I would need to know."

He looked at Fallon as he said this, but the big man only nodded.

Seemingly satisfied with this, Namza continued. "As you may know, Elihu officiated at the unicorns' great Purification Ceremony, the one that led to the birth of the Whisperer and ultimately the creation of the delvers."

"I've been told of that ceremony," said Fallon, unhappiness thick in his voice. "But try as I might, I cannot understand why he would have done such a thing."

"According to Allura, he wanted perfect creatures for the perfect world he was trying to create."

"That is correct, old one," said a new voice. "You remember the story well."

All eyes turned in the direction from which the words had come.

Standing a few feet from their gathering place was a tall, dark-skinned, golden-haired woman.

With a squeal of joy the Squijum leaped from Cara's shoulder and went running to her. She held out her hand. He leaped to take it, then scrambled up her arm and onto her shoulder. He looked as happy as Cara had ever seen him.

"Well," said Fallon gently, "this *is* a surprise. It's good to see you again, sister."

ENTER THE PLAYERS

Darkness was drawing on and the watch fires had been set in Beloved's camp when a quartet of brightly decorated wagons came rattling into the meadow southwest of the Axis Mundi. Three of the wagons were drawn by teams of four men. The fourth was pulled by an eccentric-looking man who handled it by himself, almost as if it were weightless.

The wagons had not come far past the meadow's edge when a group of twenty Hunters stood in front of them. They were led by the man named Kenneth. "Who are you?" he demanded. "What do you want here?"

"Who are we?" cried the small, roundish man who rode atop the first wagon. "Why we are the famous Strolling Players of Luster!" He sprang to the ground with astonishing agility. "I, personally, am Armando de la Quintano, leader of the Players. We travel from north to south, east to west, putting on shows for the humans who live here. Word of a new group of humans reached us not long ago, and of course we came as fast as we could. What more could Players want than a fresh audience?"

"Well, you can just turn around and travel back on out of here," snarled Kenneth. "We don't want any of your foolishness."

"You do not want entertainment?" asked Armando. He sounded astonished. "There is little in this world to lift the heart and not much for men to see or to laugh at." With a leer he added, "We, on the other hand, travel with beautiful women. Their costumes, what there is of them, are . . . lovely!"

The men behind Kenneth began to grumble. "Let's have a show!" cried one of them.

"A good way to relax before tomorrow's battle!" called another.

"A battle?" cried Armando. "Good gracious! Well, it is a fact known 'round the world that men of war grow bored without some entertainment. Restless men are not good for discipline."

"Leave this place now," growled Kenneth.

"Oh, don't be such a prig, Kenneth!" cried a Hunter. "Let's have the show!"

"A show!" cried several others. "We want a show!"

Before Kenneth could say anything in response, Armando called, "Li Yun, come out and greet our audience!"

Instantly an exquisitely beautiful Asian woman sprang from the first cart. She was dressed in a gauzy costume that covered little more than necessary. After a brief dance, she disappeared back into the cart.

The men cheered wildly and called for more.

Kenneth sighed. Though Beloved had retreated to her pavilion for the night, there were still hours to go before the men would sleep. And there *was* restlessness all across the camp. Maybe a show would be a good idea. "Oh, all right," he said. "Let's have your show, player."

"I am so pleased!" cried Armando. "We love to perform!"

Within the half hour, the main body of the Hunters was gathered on a low hill on the southern side of the camp. The four wagons formed a half circle on the lower ground, and Armando and his Players had set out enough torches to provide plenty of light. He blew a battered horn, and the show began.

About a hundred yards away were two more players. They were dressed all in black — their usual costume for performing — but instead of entering with the wagons, they had wriggled across the meadow from the far side, pausing only when they were close enough to the encampment to observe what was happening. Now they lay belly down in the grass, watching intently.

"Looks like they're in place, Bert," said one of them.

"Coo, Alfie, I hope this works. I don't want to lie here henny longer than I have to. I keep fearing the world's goin' to hopen under me belly and drop me down to lor' knows where!"

"I know what you mean, Bert. But standin', sittin', or lyin' here, there, or anywhere don't seem to make no difference. Everyplace is dangerous right now!"

First to perform were a trio of acrobats. The Hunters responded with scant applause. Next Armando brought out Li Yun and two other women, who performed a dance that was greeted much more enthusiastically.

After they were finished, an older man, gloomy-looking in the extreme, came out and launched into a story that soon had the Hunters laughing so hard tears were streaming down their faces. He looked startled at provoking such amusement, which only doubled the merriment.

When he had finished, five female acrobats did a tumbling set that had the Hunters gasping with astonishment.

Then the back door of the fourth cart opened and out stepped the eccentric-looking man who had hauled it into the clearing to begin with. His bald head shone in the flickering light of the torches. He wore an absurdly colorful patchwork coat. The front of it was crisscrossed by numerous gold chains, each of which disappeared into one of the coat's equally numerous pockets.

Following behind him, led by a much thicker chain, was the most ridiculous-looking creature anyone in the audience had ever seen. About half the man's height, it looked like a cross between a rooster and a dragon. A white cloth had been bound around its head, covering the eyes. That head itself was similar to a rooster's, though much larger and fiercer, especially around the beak. Below the head a long, scaly neck stretched down to a winged body that was also scaled, but had a thick fringe of feathers. Two stocky legs ended in clawed feet absurdly large for a creature of that size. Arcing up behind the creature was its tail. Though scaly and whip-like, it ended in a luxuriant plume of iridescent feathers.

The Hunters began to laugh, which was only natural. The creature was ridiculous, and none of them had any idea what a cockatrice was actually capable of. . . .

Across the meadow Alfie nudged Bert. "That's our cue!" he hissed. "Let's go!"

Bolting to their feet, the two men sprinted into the woods to deliver their message to the waiting dragons.

Unaware of what was happening outside, Beloved was in her pavilion, tormenting Ian. It had become a way for her to relax between the times when she was hearing reports or issuing new orders. The torments were not physical. That was too easy and did not suit her purposes. She found it far more amusing to taunt him with his failure.

Her sorry descendent was sitting up now, in a way, since he was bound to the center pole of the tent. She kept him gagged; she didn't need to hear whining excuses or pet-ulant accusations. It was sufficient to watch his eyes, which sometimes blazed with hate, other times went dark with despair and defeat.

It was a distraction — and she always needed distraction from her pain, which rose and fell in waves, but was never totally absent.

The pavilion was a bit of an indulgence, with its plethora of cushions, all beautifully embroidered, most with designs and images based on the hunting of unicorns. Oh, how many kings and nobles had heeded her urgings those centuries ago, back when the foul creatures still roamed the hills and forests of Earth, before that fool Bellenmore provided them with an escape route.

"Did you really think you could abandon me and not pay the price, Ian?" she purred now.

She was peeling an apple. Her long, slender fingers moved with languid grace. But the sense of relaxation was belied by her silver hair, which shifted and curled restlessly about her shoulders.

Ian, being gagged, made no answer.

"A pity you couldn't manage to capture that daughter of yours for me," she continued. "Things might have turned out differently if you had.

"I meant her no harm," she went on softly. The silver blade flashed as the bloodred peel of the apple descended from the fruit in a single, shining coil. "It's just that she was potentially a . . . problem. I didn't realize that at first, of course. Ridiculous to think that someone so important to me should be hidden away so thoroughly."

The peel dropped to the rug at her feet.

"Really, I was disinclined to put much stock in the prophecy about a child in whom the bloodlines of Hunter and unicorn merged. It was just too absurd. And it took time for my . . . sources . . . to find out the truth about her. She's disappeared now, did you know that? It's quite sad really. I might have thought she was simply in hiding. But I've had a hundred men out searching for her with the help of tracking packets seeded with my own blood. Blood calls to blood, as you know. Anyway, they nearly had her a few days ago. Then she just . . . vanished. It seemed mysterious at first, but the answer was obvious enough: She's *dead*, poor thing."

Neither the gag nor Ian's determination to hold himself aloof could stifle the groan that rose from his inner depths.

"The truly tragic part is, she was probably killed by one of those monsters she so foolishly thought worthy of protection. A pity, really. If we had managed to capture her earlier, we might have saved her."

She raised the apple and took a bite, her perfect teeth tearing at the fruit's white flesh.

Ian turned his head.

"Look at me!" snapped Beloved. When he did not obey, she stood, walked to him, grabbed his chin. With a grip that was remarkably powerful, she forced his head around so he was facing her once again. "A tear? Oh, dear me, Ian. I'm ashamed. I thought we had taught you to be stronger than that."

She started to say something else, but just then chaos erupted.

CHAPTER
LXXXVII

THE PIECES OF THE PUZZLE

Allura favored Fallon with a gentle smile. "I'm here for exactly the same reason you are, brother mine. I came because of Elihu." She turned to Namza. "I am sorry I could not get here sooner, venerable one. There is great risk for me in the journey, which is not done quickly. Yet even in my home, I felt it when the tree was disturbed. I have been trying to return here from that moment."

"It is a joy to see you again, lady," said Namza, bowing deeply.

Allura spread her hands in acknowledgment, then turned back to Fallon. "It has been a long time, brother."

"Millennia," he replied. "And this was the last place I expected to find you, sister."

"Surely you must have known I would be doing whatever I could to keep track of Elihu. Not having been banished as you two were, I had more freedom — though I did suffer some suspicion simply because I was so close to both of you. Even so, I journeyed here as often as I could manage to escape the notice of the Higher Powers."

"Tell me what you know of Elihu's fate," said Fallon, his voice almost pleading.

Allura sighed. "It is not a happy tale. Nor is the fact that the punishment he suffered after you last saw him —"

"A new punishment?" cried Fallon.

She nodded grimly. "A new punishment, for a new transgression. You know how his passion for whatever he was trying to create could be endearing, compelling, and infuriating all at the same time. After the two of you were exiled, it grew beyond that. I think, perhaps, he went a little mad. His passion seemed to take him over and blind pride seized him, driving him to urge the unicorns to an insane 'Purification Ceremony.'"

"Yes," said Fallon with a groan. "I know about that."

"But do you also know that in urging your unicorns to that act of pride he again offended the Higher Powers? They were already angry with him for creating Luster, of course. Having one mark against him for that previous act of rebellion, his punishment this time was swifter and far more devastating."

She paused as the ground shifted beneath them. When it began to settle, Fallon asked apprehensively, "What was this punishment, Allura?"

Looking directly at him, she replied, "The Powers transformed your *alahim* into a bestial creature that came to be known as the Dimblethum and relegated him to Earth."

Fallon groaned. Cara let out a cry of astonishment. Lightfoot shook his head in disbelief.

Allura swallowed hard, as if trying to control her emotions, then continued her story. "Confused and unhappy, but not knowing *why* he was unhappy, Elihu — now trapped in this coarse, lumbering form — made his way across Earth to the place where it connects with the Axis Mundi of Luster. It is not a spot most men can reach or even see. But despite his transformation, he still maintained a connection to this world. Once at the Axis Mundi, he was able to travel the tree back here, to the place he now considered his true home.

"I kept watch on him when I was able and did small things to try to protect him. It was not easy, for Luster was forbidden to us. Every trip I made here was dangerous for me." As she said this she stroked the Squijum, who was nestled behind the curtain of her golden hair. "I let my little companion here travel with me, until he disappeared on one of my trips."

"Hotcha good Squijum got losted," said a small voice from behind her hair.

"Yes," she said fondly, "you got losted and nearly broke my heart, you wicked creature." Looking up at the others, she said, "Happily, I see he has made friends on his own."

"You always were good at the small creatures, Allura," said Fallon wistfully.

His sister smiled at him, then continued her story. "The years — the centuries — that followed were hard for Elihu. Once so elegant and graceful, so quick of eye, deft of hand,

and sharp of wit, he now lived under a cloud, his body coarse and shambling, his keen mind dulled and foggy. He was lost and miserable, but did not know *why* he was lost and miserable. And he was intensely lonely, here in the world that he had created. At the same time, he was also intensely protective of it. Sadly, when the unicorns finally did begin to arrive, he could not remember that the main reason he had urged them to undertake that disastrous Purification Ceremony was to make them good enough for his world. He thought of them now as invaders and resented their presence."

Baffled by this, Cara intruded, asking, "But why were the unicorns coming here at all if Elihu no longer remembered these things?"

"He had informed an old magician named Bellenmore of his plans. Even though they could not find Elihu when Beloved's Hunt of the unicorns grew ever more dangerous, Bellenmore and his apprentice, Aaron, followed through on the idea.

"As you know, Elihu's spirit was a restless one. Still inflamed with a desperate desire to create, even in this form, he was always trying to make things. Yet he was ever thwarted by his clumsy paws and clouded brain. This was the true, and I think truly cruel, punishment of the Higher Powers. For his pride they did not merely cast him into this monstrous form, they blocked his deepest and most powerful urge."

She spread her hands, to indicate that she had finished her story. Cara stared at her for a long time before she finally said, "That was fascinating, but there must be some mistake. I've met Elihu!"

Allura looked at her in puzzlement.

"And I've seen the Dimblethum since then, too," she continued.

Even as the words passed her lips, Cara felt a sharp twist in her heart as she realized she was going to have to tell her story now — a realization confirmed when M'Gama said, "Tell us about this, Silverhoof."

The Geomancer's voice, always powerful, now held an air of command.

Cara glanced to her left. Her mother stood beside her, watching her with an expression she could not interpret, but that seemed to carry both fear and expectation. Lightfoot was on the other side of her mother, and Rajiv stood on the Prince's far side. Both had their hands on his shoulders, which Cara took to mean they could communicate with him mind-to-mind. Well, at least *that* would make things easier. She could tell the story in delvish and let Lightfoot provide the translation for the only two who could not understand that language.

"It happened three days ago. I was on the slopes of Dark Mountain with the dragon Graumag. We were heading for Autumngrove and had stopped to rest."

This was not the important information, but she had to build herself up to telling the full story.

"We had had a close encounter with some Hunters. We managed to elude them and were trying to decide what to do next, when Elihu entered the place where we were resting. He looked a great deal like you, Fallon, but he wore an animal's skin." She hesitated, afraid to speak the next words, but knowing she had to. "Without warning, he snatched me up and carried me away."

Fallon looked at her in puzzlement. "Elihu is powerfully built, Silverhoof, but I don't understand how he could pick up a unicorn and run off with her."

Cara drew a deep breath, then said it: "I was not a unicorn at the time."

All eyes were riveted on her. Cara could tell — by her mother's gasp and the way her hand flew to her mouth — the exact moment this information passed from Lightfoot to her.

"He had snatched me up because he had heard Hunters approaching," continued Cara quickly, before she lost her courage. "He was swift and strong, and he carried me to a cave. And there . . . there . . ."

"What happened?" demanded her mother.

Cara turned toward Martha Hunter and spoke her next words in English. "He offered to turn me into a unicorn so I could escape the Hunters, who were searching for me in my true form."

Tears rolled down Martha Hunter's face as she whispered, "And what was that true form?"

Cara's response rose on a half-choked sob. "My true form? It was the human shape I was born in." She swallowed hard. "I was called Cara, Cara Diana —"

Before she could finish, her mother flung herself forward. Wrapping her arms around Cara's neck she cried, "I knew it! I *knew* it was you the moment I saw you! I don't know why. It made no sense, it was mad, insane. But my heart knew the truth. I knew you were my daughter!"

She buried her face against Cara's silky mane and sobbed. As did Cara, who longed for arms so that she could hold her mother, as her mother held her. "Mom, Mom, Mom," she whispered, not knowing what else to say.

She felt Lightfoot pressing against her other side. "Thank the Bright Powers you're safe," he thought. "I've been so worried about you!"

She wished they could stay like this forever.

But the writhing world would not allow that.

It was Fallon who finally came to them. Putting an arm around Martha's shoulders, he murmured, "I know this is overwhelming for you, Mrs. Hunter. But the world is dying, and it will not wait for us to work out the matters closest to our hearts." Glancing at Allura, he added, "Believe me, I say this with painfully unfinished matters of my own. But we must press on in search of the truth."

Martha nodded and managed to calm herself. But she did not let go of Cara's neck.

At that moment, Rocky stepped forward. Next to him stood another delver. Rocky nudged him, then nudged him again.

"My name is Lizard," said the new delver. "I do not like

525

to bring more bad news, but I feel I should tell you that Ian Hunter is a prisoner of Beloved."

"How do you know this?" cried Cara, her joy at being reunited with her mother pierced by new terror.

"We were spying on her camp, which is in a meadow southwest of the great tree, not too far from here. We saw some delvers carry him in, bound and gagged. They took him to Beloved's tent, and later two Hunters carried him inside."

Lizard stepped back, as if embarrassed to have been speaking in front of so many people.

"We have to go get him!" cried Martha.

"First we must finish untangling this puzzle," said Fallon. "If the world fails, Ian will be lost, anyway. If we can figure out a way to save Luster, then we can work to save him as well."

Cara trembled with frustration, but knew that Fallon was right.

It was Allura who spoke next. "I do not understand how Elihu can once more be in his true form. How could he have escaped the judgment of the Higher Powers?"

At that, Lightfoot stepped into the conversation. "I fear I know the answer."

All eyes turned toward the unicorn.

"Yes?" asked Allura.

Cara could hear both eagerness and dread in her voice.

"I saw the Dimblethum at the Axis Mundi the night Beloved forced her way into Luster. He was placing the wire sphere that M'Gama called an anchor onto a pillar of stone that was clearly made by delvers. I could not understand, then, why he would have done such a thing. Now I believe. . . ."

His voice trailed off, unable to speak the terrible thing he suspected of the tortured creature who had been his friend.

After a long silence, Fallon said it for him: "You believe he betrayed Luster in return for being restored to his true shape."

"That is my fear," said Lightfoot mournfully.

"But who could have done that for him, who offered it to him?" asked Allura.

"The Whisperer, of course," said Fallon grimly.

A cry escaped Martha's lips.

Fallon turned to her. "What is it, Mrs. Hunter?"

"I almost did something as bad," she murmured. "Indeed, I might have, had the chance arisen before we met you here. This Whisperer . . . he came to me last night and promised . . . promised —"

She broke off, unable to continue right away. Silence lay across the listeners as Martha fought past her shame. Finally she said softly, "He promised he would bring me to my daughter if I would help him capture my mother." Her face blazing with self-reproach, she added, "All I can say is, do not blame this Elihu of yours too much. The Whisperer is a demon of persuasion."

"But if the Dimblethum became Elihu again, where has he gone?" asked Namza.

"Alas, the answer to that is easy," replied Allura. "Well, not where he is. But I fear I can explain the why of his disappearance." Turning to Cara, she said, "There is a thing called Transformational Magic."

"I know. I learned about it from the dragon Graumag."

"That magic would be what the Whisperer used to return Elihu to his true form," explained Fallon, his face grim. "And that same magic, stored in his body after his return to his true shape, would be what Elihu used to transform you into a unicorn." He shook his head, golden hair flowing over his broad shoulders. "After all that, he sacrificed what he had gained to save you."

"But why would he do that when Luster itself is at risk?" she cried, feeling yet another pang of guilt.

"I suspect he did not understand the full danger," said Fallon. "After returning to his true form, he must have been confused. He had spent several centuries as the Dimblethum. There is no telling what he could remember and what was lost to him."

"And he was very fond of you," put in Lightfoot. "He would have been eager to protect you any way he could."

"I am sure he was wracked with guilt for what he had done," added Allura. "He would have been looking for a way to expiate his crime, a crime committed against the very thing he loved most, the world he had created."

"So if only Elihu can heal the tree, and Elihu is now the Dimblethum again, does that mean there is no hope for Luster?" asked Lightfoot.

As if to reinforce his question, another tremor shook the world.

"There is hope," replied Fallon, his face set and dark.

"There is always hope," agreed Allura. "But in this case it is faint and comes with a heavy price attached."

"And now," said Fallon, "if you will excuse me, I have a job to do."

"Where are you going?" asked Cara.

Face grim, voice low, he replied, "I must tend to this Whisperer."

With no more words than that, he loped away from them, disappearing into the forest.

Rocky nodded to his cove. Lizard nodded back. Without a sound, the cove turned and trotted after Fallon.

The remaining group was silent for a moment, a silence broken when Martha exclaimed, "Where is Rajiv?"

CHAPTER
LXXXVIII

THE BLOODY FIELD

While the Hunters were watching Armando's show, in the forest beyond the meadow, the Gathered Glory waited tensely for the sign that the time was right to attack. Firethroat and Graumag were positioned at opposite ends of the glory's ranks. All it took was word from Bert and Alfie and suddenly two columns of flame shot straight into the air.

This was the signal the unicorns had been waiting for. With Belle and Moonheart at their front, the Gathered Glory began its first and only charge as an army, racing out of the woods and across the meadow. They moved in silence at first, but when they reached the edge of the camp they trumpeted their fury at the invasion of their home. With them came the Princess Arianna, her bowstring singing as she dispatched arrow after arrow into the ranks of the Hunters.

At the first sound, the Hunters sprang to their feet. Cursing and shouting, they drew swords, nocked arrows, raised spears. The ones in front of the audience turned their fury on the Players. As they did, Thomas whipped the blindfold off the ridiculous creature he had been displaying. The effect was immediate and horrifying: The first three men that rushed forward turned instantly to stone.

"Don't look at it!" screamed one of the Hunters. *"Don't look at it!"*

But it's hard to battle something you can't see, and at least two Hunters, more brave than wise, tried to sink arrows into the cockatrice's heart. The drawing of their bows was the last movement they ever made. Their hands froze on the bowstrings, eternally holding shafts they would never let fly.

As the other Hunters turned away or covered their eyes, the Players launched their attack. They flung themselves amongst the enemy, their lithe bodies twisting and turning as they struck out with fists and feet or slammed against the Hunters' backs, causing them to curse and stumble.

Two more of the men were foolish enough to turn back and fell victim to the gaze of the cockatrice.

Armando himself was working at ground level, rolling among the men, tripping as many as he could. They bellowed and thrust at him with sword or spear, but he was astonishingly fast for his girth. Still, he did not escape wounding, and blood flowed from several places on his body.

Tiny Li Yun leaped atop the back of another Hunter and covered his eyes with her hands. He turned, disoriented. At once she removed her hands, hiding her own face against his neck as she did.

It took her a moment to pull her legs free of his arms once he had turned to stone.

The cockatrice was tiring now, and Thomas knew it could only manage one or two more petrifications before it collapsed in exhaustion.

Another Hunter had grabbed a torch and was trying to set fire to the carts. Jacques, launching into a series of handsprings, struck him in the back. The man fell, dropping the torch. Jacques quickly rolled him over it before it could set fire to the autumnal grass.

"Jacques!" called Thomas. "Give me a hand."

Turning, Jacques saw that the cockatrice was staggering and Thomas was tying the blindfold about its eyes once more. He hurried to join his friend. Quickly, the two men finished binding the beast, then hustled it into the cart.

"Shall we?" asked Thomas as they emerged once more.

"Yes, I think we should," said Jacques. He sprang forward and leaped into the fray even as the Tinker began pulling watches from his pockets. "Ah, this one will do," said Thomas. He raced up behind a Hunter who was grappling with one of the Players, opened the watch, and clamped it to the Hunter's ear. Instantly the man shrieked with pain and fell to the ground, clawing at the watch, which clung maddeningly to the side of his head.

The Player who Thomas had rescued looked at him with wide eyes. The Tinker shrugged and said, "I had forgotten how nasty that one is."

Despite these victories, the Players were not without their losses. Already three of them lay bleeding on the ground, one beyond all hope of recovery.

The fighting on the far side of the field was even more intense. The first wave of unicorns and Hunters had met, and the unicorns had trampled a number of the men under their feet. Yet these victories came with a cost, because even when down a man can thrust up with sword or spear. Now a flow of blood, both human and unicorn, was drenching that part of the field.

The battle raged on, made infinitely more difficult for both sides by the fact that they fought not on level ground, or even on solid ground, but on the surface of a world that was bucking and heaving in its death throes. Ever and again, a spear throw or sword thrust would go astray as the world lurched and a Hunter's legs buckled beneath him. Ever and again, a unicorn would rear, only to find that the ground twisted beneath its feet, sending it crashing onto its side.

Moonheart fought furiously, silver hooves flashing and flailing in the light.

Belle seemed to be everywhere at once, striking at Hunters while encouraging the unicorns. "Fight harder!" she cried over and over again. "Strike harder!"

She noted with approval that gentle Cloudmane was pressing forward, despite some terrible wounds, pummeling with front hooves, kicking with rear, a fighting machine so ferocious that men were falling back in awe.

Even so, Belle knew in her heart that her people were not true warriors. Too many others held back their hoofblows, or struck askance, because their gentle hearts quailed at the thought of killing instead of healing.

"You fight for your lives and for the lives of your brothers and sisters, your mothers and fathers!" trumpeted Belle. "Fight, unicorns! Fight without pity or mercy! Fight, or we all die this night!

The dragons remained at the edge of the battle. The combat was so close that to shoot flame would only wound as many friends as it would burn enemies.

In frustration, Firethroat finally plucked two of the men from the edge of the battle and simply ate them. Graumag, on the other hand, decided that this might be a good time to set the tents ablaze.

A moment later, Firethroat soared into the air. Turning, she flew away from the battle. . . .

From the edge of the forest, Amalia Flickerfoot, Feng Yuan, and Alma Leonetti watched with mingled hope and horror.

The hope was because it seemed the unicorns might actually succeed in driving the Hunters out of Luster. Even now some were turning and fleeing in the direction of the Axis Mundi.

The horror came as they saw how many unicorns had already fallen in defense of their world.

Still, it will be worth it, thought Amalia, *even with all the deaths, all the blood, if the threat of the Hunt is ended forever.*

But then, just as it looked as if the enemy might indeed be ready to flee or surrender, a bloodcurdling ululation rose from the west side of the field. At first Amalia couldn't see the source of this cry, but a moment later she groaned in despair.

An army of delvers had come racing into the battle.

CHAPTER LXXXIX

SAVING THE SAHIB

Rajiv had been horrified to learn that his friend the sahib was being held prisoner not far from where they stood. In the intensity of the revelations that followed, it was not difficult to slip away and disappear into the depths of the forest. Let the others fuss about the past. He was going to rescue his friend!

Because his sense of direction was good, and because he had known where they were coming from when they returned to the great tree, it did not take him long to figure out which way was southwest. However, he quickly discovered three great difficulties in actually moving through the forest. The first was the darkness that had fallen; oh, there was a half-moon, but in the deep woods its light hardly penetrated. The second was the gaps that had opened in the ground; avoiding those slowed him considerably. The third was the number of trees that had toppled as a result of the quakes. Some were huge and created massive barriers, their trunks as high as walls — though in at least one case the trunk of a fallen giant served as a bridge across a gap he might not otherwise have been able to cross. The world shook while he was on that bridge, which was terrifying, but he immediately dropped to his belly and clutched the trunk until the tremor ended. The tree rolled a quarter turn, and climbing back to the upper side was made more difficult because the bark was smooth.

He made it a point not to look down while he was doing this.

He had not traveled more than another ten minutes when he heard the sound of a great battle. The unexpected sound confused him, but did seem to make it clear he was heading in the right direction.

When he emerged from the woods he saw a meadow. Though much of it was illumined by the half-moon that hung low in the sky, large sections were obscured by clouds of smoke that rolled from a fire raging at the meadow's far side, almost as if light and dark themselves were battling for dominance. In that lurid mix of moonlight, firelight, and smoky shadow, Rajiv could see hundreds of men, unicorns, and delvers locked in ferocious combat. The boy watched, sickened, as one of the Hunters — not five paces from where he stood — slashed across a unicorn's chest with a shining sword. Blood, silvery-crimson, spurted out in a graceful arc. The unicorn, screaming, pummeled at the man with flashing silver hooves. Only one blow connected with the man's head. One was all it took. Rajiv heard a horrible, dull thud then saw the man fall. Trumpeting defiance, the wounded unicorn reared, its shining hooves pawing the smoky air, then bent sideways and collapsed on top of the fallen man, their blood mingling. The boy could not tell if either of them was alive or dead.

He sprinted forward. Despite the times he had longed to be bigger, he now blessed his small size, which let him zigzag across the field largely unnoticed by man and unicorn alike. Each had greater dangers than him on which to concentrate. Even the delvers, who were about his size, were so focused on battling the unicorns that they largely ignored him.

A few minutes later — minutes during which he saw more blood and pain than a lifetime on the streets of Delhi had shown him — he stood at the edge of a small village of tents. The ones farthest from him were aflame, a fire that was spreading rapidly. The tents were all alike save one, larger and far more grand, that stood at the center of the grouping. He made for it at once, thinking it the most likely place to find the sahib.

The front of the tent was open. The sight was tempting, but entering there seemed unwise. Despite the battle, despite the fire, it was possible the sahib was guarded. That assumed, of course, that this was actually where he was being held.

Rajiv circled to the back of the tent. To his disgust, he could not lift its edge, for it was attached to a floor, much like the one he had shared with the sahibs on their journey into the Himalayas. He drew his sword, thinking it was a very good thing that the sahibs had seen fit to arm him back at the castle. He looked at the blade for a moment, then wriggled out of his shirt and used it to wrap the glinting edge. Now that it was safe to clutch, he cautiously and quietly used the tip to make a tiny opening in the material, close to the bottom. He widened the hole a bit with his finger, then, lying on his side, peered in.

The sahib was bound to a pole in the center of the tent.

He was the only one there.

It would have been easy enough to return to the front of the tent now and enter that way, but Rajiv was not feeling kindly toward the sahib's captors. So he simply unwrapped his blade, slid back into his shirt, then sliced an opening in the back of the tent.

Ian struggled to turn so he could see what was happening, but his bonds held him too tightly.

"No need to fear, sahib. It is me, Rajiv. I have come to free you."

He spoke the words softly, moving to the sahib as he did. Once beside him, he quickly sliced the gag that covered Ian's mouth. When the cloth fell away Ian whispered, "Rajiv! What are you doing here?"

"Oh, sahib! You did not think I would leave you in such a situation, did you? Do not move. I am going to cut the ropes that bind you, and I do not want to hurt you."

It was the work of but a moment to saw through the bonds. With a cry of relief Ian tried to get to his feet, but staggered and fell.

"Sahib!"

"It's all right, Rajiv. I should not have tried to stand so quickly. My legs have fallen asleep. I just need a moment."

"We should not take even a moment. We must go! Lean on me, and we will begin." But as they were leaving the grouping of tents, they stumbled over a body. Ian looked down and groaned.

"What is it?" asked Rajiv.

"Help me get him to his feet," replied Ian. "We have to take him with us."

THE WRESTLING MATCH

Lizard and his cove stood outside a small clearing. The space within was nearly dark, the half-moon's light blocked by the towering trees that surrounded them. This was no problem for the delvers, whose eyes were made for such conditions. They could see everything quite clearly. And what they saw now was Fallon, who stood in the center of the clearing, stripped to the waist.

Stretching out his powerful arms, the big man roared, "I call you, Whisperer! I call and command, as you are bound to me by the fact that you came from the creatures I created. Appear to me. *Appear to me!*"

"What is he doing?" asked Pebble breathlessly.

Before Lizard could answer, a voice seemed to come from nowhere. Though soft, it somehow filled the clearing, whispering in seductive tones, "Why don't we just talk instead?"

The delvers looked at each other uneasily. They had not wanted to believe Rocky's horrible story, but this must indeed be the voice he had spoken of, the voice that had driven their king mad. And if that were so, then perhaps the rest of the story was true and this Whisperer really had put part of itself into a tribe of dwarves, and from them created the delvers. And if *that* were so, he was both their creator and, in a way, their destroyer.

Lizard heard a sniffle and turned to glare at Waterfall. Wiping at his face, the delver nodded and fell silent.

"APPEAR TO ME!" roared Fallon again.

The voice chuckled. "Do you really think that just because we are linked you can command me?"

"APPEAR TO ME!"

A sigh rustled through the clearing. A moment later a mist formed in front of Fallon. At first it was little more than slowly swirling tendrils, dark and murky, of a vile color.

"You cannot think to defeat me," purred the mist, as it curled around itself. "I am of you and of your creatures, but magnified a thousand times. So I am far better, and far stronger, than you could ever dream of being."

Now the watching delvers clung to one another. Lizard wanted to bolt, but knew that if he did the others would follow. And this was the task they had been given by the leader of their cove: to be present at this intimate battle.

Fallon's next words were nearly as soft as those of the Whisperer's, yet somehow even more compelling. He did not shout, but simply said with power and authority, "As the creator of the unicorns, from which you were yourself created, I command you: Appear to me, Whisperer."

The mist swirled faster, angrily winding into and around itself. Slowly, excruciatingly slowly, it took on shape and substance, revealing the form of a man like Fallon, but twisted somehow. This twisting was not merely physical, though it was clear that something about its almost-beautiful body was not quite right. No, it was twisted in all ways, an external indication of its internal wrongness.

"Appear to me," repeated Fallon, the command now given through gritted teeth.

With a cry of rage the Whisperer did just that, finally coalescing into a solid presence, its body almost that of a man yet warped out of all proportion. Its face was so distorted by anger and fear and greed and base desire that it was terrifying to see.

"So," said Fallon, gazing at it sadly, "you are the worst of me."

"Of you and from you," replied the Whisperer maliciously.

"I reject you, utterly."

The malformed face twisted as it sneered and said, "Reject your own heart then, for I am born and built from its darker parts."

Fallon stared at the Whisperer as if looking into some evil mirror. Finally he smiled grimly and said, "I correct myself. I do not reject you. I simply claim what is mine . . . claim it — and conquer it!"

With that, he launched himself at the Whisperer. Their

bodies struck with a meaty smack, making it clear that the Whisperer was now fully carnate.

In the first moments, Fallon seemed to have the advantage, by virtue of surprise more than strength. The Whisperer staggered backward, until it fell against a tree. Fallon pressed forward, pinning his counterpart to the bark. But just as it looked as if it the battle might be over almost before it began, the Whisperer emitted an unearthly scream and flung Fallon away. The big man struck the ground with a jolt that drove the breath from his lungs. Before he could catch it again, the Whisperer hurled itself upon him.

Now began a long, strange time as the two beings grappled on the forest floor. From moment to moment, the watching delvers could not tell who was winning and who losing. The wrestlers rolled and cursed, shouted and shrieked, first one on top and then the other, one pinned and breaking free, then the other doing the same.

The cove of delvers watched, scarcely able to breathe, as Fallon and the Whisperer grappled across the leaf-strewn ground, which bucked and trembled beneath them. More than once the wrestlers struggled at the edge of some fresh gap in the soil, a newly opened fissure that might easily swallow both of them. Each time, finally, they rolled away, back to solid ground, only to smash themselves — seemingly without care — against the roots of the greater trees.

Fallon was bleeding now, his mighty torso crisscrossed by trails of crimson and silver blood. Finally, panting, he fell, taking the Whisperer with him. They grappled for another moment then suddenly the Whisper was straddling him. The twisted creature wrapped its hands around Fallon's throat and began to choke him, slowly closing its powerful fingers on the muscular neck.

Fallon fought desperately, but could not dislodge his opponent. The Whisperer bent toward him. "Did you really think you could defeat me?" it hissed, squeezing its hands still tighter.

Fallon beat his own hands against the ground, then twitched and lay still.

"Noooo!" screamed Lizard.

Without thinking, the delver raced into the clearing, the rest of his cove at his heels. They jabbed at the Whisperer with their spears, cursing it in the name of their people. Shrieking in astonished fury, it turned and struck out at them, sending Wart and Diamond flying.

That moment of relief was all Fallon needed. He sucked in a gasping breath, then with one smooth flip of his body reversed the situation and pinned the Whisperer.

"Stand back," he rasped to the delvers.

They did as he asked.

The Whisperer writhed beneath him, spitting, clawing, shrieking furious curses. Then, suddenly, it lay still and whispered, "Have mercy on me. You are wise and powerful. Oh, have mercy, my creator, for you are the source of all that I am."

Fallon said nothing, simply stared into the creature's eyes, a long, searching gaze filled with horror and compassion.

Finally after what seemed to the watching delvers an eternity, he leaned down and kissed his dark twin on the forehead. Whispering himself, he said, "All right, at last I know you. That is what I needed."

Then, with a wrenching movement that made his muscles bulge, he tore away a piece of the Whisperer's back.

"This is for my *alahim*," he growled as he flung the piece skyward. The Whisperer screamed as the bloodless flesh arced upward, then spread out and . . . vanished.

Fallon tore off another piece of the creature's flesh and again flung it toward the stars, this time crying, "And this is for my unicorns!"

Again the Whisperer screamed.

Again the flesh expanded, dissipated, vanished.

"Mercy!" pleaded the Whisperer. "Oh, show me mercy!"

"So you can destroy more lives?" cried Fallon.

The Whisperer was writhing in his grip now, raking the big man's arms with fingers that still had uncanny strength. It had no effect. Fallon simply clasped his foe even closer and, his own voice now little more than a whisper, said simply, "You are of me, and from me, and I *shall* see to your ending."

Then he ripped away another piece of the coalesced darkness.

"This," he said fiercely, "*this* one is for the delvers!"

Slowly, surely, with every ounce of strength left to him, Fallon continued the dismemberment, pulling apart the Whisperer until nothing remained but the still-beating heart.

He moved as if to fling this away, too, then sighed wearily. Turning toward Lizard, he said, "This ending must be sealed, or the creature might yet reassemble itself."

With those words, he pressed the last remnant of the Whisperer to his own chest. The heart blazed with dark fire for a moment, then disappeared, as Fallon took in some of his own darkness.

"It is finished," he murmured.

Then he collapsed in a dead stupor.

Lizard nodded to the others. They gathered around Fallon's beautiful body, which was scored with dozens of wounds. Without speaking, and in perfect coordination, they lifted him and carried him into the darkness.

CHAPTER
XCI

ON FIELD OF BATTLE

Their screams alone are enough to make your blood run cold, thought Amalia as the delvers, uttering a fierce ululation, poured onto the field of battle. Small and fast, they darted among the unicorns, jabbing at their bellies with spears, tangling their feet in nets, tripping them with ropes.

Watching from their observation post, Feng Yuan thought to the Queen, "They are holding back!"

"What do you mean?" asked Amalia.

"For some reason, the delvers have the same problem as your unicorns. Look at how fiercely they fight. Yet despite that, most are not going for the kill."

"Thank goodness for that," replied Amalia grimly.

"What are those flashes of light?" asked the girl.

"I believe it is my friend, Thomas the Tinker. He specializes in minor explosions."

"A very useful friend," replied Feng Yuan. "As are the dragons — though in close combat like this they cannot unleash their full power."

The dreadful scene was lit by a strange mix of moonlight and the ghastly orange glow of burning tents. In places, the light was blocked by dark swirls of smoke. The acrid scent now reached all the way across the meadow.

The delvers' arrival gave heart to the Hunters, who raised a great cry and began to fight more brutally than ever.

"The delvers are not well organized," observed Feng Yuan. "If they were smart they would attack in groups. They're spreading themselves out too much."

"I welcome their foolishness," replied Amalia. "Even so, they've rallied the Hunters."

"Alas, that is true. But look at Belle. She is doing her best to rally *our* forces!"

Indeed, Belle seemed to be everywhere at once, racing from one melee to another, striking at Hunters, using her teeth to wrench an arrow or spear from the side of a wounded but still-standing unicorn, aiming her back hooves in sudden kicks that sent Hunters flying. Her clear voice rose above the battle as she shouted encouragement everywhere she went.

Which was why the Hunters, the ones who realized what she was doing, decided to concentrate on her.

"Look!" thought Feng Yuan in alarm.

She pointed to a group of Hunters who had clearly recognized Belle as one of the unicorn leaders. They had formed a wedge and were pushing their way through the battle, obviously intending to strike her down.

"We have to help her!"

"You have cautioned me repeatedly that it is folly for a general to join the battle proper," replied the Queen.

"I have changed my mind! It may not be wise, My Queen, but tonight I say wisdom be damned. I have only a dagger, but even one blade can sway a battle. I say let us fight!"

"Let us fight!" trumpeted Amalia. She reared and pawed the air, then planted her feet solidly on the shaking ground. Swiftly Feng Yuan scrambled onto the Queen's back. Together they galloped into the fray.

Feng Yuan longed to shout, "To the Queen, to the Queen!" But she knew none of the unicorns would understand her. She need not have worried. Cloudmane started the cry on her own.

Because of her connection to Amalia, Feng Yuan could understand the unicorn's shouts and saw the results as several unicorns picked up the call and quickly rallied to their side.

Belle, unaware of her danger, had reared and was pummeling a pair of delvers who cut at her with their spears. As Amalia drew closer, Feng Yuan was horrified to see what had been invisible to her from farther off: Streams of crimson and silver blood flowed along Belle's heaving flanks.

The approaching Hunters, most carrying swords but two with spears, were only a few feet away now. One of the spearmen flung his weapon. It lodged in Belle's shoulder. With a cry of defiance she bent her neck and yanked the spear out, loosing an arc of blood that spattered on the delvers she had been battling. The other spearman raised his weapon — and fell beneath the hooves of five unicorns, led by Amalia Flickerfoot.

Feng Yuan leaped from Amalia's back, onto the back of one of the Hunters. He staggered, and she twisted, throwing him further off balance, so that he fell to the ground. She sprang away. A unicorn did the rest. . . .

She was heading for the Queen when another Hunter grabbed her and spun her around. To her horror, she found herself staring into the eyes of her old teacher, Wu Chen.

"Oh, Feng Yuan!" he cried. "That you would betray us so!"

"Master, you don't understand!"

"I understand treachery," he said. Tears filling his own eyes, he raised his sword to kill her. The blade whistled toward her, but before it could reach her flesh Belle struck from behind, crushing his skull. A wail burst from Feng Yuan as he crumpled to the ground, for Wu Chen had been her true teacher and had taught her the ways of war.

She caught her breath and straightened her shoulders. *Such is the way of war,* she thought. Dagger raised, she flung herself on the nearest Hunter.

The Maidens of the Hunt, who had returned to the main encampment with their Hunters, had fled their tents. Some were screaming and near delirium. Others, more well-trained, had searched for weapons and were racing past the blazing tents to join the fight.

Observing the battle from one of the watchtowers, dark smoke snaking around her as the tents burned, Beloved stretched her arms to the darkened sky and cried, "Where are you? Friend, where are you? How could you abandon me now of all times?"

No answer came from the darkness.

Drawing a deep breath, she spat into her hands, then rolled air between them until she had a glowing ball of red light. She hurled it at the closest unicorn. It struck him in the chest. He reared, trumpeting in pain as the light spread over him, burning at his skin. Screaming with agony, he collapsed, hitting the ground with a thud.

Beloved's shout of triumph was cut off when she felt her knees buckle. She cursed herself for giving way to her frustration. She knew very well that the kind of magic she had just used drew too much power. She would need time to recover before she could launch another such blast.

Still, the painful death of that unicorn had been satisfying to watch.

As she leaned against the rail of the watchtower, trying to regain her strength, a coil of smoke made her cough. Looking down, she saw that flames were licking at the tower's base. With a cry of panic, she began to descend the ladder.

The flames stretched for her scarlet robe. . . .

*   *   *

With Feng Yuan once more clinging to her back, Amalia galloped across the smoky field, rallying her troops. Suddenly they saw Moonheart. Hooves flashing in the moonlight, the big unicorn was battling three delvers and a pair of Hunters. An arrow protruded from his right shoulder, and blood flowed from a gash on his side. Behind him lay the plump form of Armando de la Quintano. The man was wounded and struggling to rise, and Moonheart was protecting him.

Despite his wounds, the big unicorn was fighting with full force. Before Amalia could reach his side he had struck down the closest Hunter and disabled two of the delvers. But just as Amalia thought he would be safe she saw a well-placed spear pierce Moonheart's chest. With a shriek he crashed to his side. He struggled to rise, then fell back, flailing his hooves and bellowing in rage.

"Brother!" cried Amalia. Screaming in fury, the Queen leaped forward. She dashed the Hunter whose spear had struck Moonheart to the ground, then trampled him beneath her vengeful hooves.

Though Feng Yuan could not hold on to the Queen's back, she landed lightly and turned to slash at an approaching delver.

And, moment by moment, the shaking and heaving of the ground beneath them grew ever more violent.

CHAPTER
XCII

TO THE TREE!

In the forest near the Axis Mundi, unaware of the battle raging in the southwest meadow, Lightfoot said to Martha, "It is easy enough to guess where Rajiv has gone. He is deeply attached to Ian. Once he knew your husband had been captured, he would not be interested in any stories being told here. I'm sure he is heading for Beloved's camp to try to free him."

"We have to go after him," said Martha. She was still clinging to Cara's neck but had one hand on Lightfoot's shoulder as well.

Lightfoot shook his head. "Rajiv might slip past any guards they have, but I cannot enter that camp, nor can Cara, nor can you."

"But what are we to do?"

Rocky, who was standing nearby, asked what the problem was. After Cara explained, he said, "I can go. Since the delvers and the Hunters are now allies, I may be able to enter the camp. I doubt the Hunters are aware that I am an exile."

"Why would you risk this?" asked Cara.

"Your father saved my life not long ago. I am in his debt."

Martha, who received this information through her connection with Cara and Lightfoot, said urgently, "Please do!"

"It will be faster if you ride on my back," said Lightfoot. "I can take you to the edge of their encampment, then let you go forward on your own."

"You would do that?" asked Rocky. "Let me, a delver, ride you?"

Lightfoot grimaced. "I will not pretend the idea does not give me shivers. But, then, the whole world is shivering now. Everything is changing. I can, too."

"Then let us go!"

Lightfoot knelt and Rocky climbed onto his back. No sooner had he done so than both unicorn and delver cried out in surprise.

"What is it?" asked Cara.

"I cannot say for sure," replied Lightfoot. "But . . . I felt a strange charge of energy."

"And I . . . I felt a calming, as if some uneasiness that has been with me all my life was quieted," said Rocky.

"Fascinating," said Lightfoot. "Alas, we have no time to try to understand what it means."

With that he galloped into the woods. "Yaahhh!" cried Rocky. Leaning forward, he clutched Lightfoot's neck, trying desperately not to fall off.

*　　*　　*

Across the writhing meadow, M'Gama stood at the base of the Axis Mundi, staring at the tree with bleak despair. Namza, who was at her side, pointed up and said, "What is that odd piece of wood embedded in the trunk?"

"It is a chunk of rootwood, from one of the great trees that grow at the center of the unicorns' seasonal resting places. I was using it — I had a piece from each of those trees — to cast a protective spell. Unfortunately, the delvers captured me before I could finish."

Namza sighed. "For that I am sorry. But do not think your work was in vain, M'Gama. I can tell that, had you not done this, the tree would have split already and with it, our world. Now we must do what we can to try to hold things together."

"I thought you said you could not heal the tree?"

"Alas, that is a magic far beyond me. The best we can do is try to stave off the last moments and hope for a miracle. Let us go into the ground and see if we can soothe these troubled roots."

Lying side by side at the base of the tree, their bodies tossed by the constant shifting of the tormented roots, the two wizards joined hands, then joined magics and began to try to hold off the end of the world.

Despite their new invigoration, the unicorns were losing ground.

We fought valiantly, even if we have lost, thought the Queen. Then she stamped her foot and recalled the words she had so often spoken to Cara during the days that she, Amalia, was a human: *If you're alive, you have a chance.*

With a defiant cry, she charged again into the fray. But even as she erupted forward Feng Yuan cried, "Look! Oh, look, My Queen!"

Amalia turned in the direction the girl was pointing and cried out in joy.

Firethroat had returned! Wings spread wide, the massive dragon swooped low over the battle. She made a quick dive and snatched up a Hunter. She reversed course, flew up about a hundred feet, then dropped him.

He fell screaming to his death.

New chaos erupted on the battlefield. And into that chaos charged the ones Firethroat had flown off to fetch, the ones she had accidentally misdirected earlier that day, before she knew the Queen's true plan. Towering over all the combatants, Arkon's warriors — fifty-one centaurs fresh and eager for the fight — thundered onto the field. Whooping their savage war cries, some were wielding swords, some hefting spears, some clutching bows with arrows nocked and ready to fly. A few swung double-headed axes so sharp-edged they could slice flesh just by touching it.

The Princess Arianna, fighting near the center of the field, cried out in joy at the sight of her fellow centaurs charging into the battle. Despite the wounds she had taken, and the arrows in her flank, she trampled two men beneath her in her eagerness to join them.

"Arkon!" she cried, rushing forward.

He turned and shouted her name. In that same moment a Hunter's arrow struck her directly in the chest.

Arianna reared back with a scream, then defiantly ripped the arrow from her breast and charged forward. She managed three steps before she stumbled and fell.

With a roar, Arkon fought his way toward her, slicing at Hunters with his sword, trampling delvers beneath his oversized hooves.

The glow of the burning tents was lurid as Ian Hunter bent to help the man over whom he had nearly tripped to his feet.

"Who is it, sahib?" asked Rajiv.

"A friend of my wife's family," replied Ian, not taking the time to explain that Jacques had briefly been married to his wife's mother and might indeed be her father. Once he had the old man's arm around his neck — he was conscious, but just barely — Ian said, "All right, you take the lead, Rajiv. How do we get out of here?"

Before the boy could answer, Jacques's legs buckled, nearly pulling Ian down. Rajiv immediately moved to the man's other side. He lifted the man's hand and placed it on his shoulder. "All right, sahib," he said. "We'll go this way."

Ian groaned.

"What is it, sahib?"

"You will have to be my eyes, Rajiv. I have lost my sight again."

The boy nodded, realized that was useless, and shouted, "You first hired me to be your guide, sahib. I am glad to continue."

Brushing away a bit of burning canvas, Rajiv began to lead the two men out of the inferno.

Beloved's robes had caught fire as she scrambled to escape the burning watchtower. Silently she leaped from the ladder and rolled upon the ground. Though serious burns scored her body, she was no stranger to pain and did not let it stop her now. She stripped off her outer robe and strode toward the battle, pausing only to pull a sword from the body of one of her Hunters. Swinging it once, she vowed she would draw blood of her own before this was done.

A sudden roar attracted her attention. She pivoted to her right, then cried out in fury. Even from where she stood, on the far side of the battlefield from where they entered, it was easy to spot the centaurs, since they towered above everyone else in the fray.

"No!" screamed Beloved as she watched them gallop into the battle. "No, this cannot be!"

Their arrival was too much for the Hunters. Their ranks began to break.

"To the tree!" cried one of them. "To the tree and back to Earth! This is madness!"

"To the tree!" cried another, and then another.

Their cries began to swell. Suddenly, as if seized by a

rapidly spreading infection, Beloved's army turned and moved into full retreat, plunging into the forest that surrounded the battlefield.

With a cry of triumph the unicorns gave chase.

Screaming in rage, Beloved bolted after them.

Behind them, the site of the first battle ever fought in Luster was strewn with the bodies of Hunters, unicorns, delvers, and one centaur.

Some of the fallen were merely wounded and unable to rise.

Others would never rise again.

Beside one of those who would never rise, a female centaur of uncommon beauty, knelt the newly named Chiron. He held her close in his muscular arms. She lifted a cold hand to stroke his cheek. "You came," she whispered. "You came. Oh, Arkon, I knew you would not fail me."

He pulled her close. "Arianna!"

"I have to leave you now, my love," she whispered, her voice hoarse. "Forgive me."

"No!" he screamed. He pulled her closer, buried his face in her chestnut hair.

Breathing her last, Arianna collapsed in his loving embrace.

Arkon continued to hold her as heaving sobs wracked his chest. At last he lowered her carefully to the ground. Rising, he hurled a defiant cry of grief to the smoke-smeared sky. Then he turned and thundered into the woods, in pursuit of the fleeing Hunters.

CHAPTER
XCIII

DRAGON BINDING

Because the forest through which the Hunters fled was too dense for dragonflight, Graumag and Firethroat went above it. As a consequence, the two dragons arrived at the Axis Mundi well ahead of the fleeing Hunters. But as they swooped over the meadow surrounding the great tree they saw — could not help but see — a heart-stopping sight: The ragged gap that Beloved had opened at the tree's base now extended up the vast trunk for hundreds of feet. The upper branches were trembling, and it appeared the tree might soon separate, its gigantic halves crashing to the ground.

"If the tree splits, all is finished!" cried Graumag.

"If the tree splits, Luster dies," agreed Firethroat.

No more needed to be said. Both dragons knew what must be done. It was a temporary solution and could not last for long. But moments, seconds, counted right now. Without another word, they dove toward the dividing tree, then attached themselves to the trunk some hundred and fifty feet above the ground.

Moving quickly, and with remarkable grace, the dragons wound themselves around the wood, overlapping each other until that section of the tree looked like nothing so much as a giant caduceus, the ancient symbol of healing still used by Earth's physicians. Once the intertwining was complete, the dragons twisted the tips of their tails together, then stretched around the trunk to join claws.

"I do not know how long I can hold on," gasped Graumag, who was the smaller of the two.

"Nor do I," replied Firethroat. "I do not even know if there is any reason to do so. This tree is dying, and I see no hope of saving it. But what else shall we do? Die on the ground as Luster perishes? Let it not be said that you and I did not battle against the end of the world until the last moment."

Her words were answered by a groan of anguish from Graumag: "Sister, I feel as if I am being torn apart!"

Firethroat tightened her grip on Graumag's legs. "Hold fast! *Hold fast!*"

But she could feel the tree pressing out against them, its great weight threatening to pull them apart. Soon Firethroat, too, cried out — first in pain, then defiance. "I will hold on! Past pain, past agony, I will hold until the tree itself rips me asunder!"

Graumag's answering scream was wordless, yet Firethroat knew her Flame Sister was making the same promise.

And still the wounded tree pressed out against them, the slow creak of its splitting wood like a vast scream of its own.

CHAPTER
XCIV

AT THE CENTER

The Dimblethum had been lurking in the forest that surrounded the meadow of the great tree. He was confused and unhappy, but did not know what to do. All he really understood was that he had done something bad and then tried to make up for it by doing something good. After that, everything had gone all hazy again.

He flexed his great claws, wishing there was something he could tear apart. Not the trees, though. He loved the trees, the big tree most of all. But that was in trouble. The hole in its center was growing. Its roots were twisting and its branches shaking. He feared it was dying, and his longing to fix it was so urgent that it pained him. But he had no idea how to do it.

He growled angrily. Why couldn't he ever make something without it going bad?

When he heard the noise — shouts and cries and screams — coming in his direction, he wanted to hide. Not out of fear. The Dimblethum did not fear things. He simply wanted to be alone. He ran to the left, circling trees and leaping over exposed roots, but the cries were still coming. He reversed course and ran right, but heard more shouts and screams from that direction. He groaned. Was no place free of these invaders?

A moment later he saw the men. He knew they were called Hunters.

The Dimblethum remembered that he did not like Hunters.

And he was unhappy.

This combination was not a good thing for the Hunters.

Lightfoot and Rocky had nearly made it through the forest to Beloved's encampment when they were startled to see a flood of men and delvers surging toward them. Among them, too, ran the Maidens of the Hunt, all clad in white. Lightfoot could feel the unwanted surge of desire to help them, but fought it down.

Coming behind the men and the maidens, driving them forward, were the unicorns of Luster, beautiful in their fury, glorious in their power. With them ran dozens of centaurs, brandishing spears and swords and rending the air with savage war cries.

Lightfoot longed to join this chase. But he had promised to help find Cara's father. So with Rocky still clinging desperately to his neck, the Prince veered sideways to avoid the first flow of the Hunters. Ignoring brambles, nimbly leaping over roots and cracks in the surface, he raced parallel to the oncoming Hunters, like a runner speeding along a beach as a wave is coming in. When he came to the end of their line, he swung around and past them and turned once more toward the encampment.

It didn't take long after that to reach the abandoned battlefield, but the dreadful sight that greeted them — so many wounded, so many dead — nearly drove Lightfoot to his knees in grief.

He headed straight across the body-strewn meadow, picking his way among the dead and the wounded, until one familiar form caught his eye — and his heart.

"Moonheart!" he wailed.

Now he did fall to his knees. Ignoring Rocky's protests that he could not afford to attempt a healing now, he pressed his horn to his uncle's side. His heart went cold when he realized no energy would flow from him to the fallen warrior.

Unicorns can heal, but they cannot resurrect.

Staggering to his feet, half-blinded by tears, the Prince forced himself to move on toward the still-blazing tents.

The forest floor bucked and heaved as the Hunters fled toward the Axis Mundi. The quakes — "tremors" was no longer a sufficient word, the world was clearly tearing itself apart — were growing stronger and more frequent than ever.

Passage through the woods was difficult. Everyone involved in that desperate chase — man or woman, delver, unicorn, or centaur — was repeatedly knocked to the ground. Far more terrifying, new fissures continued to open in the forest floor, some directly at the feet of the runners.

On the far side of the Axis Mundi, seven delvers also made their way through the forest toward the meadow. They traveled single file, arms upraised, bearing the unconscious body of Fallon. The trip would not have been difficult — he was big, but surprisingly light for his size — if not for the wretched heaving of the ground.

At least, thought Lizard, *we haven't fallen into any crevices.* After another spasm in the forest floor he added the thought, *Well, at least, not yet.*

It was obvious the danger of that was growing worse. So he was relieved when a beautiful voice said, "Let me take your burden, delver."

Cara and her mother had braved the meadow's upheavals and were making their way to the tree, which now appeared to be surrounded by an odd band of calm. They both had the same idea, but in each case it was for the other.

"You should go through the tree right now," urged Cara as they approached. "You can get back to Earth where it's safe."

"Not without your father," replied Martha firmly. "But you should go now. I want you out of this."

"And what would I do on Earth as a unicorn? Luster is my world now, Mom." She paused, then added to herself, *At least, for as long as it lasts.*

They heard a shout from behind, turned, and saw a row of men approaching. The first wave of Hunters had arrived. Though their progress was slowed by the meadow's ever-worsening disruptions, their intent was made clear by the man in front, who bellowed, "By god, I'll get one more unicorn before I go!"

Drawing his sword, he rushed toward Cara.

Stepping in front of her daughter, Martha Hunter also drew her sword.

"It is good you came, Sahib Lightfoot," said Rajiv, placing a soot-smeared hand on Lightfoot's shoulder. "Sahib Hunter and I were having a hard time with the old sahib. I do not think we could have got him back to the others without your help."

"I'm glad you've come, Lightfoot," said Ian, supporting the older man with one arm while he placed his right hand on Lightfoot's other shoulder.

"I'm here, too," said Rocky, sounding offended.

Ian sighed. "Forgive me, friend delver. I cannot see right now, and . . ."

"Cannot see?" cried Rocky.

"It will pass," said Ian. "But I will need help until my sight returns."

The older man groaned and rolled his head.

"It's Jacques!" thought Lightfoot, seeing his face for the first time. "Is he in mortal danger?"

"I don't think so," replied Ian, "though he would have been had Rajiv not rescued me. We found him among the burning tents as we began our escape. I think he just needs time to recover."

"Then it would be better for me to carry him than try to heal him, since that would leave me unable to walk myself."

"That makes sense. Thank you for being willing to do that. I do not want my wife to miss the chance to meet this man."

"Nor would Amalia Flickerfoot ever forgive me if I let him perish here," replied Lightfoot. "Let us try to get back to the center. There may be time for one last good-bye before the world falls to pieces."

The Dimblethum was lost in his rage against the Hunters, the latest and most destructive of Luster's invaders. He had quickly dispatched four of them when the first wave of the fleeing men reached him. Now he pursued them into the fray in the meadow, stumbling and staggering across the troubled ground, bellowing in anguish for his wounded world. Most Hunters and delvers simply fled before him, terrified by his size and ferocity. Some turned to fight. The battles were brief, and the Dimblethum quickly flung aside their battered, broken bodies. Still, these victories did not come without a price; he was bleeding now from a score of wounds.

It made no difference. His despair was complete, and nothing made a difference now.

At least, not until someone, someone he cared for, called his name.

Untrained in the use of the sword, Martha Hunter would have been at a huge disadvantage if not for the wild gyrations of the meadow. On that unstable ground no one could hold steady, parry a blow, strike with confidence. Two more Hunters followed the first; more were following after them. When the lead Hunter was only a few feet from Martha, he thrust his blade toward her. She countered the move, but in a flash he knocked the sword from her hand. He laughed at the look on her face, then pushed past her to attack her daughter.

The mockery died on his lips when the smaller blade that Martha carried in her boot found a home in his back.

Cara was battering at another of the men with her hooves. She struck him a glancing blow, destroying his shoulder, before she was knocked to the ground by another heave of the meadow. Screaming with pain, the man flung himself toward her. Martha did the same, shouting, "Don't touch my daughter!" She wrapped her arm around the Hunter's throat and began choking him with a strength she had not known she possessed. He pulled and scratched at her arm. She spotted a fallen arrow, snatched it up, and thrust it into his neck. He gasped and fell from her grip.

Cara struggled to her feet. Three more Hunters were approaching, blades drawn. As the first lunged toward her, she heard a fierce shriek from above.

"Gaaaah!"

Looking up, she saw Medafil plunge from the sky. Talons outstretched, a mighty roar bursting from his throat, the gryphon raked his claws across the face of one of the Hunters. As the man screamed and fell to his knees, Medafil sank his beak into the shoulder of another. The Hunter flailed at him with his free hand, but Medafil flew upward, just as Firethroat had done with the Hunter she had plucked from the battlefield. But Medafil was much smaller than the dragon, and the man's struggles caused the gryphon to falter and lose his hold.

It was only a short drop; the Hunter would have landed safely, had he not managed to squirm free of the Medafil's grip directly above a widening crevice.

The man's scream went on long after he had disappeared from sight.

A volley of arrows flew in Medafil's direction as more Hunters entered the field. Most were badly aimed because no one could take a firm stance, and the gryphon ignored them at first. Then a lucky shot burst through his right wing, sending big feathers scattering. Medafil screamed in outrage, but managed to keep flying.

Another arrow struck, and then another.

"Gaaaah!" he cried as he fell to the shaking ground. Ragged wing limp at this side, he surged to his feet. "Do your worst you frib-jabbled Hunters. I will slice you till my last breath!"

Most of those who had survived the flight through the forest had made it to the meadow by this time. The restless surface was nearly covered by a surging mass of men and delvers, unicorns and centaurs.

The men were running for the tree.

"They're fleeing!" thought Feng Yuan, who was still clinging to Amalia Flickerfoot's back. The two were in the first wave of the unicorns to reach the meadow. "Press the advantage, My Queen. Drive them out!"

"Drive them out!" trumpeted Amalia. "Drive the Hunters out of Luster!"

It was hard to be heard above the shouts of the men, the screams of the dragons, the rumbling and grinding of the splitting world. Even so, the unicorns nearest to the Queen took up the call: "Drive them out! Drive the Hunters out of Luster!" Across the field spread the rallying cry: "Drive them out! Drive the Hunters out of Luster!"

King Gnurflax had been seized by the bloodlust that can come in battle. The group of delvers he now led across the meadow attacked anyone they could reach, unicorn or Hunter, without distinction. Beloved had destroyed Delvharken. The Whisperer had abandoned him. To the berserk king, everyone — *everyone* — was now the enemy.

As his band of delvers fought their way toward the center, Gnurflax spotted a particularly tempting trio: a gryphon, a unicorn, and a human, all standing together.

"That way!" he cried.

Screaming their battle cry, the delvers sprang from behind, swarming over Cara, Medafil, and Martha.

Martha bellowed curses and fought like a madwoman.

Medafil struck out with beak and talons, snapping and clawing with the fury of a cornered beast.

The majority of the delvers went for Cara. She bucked and kicked as she tried to shake them off, but there were too many, and their battle lust had doubled their strength. Trumpeting defiance, Cara toppled sideways. As she fell she spotted a hulking figure. He was looking around at the chaos as if he did not know what to make of it. "Dimblethum!" she cried desperately. "Dimblethum, it's me, Cara! Help me! Help —"

572

Her plea was cut off by a delver pinning her head to the ground. But at her call the Dimblethum had turned. An instant later, he hurled himself into the fray, roaring as he came.

Delvers flew left and right as he plucked them from Cara's side. They screamed as he flung them into the air, heedless of where they might fall. Others cried out in agony as he stomped them beneath his mighty feet.

The delvers turned from Martha and Medafil. Here was their great enemy!

"Kill him!" cried Gnurflax. "Kill the Dimblethum!"

They swarmed over him.

Bellowing in rage, the Dimblethum yanked the attackers from his body. They clung like leeches and took chunks of flesh with them, but in the blood haze that now possessed the Dimblethum such wounds meant nothing.

The world rumbled and shook again. The Dimblethum staggered, then fell, crushing two delvers beneath his great bulk. Cara, Martha, and Medafil threw themselves back into the fight, trying to drag the little monsters away from the great beast battling on their behalf.

Cara felt a strange elation as she used her wonderful new body in ways she had not known possible. Silvery hooves flashing, she struck down delver after delver. When one leaped onto her back, she twisted her lithe neck and gripped his arm in her powerful jaws. She heard him scream, felt the bone break. With another twist of her neck, she wrenched him into the air, then sent him flying. He landed at the edge of a newly opened crevice and scrabbled wildly to avoid tumbling into its unknown depths.

As if their fellows' screams had alerted the delvers to how severe the quakes had become, they made a sudden retreat, leaving Cara standing alone, panting for breath, trying to keep her balance as the world continued to writhe around her. Turning, she saw that the Dimblethum was on his feet again. Gnurflax was clinging to the beast's great leg, which was like a small tree trunk. Stabbing at it with his stubby sword the delver king shrieked, "Die! Die, beast!"

Oddly, he was weeping as he did this.

The Dimblethum collapsed. Gnurflax, still weeping, leaped away from him, waving his sword in triumph.

Screaming in rage, Cara reared. With flailing hooves she rained a hail of silvery blows upon the delver king. He toppled beneath her onslaught and rolled away.

As he did, the ground opened and swallowed him.

The rest of the delvers fled, wailing in fear and despair.

CHAPTER
XCV

TRANSFORMATIONS

A strange silence had fallen over the meadow. It was not a complete silence. The shifting ground continued its ominous and ever-worsening rumbling. Firethroat and Graumag still shrieked with the pain of holding the tree together. But the battle proper had ended. Most of the Hunters and the maidens had fled through the tree. The ones left were too wounded to travel across the tortured and riven meadow and did not pose an immediate danger. One maiden lay crumpled at the base of the tree, as if her strength had run out before she could make the final sprint into the tunnel. Her white robes covered her like a shroud.

Though the enemy had fled, the greatest threat remained: Luster was about to rip itself apart. Yet the knoll surrounding the tree was oddly peaceful. This untroubled patch, which extended about twenty feet out from the trunk, was the work of Namza and M'Gama, whose bodies lay nearby. Their true selves were woven into the soil, working to calm the troubled roots. With the dragons binding the tree from above, and the wizards of earth and stone soothing the roots from below, the death of Luster was held off for at least a few more moments. But all four knew it was a delay, not a victory. The end was still coming.

As if in defiance of the approaching doom, the unicorns had spread back across the meadow and were moving from there to the main battlefield, in search of healing work. The Queen had ordered them to heal the unicorns first, but then, when possible, to turn their attention to others who had fallen that day, whether Hunter or delver. Hunters were to be healed with care, and only with at least two other unicorns at hand to keep them in control should they choose to attack.

Amalia Flickerfoot herself remained at the center, as it seemed the best place for her new seat of command, however briefly that command might last.

She had not been there long when into that circle of calmer ground stepped Allura. She was surrounded by seven delvers, who continually glanced up at her in awe. On her shoulder rode the Squijum. In her outstretched arms she carried Fallon's unconscious body.

"Awake, brother," she whispered. "You've earned your rest, but one last struggle remains."

She knew, and dreaded, the thing that must be done next — or, at least, attempted. She did not know if her brother had the strength for it, or if he did, if it was even truly possible.

"Awake, brother," she whispered again.

Fallon stirred and groaned. He looked at the tree and groaned again, the sound this time not one of physical pain, but of heart-deep despair.

As Allura helped her brother to his feet, she gasped. Fallon turned to see what had caught her attention.

They had been joined in the circle of peace by Ian, Martha, and Rajiv. With them came an old man Fallon had not met and the delver called Rocky. Behind the four humans and the delver, walking side by side and in perfect unison, were Prince Lightfoot and the unicorn Fallon had come to know as Silverhoof, but who he now understood to be Ian Hunter's daughter, Cara. Stretched across the backs of the two unicorns was the body of a creature that could only be the Dimblethum.

Fallon cried out in grief.

"He is not dead," said Ian, moving quickly to his friend's side. "But his wounds are severe."

The unicorns knelt. The Dimblethum rolled to the ground, where he lay upon his back, his eyes open but unseeing.

With two quick steps, Fallon crossed to his *alahim*. He looked down with sorrow at the wounded form of his oldest, dearest friend, then glanced at Cara. "You remember what I told you about Transformational Magic?"

Cara nodded.

"When Elihu transformed you into your unicorn self, he did so by passing to you the Transformational Magic with which the Whisperer had returned him to his true form."

Cara shuddered with guilt. Elihu had been as beautiful as Fallon. Now he was, again, simply . . . the Dimblethum. He had sacrificed his heart's desire to save her from the Hunters.

"Can I return the magic?" she asked. "Change him back?"

"You may try," said Fallon. "We need him — he is the only one who can possibly stop the destruction of Luster."

Cara went to her dear friend and protector, the first being she had ever met in Luster.

So many wounds! she thought, gazing down at him in sorrow. She remembered how fiercely he had resisted the first time she tried to heal him. Now she understood that it was because he did not want to let her return the Transformational Magic, though in his muddled state he might not even have completely understood that. Cara knelt and pressed her horn to his chest. Instantly she felt a surge of energy pour out of her.

So this is what a healing is like, she thought.

Yet she did not lose consciousness as had happened with Lightfoot in the past.

The Dimblethum's breathing steadied. Some of his wounds healed. But he remained in his bestial form.

Fallon stepped beside her. "It is too late, Silverhoof," he said softly. "The Transformational Magic has been in you for too long. It has settled, and you do not have the knowledge to return it."

"Is there nothing to be done?" she cried in horror.

"Step aside," said Fallon.

Without another word, he straddled the Dimblethum's body. Reaching down, he grasped the great, brutish paws in his own hands, which — despite their size — were oddly delicate in comparison. He stared down at the bestial form of his *alahim*, then closed his eyes and began to murmur.

Light began to shimmer around them.

Fallon's face twisted and he cried out in pain as his body began to tremble, then shake violently.

The transformation began with Fallon's hands, which grew thick and coarse. His smooth arms sprouted dense fur. What was left of his clothing after his fight with the Whisperer tore away as his limbs grew thick and bulky. And his face . . .

Cara had to turn away as Fallon's once beautiful face grew coarse and bestial, the jaw extending, the upper lip and straight nose merging to form a snout.

Allura was standing close, her face contorted by grief. Tears flowed down her cheeks.

Unable to resist, Cara turned back to the transformation and gasped yet again. The Dimblethum was changing in a way opposite to Fallon. His bearlike traits faded, his snout shrank, his fur vanished, until he was once more the exquisite Elihu.

From above, Cara could hear the screams of dragons. She wondered, vaguely, at the cause, but could not tear her eyes from the scene before her.

Finally the metamorphosis was complete. With a roar, Fallon wrenched his paws from Elihu's hands, then fell sideways. On the ground, he let out a gasping sob, a strange and horrible sound to hear coming from his hulking, bear-like body.

Elihu sat up. When he saw the new Dimblethum beside him he moaned in horror. "It's Fallon, isn't it?" he asked.

"Yes, my love," said Allura. "It is him."

Elihu extended his shapely hands toward his *alahim*.

"Don't!" cried Allura, before Elihu could actually touch the new Dimblethum. "If you make that connection the Transformational Magic will flow back to you. Fallon did this of his own free will, Elihu. He did it because . . . because you are needed here."

She gestured toward the tree.

Elihu turned and cried out when he saw the vast cleft that was destroying the tree, the tree that had grown from a stolen seed, a seed quickened by his own blood.

"You have no time to waste," said Allura gently.

Elihu looked down at Fallon, and a sob choked in his throat. "Thank you, my friend," he murmured. "My *alahim*. Thank you for freeing me to do what must be done. Had I known this would be the end, that you would pay this price, I would never have begun."

All eyes had been riveted on the drama occurring between Fallon and Elihu. So no one had noticed when the white-clad figure lying at the base of the tree had risen.

No one had noticed when she crossed to join them.

No one noticed her at all, until a chillingly cold voice said, "No one is going to do anything right now."

Then they did indeed notice that the figure that had been lying at the base of the tree had not been one of the Maidens of the Hunt, but Beloved herself, who now stood with a knife at Martha Hunter's throat.

From the far side of the massive tree came a dozen Hunters, led by the man Kenneth.

"Let her go, Grandmother Beloved," said Ian, struggling to keep his voice calm. "It's over. The Hunt is done."

Beloved spat on the ground. "The Hunt is done, but my task is not." The sense of confident command in her voice was terrifying, as if there were no question in her mind that now, at last, she held the outcome in her hands.

"This world has very little time left, and I do not mind dying with it if that is what it takes to end the curse of the unicorns. Nor do these men, who are neither traitors nor cowards like you, Ian. There are not enough of you to overcome us. All we need to do is wait — or, if you insist, fight you to a standstill. Either way, it is but minutes before Luster will perish, and with its death throes take every last one of the unicorns." She smiled, a look of ice and venom. "It matters little to me if I die along with you. My grand task will finally be complete."

Far above, unaware of the drama playing out at the base of the tree, Firethroat could feel the convulsions of the Axis Mundi growing worse. It was not just that the terrible pressure had increased. She felt a kind of sickness in the tree that seemed to flow from it directly into her spirit, a dark sense of dread and loss and approaching oblivion that made her fear she might swoon.

"Sister," she said, "our work is nearly finished. We have done what we could. When the tree can stand no longer, we must release it. Once we do, we can fly between worlds. It is not easy, but I have done it. I will show you the way."

"I do not think I will be able to go," replied Graumag, her voice weak and strained.

At the sound of her Flame Sister's words, Firethroat felt a twist of grief. "Graumag, are you all right?"

"I fear not, Sister," hissed the other dragon. "I fear not."

Though the dying world rumbled louder than ever, a dreadful silence gripped the humans and creatures gathered at the base of the tree.

After a moment, Beloved said with casual cruelness, "I wonder how much longer this will take."

Cara glanced at Elihu. His jaw muscles were clenched, his once-more beautiful face dark with suppressed rage. She wondered if he was about to launch an attack.

"Let Martha go," pleaded Ian.

Beloved's laugh was cold, mirthless. "After the way you betrayed me, you expect mercy, Ian? You're even more of a fool than I thought. It's a pity that daughter of yours isn't here to share these last minutes. She was the only one I ever really feared, you know. The Whisperer told me long ago that only someone who carried both the blood of the Hunters and the blood of the unicorns could defeat me. I thought the idea was mad the first time I heard it. How could such a thing be, that these bloodlines could merge? Then, slowly, I learned the truth about your daughter's heritage. I can't tell you what a relief it was when she disappeared and it became clear that she was dead."

Amalia and Jacques cried out in grief at these words. As they did, the world shook — and shook again.

"I can hold no longer," gasped Graumag.

Firethroat loosed her grip on her Flame Sister's front legs. To her horror, the smaller dragon toppled backward. She twisted downward, clawing at the trunk as she did. She tried to cling to it, but her body grew limp.

Firethroat wanted to reach for her, to help, but could not think how. Worse, her own body was still held to the tree by the way the lower part was wrapped with Graumag's around the trunk.

She felt that change as Graumag's coils grew slack, the muscles relaxing, her body unwinding. The smaller dragon groaned, a sound from deep within. Firethroat writhed and slithered, trying to pull herself loose.

Suddenly Graumag's body broke free, the lower part whipping around as it was pulled from the tree.

The bronze dragon made no cry as she fell.

Feng Yuan gasped. "Look!" she cried, pointing upward.

Beloved laughed, as if she could not believe anyone would try such a foolish stunt.

An instant later, Graumag's massive body crashed down between the two groups. The leading bone on her right wing struck three of the Hunters, killing them instantly. A fourth lay on the ground, screaming with pain. Beloved leaped backward, barely avoiding being sliced in half by one of the spines in the dragon's crest. Martha twisted free of her grip.

The impact of Graumag's fall seemed to reawaken the sleeping ground. At once the tremors that had been held at bay began again, so that the ground was as restless here as in the rest of the meadow.

Deep in the soil below, Namza and M'Gama, tangled in the tree's roots, felt their spirits being wrenched apart.

As Cara cried out in horror at the fall of her friend, Ian, Jacques, and Elihu vaulted over the dragon's still and silent body. Ian snatched up Martha. Jacques and Elihu grabbed Beloved and pinned her arms behind her.

The unicorns and Rocky's cove hurried around Graumag's body, but were only in time to see the last of the Hunters escape into the tree.

Kenneth alone remained to defend Beloved, and he was swinging his sword at Ian when he suddenly howled and fell to the ground.

"It is not good to try to hurt my friends," said Rajiv,

who had crawled up behind Kenneth and slashed the tendons in his right knee.

The street boy calmly slashed the tendons in the other knee, then stepped away as Kenneth fell.

"Hold her," ordered Elihu, thrusting Beloved toward Ian.

The ancient enemy of the unicorns screamed and writhed as Ian and Jacques grasped her arms and held them tight behind her back. Her eyes blazed and her long white hair lashed out violently, like whips made of moonlight. Ian and Jacques had to close their eyes against its stinging strands.

Without a word, Elihu turned and sprinted toward the tree, then leaped into the gaping wound Beloved had ripped open in its trunk.

He began to chant, calling out in a language that even Cara, with her gift of tongues, could not understand. She knew only that the words he uttered sounded as if they were wrenched from a place deep in his soul and were ancient beyond understanding. She seemed to feel them in her skin.

A strange glow began to emanate from Elihu. His body growing, he stretched upward, extending his hands so that he was touching the edges of the tree's wound.

He continued chanting.

Cara gasped as light blossomed around him.

In that moment, the wound created by Beloved began to close, sealing itself from the top down.

"Elihu!" called Cara. "Elihu, the tree is healing now. Come out! *Come out!*"

Near her, the new Dimblethum pushed himself to his knees and let out a roar. Cara could not tell if what came from his mouth was a sound of triumph or of loss. Probably both, she decided. Turning to Allura, she asked, "Why doesn't Elihu come out?"

"He cannot," replied the golden-haired woman, her voice thick with pain. "He's feeding his own life force into the tree, giving it his power to bring it back to health." She watched for a moment longer, then murmured, "It's not enough. It's not enough!"

Cara looked back at the tree. The gap at its base was pulsing, growing wider, diminishing, growing wider again, as if it wanted to close but could not.

Suddenly Allura took the Squijum from her shoulder and placed him on Cara's back. "Stay here and be happy," she said fiercely to the little creature.

Then she sprinted toward the tree.

The Squijum screamed as he watched her go.

Even through the blaze of light surrounding him, Cara could see that Elihu was horrified at Allura's approach. She expected him to cry out to the woman to leave, then realized that he could not stop his chanting. Allura tucked herself behind him, wrapped her arms around his bare chest, held him close, resting her head against his shoulder. The light surrounding them blazed with new intensity.

"She's adding her power to his," murmured Amalia in awe.

Elihu continued to chant as Allura's voice merged with his, twining around it like a vine. The sound was so pure, so beautiful, that Cara longed to listen to it forever.

With a lift of her heart, she realized the world was growing quiet, the ground becoming still and solid once more.

The hole in the tree was closing faster now, closing in on Elihu, who had made this world and was giving himself to save it, and Allura, who was giving herself as well, merging with her loved one in his final act of creation and healing.

"Elihu!" roared the new Dimblethum, staggering to his feet and stretching his paws toward the tree. "Elihu! *Alahim!*"

"Farewell, *alahim!*" cried Elihu.

"Farewell, brother!" cried Allura.

With a final rush, the tree sealed itself around them.

In that instant the ground ceased its trembling.

Where Beloved's tunnel had been was now only a scar, a tall, wide mark in the once perfect trunk.

The Squijum leaped from Cara's shoulder and raced to the tree. He pressed himself to the bark where the trunk had sealed itself and clung to it, weeping as if his tiny heart would break.

CHAPTER
XCVI

FIRE ATTEND THEE

Crouching beside her sister dragon, Firethroat ignored the babble around them. Beloved and Cara's family were behind Graumag's body, closer to the tree. She did not care.

Several unicorns came forward, across the now peaceful meadow.

"Can you heal her?" asked Firethroat, speaking to them in their own language.

One of the unicorns — it was Cloudmane — stepped forward, knelt beside Graumag's still body, touched it with her horn. Rising, she turned to Firethroat. "We will try, but there is not much life force left. We can heal. But we cannot resurrect."

"Try!" urged the dragon. *"Try!"*

The unicorns did try, six of them at once pressing their horns to Graumag's neck. The dragon's great body flinched and twisted. She uttered a soft moan and attempted to raise her head, but was only able to get it a few inches from the ground before it dropped back again.

The unicorns staggered and fell. Cloudmane managed to gasp, "We did what we could. I am sorry it was not enough."

"You did what you could," agreed Firethroat. She placed her long neck beside Graumag's, so that her own vast head was close. "We did a mighty deed this day," she murmured into her Sky Sister's ear. "We saved the world that has given us shelter these last centuries."

"I'm glad," whispered Graumag, her voice barely audible. "I owed my life to Luster. Now the debt is repaid. Oh, Sky Sister, I will not last much longer. I feel the darkness coming and into it I must go."

"Fire attend thee," whispered Firethroat.

Then she drew back, hissing in astonishment.

Graumag had begun to shrink, her body to transform.

"It hurts!" cried the smaller dragon. "Sister, yet again it hurts!"

Moments later the transformation was finished.

On the ground before Firethroat lay not a dragon, but a beautiful woman, naked save for the flaming red tresses that shielded her body.

CHAPTER
XCVII

GENERATIONS

Oblivious to what was happening with the dragons, Beloved screamed and raged, writhed and twisted, spat and cursed. Yet try as she might, she could not break free of the grip in which Ian and Jacques held her.

Arrayed in front of her were Amalia Flickerfoot, Martha Hunter, and the unicorn known as Silverhoof — three generations, in the youngest of whom the blood of Hunters and unicorns had merged.

Only Martha was now in human form. Her voice sharp, she said, "You were wrong, Beloved. Cara is not dead."

Jacques and Amalia cried out in relief at these words. Beloved stopped her ranting and stared at Martha. "What do you mean?"

"She means," said Cara slowly and clearly, "I am not dead, simply transformed."

Her father and grandfather were so startled they nearly lost their grip on Beloved's arms. Without thinking, both men opened their eyes — which had been closed against the miniature whips of Beloved's hair — to gape at her. Fortunately, Beloved herself had gone still when understanding overtook her. Slowly her face twisted in bitterness, as if this were the greatest betrayal of them all. Voice now weak, she said, "Then kill me. Kill me at last, and at least end this endless pain. You are the only one who can end it, you hell-born child. So do it. Do it now!"

Cara stared at Beloved, who had wrought so much death and destruction. She thought about how the woman had been driven, both by her endless agony and by the treacherous urgings of the Whisperer, who had come from the unicorns themselves. And in that staring, in that moment before the choice must be made, which is the only moment of freedom anyone ever really has, she found herself torn between loathing and compassion.

All attention was now focused on Cara, but she was aware only of Beloved, whose blazing eyes stared back at her with hate and pain and defeat.

Cara took a deep breath. "Hold her tight," she cautioned her father and Jacques. Then, to Beloved, she said, "If I am the only one who can kill you, then perhaps I am also the only one who could heal you."

She glanced back at her mother and her grandmother.

Amalia made a gentle nod. Martha's face was rigid.

Please let me get this right, thought Cara. As her father and her grandfather held Beloved, Cara stepped forward.

It's in her heart, she thought. The idea was frightening, and there was no guide for this, but it seemed that only one thing would work. Extending her neck, she braced her legs, then thrust her horn into Beloved's chest, driving on until she reached the enemy's heart.

No matter how many times she had seen Lightfoot do this, and seen what it had cost him, no matter that she had tried to heal the Dimblethum and felt some flow of energy then, nothing had prepared Cara for the way this healing pulled at her strength and vitality. The sensation was both exhilarating and excruciating, an odd mix of pain and ecstasy. It was too much to bear, and she wanted to pull back, but braced her legs and forced herself to continue.

Beloved's scream when the horn entered her heart seemed to shred the growing dawn. She spasmed, twisting uncontrollably as she tried to pull herself from the horn. Cara, fearing she had made a mistake and was only wounding Beloved further, tried to pull back. She could not. She felt her knees buckle. Terrified she would collapse with Beloved still impaled on her horn, she tried again to wrench free. The horn was stuck fast, as if she and her ancestress were now locked together in some unholy circle of energy.

Then something changed in the energy flow. With a sudden gasp, Beloved cried out one last time, then fell back, the bond broken.

Cara, too, staggered backward, then fell to her side. She heard her mother gasp. Gazing up, she saw that an astonishing look of peace had come over Beloved's face.

"What have you done?" she whispered, her voice filled with wonder.

Even as Beloved spoke these words, age came upon her at last, the age that had been kept at bay all the centuries of her mad quest to destroy the unicorns.

Her hands grew gnarled. Her moon-white hair fell limp. Lines began to rive and ravage her once-smooth face. She lifted her fingers, and a look of horror crossed her coarsening features as she saw them shrink and wither. But she closed her eyes, then shook her head. In the papery remnant of a voice that was left to her, she murmured, "It's all right. It's all right. At last the pain is gone."

She collapsed to the ground and made a sound that was half sigh, half sob.

A moment after that she curled and shriveled into herself until there was nothing but dust where she had lain.

Cara, exhausted in a way she had never imagined possible, lifted her head to her mother. "I killed her!" she wailed. "I only wanted to help, only wanted to heal her. And now she's dead."

Martha Hunter knelt and lifted her daughter's head into her lap.

"It's all right," she whispered, stroking Cara's silken mane. "It's all right, dear one. You did what only you could do. You brought her peace at last."

CHAPTER
XCVIII

SCARS AND HOPE

The weeks that followed the healing of the great tree were painful. Luster was badly damaged and had seen more death in the five days of the invasion than in all the centuries that preceded it.

Amalia Flickerfoot established her base in the meadow of the Axis Mundi; she had much to do, and the center of the world seemed the best place from which to do it.

The major problem with this decision was that great rifts still scored the land all around — gaping crevices that made it hard, even dangerous, to approach the tree. On the other hand, this was true all over Luster — though in time it became clear that the worst of the damage was at the center, and the farther from the tree you went, the less catastrophic was the destruction. This is not to say it was not bad — cliffs had crumbled; forests had fallen; entire valleys had vanished under the debris of shattered mountains.

*   *   *

The first task was to complete the healing of the unicorns who had been injured in the battle. This took much time and energy, for the wounds were deep and numerous.

A tally was made of the unicorns who had not survived; the list was long and painful to read. When their bodies had faded, as is the way of unicorns, Thomas the Tinker collected their horns. He placed them in his cart — the cockatrice was still there, too — and carried them to the Cavern of the Unicorn Chronicles. In later times a special space was made for them, an underground hall of honor, where each horn stands as proud reminder of those who fought to save their world. Their names were inscribed in a scroll that is kept at the front of this room, and once a year, on the anniversary of Beloved's invasion, their names are read aloud in loving memory. Moonheart's is first among them.

They found the bodies of M'Gama and Namza next to the tree, about a quarter of the way around from the scar that marked where Elihu and Allura had closed the wound. At first the unicorns feared that the two magic makers were dead. But careful examination showed that their hearts still beat, their lungs still moved, if only very, very slowly.

The Queen's Council debated long over whether they should try to wake them with a healing. In the end, Amalia Flickerfoot said, "It may well be that they are yet working their magic among the roots of the Axis Mundi." After a consultation with Rocky, she decreed that a shelter should be built above their bodies to keep them safe.

No one, including the Queen, knew if she had made the right decision, and worry over it kept her awake many long nights thereafter.

As for the delvers, without a king and with their ancient home in shambles, they were cast into despair. That something had also changed *inside* them only added to their confusion.

That internal change, which had come with the death of the Whisperer, was modest. Yet all felt it . . . a kind of easing of the heart and a lessening of long-held anger.

Rumors began to spread that any delver who rode a unicorn would experience a deeper peace. Most scorned the idea, and some thought it was a lie, created by the unicorns to trick them yet again. Even so, almost everyone, even the skeptics, secretly longed to try it.

Because Rocky's cove was the only one that had not succumbed to the panic, and because they knew more than any about what had actually happened in those last terrible hours, the delvers turned to them for guidance.

Which was how Rocky became the new king of Delvharken. This decision was made easier for the delvers by the lines now scored in his face from his time in the Stone, which all took to be a sign of great bravery and wisdom.

The kingship was not an easy task to take on, for

Gnurflax had left the People of the Stone in chaos and despair, and their underground home was shattered. At first Rocky tried to decline the crown. But his cove convinced him that it was what his teacher would have wanted, and with this he could not argue.

The younger delvers, especially, were happy with the choice. Though they had not dared to speak of it in the days of the old king, many had come to hate and fear Gnurflax.

Taking nicknames became a fad among those who admired their new leader.

Most of the Hunters had fled through the opening in the tree before it was sealed. Even so, dozens remained in Luster. They fell into two categories. First were those who had fled the battle as it turned against them, but had not made it to the tree. These had disappeared into the wilderness, and there was no way of knowing how many there were. Second were those who had fallen in battle, but were only wounded, not dead.

"We'll heal the ones we can," decreed the Queen.

"You will heal the enemy?" replied Feng Yuan, aghast.

"We are healers," replied Amalia Flickerfoot, "and we are not vengeful. But neither are we fools. Once healed, they will be put into the Deep Sleep."

Cara remembered the story of Martin Hunter, who had tracked her grandmother when she was a teenaged girl named Ivy Morris. "Where will you keep them?" she asked.

"Martin Hunter sleeps in a cave attached to Grimwold's Cavern. We'll put the others there and wake them one at a time. They will be given a choice — we will escort them to one of the gates so that they can leave Luster, or they can prove themselves with service and make a life here."

"Most will probably want to return to Earth," said Ian. "However, now that Beloved is gone, some may indeed want to stay. I think it more likely that some of the Hunt maidens will choose to remain. Feng Yuan has told me there are five who did not make it through the tree."

At the Queen's request, Belle and Feng Yuan agreed to work with the maidens to see if they wished to return to Earth or wanted to try to make a home in Luster.

All that remained in that regard was the disposal of the Hunters who had died in battle. It did seem to please Feng Yuan when the Queen ordered that the corpses simply be rolled into the seemingly bottomless crevices.

"For your help in our time of need, I thank you, Firethroat," said the Queen. "I know it cost you dearly."

"This was always your world," replied the dragon, "and we know we came as uninvited guests. Yet I would now make claim that Graumag has paid the price for all of our entry."

"Indeed, she has," agreed Amalia, "many times over. I mourn that Luster no longer has seven dragons."

Firethroat twitched one nostril, then said, "Actually, it does."

The Queen looked at the dragon in puzzlement. "I do not understand."

"There has always been another. For reasons of our own, we do not speak of him. But there are indeed still seven dragons in Luster." She looked past Amalia as if considering something, then stretched her great wings and said, "I am returning to my cave now. In time there will be a dragon-moot to mourn the loss of Graumag. Our period of grieving is long, so do not expect to hear from me anytime soon." She paused yet again, then added, "It would be wiser not to disturb us for now."

The Queen nodded and said gently, "We will leave you to your sorrow."

When Arkon presented himself to the Queen, as had been requested, she said, "Your help was most timely, Chiron, and our appreciation is enormous. What boon may I grant you in return?"

"We ask only free passage through Luster."

Amalia shook her head sadly. "That you have always had, my new friend. It was by the choice of the old Chiron that your people remained in the valley, not by our command."

Arkon looked startled, but bowed from the waist and said, "May there be new friendship between our people."

"In this, Chiron, we are in agreement. You and I and the Delverking are all new to our positions. It is a good time for change."

Two days after the healing of the tree, Rajiv stood in front
of Ian and said, "Sahib, you know I am fond of you. But I
must work. It is the rule of Luster that for a boy to stay
he must earn his place. Sahib Jacques and Sahib Armando
say that I may join the Players. They will teach me many
things I wish to learn. You have the memsahib and your
daughter, though she is a unicorn, which seems to me very
strange. So you will not be lonely, even though Sahib Fallon
is gone. And we will see each other again, I believe. I have
been learning about this Luster you have brought me to. It
is a big world, but not so big as all that. It is a good size for
a boy to explore. I know our paths will cross again."

"*Namaste,* Rajiv," said Ian, pressing his palms together
and bowing to the boy.

"*Namaste,* Sahib Hunter," he replied. Then his lips trembled. Ian knelt and scooped him into his arms.

"I shall miss you, sahib," murmured the boy, flinging his
arms around Ian's shoulders.

"Oh, and I shall miss you, my partner in adventure!"

With a last, quick embrace, Rajiv slipped free and
scampered off to where Armando de la Quintano stood
waiting.

That Ian and Martha would stay in Luster was not a matter
of question, since Cara could not leave. So on the evening of

the second day after the healing of the tree, when the first crush of Amalia's duties had eased, Martha Hunter went to speak with her mother.

Their conversation was long and painful, and — as it turned out — only the first of many it took to heal the breech between them. Not all things can be made better by the touch of a unicorn's horn.

Theirs would be a slow healing. But it had begun.

While they were speaking, Cara went to Jacques and said, "Why won't you ask my grandmother if you are truly my grandfather?"

The old man's woebegone face twisted as if trying to smile. "Oh, my dear girl," he murmured. "As long as I do not know, it remains a happy possibility. And knowing would change nothing. In my heart I long ago claimed you as my grandchild, and I love you as ever much as I could whether the bond of blood is there or not. Much is made in this world of the ties of blood, but I tell you truly the heart is stronger than mere blood, and love needs no such link to blossom and be true. I need neither the joy of assurance nor the sorrow of unhappy knowledge that perhaps another took my place in your grandmother's affections. Between your heart and mine, nothing will change."

One week after the healing of the Axis Mundi, Cara stood beside Lightfoot. They were looking out at the meadow that surrounded the tree. Shoulders touching, they spoke mind-to-mind.

"Do you wish you could return to human form?" asked Lightfoot.

"I don't know. I miss having hands." She paused, feeling a pang of sorrow as she remembered how Finder had once told her that hands were the single thing he envied about humans.

"But . . ." prompted Lightfoot, after several moments had passed.

"But I love being a unicorn. I've never felt so free, so powerful." She paused, then asked shyly, "Does it bother you?"

"No! I mean, no — it is fine with me, though it will take some getting used to."

"It will be harder for me to tease you," said Cara. "I'll miss trying to wind flowers in your mane."

"I won't!" said Lightfoot.

She moved away. He shifted to once more press his shoulder against hers. "I was teasing, too," he said gently.

She leaned back against him, but said nothing. She didn't need to.

The sky was growing dark, stars starting to appear. Her mother and father came to join them. Walking behind them were Amalia Flickerfoot and Jacques. Seeing them, the four of them, Cara felt such a sudden surge of warmth and happiness that she had to blink back tears. Looking away, she noticed something that surprised and thrilled her. "Look!"

she said, gesturing with her horn. "That rift — it's smaller than it was yesterday!"

All eyes turned to where she was pointing. After a long silence her grandmother said, "The world is starting to heal. I wonder if Luster is doing this on its own or if M'Gama and Namza really are still working among the roots."

Her voice had a wistful note, and Cara knew she was hoping she had made the right decision.

"Perhaps it's them," said Lightfoot. "Or it might be that Elihu and Allura, even from inside the tree, are working to mend the world he created."

His voice held a kind of wistfulness, too, and Cara knew — not because she was connected to him, but just because she knew him — that he was thinking about his lost friend.

"Perhaps," said Martha, "they are all working together."

"Whatever the cause," said Ian, "it seems Luster may someday be whole again."

How long that healing would take, they did not know. All Cara knew was that the world to which she had given her heart, and for which her beloved Dimblethum had given his life, would survive.

That was enough for now.

With Lightfoot at her side, her mother and father standing nearby, and her grandmother and Jacques close at hand, she felt, for the first time in her life, that she was home.

And it was good.

GRIMWOLD
SPEAKS

All these things I know, for it is my job to know them.

Some I know because I was there when they happened.

Others I know because the pieces of the puzzle were brought to me.

All must come to tell me their tales. That is the law of Luster and what it means to be Chronicle Keeper.

In some few places, I have had to guess at what happened or what was being thought. I believe these guesses to be true, or I would not have included them in this record.

So. Now I have written this tale, as was my duty, and I do not think any I have ever penned has given me such sorrow nor yet held the seeds of so much hope for what may come to be.

Only one last thing do I wish to record before I lay down my pen, and it is this: Every night the Dimblethum, the new Dimblethum, comes to the base of the great tree.

Most nights the Squijum is with him. They annoy each other, but only a little. Mostly they rest in sorrowful peace, side by side, gazing at the tree and wishing for the ones they love, the ones who were lost, and will not come again.

As do we all.

As do we all.

Grimwold

Fourth Keeper of the Unicorn Chronicles
The Queen's Forest, Luster

CAST OF
CHARACTERS

HUMANS

Cara and Her Family

Beloved – matriarch of the Hunters; greatest human enemy to the unicorns; ancient ancestress of Cara; kept alive for centuries by a piece of unicorn horn embedded in her heart, which is both ever-wounding and ever-healing

Cara Diana Hunter – granddaughter of Ivy Morris, who became the unicorn queen Amalia Flickerfoot; Queen Arabella Skydancer's great-great-granddaughter; she is the only being in whom the bloodlines of Hunter and unicorn are merged

Ian Hunter – Cara's father; a direct descendant of Beloved; recruited by her to the Hunt until he switched sides and joined the unicorns to be with his daughter

Ivy Morris – born Amalia Flickerfoot, but transformed when young to the human Ivy Morris; recently restored to her true form; now Queen of the unicorns

Jacques the Tumbler – a melancholy older man; possibly Cara's grandfather since he was once married to Ivy Morris

Martha Hunter – Cara's mother; her own mother is Ivy Morris, from whom she is estranged because Ivy kidnapped Cara to save her from Hunters, but never had a chance to explain why

The Humans of Luster and Earth

Aaron – a magician who helped open the way to Luster for the unicorns

Alma Leonetti – the oldest human in Luster; as a girl she persuaded Arabella Skydancer to establish the "Guardians of Memory"

Armando de la Quintano – leader of the Queen's Players

Bellenmore – the other magician who helped open the way to Luster for the unicorns

The Blind Man – a repository of arcane information, he told Ian how to enter the Rainbow Prison in return for occasional use of Ian's sight

Felicity – former wife of the Blind Man; now held captive in the Rainbow Prison

Feng Yuan – one of the Maidens of the Hunt, which are girls used by Beloved to entrap unicorns

Kenneth Hunter – one of Beloved's chief helpers

Li Yun – a petite tumbler who performs with the Queen's Players

Martin Hunter – a servant of Beloved who was on the track of Ivy Morris

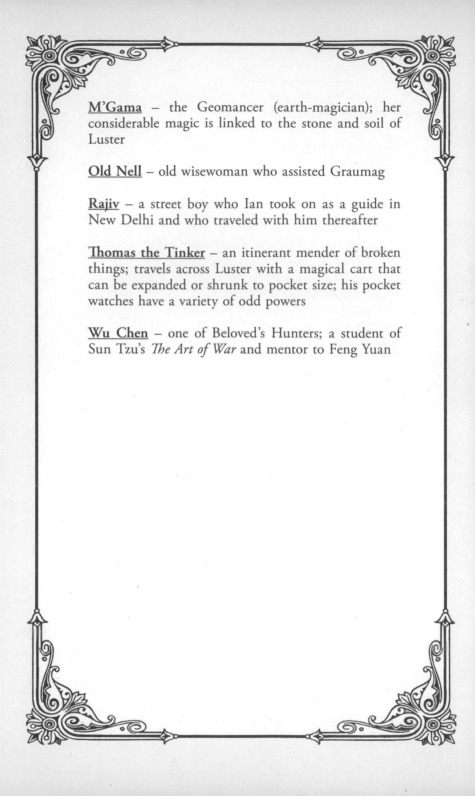

M'Gama – the Geomancer (earth-magician); her considerable magic is linked to the stone and soil of Luster

Old Nell – old wisewoman who assisted Graumag

Rajiv – a street boy who Ian took on as a guide in New Delhi and who traveled with him thereafter

Thomas the Tinker – an itinerant mender of broken things; travels across Luster with a magical cart that can be expanded or shrunk to pocket size; his pocket watches have a variety of odd powers

Wu Chen – one of Beloved's Hunters; a student of Sun Tzu's *The Art of War* and mentor to Feng Yuan

GREAT POWERS

Allura – a beautiful female who has been in contact with Namza

Elihu – Fallon's long-lost friend; a mysterious but powerful presence in Luster

Fallon – an exile who joined forces with Ian in New Delhi in order to further his search for Elihu

UNICORNS

Amalia Flickerfoot – Queen of the Unicorns; spent decades in human form as Ivy Morris; mother of Martha Hunter and grandmother of Cara

Arabella Skydancer – the former unicorn queen; Cara's great-great-grandmother

Belle – one of the fiercest of the unicorns; a leading member of the Queen's Guard

Cloudmane – first female Guardian of Memory

Finder – explorer of Luster; killed in a delver attack

Fire-Eye – member of the Queen's council

Goldenwords – wanted to purge darkness from the unicorns

Guardian of Memory – formal title of the unicorn who volunteers to spend twenty-five years on Earth to keep the memory of unicorns alive

Laughing Stream – one of the Queen's messengers

Lightfoot – Prince of the Unicorns; Cara's special friend

Manda Seafoam – member of the Queen's council

Moonheart – Lightfoot's uncle

Silvertail – member of the Queen's council

Whiteling – tried to heal Beloved's illness when she was a child; killed in fight with Beloved's father; a piece of his horn remains lodged in Beloved's heart

Windfoot – first Guardian of Memory

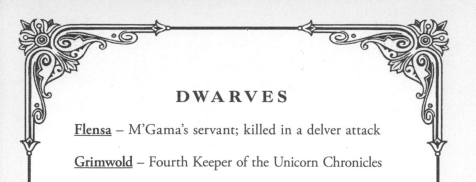

DWARVES

<u>Flensa</u> – M'Gama's servant; killed in a delver attack

<u>Grimwold</u> – Fourth Keeper of the Unicorn Chronicles

DELVERS

<u>King Gnurflax</u> – The Delverking

<u>Metzram</u> – Namza's teacher; previous wizard to the Delverking

<u>Namza</u> – the Delverking's wizard

<u>Rocky</u> – previously known as Nedzik; rebel delver who became Cara's friend

<u>Rocky's Cousins</u>

Erkza, nicknamed "First"

Gergga, nicknamed "Waterfall"

Gratz, nicknamed "Pebble"

Razka, nicknamed "Diamond"

Rendzi, nicknamed "Hammer"

Wurtza, nicknamed "Wart"

Zagrat, nicknamed "Lizard"

DRAGONS

Ebillan – a fierce and bad-tempered dragon; one of the last to arrive in Luster because he did not want to leave Earth

Firethroat – dragon who gave Cara the "gift of tongues" as a boon in return for releasing her from an enchantment

Graumag – dragon with a mysterious past; she came to Luster because she did not fit in on the world the dragons fled to when they had to leave Earth

Other Dragons of Luster

Bronzeclaw

Fah Leing

Master Bloodtongue

Red Rage

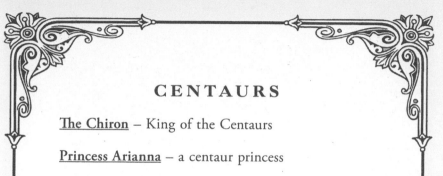

CENTAURS

The Chiron – King of the Centaurs

Princess Arianna – a centaur princess

Arkon – leader of the centaur guard

Basilikos – friend of Arkon

Danbos – a guard in the Chiron's court

Kallista – beloved of Basilikos

OTHER CREATURES

The Dimblethum – a bearish humanoid; an early inhabitant of Luster

The Squijum – Cara's monkeylike companion

Medafil – a sensitive and loquacious gryphon

The Whisperer – the unicorns' worst enemy; created from their own darker urges after they performed the Purification Ceremony

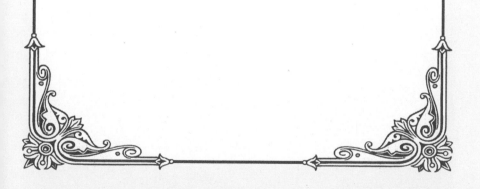

ABOUT THE AUTHOR

BRUCE COVILLE grew up in a rural area, around the corner from his grandparents' dairy farm. He considers himself especially lucky to have had a swamp and a forest behind his home.

His writing for children was affected by his own early reading, which included lots of pulp fiction and comic books but also had a healthy dose of myths and legends—a taste he first developed when one of his teachers read aloud the story of Odysseus. He has been reading fantasy ever since and has long dreamed of creating an epic series like The Unicorn Chronicles.

In addition to being the author of nearly 100 books for young readers, Bruce Coville is the founder of Full Cast Audio and has directed and performed in dozens of audiobooks. He lives in an old brick house in Syracuse, New York, along with his wife, illustrator Katherine Coville, and an assortment of cats.

Visit Bruce at both of his websites:
www.unicornchronicles.com
www.brucecoville.com